RAVE REVIEWS FOR DEBRA DIER!

A QUEST OF DREAMS
ROMANTIC TIMES REVIEWERS'
CHOICE AWARD WINNER

"Ms. Dier has created a rich tapestry woven with characters who come vividly alive and walk right off the pages, a plot line that is tightly crafted, and a magical blend of fantasy, fact, and dreams."

—*Rendezvous*

"The action never stops in this wonderful and heart-stopping fantasy adventure that sweeps the audience into a world rarely glimpsed by civilization."

—*Affaire de Coeur*

MacKENZIE'S MAGIC

"Debra Dier always brings something new and special to the genre, and she has done it again."

—*Romantic Times*

"Debra Dier has written a refreshingly delightful time-travel romance that will provide much entertainment."

—*Midwest Book Review*

SCOUNDREL

"This great romance has a cast of lively characters and fast-paced action that brings you right into the story. A thoroughly enjoyable book!"

—*Rendezvous*

"Another great read for Ms. Dier, *Scoundrel* sizzles with romance, intrigue, and memorable characters."

—*Paperback Forum*

BEYOND FOREVER

"Once again, Debra Dier gifts her numerous fans with another extraordinary tale of timeless love. *Beyond Forever* is a wonderful tale. . . . This is a great book to curl up with."

—*Affaire de Coeur*

"Debra Dier takes us on a journey that is peppered with tantalizing passion and spiced with intrigue. The exciting cast of characters is well-defined, showing remarkable strength and sensitivities. The conclusion will delight you."

—*Rendezvous*

MORE PRAISE FOR DEBRA DIER!

SAINT'S TEMPTATION

"Ms. Dier, with deft turn of phrase and insight into human nature, wrings an emotionally charged tale from her characters which engages both the interest and empathy of her readers!"
—*The Literary Times*

DEVIL'S HONOR

"Debra Dier will keep you turning the pages in this entertaining, fast-paced tale. . . . It both charms and delights with a little mystery, passion and even a bit of humor."
—*Romantic Times*

LORD SAVAGE

"Exhilarating and fascinating!"
—*Affaire de Coeur*

MacLAREN'S BRIDE

"The talented Ms. Dier captures the English/Scottish animosity to perfection and weaves an exhilarating tale that will touch your heart and fire the emotions. Great reading!"
—*Rendezvous*

DECEPTIONS & DREAMS

"An exciting and action-packed adventure. . . . Once again, Debra Dier proves that she is a sparkling jewel in the romantic adventure world of books."
—*Affaire de Coeur*

DREAMY DESIRE

"I suppose you think it's silly, making wishes on the stars."

"I've got nothing against wishes." Devlin rested his hands on the railing and turned his face into the creamy flow of moonlight. "As long as you aren't too disappointed when they don't come true."

"Is there anything you believe in, Mr. McCain?"

The look in his silvery blue eyes made Kate's breath catch in her throat. So full of heat, so full of sensual promise, that look in those beautiful eyes, as though he wanted to hold her, kiss her, touch her in ways she could only imagine possible.

"I believe in the smooth curve of your cheek," he said, sliding the backs of his fingers over her cheek, a gentle stroke of warmth that set her legs to trembling, like a willow in a summer storm. "The softness of your lips."

"Oh," she whispered, a curious tingle vibrating deep in her belly. "Mr. McCain, are you always so brazen with women?"

A Quest of Dreams

DEBRA DIER

LEISURE BOOKS   NEW YORK CITY

To Denny, my brother, my friend.
Thank you for always being there for me.

A LEISURE BOOK®

September 2002

Published by

Dorchester Publishing Co., Inc.
276 Fifth Avenue
New York, NY 10001

ISBN: 0-8439-4485-4

The name "Leisure Books" and the stylized "L" with design are trademarks of Dorchester Publishing Co., Inc.

Printed in the United States of America.

Visit us on the web at www.dorchesterpub.com.

A Quest of Dreams

Chapter One

Rio de Janeiro, 1886

"Miss Whitmore, you really don't want to be going in there right now." Barnaby rushed to keep up with Katherine Whitmore's determined strides, his footsteps pounding on the worn planks of the casino floor.

"Mr. Shalleen, your employer has managed to be otherwise occupied whenever I have tried to see him for the past three days." Kate glanced at the stage, her back growing stiff. Four women dressed in red skirts that barely brushed the tops of their thighs were kicking their feet onstage, in time to the raucous sounds of a badly tuned piano. Apparently Mr. McCain had little respect for women.

"Miss Whitmore, I'm thinking he'll be agreeing to see you, if you'll only be agreeing to wait until I can talk with him."

"I waited two hours in his office yesterday morning, as I recall."

"He was tied up, as it were," Barnaby said, grabbing her arm.

Kate halted. She glanced down at the small male hand spread against her ivory-colored sleeve, then glared straight into Barnaby Shalleen's dark blue eyes.

He snatched back his hand. "I'll be begging your pardon, miss."

"Mr. Shalleen, we plan to return to Pará tomorrow. It's imperative I speak with him today." She resumed her march across the dingy casino. The scent of stale beer and spent tobacco followed her into the hall leading to Devlin McCain's office, specters of dissipation haunting the place even in the light of day.

"But Miss Whitmore, you don't understand. At this time of day Dev is usually—"

"I understand Mr. McCain has been avoiding me. I cannot afford to give him the opportunity to avoid me today. I must speak with him."

"But Miss Whitmore, I'm thinking you—"

Without knocking, Kate opened the door to the office and marched across the threshold. "Mr. McCain, I . . ."

Her words fled with the air rushing from her lungs. Devlin McCain was stepping out of a slipper bath that had been placed beneath the windows on the far side of the small room. He paused when the door opened, with one foot still planted in the water and both eyes focused on Kate.

Oh heavens! She had never before seen a man without his shirt, let alone without anything else. Curious, mesmerized, she stared. She couldn't help herself. She studied him as she might have studied a magnificent wild creature poised on the bank of a stream. It was impossible to drag her gaze from him.

Damp, black waves tumbled around his face and curled just below his earlobes. His features were carved with strong lines and curves, too potently masculine to meet the genteel Victorian fashion of male beauty. Yet compelling. Overwhelming. Like a prince from an ancient race.

Afternoon sunlight slanted through the slats of the closed shutters, stroking golden lines across the smooth, moist skin of his wide shoulders, the thick curves of his upper arms, the lean lines of his torso.

Power radiated from the man. It throbbed in the thick muscles of his arms, his chest, his legs. And with that power he seemed to be devouring all of the air, like a hungry flame, until she could scarcely draw a breath.

A thick pelt of luxurious black fur covered his wide chest before narrowing into a thin line that rippled over the ridges of his flat stomach. It widened once more around . . . Good heavens! A tremor quivered inside her, spiraling outward in all directions. She yanked her gaze upward and collided with his eyes.

Those eyes! Even in the dim light his eyes shimmered like silver in the moonlight. Like a beautiful wild beast, he showed no embarrassment at his own nakedness, only a mild amusement at what his state of undress was doing to her. And she had little doubt he knew exactly what he was doing to her.

Kate spun on her heel, turning away from him. Her cheeks flared with the same heat that seared his stark male image across her memory. And somehow, in a way she had never felt before, the heat of her blush smoldered deep within her, somewhere low in her belly. "Mr. McCain, why are you bathing in your office?"

"Well, now, Miss Whitmore—It is Miss Whitmore, isn't it?" His voice was deep, gravelly, faintly colored with a drawl that reminded her of the few sultry days she had once spent with her father on a speaking engagement in New Orleans, as though time and distance had faded the accent of his youth.

"I'm Katherine Whitmore. Frederick Whitmore's daughter." She shut her eyes at the soft sound of a towel being rubbed across skin. Although she tried, she couldn't halt her imagination from conjuring the image of soft, white linen stroking smooth, golden skin.

"You'll excuse me if I wait till I put on my trousers to take your hand."

She could hear the amusement in that sultry voice. Mr. McCain was taking great pleasure at her expense. "Do you always use your office as a bathroom?" she demanded.

"I'm afraid this building hasn't much in the way of indoor plumbing. My office is a whole lot closer to the kitchen than my bedroom, which is upstairs, in case you want to take a look at that too."

There was a subtle shading in his words, an emphasis that left little doubt he had noticed the thorough look she had given him. How could he not have noticed? She had stared like a fascinated child.

"Of course I don't wish to see your bedroom." A fresh wave of fire scorched her cheeks. "Do you always bathe in the middle of the afternoon?"

"People who work nights usually sleep a few hours during the day."

"I'm sorry, Dev. But there was no stopping her."

Kate glanced down at the man standing beside her. The top of Barnaby's copper-colored head rose halfway between her elbow and her shoulder. He was looking up at her with dark blue eyes, his ruddy cheeks crinkled in a wide grin, looking as impish as a leprechaun who had just managed to trick someone out of finding his pot of gold.

"Mr. McCain, I apologize for coming in unannounced. But it's important I speak with you. Perhaps I could wait in the casino." Even though she didn't care to watch those poor women make spectacles of themselves onstage, it was preferable to making a spectacle of herself in here.

"We don't have anything to discuss," Devlin said, his words accompanied by a soft rustle of cloth.

"But Mr. McCain, I have come here to—"

"I know why you're here, Miss Whitmore. And I'm going to tell you the same thing I told your father, Lord Sinclair, and that man from the British Museum. I don't intend to go back into that green inferno just to chase after some man's misbegotten notion of finding a lost city that exists only in his head."

Kate clenched her hands into fists at her sides. She had heard too many people laugh at her father and his research into Atlantis. "It is not a misbegotten notion. The city exists."

"A man would have to be insane to trek into the center of Brazil with an old man full of moonshine and a green girl."

"How dare you!" She pivoted to face him. He was fastening the few remaining buttons in the front placket of his trousers, his hands moving leisurely upward across the black linen. "My father has spent his entire life searching for traces of Atlantis. And he has found them."

"What your father has is a map and journal sold to him by some old man who claims to have found them in a load of junk."

"In a box of books he bought at an auction. The man is a dealer in rare books."

"The man is a dealer in hogwash. And he knew your father was willing to pay very well for it." Devlin tossed open the shutters. Sunlight rushed through the open windows, eager to touch his face, to stroke golden light across the bare skin of his shoulders, to ignite dark chestnut highlights in his black hair.

"Mr. McCain, what we have come across is a journal written by a man who found an ancient city he called Avallon more than eighty years ago."

"And this journal just happens to have turned up at an auction in London four months ago." He turned to face her.

Sunlight shimmered around him, filling his thick hair, drenching his wide shoulders. Behind him ships crowded the harbor, masts swaying, gray plumes rising from black smokestacks. Across that expanse of glittering water Sugarloaf Mountain rose, emerald jungle climbing the steep slope. The scene was elemental, primeval, beautiful, like the man.

The beauty of wild, untamed creatures, of rugged, untouched nature, were all personified in this man. Framed by the open windows, he stood as a portrait of potent male beauty. She wondered if she could ever capture the essence of this man on canvas.

Good heavens! What was wrong with her? Thinking such things about this man.

"Connor Randolph, the man who wrote the journal, lived in London. When he died, his possessions must have been sold and . . ." She hesitated, knowing by the look in his eyes that Devlin McCain was not believing a word she was saying. "Mr. McCain, perhaps we don't know precisely how the journal came to be at the auction, or why Connor Randolph never made his discovery public. But the journal is genuine."

"How can you be so sure?"

"This isn't the first time the city has been discovered. A Portuguese explorer filed a document with his government in 1754, describing a city he had discovered on a mountain in the interior."

"Apparently his government didn't take him seriously."

"No, they didn't. Perhaps because he didn't outline clear enough directions to reach it."

"But Randolph managed to use those sketchy directions to find the city."

"That's right."

"And this journal of Randolph's gives the precise location."

"He drew a map."

"That was nice of him." Devlin gave her a look of pure skepticism.

"There were notes in the journal, ancient symbols found on buildings, symbols my father has traced back to Atlantis."

The door closed softly behind her. Kate glanced back to find Barnaby had left her alone with McCain. Alone with a man who seemed more primitive than civilized, a man savage enough to survive the wilds of the rain forest. A man who was staring at her as though she were some rare curiosity, appraising her in a way that made her wonder if the buttons of her bodice were still fastened.

She clasped her hands at her waist and forced her back to stiffen. She had suffered appraisals like McCain's before, from men who looked at her as though she were a pastry to be consumed, men who didn't care if she had a brain in her head, men who wanted her as a decoration. Yet she had never felt the heat of a man's gaze scorch her the way Devlin McCain could with one look from his silvery blue eyes.

"We found the same symbols on rocks in Cornwall and Wales, and in Ireland and the highlands of Scotland," she said, trying to focus on something other than the disturbing way McCain stirred the blood in her veins. "The same symbols in Egypt, on the walls of pyramids in Central America, and in caves in Iceland. They have a common source—Atlantis. They are symbols left by colonists from that ancient civilization."

Devlin lifted a fresh white linen shirt from the back of a wooden armchair near the tub. "If I were going to sell a journal and map leading to a mythical lost city, I'd look up a few symbols in one of the books your father has written and sprinkle them through my journal."

A warm breeze drifted through the windows, brushing his skin before touching her face with the intriguing fragrance of sandalwood and spices and man. That scent spilled over her, filling her, sparking along her nerves in the most disconcerting manner.

"My father is an expert." She tried not to watch the way the muscles in his chest flexed as he slipped into his shirt. She really must not wonder what it might be like to touch him. "It would take more than a few symbols sprinkled through a journal to convince him."

"Even if that journal is genuine, even if there is an ancient city planted in the heart of Brazil, colonized long before Egypt"—He fastened the buttons lining the front of his shirt as he spoke—"you'd be marching through hell to go looking for it."

"My father has been looking for some trace of Atlantis all his life. In his journal, Connor Randolph described the architecture, the carvings he found, and drawings on the walls of buildings. They can all be traced back to Atlantis. Don't you see, this city could very well have been a colony of Atlantis. Finding it would prove all of my father's theories."

"Not with me as a guide."

"But you've been there. You've followed the tributaries. You know what to expect. In Pará we were told by the British Council you would be the best man to lead us through the jungle. The only man."

Devlin frowned as he held her gaze. He couldn't understand why the British Council had recommended him. There was more than one person in that consulate who thought he was a murderer.

"With your help, we can do it, Mr. McCain."

Faith, complete and unflinching, radiated from the woman. Faith and confidence in him. It was tempting. Just as the mystery of a lost city was tempting. Yet Devlin knew what was waiting out there in the jungle. He knew dreams couldn't survive in that green hell. "I spent a year in the jungle. Nothing is going to make me go back."

She hesitated a moment, clasping her hands at her waist, studying him as though she were figuring the best way around a brick wall. "I would think that for the right amount of money, you might."

"I'm not for sale." Money was what had lured him into the jungle. He had been hungry then, foolish to think he could drag enough gold out of the rivers to buy some respectability. He had found enough gold to buy an old warehouse and turn it into the Paradise Casino. Not very respectable, but it was his, the first thing he had ever owned in his life.

"Mr. McCain, there is no one else who can help us. We need you."

"Lady, I'm no one's hero."

He looked at the woman standing a few feet away from him. She was neither tall nor short, and she was slender, though the way her bodice stretched across her breasts as she drew a deep breath suggested a nice curve of feminine flesh hidden beneath. One glance might suggest she was nothing but a plain spinster. But he had taken more than a glance at this woman.

"Mr. McCain, there must be some way I can make you see how important this expedition is."

She was looking at him with eyes the cool, clear blue of a summer sky, large eyes set beneath the delicate, arched wings of light brown brows. The small lenses of her spectacles didn't disguise the beauty of those eyes. The spectacles perched on her slim nose couldn't spoil the pure oval of her face or tarnish her finely chiseled cheekbones. And they couldn't hide the hunger he saw in those pale blue depths when she looked at him.

There was an odd mixture of innocence and passion in this woman, a blend that had triggered an instant response in him, like a match tossed on whiskey. If she hadn't turned away from him when she had, she would have seen how hot and hard she had made him just by looking at him. Standing naked before her, he would have had no way to hide.

"We are on the verge of discovering the remains of a civilization that was established more than ten thousand years ago. Think of it: the remains of a people who gave civilization to the Egyptians. My father has spent his entire life looking for proof that civilization existed. Think of it, Mr. McCain." She moved toward him as she spoke, stepping into the sunlight flowing in a river of gold through the windows.

Despite the brutal way her hair was pulled back into a tight bun, she couldn't hide the luster of that glorious mane. Her golden hair captured the light, spinning each silken strand into shimmering sunshine. The woman was beautiful. And he suspected it was the last thing she wanted anyone to notice.

"Think of the mysteries." Her face glowed with the radiance of her dreams. "Why, there could be something as valuable as the Rosetta stone in that city. Think of the possibilities."

Right now he was thinking of what her golden hair would feel like spilling across his chest, silky strands sliding against his skin. "There's no place for innocence in the jungle. Go back home, be safe, Miss Whitmore."

She paused a foot in front of him, so close he could catch a breath of roses rising with the heat of her skin. "I'm not a little girl who needs protecting," she said, her chin rising. "I'm an archaeologist. I have gone down the Nile, Mr. McCain. I have spent weeks living in tents, sleeping on the ground."

"The Nile isn't the Amazon, Professor." He stroked his fingers over the curve of her cheek. Her skin was every bit as smooth as it looked, like warm silk. And he'd bet she would taste every bit as good as she felt. "You have no idea what you'd be getting into. A little English rosebud like you wouldn't last a week in the jungle."

She stepped back, lifting her fingers to her cheek as though he had slapped her rather than caressed her. "Mr. McCain, this is an opportunity to touch another world, to take a look into the past, maybe glimpse the future."

"Sorry, I've never believed in fairy tales."

"Fairy tales." She stared at him for a long moment before she spoke, her expression dissolving into disgust. "You have no right to say my father's beliefs are no more than fairy tales. You have no right to ridicule him."

Devlin hadn't meant to ridicule anyone. He knew too well what it felt like to be ridiculed. This quest of Frederick Whitmore's was nothing short of suicide. He had only wanted her to see that. And now he wanted to show her he wasn't cruel, he wasn't unfeeling. He understood dreams. All too well. Yet the look in her eyes froze the gentle words in his throat.

"I don't know what made me think a man like you could understand."

The muscles in his chest tightened. She was looking at him with the same contempt he had seen in too many eyes, a look he had known all his life. People had stared down their noses at the orphan in threadbare trousers that were too short for his long legs, then later at the young man in dirty Levi's who had taken any job he could find just to put food in his belly.

And finally they stared with contempt at the gambler, even though his clothes were clean, even though he always played a fair game. He was still trash.

"You should be wearing animal skins and carrying a club. Your mind is too narrow to even conceive of the possibility of something so fantastic as a colony settled by people from another lifetime. You can't see past the smoke in your filthy casino."

Devlin forced his lips into a smile. "Some of us weren't born rich enough to go chasing after moonbeams."

She clenched her hands into fists at her sides, her shoulders rising with the effort to control her fury. "My father is a scholar, Mr. McCain."

"Your father is a damn fool if he goes looking for that city. And a murderer if he lets you go along."

She slapped him so hard his lower lip scraped against his teeth, tearing his skin. "You have no right to talk about my father in that disparaging manner."

He grabbed her arm as she turned to leave. She pivoted, drawing back her hand to slap him again. He grabbed her wrist in midflight and dragged it behind her, pinning her hand to the small of her back, slamming her against his chest.

"Let go of me!" She tossed back her head, staring at him with blue eyes inflamed with rage. "You have no right to—"

"What gives you the right to come barging into my office, Professor? Tell me. Is it money? Does money give you the right to treat someone as though he's nothing but dirt?"

"Barbarian!" She twisted in his grasp, brushing her breasts against his chest.

In spite of his anger, he felt his body respond to the siren call of woman to man. His own response disgusted him. At the moment she was the last woman on the face of the earth he wanted. Issuing an oath under his breath, he pushed her away from him.

With a swirl of her ivory linen skirt, she turned and marched across the room. She flung open the door and paused on the threshold, hesitating a moment before she turned to face him, color high on her cheeks, her hands tight balls at her sides. "With or without you, we will find that city, Mr. McCain. We will prove to the world how great a scholar my father really is. We will make everyone see how foolish they were for laughing at him."

Devlin watched her leave, her golden head held high and proud, her footsteps tapping the bare planks with a determined rhythm. Music from the main room of the casino swirled around him. The girls were expecting him to attend their rehearsal to see their latest tricks.

He drew a finger across his throbbing cheek and pressed the tip of his tongue to the jagged flesh on the inside of his lower lip, tasting the salt of his blood. It would be a long time before he forgot Miss Katherine Whitmore.

Barnaby appeared in the doorway. "That's one determined female."

"Determined to get herself killed." Devlin tucked his shirt into his trousers as he continued. "If her father leads her off into that jungle, neither one of them is going to walk back out alive." He released his breath in a long sigh, trying to release the tension that had drawn his stomach into a tight knot. "Well, it's none of my business what they do."

Barnaby climbed into an armchair near the door. "They would have a better chance with you leading them," he said, settling against the curved wooden back, his feet dangling a foot off the floor.

Devlin arched one dark brow as he looked at Barnaby. He had met the little man six months ago, a few days after he had opened the Paradise. Devlin had plucked him out of the middle of a fight in his casino and Barnaby had been with him ever since, as cook, bookkeeper, and friend—one of the few friends Devlin had ever known. "Think you're in my will, do you?"

"Ah, Devlin, my lad, I've been looking for a real adventure since I left the cool climes of county Kildare." He rubbed his small hands together as he continued. "And this sounds like a roaring good one."

Devlin shook his head. "I've had all the adventure I need for one lifetime."

"And what about the money? I thought you had dreams of getting out of this place, Devlin. I thought you had your heart set on owning a piece of the rolling green hills of California."

Devlin sank into the worn leather chair behind his desk and pulled on his socks. "I'll get it on my own."

"You'll be too old to run a ranch by then. What with the fights and the cheats and the money you pay the help, you lose more in a week than you gain." Barnaby lifted his foot and studied the pointed tip of his black shoe. "You're too honest to become rich in this business."

"Forget it."

"So you're just going to let them wander off into the jungle alone?"

. "If they want to go hunting for some fairy-tale city, I can't stop them."

"Pity. I'm thinking that's one fine female. Hate to see her end up in a cooking pot."

As much as Devlin hated to admit it, the woman intrigued him. She was filled with dreams, a little girl on a treasure hunt. He didn't want to let her walk into that hell. There was something about the woman that made him feel protective, something that made him want to be the hero she was looking for instead of the bastard she now thought he was. He shoved his feet into his shoes and pushed away those romantic notions. He couldn't afford to be romantic.

Eighteen months ago Devlin and his partner, Gerald Fielding, had taken a boat full of trinkets and headed out on the Amazon to pan for gold. On one of the tributaries they had found a tribe of friendly Indians who were willing to work for them with trinkets as payment. Yet there were other tribes in the area, tribes who wanted to kill them for the same trinkets.

Devlin had spent a year with a rifle by his side, each night afraid to go to sleep. And every day there had been the insects and the snakes and the constant threat of attack. God, he hated the insects worse than anything.

Three days before they had planned to return to Rio, Gerald had been killed by an Indian hunting party. Devlin had survived both the jungle and the murder investigation afterward. And he had the Paradise. And maybe one day it would be enough to take away the emptiness inside him.

"Katherine Whitmore is an aristocratic little snob who thinks I'm a caveman." Devlin shrugged into his black linen coat. "I shouldn't give a damn what happens to her."

"No, I'm thinking the lady didn't leave you with a warm glow in your heart." Barnaby chuckled deep in his throat. "More of a warm glow on your cheek."

Devlin rested his hands on the windowsill and stared out at the bay. Sunlight spread across the rippling water like a blanket of shimmering gold. It was beautiful. Yet he had never seen land more beautiful than the coast just south of San Francisco.

Brazil had been Gerald's idea. The two men had met in a casino on the Barbary Coast. They had known each other less than a month when Gerald had coaxed him into panning for gold on the Amazon. It hadn't taken much coaxing.

Devlin had been looking for something all his life, and he believed the gold might help him find it. But it hadn't. And now, at 32, he was beginning to realize it was time to stop looking for it. It was time to settle down on a piece of gorgeous California land and raise horses, a dream he couldn't afford.

He thought of Katherine Whitmore, of the way the sunlight had come to life in her hair, of the way her skin glowed when she spoke of her dreams. His cheek throbbed. Without looking in a mirror, he knew her hand was etched in red across his face; he could feel the imprint of each slender finger along his cheek.

"You've never met anyone like her, have you, Dev?" Barnaby asked, his voice oddly gentle.

"If I'm lucky, I won't meet anyone like her again." But even as he spoke the words, he knew they weren't true. The woman intrigued him with her special blend of innocence and passion. She was a beautiful woman hiding behind high collars and ugly buns, a goddess dressed up like an old-maidish schoolteacher. And she was headed for disaster.

Devlin curled his hands into fists against the windowsill. It was none of his business what she did. The lady was nothing but trouble. If he were smart, he would stay clear of the beautiful little snob. If she were smart, she would forget all about chasing a fairy tale called Avallon.

Avallon. He had to admit, it sounded intriguing. During his months in the Amazon, Devlin had heard legends of an ancient city perched high on a mountaintop in the heart of the interior, tales of the fair-skinned people who lived there, like the gods of Olympus. Yet he knew the stories for what they were—nothing but smoke. And he knew better than to believe in fairy tales.

Avallon. Brianna stood on the rocky brow of the hill behind her house staring into the valley below. Crystals trapped in black stones glittered in the sun like a vision from a fairy tale, rising from the valley floor to shape the temple and surrounding buildings of ancient Avallon. These were the remains of a city built by her husband's ancestors, the first of many that had borne that name.

The breeze whispered softly here. Perched high on the top of a rugged mountain, the Avallon that flourished today was blessed with a climate much milder than the extremes suffered on the surrounding plains, much more temperate than the humid jungle shimmering dark emerald miles beyond.

For more than 30 years this mountaintop had been Brianna's home, since the day she had married Rhys. Since the day he had carried her from her home in Ireland to this hidden paradise of mystery and wonder. Yet there was a part of her still locked to the other world. A part of her lost long ago.

She sensed rather than heard her husband approach; as always Rhys moved silently, but the breeze changed upon her cheek, grew warmer with his presence. He had been born here, trained in the ancient ways, just as their son had been trained.

The teachings dated back 10,000 years, back to the ancient ones. Teachings that had caused people of that simple world long ago to murmur of witches and fairies and magic when her husband's ancestors had tried to live among them after a cataclysm had destroyed their island nation. Eventually, those murmurs and the danger of discovery had sent his ancestors looking for a safe haven.

Six thousand years ago her husband's ancestors had come to this mountaintop. Still, she wondered if the ancient training would be enough to keep their son safe on the quest he would soon face.

"You're troubled, my *Edaina*."

Her husband's voice brushed her like warm sable. *Edaina*, soul mate. They were two halves of one whole. Yet there were times when he remained a mystery to her. She turned to face Rhys, the cool breeze lifting her unbound hair, strands of gold streaming across her face. Sunlight fell soft and shimmering upon his features, the shining rays slipping into the thick waves of his black hair.

He looked commanding, beautiful, like a young prince, his skin as taut and smooth as the day she had met him, his tall, broad-shouldered body still finely muscled. No more than 35 summers, that was how young this man seemed, though 62 had passed since his birth.

Here in Avallon they had discovered the secret for slowing the inevitable tide of time. It existed in the forest. It existed in the plants and the trees and the insects. It existed with the other medicines, the cures for all manner of disease.

"I was just thinking," Brianna said, "that for all the advances the people of Avallon have made through the ages, in many ways they still live in a distant century, in a time when knights were sent on dangerous quests to prove their worthiness."

Rhys slid his fingers across her cheek, brushing the hair back from her face. "You're worried about our son."

"I want to go to him. I want to tell the council to go to blazes and take all their cautions and rules with them."

"I understand how you feel." He slipped his arms around her and held her close. She pressed her cheek against the soft, black linen covering his chest, taking comfort in his heat, in the strong, even rhythm of his heart. "But what would become of our son if we turned our back on the council?"

"And what will become of him on this quest?"

"If he succeeds, he will have his chance to become a Lord of the Inner Circle. It is his birthright, the highest honor my people can bestow."

"And if he fails, he could die, all for the sake of honor." Brianna lifted her face and looked up into his eyes; the swirling blue-green of the Caribbean was in his eyes; the pain and suffering she had known for years was there in his eyes. "What of these people? Whitmore and his daughter, the others who will go on this expedition. They're being deceived, manipulated as though they were pawns on a chessboard, all because of the Central Council and their stubborn insistence on this test. It's dangerous. These people could be injured or killed."

"Their own thirst for knowledge has brought them here."

"And our son, we might never see him again."

"I've done all I can, my love." He slipped his hand beneath her hair, stroking her nape with his warm fingers.

"I know. But I'm torn. In my mind I understand the council's decision, the need to test our son's integrity. But in my heart I can't sanction this dangerous game."

"If I didn't believe he would triumph, I would go to him today, the council be damned." Rhys held her close, enfolding her in his warm embrace. "We must trust in our son. We must trust he will pass this gauntlet. It's the only way he will be whole again."

Chapter Two

"The man is a barbarian." Kate pivoted as she reached the pale green painted wall. Without pause she continued her pacing, reversing her direction, heading back toward the open doors leading to the balcony on the far side of the sitting room in her father's hotel suite. "We are better off without him."

"No, I'm afraid we aren't. He would be invaluable to us." At the sound of the derisive huff his daughter made, Frederick Whitmore glanced up from the map of the Amazon that was spread across his lap.

Kate paused in front of the open doors and stared out at the distant bay. Emerald mountains surrounded the city, rising in great, jagged peaks like a giant serrated shell open to display its pearl. Gold and scarlet rays of the late afternoon sun spilled into the room with a humid breeze, stroking her face with warmth, drenching her senses with the fragrance of orange blossoms and jasmine from the nearby gardens. "I doubt we could trust him, even if he did decide to act as our guide. Any man who would trick poor, unsuspecting Indians into panning for gold for the promise of a few trinkets is a man without scruples."

"A pocketknife is more valuable to the Indians than gold," Austin Sinclair said.

She glanced over her shoulder at the man sitting in an upholstered armchair across from her father. Although she had known Austin only a short time, she felt as though they had been friends all their lives. Six months ago this tall, elegant man with thick, black hair and pale blue-gray eyes had come to their town house in London, anxious to discuss her father's latest book. Through their mutual passion for Atlantis, Lord Austin Sinclair, Marquess of Somerset, son of the Duke of Daventry, had become a dear friend of both Frederick and Kate. It was only natural to invite him to join them on this adventure.

"I'm not sure why you're defending him."

Austin looked at her, his gray eyes filled with mischief. "Perhaps because he isn't here to defend himself."

"Oh, that isn't fair. You make me sound like a bully." She spun away from the open doors and started back toward the wall, her ivory skirt swirling around her.

Although her gown was new, it was not made in the current fashion. Kate found nothing appealing in bustles; they were impractical, constricting, and made a woman look like a deformed camel. And, as far as she was concerned, the materials currently being used to fashion those monstrosities looked better draping furniture than they did women. Four years ago, when she was 22, she had started designing her own clothes, much to her dressmaker's horror.

"Devlin McCain is a scoundrel," she said, defending her stance.

"Interesting," Frederick murmured, watching his daughter's agitated movements. "I'm surprised he made such an unfavorable impression on you. I must admit, I found the man quite likable."

"Likable!" Kate paused beside the round pedestal table which stood beside the sofa where her father was sitting.

"Do you know he has women dancers in his casino?" She clasped her hands at her waist, affecting what her father had often called her schoolmarm pose. "Women who wear barely anything at all and bounce around onstage kicking their feet and lifting their short skirts above their heads."

"Really?" Frederick looked at her over the narrow lenses of the reading glasses perched on his slim nose. Sunlight brushed the tousled mane of his hair, silvery strands streaking the thick, dark brown waves. "I didn't see any dancing girls when I visited Mr. McCain."

Kate frowned. "You sound disappointed."

He smiled, deep lines creasing the tanned skin around his dark brown eyes. Although he owned one of the largest shipping companies in England, Frederick Whitmore preferred to spend most of his time indulging his passion for archaeology in general, and Atlantis in particular.

"Sometimes, my darling daughter, you are far too serious." He began folding the map as he spoke, fighting with the natural creases in the paper. "And far too critical of the other half of the population."

She lifted her fingers to her cheek, remembering the soft touch of Devlin McCain's fingers gliding across her skin. McCain probably thought women would melt at his touch. No doubt most women did. "You don't understand. The man thinks women are ornaments. He believes we were placed on the earth to be nothing more than playthings for men."

Frederick studied her a moment before he spoke. "I would suppose most women find Mr. McCain attractive, decisively so."

"Only women who would like to be clubbed over the head and dragged to a nearby cave."

Austin's deep laughter rumbled in the room. When Kate turned to give him a chilling look, he rose from his chair, his lips a smiling curve in the neat fringe of his full, black beard. "I'm going to take a walk before dinner. Maybe I can think of some inducement to coax the scandalous Mr. McCain into doing his proper duty. See you both later." He left Katherine and Frederick alone in the sunny room.

"Pity Mr. McCain isn't going with us on this journey." Frederick turned the wrinkled mass of the map over in his hands. "I have a feeling he just might be the man who could change your mind on a few matters."

"If you mean marriage, I can assure you Devlin McCain is the last man in the world who could make me change my mind about that institution."

"He has qualities, Katie."

"None of which I find the least bit appealing. I have no intention of becoming any man's chattel. No man shall steal my identity, especially a man like Devlin McCain."

"Marriage to the right person makes us more, not less." He slipped his glasses onto his forehead. "I don't think your mother ever felt as though I had stolen her identity."

"That was different." Although Kate's mother had died giving her birth, she knew her through her father's impressions, soft memories of the woman he had adored. "You aren't like most men." She sank to the sofa beside her father and placed her hand on his arm. "You're caring, understanding. You have never tried to hold me back, to make me less because I was born female. You are rare."

"I raised you like a son." Frederick patted her hand. "I didn't know any other way. But I hate to think my ignorance has caused you to shut out a part of your life that can be one of the most rewarding experiences in the world."

Kate shook her head. "There is nothing a man can offer a woman to compensate for the loss of her independence."

Frederick pursed his lips, his dark brows raising slightly. "There are one or two things a man might offer a woman."

"If you imply something of a carnal nature, I'm not interested. Intellectual pursuits are far more rewarding, I'm certain." Into her mind crept an image of Devlin McCain as she had first seen him, every inch of him naked power and animal beauty. The memory sparked an odd tightening of her muscles deep inside her, a foreign flare of heat that shocked her.

"There are some experiences one should not miss in this life, Katie. Love, both emotional and physical, can be most rewarding."

She had been raised a scholar, taught to explore her curiosity about everything. And her father had long ago indulged her curiosity concerning what Kate had called the "human mating process." She would never forget the blush that had risen to her father's cheeks as he had explained the fundamentals of the process. And she would always be grateful he had never tried to nurture a false ignorance in her.

"Father, are you hoping I might jump into the arms of any man who comes along?"

Frederick smiled. "I was hoping you might jump into Austin's arms. But you seem to consider that handsome young man a brother rather than a possible lover."

"Father, really." Kate raised her brows in mock indignation. "You positively shock me."

"My darling daughter, if I had raised you properly, talk such as this would shock you."

"You wouldn't have me any other way," she said, taking the mangled map from his hands. "And tell me, just what would you do if I ran off with some man?" She opened the map and began folding it precisely along the precreased lines as she continued. "Can you really imagine going on an expedition without me?"

"I've been selfish. I should have sent you to proper schools instead of hiring tutors, instead of keeping you with me, dragging you around the world. But you were such a joy, Katie, such a comfort to me."

"And now you want to marry me off, to be rid of me." She laid the neatly folded map in his lap.

"You need someone in your life. I won't always be around. I hate to think of you all alone."

"Don't talk that way." She slipped his glasses from his brow. She folded them and slipped them into the inside pocket of his light gray coat, patting his shoulder as she continued. "You're far from old."

"The years creep up on us all." He took her hand between both of his. "I'm so very glad I have you, Katie. And I wonder who you will have when you're my age."

"I have my work." She felt a tremble deep inside of her, a tiny echo of longing that could fill her if she didn't fight it, as it often filled her at night when she was too tired to force it into abeyance.

"Will work be enough?"

"A husband would never allow his wife to go traipsing all over the world in search of lost worlds. He would expect me to give up my work. He would want me to be a docile little ornament, to hold teas and dinners and . . . and I don't know what else. I would be so terrible at it, don't you see? And in time he would hate me as much as I hated him for turning me into something I am not."

Still, there were moments when she wondered what it might be like to share her life with someone special, to feel a man's arms around her. "If I could meet a man who would allow me to keep my independence, who would be a true partner . . ." Ah, but where was that man? She had come to believe he didn't exist.

"Austin seems like the kind of man who would never try to chain you."

It was true. At least it seemed to be true. But how could you be sure a man wouldn't change after the marriage ceremony? How could you be sure you wouldn't find yourself trapped? "I'm certain Austin has never once thought of asking me to marry him."

"With some encouragement, he might."

Dear Austin. He was intelligent and kind and witty and, she had to admit, pleasant to look at, everything a woman could desire in a mate. And yet only the warmth of friendship flickered between them. It wasn't enough.

Once again the image of Devlin McCain invaded her thoughts, and with it came that intriguing wave of heat, making her feel oddly restless. She stood and snatched a glass from the silver tray on the table beside the sofa. "I'm not sure how you could even suggest I would consider marrying a man like Devlin McCain."

The look in her father's eyes made her realize how revealing her father found the sudden turn in her conversation. She lifted an earthenware pitcher in the shape of a toucan—what the natives called a *moringue*—from the table and poured water through the beak into her glass. "I assure you, I do not find the man the least bit attractive."

"I shouldn't drink that."

Kate glanced down into the glass and found an inch-long cockroach, a *barata,* swimming in the water. A shiver of revulsion coiled along her spine. Insects thrived everywhere in this climate. That was the reason the floors were bare; fleas liked to infest carpets.

She still wasn't accustomed to finding the huge, dark cockroaches, and she was likely to find them anywhere. This morning one of the creatures was sleeping in her shoe. Since her father didn't share her aversion to the ugly beasts, he saw no reason to slaughter them when he found them. He had even started naming a few of them he saw on a regular basis.

"Father, I do wish you wouldn't keep your pets in the water pitcher."

"I caught Horatio chewing on the cover of my journal last night," Frederick said, watching his daughter carry her glass toward the open doors leading to the balcony. "The little devils love to eat leather."

Without glancing over the wrought-iron railing, Kate dumped Horatio over the railing and started back into the room. A startled gasp followed by a deep rumbling curse brought her up short.

"Good heavens!" she murmured, glancing at her father.

Frederick tilted his dark head, a smile curving his lips. "I think you should have looked before you tossed poor Horatio from the balcony."

She rushed back onto the balcony and glanced down to find Devlin McCain staring up at her from the grassy court-yard 20 feet below. The fading sunlight glittered on the water

dripping from his dark hair. With her eyes, Kate followed
a glistening droplet as it slid down the curve of his cheek
and the strong column of his neck before slipping beneath
the collar of his white shirt. Her imagination completed the
journey of that glistening droplet into the thick, black curls
she knew covered his wide chest.

Devlin drew a deep breath and released it between his
clenched teeth when he saw her. "I should have known."

She felt a nervous tickle in her stomach, a giggle that
scampered upward until she had to bite her lower lip to keep
it from escaping. "I'm terribly sorry," she said, her apology
marred by a wayward trickle of laughter.

One dark brow quirked upward as Devlin held her amused
gaze. "Sorry you didn't throw the glass as well?"

"Now that you mention it, yes."

"Mr. McCain, please forgive my daughter." Frederick
rested his hands on the railing beside Kate. "I'm afraid
she has a rather distorted sense of humor. Do come up.
There are fresh towels in the room. Number two-oh-three."

Kate watched McCain disappear beneath the balcony, then
turned to face her father. "Why do you suppose he's come
here?"

"Perhaps he's changed his mind," Frederick said, walking
back into the sitting room.

Kate followed him, tapping her fingertips against the
glass she still held. "He thinks we're fools for believing
in Avallon."

"He is pragmatic, dear."

"An ignorant boor, if you ask me." Kate set the glass
beside the pitcher on the table and glanced down at her palms.
They were damp, and it had more to do with Devlin McCain
than the moist glass she had been holding. She jumped when
someone knocked on the door.

"Do you know you're blushing?" Frederick asked as he
walked toward the door.

"Father, please, don't be vulgar," she whispered, resisting
the urge to hide her warm cheeks behind her hands. She drew

a deep breath and tried to calm the sudden fury of her heart. Good heavens, she was acting like a woman infatuated with a ruthlessly handsome man. The silly sort of creature she could never tolerate. Well, she would have none of this nonsense.

Kate stood by the sofa as her father opened the door and greeted Devlin McCain. She had always thought of her father as being tall. Yet McCain towered several inches above Frederick's slender six feet. For a moment, McCain filled the doorway with his broad-shouldered frame, and then her father was inviting him inside. McCain moved into the room with long, graceful strides, a giant of a man.

Once again the raw power of this man overwhelmed her. It surrounded him, it radiated in his every move, it brushed against her like a hot desert wind. Images came to her mind of immortal gods living on lofty mountaintops high above the fragile humans of their kingdom.

She had read in Celtic lore of magical men who would carry mortal females to their palaces in the heavens, where they would never again know the cold touch of time. Immortal. To live forever with this power and majesty.

Nothing more than fables, she reminded herself. McCain was nothing more than a man. And barely civilized at that. Still, she felt a shaking deep inside her, a frightening weakness that came from nothing more than looking at this man, a flaw within her she had never realized existed.

Most of the men she knew were scholars or aristocrats. She had never met anyone like Devlin McCain. That must be the reason she found him fascinating, she assured herself. It had nothing to do with being attracted to the primitive barbarian. It had everything to do with being a scientist.

She was not the type of woman who could be overwhelmed by a handsome face and finely chiseled body. She was just curious, that was all. Yet she couldn't keep herself from wondering what it might be like to touch him, to feel the warmth of his skin beneath her palm. He had such warm, smooth-looking skin. McCain glanced straight at her and caught her staring. Once again.

Shades of blue and gray mingled like storm clouds in irises that darkened to midnight blue around the edges. Caught in McCain's silvery blue gaze, she couldn't move, couldn't breathe.

He penetrated her with his eyes, touching her as no one had ever touched her. With those eyes he seared away the masks she might have tried to hide behind. He stripped her bare, exposing her, making her feel as though he had read her diary, as though he knew all the secrets there and all the secrets she had never been brave enough to admit, even to herself.

Her father was speaking, yet she couldn't hear the words above the pounding of blood in her ears. McCain was moving toward her, offering his hand, filling her world.

"Miss Whitmore, I thought we . . ." Devlin hesitated, drawing a sharp breath.

"Is something wrong?" Kate asked.

Devlin twitched, reaching behind him, shoving his hand down the collar of his shirt as though he had a hot coal down his back. "Something is . . ." He jerked his shoulders. "Something . . ."

Kate stared at him, watching his erratic motions, realization slowly dawning inside her. She glanced at her father just as Frederick turned to look at her.

"Horatio!" Kate and Frederick spoke the single name at the same time.

"Horatio?" Devlin asked.

"Father's pet cockroach," Kate said, fighting down the giggle that was tickling her throat. "He was in my glass."

Devlin's eyes widened. "Bathroom?"

"In there," Frederick said, pointing toward a door on the far side of the room.

Devlin McCain rushed across the room, twitching, stripping off his coat, snatching at the buttons of his shirt. Kate pressed her fingers to her lips, trying to catch the giggle tumbling across her tongue as McCain disappeared into the bathroom, closing the door behind him.

"Katie, this isn't a laughing matter." Frederick looked at his daughter, the smile tugging at one corner of his lips spoiling the severe cast of his features.

"Did you see his face?" Kate surrendered to the laughter bubbling inside her. "He looked horrified."

Frederick cleared his throat in an obvious effort to stop his own chuckle. "Hush, Katie. He'll hear you."

Kate hugged her arms to her waist and fell back, dissolving into giggles on the sofa. "The brave Devlin McCain. He faced headhunters . . . cannibals . . . and Horatio made him . . . blanch."

"I should guess I might react much the same." Still smiling, Frederick glanced over his shoulder at a knock on the door. "I wonder who that is?"

Kate drew a shaky breath and tried to stop her giggles. Through tears she watched her father cross the room and answer the door. What happened next drove the laughter from her heart.

Chapter Three

Two dark-haired men surged across the threshold. One man, the smaller of the two, thrust a pistol into Frederick's chest as he forced him backward into the room. The other, a man who stood over six feet tall and looked equally as broad, lumbered toward Kate.

Kate scrambled to her feet. "What do you want?"

The big man didn't answer. He just kept advancing, like a slow-moving bear, his small, dark eyes fixed on her face. Kate turned to run. The big man lunged for her, grabbing her arm, hauling her back so quickly she lost her balance and plowed into him.

Before she could catch her breath, he clamped one thick arm around her waist and dragged her upward, her back sliding against his chest until her feet dangled several inches above the floor. Kate opened her mouth to scream. A hand the size of a ham slammed across her mouth, cutting off her words.

"Let go of her!" Frederick shouted, taking a step toward his daughter. He halted as the big man holding Kate pressed a knife to her throat, dying sunlight shimmering scarlet against the long, curving blade.

"You do what we say and nobody gets hurt," the smaller man said. "We only want the map. Give it to us, and we leave."

The smaller man was from the United States, probably New York, Kate decided, basing her judgment on the flat sound of his vowels. Still, Rio was filled with people from all nations. They could have been hired to come here by anyone.

The cold steel bit into her throat. She wanted to swallow and couldn't, too afraid any movement might force the blade into her skin. She stared at her father. She tried to calm the muscles trembling in every part of her body. Calm. She must be calm. Only a calm mind could figure a way out of this predicament.

"The map is in a safe in London." Frederick kept his eyes focused on Kate. "My daughter has it memorized. But I doubt she can draw it for you if you cut her throat."

Kate bit her lower lip. They had both memorized the map; this was her father's way of shifting the importance, of making her more valuable alive than dead. But in doing it, he had placed his own life at greater risk.

"All right, Jocko," the smaller man said, keeping the pistol directed at Frederick, staring at Kate with dark brown eyes that were squinting as though the sunlight slanting through the windows bothered him. "Let her down."

Kate's knees threatened to buckle when her feet touched the floor. Silently she admonished herself for the weakness. She had to remain calm, for she doubted these two men intended to leave behind any witnesses to their crime.

"All right, lady," the squinting man said. "You got a desk over there. Get to making that map."

Kate forced her feet, which had somehow turned into clay, to carry her toward the desk. As she sat in the rosewood chair at the desk, she wondered how they would know if she gave them an accurate map. She pulled out a sheet of white parchment and decided to draw an interesting map that might lead them to Piccadilly as well as the lost city of Avallon.

"Don't get cute, little lady," the smaller man said. "We been told you both got the map in your head. When you're done, we're gonna ask your father to draw one. If they're different, we're gonna cut off your little finger. For starters."

Out of reflex Kate curled her fingers against her palms.

The man with the gun laughed, a cackle high in his throat. "And we want everything, including those funny marks that tell you if you're going the right way."

Kate frowned as she opened the ink pot. How would these men know both she and her father had memorized the map? How would they know about the symbols? Had someone seen the original?

She dipped the pen into the ink pot and stared down at the blank sheet of paper. Should she risk giving them a fake? Did it matter? Unless they thought of some way out of this, both she and her father would be dead. She was sure of it.

"Get to it."

The growl had come from the big man standing behind her. Kate moistened her lips and pressed the tip of the pen to the paper.

A low gasp of pain ripped through the room.

"Father," Kate whispered, turning in her chair, looking past the giant standing behind her.

She had expected to see her father bent over in agony. Instead she saw Devlin McCain crouched beside the crumpled figure of the other brigand, reaching for the man's gun. Slowly Devlin straightened, rising in a shaft of sunlight like an ancient warrior awakened from an eternal sleep, golden light flowing over the smooth contours of his bare shoulders and chest.

"Stand away from the woman," Devlin said, pointing the pistol at the giant guarding Kate.

Even half a room away, Kate could feel the savage fury emanating from McCain's big body. It prickled her skin, exciting her and frightening her at the same time.

"You hit Frankie." Jocko sounded more like an overgrown child than a furious adult.

Kate came to her feet, wanting to put as much distance as possible between herself, the big man behind her, and his knife. As she stood, Jocko snagged his arm around her waist and hauled her in front of his body, holding her like a shield.

"Take your hands off me," she shouted, twisting in his grasp. She froze when the cold, flat edge of a blade slapped her cheek. Fear rolled inside her like a bitter wave as he slid the blade downward, stroking her cheek, pausing when the steel pressed against the pulse in her throat.

"Drop the gun."

The man's chest rumbled against her back as he spoke. Devlin frowned, looking at Kate as though he would like to strangle her. After an eternity, during which time Kate was certain Mr. McCain intended to let the man cut her into small pieces, he dropped the pistol.

"Kick it over here."

Devlin kicked the revolver. The pistol slid across the smooth, wooden planks, coming to rest a few feet in front of Kate. Without moving her head, she stared at the weapon, knowing once it was in the big man's hands they would all once again be at the mercy of these brigands. She squeezed her hands into fists, feeling the smooth length of the pen against her palm.

She glanced from her father's worried face to McCain. McCain was standing with his hands loose at his sides, balanced evenly on the balls of his feet, poised like a jaguar about to pounce. And if he did, he would die. Even with all the agility in the world, she doubted McCain could reach the pistol before the big man. She had to do something.

Jocko loosened his grip on her and bent to retrieve the pistol. Devlin dashed toward that same pistol. Kate lunged, ramming the pointed tip of the pen into Jocko's neck. He howled like an injured bear, lashing out with his arm, catching her just above her waist. The sudden flash of pain drove the air from her lungs. Kate staggered back, clutching her arms to her waist.

Devlin reached the pistol first, but as he rose, Jocko rammed him, butting Devlin's chest with his shoulder. The impact toppled both men. They crashed to the floor, Jocko falling across Devlin in a tangle of legs and arms.

"Katie, are you all right?" Frederick asked, dragging her a few feet back from the battle, his hand hard around her upper arm.

Kate sucked air into her burning lungs. "Help him," she whispered, staring at Devlin as he struggled to retain control of the pistol.

Devlin and the other man rolled toward the sofa. Two arms surged outward along the floor, one bare, the other swathed in black cloth, a pistol thrust between their clasped hands. The revolver arced as they rolled, tracking a line upward along Kate's body. She tried to move, but everything had turned to slow motion. Each footstep took a lifetime, and the revolver always seemed to move with her.

She heard a metallic click. Devlin's gaze locked with hers. In that instant she saw her fate in his silvery blue eyes—she was about to die by the pistol he held in his hand. He knew it as potently as she did. Devlin groaned, his face contorting with the strain as he forced Jocko's arm upward.

The pistol fired. The explosion ripped through the air, followed by the rattle of plaster falling against wood, the bullet lodging in the ceiling. Kate pressed her hand to her heart and fought to keep her legs from crumpling beneath her.

"Katie, get out of here," Frederick shouted, pushing her toward the door leading to the hall.

Kate stumbled a few steps, then turned. Her father was shifting back and forth on his feet near the two men who struggled on the floor, looking for a way to enter the fray. If Jocko got control of that pistol, both her father and Devlin could be dead by the time she brought back help.

She dashed to the table near the sofa and grabbed the pitcher. Behind her shouts echoed down the hall. The pistol shot had drawn attention. Yet they wouldn't be in time to help Devlin. Jocko had gained the upper hand; Kate could see it as she rushed toward them. He was on top of Devlin holding his hand against the floor, trying to force the pistol from Devlin's grip.

She lifted the pitcher over her head and started it in a downward plunge toward Jocko's head, aiming for a small bald spot near his crown. The men rolled. Now the pitcher was aimed at the thick mane of Devlin McCain. Kate tried to stop the missile, but it was too late.

The pitcher hit Devlin's head with a dull thud. Water spilled over the edge of the pitcher, splashing both men on the floor, the sturdy earthenware remaining intact in Kate's trembling hands. A low groan slipped from Devlin's lips as he slumped against Jocko. She heard the air leave Devlin's lungs in a soft rush and bit her lower lip.

"Is everything all right in there?" a man shouted, pounding on the door leading to the hall.

Distantly Kate heard her father shout. The door opened. Men shouted. Jocko scrambled to his feet, taking the pistol. Kate sank to her knees, thumping the pitcher against the floor.

Devlin was lying on his side with his back to her, one arm flung wide, the other folded beneath his body. Scarlet sunlight streamed across the smooth contour of his shoulder, as if trying to awaken this sleeping prince.

"Mr. McCain," she whispered, gently rolling him to his back. His eyes were closed, his lips parted. He didn't seem to be breathing.

She cradled his head on her lap and stroked his face, touched his lips with her fingertips. Dear Lord, he couldn't be dead. "You must breathe. You must."

"Don't nobody come near me."

Kate glanced over her shoulder. Jocko was sidestepping toward the open door, the pistol in his hand, his smaller companion draped over his beefy shoulder. Several men stood in the doorway, several others in the hall, a few Kate recognized as fellow Englishmen staying at the hotel. Edwin Melville, curator of the British Museum, stood amid the crowd, staring into the room. They parted to allow Jocko to pass.

"How is he?" Frederick asked, crouching down on the other side of Devlin.

"I don't know." Kate pressed her hand over Devlin's heart, holding her breath. Silky curls, warm skin, and a slow, steady beat greeted her palm. She nearly collapsed with relief. "He's alive," she whispered, bowing her head over Devlin's.

"You don't carry salts, do you, Katie?" Frederick lifted Devlin's wrist and patted his hand.

"I've never fainted in my life."

"No, of course not."

"Good God, Frederick, what happened here?" Edwin Melville asked, grabbing Frederick's shoulder.

"Two men, after the map," Frederick said, rising to his feet.

"Did they get it?"

"No," Frederick said. "Mr. McCain intervened in time."

"Katherine, dear, are you all right? You look dreadfully pale."

"I'm fine." Kate dragged her gaze from Devlin McCain's still features to look up at the tall, angular man standing beside her father. It seemed she had always known Edwin Melville and his son Robert. Although Edwin and Frederick spent most of their time arguing, their friendship went back to their days as students at Oxford. "Father, we must do something for Mr. McCain. Perhaps some water."

"Water. Yes, I'll get him some water. Don't worry, darling. I'm sure he'll be all right. He's made of sturdy stuff." Frederick turned to Edwin as he continued. "You take care of these people, and send someone for the police."

"The police." Edwin stared at Frederick as though he had just escaped Bedlam.

Although they were the same age, at 52, Edwin looked ten years older than Frederick. Only a few strands of dark brown streaked his thick, gray hair, deep lines fanned out from his

dark eyes, crevices sank from either side of his nose into the
fringe of his thick, drooping gray mustache. There was little
doubt Robert had taken a toll on his father, Kate thought.

"I think we really must call the police, Edwin," Frederick
said, walking toward the bathroom.

Edwin followed him. "Yes, I suppose we do need to
involve the police. I'll handle everything."

Devlin stirred, groaning softly, turning his head on Kate's
lap. "I'm sure you'll be all right," she whispered, stroking
his cheek. His skin was warm, taut over the high crests of his
cheekbones. "But I'm afraid you're going to have a horrible
headache."

Behind her, Edwin was clearing the room, his voice cutting
through the babble of curious spectators. She brushed a damp
lock of hair back from Devlin's brow, the silky strands sliding sinuously around her fingers, cool strands that warmed
near his scalp. On expeditions, she had often trimmed her
father's hair, but feeling McCain's hair slide through her
fingers was something altogether different. Was her father's
hair this soft? She had never really noticed.

"Mr. McCain, do wake up." With her fingers, Kate combed
the hair back from his temple, brushing his warm scalp with
her fingertips. She had never realized how pleasant it might
be to feel a man's hair brush against her skin.

She glanced down at the thick pelt of fur covering his
chest, full across the thick plane of muscle, tapering as it
plunged down his belly. How peculiarly masculine. Her fingers curled in the hair at his nape, but it was that intriguing
pelt of fur that held her gaze and her imagination. Had those
small black curls really felt silky?

"Here we are," Frederick said, kneeling beside Devlin.

Kate glanced at her father, heat creeping into her face, as
though her wayward thoughts of Devlin McCain were being
etched in scarlet across her cheeks. For heaven's sake! Of all
the things to be thinking at a time like this. At any time.

Frederick tilted the full glass of water he held and flicked
water from the rim onto Devlin's face. "This will do the

trick." As he spoke he tilted the glass just a little too far, sending a torrent of water into Devlin's face. Devlin came awake with a start, jerking his head, coughing.

"Father!" Kate shouted, pushing the glass upright in her father's grasp. "For heaven's sake, you nearly drowned him." Absently she smoothed the water from Devlin's face with her fingertips. "Please, fetch a towel. You've soaked him through."

"Yes, yes, of course," Frederick said, scrambling to his feet. His footsteps rapped against the bare planks as he rushed toward the bathroom.

"What happened?" Devlin asked, pressing his hands to his temples. "Where's that grizzly bear in the black suit?"

"I'm afraid he got away." Kate pulled a lace-edged handkerchief from the pocket of her skirt. She shook out the folds and dabbed at Devlin's cheeks.

The fragrance of roses drifted from the linen of her handkerchief to fill his senses. Devlin tried to sit up. Blood pounded behind his eyes. A wave of dizziness forced him to fall back against the cushion of her lap.

"Please, Mr. McCain, don't try to move." She rested her warm palm against his shoulder. "Not yet. I fear you need a little time to gain your sense of balance."

He opened his eyes and stared up into her face. The hazy rays of the setting sun streamed through the windows behind him, touching her face as though her lovely features were the last they wished to caress before dying. A thick lock of hair had escaped the ugly bun at the nape of her neck. The shimmering coil streamed down her neck, across the curve of her breast, to form a puddle of gold on his shoulder. With each breath he took those silky strands stroked his skin.

Devlin bet all of that hair would fall to her hips if she ever released it. But he had a feeling the golden cascade went from ugly bun in the day to tight braids at night. Pity. She might be one hell of a woman if she ever gave it half a try. "Anyone hurt?"

She bit her lower lip. She lowered her eyes, refusing to meet his gaze as she replied. "The man you knocked unconscious and, ah, you."

"I didn't see him coming." Devlin searched for the bump he could feel throbbing at the back of his head. When he touched it with his fingertips, he groaned. It was already the size of an egg. "What did he hit me with?"

"You were struck by a water pitcher." She folded her handkerchief into a neat square, keeping her eyes averted from his.

Devlin frowned, watching her expression, seeing how uneasy she was. There was something she wasn't telling him.

"I'm certainly glad to see you join the living again," Frederick said, kneeling beside him.

Kate took the towel her father offered and began scrubbing the water from Devlin's chest as though he were a table in need of a good polishing. He was about to tell her the hair was supposed to be there when Frederick spoke.

"That was one nasty rap on the head Katie gave you."

"*You* hit me with a pitcher?" Devlin asked, looking up at her.

"I . . . yes. I did."

He watched her blush spread upward from her starched white collar, until her cheeks were stained a dark rosy color. "Coming to my rescue, Miss Whitmore?"

"I was only trying to help. I thought that man was going to win, and then you turned, and I couldn't stop."

She folded the towel lengthwise as she spoke, once, twice, a third time, until it formed a narrow tube in her hands. Then she stared at it as though she wasn't sure what to do with it.

"I'm sure I didn't hit you as hard as I had intended to hit him," she said, laying the towel on the floor beside her.

Devlin forced himself into a sitting position. "I'm heartily grateful for that."

With the help of Frederick's strong arm, Devlin came to his feet. Blood surged before his eyes. His legs wobbled. He had the sensation of the floor dissolving beneath him, his body growing cold and moist all over. In spite of Frederick, he would have fallen flat on his face if Kate hadn't grabbed his free arm. Her hand was warm and surprisingly strong.

"Better sit," she said.

Devlin obeyed as Kate directed him toward the sofa, taking the few shaky steps, supported on either side by Frederick and his daughter. After he sank to the smooth, pale green cushions, Kate ran into the bathroom. Through the low throb of blood in his ears, he heard the splash of water in the sink. A few moments later she returned carrying a towel.

"This might help a little." She handed Devlin the towel.

The towel was cool and wet, a sharp contrast to the warm fingers that grazed his hand as he took the white linen from her. She snatched back her hand at the brief contact, as though the last thing in the world she wanted to do was touch him. He wondered if all men frightened her as much as he did.

"Do you have any idea who sent those two thugs?" Devlin asked, pressing the towel gingerly to the bump on his head.

Frederick shoved his hands into his trouser pockets, frowning as he looked down at Devlin. "None at all."

Devlin leaned back against the thinly padded cushions. "Apparently someone else believes in this fable of a lost city."

"It isn't a fable," Kate said, clasping her hands at her waist.

She looked like a teacher confronting a wayward student. He might have spent more time in class if the teachers at the orphanage had looked like Katherine Whitmore. "Who knew about the map?"

"We told no one, except of course Edwin Melville, and Lord Austin Sinclair. You met both Edwin and Austin the other day." Frederick rocked back on his heels, pursing his lips. "They both read the journal, but no one except Katie and I has done more than glance at the map."

"Do you think there's a chance this Sinclair could be involved in—"

"Lord Sinclair would have nothing to do with a scheme to steal the map," Kate said. "Obviously someone has overheard one of our conversations. Or perhaps the dealer who sold us the journal allowed the information to fall into the wrong hands."

Devlin released his breath in a long sigh. The lady was quick enough to jump to this Lord so-and-so's defense. From what he remembered, Sinclair was a handsome man in his early thirties, just the type who might make a woman like Katherine Whitmore start decorating a church. Well, it wasn't any of his business.

"What is so valuable about this city, if it does exist," Devlin said, glancing at Kate, "that would make someone desperate enough to send those two choirboys here to get the map?"

"How could I even try to quantify the value of such a discovery?" Frederick smiled like a little boy on Christmas morning. "Aside from what we might learn from the architecture, from the writings and drawings we might find, there would be artifacts from ten thousand years ago. Why, they would be priceless. Imagine, if you will, being the first people to discover the pyramids. We are talking of a discovery of that magnitude. Think of what we might find."

Devlin draped the towel over his eyes. A warm breeze drifted through the open doors, brushing his face with jasmine and orange blossoms, mingling with the scent of roses—her fragrance—clinging to his skin. He caught himself breathing deeply, trying to draw her essence inside him. Only a fool would start having warm thoughts about that frigid little aristocrat. "I suppose you never figured anyone would want some of those valuable artifacts for themselves."

"My father is interested only in the scientific aspects of this expedition. We never gave a thought to any monetary factors involved."

Devlin lifted one corner of the towel, just far enough so he could see her. She looked as though someone had shoved a fence post down the center of her body. He had never in his life met a woman who held herself more stiffly.

Yet he remembered the way she had looked when she talked about finding that lost city; all the hard edges had softened, giving him a glimpse of the woman hidden beneath her prudish veneer. It might be worth a trek back into hell just to meet that woman. "You won't be safe here." He dragged the towel from his eyes.

"I suppose we could try to find a room in another hotel. But with the scarcity of hotels in this city . . ." Frederick shook his head as if dismissing the possibility. "I doubt they will come back here and try anything. We should be quite safe."

Devlin wasn't sure which one of these two people was more naive, Frederick or his daughter. "You can stay with me tonight."

"Does this mean you've changed your mind?" Kate asked. "Will you be our guide?"

She was looking at him with those huge, blue eyes, expectation and excitement dissolving the schoolteacher into an eager little girl. Devlin leaned back on the sofa and closed his eyes, wondering if that bump on the head had knocked him senseless.

He had come here to talk them out of this crazy expedition. The last thing in the world he needed was to go back into the jungle. The last thing in the world he needed was a woman like Katherine Whitmore in his life. She was a rich little snob who thought he should be wearing animal skins and carrying a club.

"We can find the city, Mr. McCain," Kate said, her voice pouring over him like warm honey. "With you as a guide, we can do it."

She was also an intriguing woman who was so filled with dreams Devlin could feel them radiating from her when he was near her. She made him remember all the dreams he had once believed in, all the dreams that had never come true.

White trash. He would never be anything else in this woman's eyes. And yet . . .

Here he was, imagining all that golden hair tumbled around shoulders he knew would be as smooth and pale as ivory satin. Innocence and passion—he had never realized they could combine into such an intoxicating blend.

The woman would bring him nothing but grief. He would be a damn fool if he agreed to go anywhere with her. Still . . .

"Fifty thousand dollars." The words came before his judgment. But Devlin would stand by them. That kind of money just might buy a dream. If he lived to collect.

She blinked. She straightened, staring at him as though he had just asked her to take a ride to the stars. "You want fifty thousand dollars to be a guide?"

"You want me to risk my life, Miss Whitmore."

"The price you're asking is exorbitant."

Apparently the lady thought his life worth considerably less than the sum he had demanded. It made him angry. It made him want to grab her shoulders and shake her. It made him want more, so much more than he would ever have. "What price do you put on a man's life?"

"Quite right," Frederick said. "You should come away with something substantial, Mr. McCain. Especially considering the risks."

"And considering the risks, I think it would be better if Miss Whitmore took the first steamer back to England."

"You can't be serious," Kate said.

Devlin tossed the wet towel on the silver tray atop the table beside him. "The jungle is no place for a woman."

"I see." She stared at him a long moment, undiluted anger in her gaze. "Take a good, long look at me, Mr. McCain. I am not crippled in any way." She raised her arms as if to prove they were straight and capable. "Female, yes, but it doesn't make me less than you. Still, I suppose a woman's equality would be a foreign notion to a man like you."

She was looking down her slim little nose at him as though he were nothing more than a pile of garbage littering the sofa.

"You have no idea what waits out there." Devlin stood, blinking against the sudden rush of blood before his eyes. "There are anacondas thirty feet long, big enough and nasty enough to swallow you whole. Indians who would love having you as the main course at dinner. Insects that eat you more slowly, nibbling the flesh from your bones. And someone who apparently wants to get to that city every bit as much as you do. I doubt he's going to stop trying. Next time, someone could get hurt."

She shook her head as if she were impatient with his warnings. "I know about the danger. And I choose to take the risk. It's my right to take the risk."

Devlin turned to Frederick Whitmore. He was standing a few feet away, studying them, rubbing his hand across his chin. "You can't mean to allow her to go."

Before Frederick could answer, Kate grabbed Devlin's forearm and forced him to look at her, her fingers digging into his bare skin. "I'm an adult, Mr. McCain. I am capable of making decisions concerning my life."

"Go back home, Rosebud. Back to your English garden."

Her eyes narrowed behind the lenses of her glasses. "I'll go with or without you, Mr. McCain. I memorized the map. I have my own resources. I will find that city."

Devlin stood for a moment staring down into her fierce blue eyes. Color had risen in her cheeks, deepening the smooth ivory to a dusky rose. It didn't seem possible, but the woman was even more beautiful when she had a full head of steam. He couldn't stop himself from wondering what she would be like if he could manage to turn all that fury into something much more inviting.

"Mr. McCain, I couldn't deny my daughter the opportunity to travel in our company. I hope this will not change your decision about acting as our guide."

Devlin knew it was true. They would go with or without him. And take his 50,000 dollars to their graves. What the hell difference did it make to him? If the spoiled little bitch wanted to risk her life, who was he to stop her? "I agreed to act as your guide. If your daughter is foolish enough to go along, it's her business."

Devlin kept his gaze on her face as her father's words pounded against his throbbing skull. Excited words of steamships to Pará and preparations for the long trip to a city called Avallon.

Kate held Devlin's gaze, the look in her eyes something more heated than loathing. It occurred to him how much he would like to see something different in those eyes, something he couldn't even allow himself to think about.

The last thing in the world he needed was to fall for a rich little snob who thought he should be living in a cave. No, the farther away he stayed from this English rosebud, the better. Yet he wasn't sure how he was going to manage that when they were going to be together for the next few months.

He was headed into the jungle with a naive old man and a woman who thought he was just one step below a toad. A woman who made the blood simmer in his veins, simmer with anger and lust.

Devlin, you're headed for rough waters.

Chapter Four

The moon, well into its long trek across the evening sky, cast silvery light on the waves crashing against the beach below Leighton Van Horne's residence in Rio. Lady Judith Chatham huddled in the shadows of the balcony, watching Van Horne, who seemed oblivious to her presence. *If only he were,* she thought. If only she could leave here a free woman. But Leighton had a leash around her neck, a leash he could turn into a noose at any time.

Van Horne had rented this house for six months, though he expected to stay here less than two weeks. He preferred to rent private dwellings over staying in hotels. At times he bought a mansion when a suitable one for lease could not be found. The huge inheritance he had acquired upon his father's death allowed Leighton to buy anything he chose, as well as nearly anyone he chose. Lady Judith suspected this wealthy young American believed he was royalty. Perhaps that was the reason he spent more time in London than he did in New York City, where he and his sister had been raised.

Leighton stood with his hands against the wrought-iron railing, his face lifted to the wind that swept in from the bay. Moonlight glinted against his flowing blond hair, the silken strands nearly brushing the shoulders of his white linen coat.

"It seems we still don't have the map."

Although the resonance of Leighton's voice betrayed nothing, Lady Judith sensed the anger behind each word molded in that smooth, tenor voice. She clenched her hands into tight balls, wondering what spurt of violence might follow his soft words.

"We would've," Frankie said, rubbing the back of his head. "But this guy came out of nowhere."

Leighton glanced over his shoulder, his blue eyes piercing the shadows. Not for the first time, Judith thought she knew what it must be like to watch the devil at his trade. She had first met this tall man with the angelic face a year ago, at one of those lifeless parties the aristocracy were so fond of giving. He had been so attentive, so attractive, so exciting. Perhaps he had noticed she was restless. Perhaps he knew what she craved. Perhaps he recognized her weakness.

Leighton had lured her into his circle of private pleasure and unspeakable perversion. The price had been her soul, and she had paid without even knowing the cost. But then, Leighton took special delight in ensnaring British aristocrats, men and women alike. He collected them, as he collected the sons and daughters of rich businessmen, the way some men collected butterflies.

Leighton turned and rested one arm along the railing, smiling, his even teeth inhumanly white in the moonlight. "I am disappointed in you, Frankie. And you, Jocko."

Judith stared at the two men who stood in front of Leighton. The hulking brutes looked as though they were looking into the face of their executioner. But then, they knew what Leighton might do to them. They had often carried out sentencing on someone who had fallen from grace in Leighton's eyes.

Frankie dragged a hand over his narrow brow, wiping away the beads of sweat that glistened in the moonlight. "Give us another chance, boss."

Leighton laughed, the soft sounds melding with the crash of the waves, with the rustle of the wind through the two tall palm trees swaying near the balcony. "You know I have my heart set on seeing that city."

"We'll take care of that guy next time, boss." Jocko smashed his fist into his open palm. "You'll see. We'll get that map."

Leighton moved toward Judith, the breeze tossing a long lock of silvery blond hair across his brow. She forced a smile to her lips as he slipped his arm around her waist. The man was capable of anything, including murder should she try to leave him.

"What shall I do with these naughty boys, my queen?" he asked, lifting a dark brown curl from her shoulder.

"Give them another chance."

"Ooh, you are so charitable." Leighton laughed as he slipped his fingers under the ornately carved gold necklace he had slipped around her neck after dinner. "How does it feel, knowing this once graced Cleopatra's neck, and now the timeless gold touches your skin?"

She had first admired the necklace several weeks ago while at a reception she had attended at the British Museum with Leighton. She knew the necklace was real; Leighton wouldn't own a fake. She knew he would insist she wear it as long as it suited him. She didn't want to know how he had obtained it.

Leighton was addicted to artifacts. There was a hidden salon in his house in New York filled with treasures from ancient Egypt, Rome, Greece, relics said to have belonged to King Arthur, jewels from Mary, Queen of Scots, and hundreds of other pieces, all rare, all belonging in a museum.

Smiling, Leighton slid his hand lower, over the embroidered lace trimming the round neckline of her blue silk gown. Judith glanced at the two men standing nearby. They were staring, two dogs waiting for their master's orders. "Leighton, please don't. Not in front of them."

"Oh, but you won't tell me no, will you, my sweet?" He slid his hand into the top of her bodice, his long fingers curving over the naked slope of her breast. "I wonder what would your husband, the right honorable Lord Chatham, Baron of Hempstead, think if he knew you were with me instead of visiting the good Mrs. Pennyfield."

Judith bit her lower lip. Her husband wouldn't care. Her husband was too busy with his own diversions to notice what she did.

She had been 18 when she married Oliver Chatham, too innocent to understand why her handsome young husband had no taste for the marriage bed. After five years of trying to win his favor, five years of thinking it was some fault of her own, she had come to fully understand her husband's preference. Her understanding had come only after she found him in bed with one of the stableboys. A few months later she had met Leighton. And he was still only beginning to teach her the true understanding of her own need.

Leighton rolled her nipple between his fingers, the spiraling sensation filling her with sharp-edged hunger, and a familiar self-loathing. "The map, the city," she whispered, hoping to divert him. "What are you going to do?"

"I have ways." Leighton glanced over his shoulder. "My queen has granted you clemency. Leave us now."

Frankie and Jocko hurried through the open door leading to the parlor. Judith leaned back against the stone wall as Leighton unfastened her gown. She both craved and dreaded what would follow.

He ran his hands over her shoulders, his soft palms sending shivers across her skin. The blue silk rustled as it drifted to the floor. He unfastened her petticoats and pushed them from her hips, then lowered his gaze to where the swell of her breasts peeked above the lace-trimmed edge of her white corset. Judith glanced down to her own body, feeling her skin grow moist beneath his stare.

"Don't worry about the map." Leighton unfastened the buttons in the front placket of his white linen trousers as he continued. "One of my friends will be on that expedition with the Whitmores. Someone who will make sure we have no trouble following them if we cannot secure a copy of the map."

Judith shivered in the warm evening breeze. "Who?"

"Curious little cat, aren't you?"

Leighton slipped his hand around the base of her throat. He pushed his thumb into the soft skin beneath her chin, forcing her head back until she was staring up at the stars.

"Did I ever tell you I could read the future in the stars?"

She felt his hand slide upward along the sheer white lawn covering her thigh. "What do you see in the stars?"

"I see a great tragedy ahead." He slipped his hand between her thighs. He pressed his palm to the sensitive mound of flesh, his long fingers sliding against the slit in her drawers.

The hot sting of tears pricked her eyes. Humiliation. Horrible humiliation. Because she wanted this. She needed this. He pressed into her, his fingers finding no resistance, her body aiding his entry.

"The entire Whitmore party is going to disappear, killed in the jungle." He chuckled softly under his breath. "Was that a shudder of revulsion I just felt? Or do you want me so badly?"

Both, she thought. His thumb passed over the sensitive nub of nerves hidden beneath soft curls. Judith closed her eyes and tried not to move against his hand. Impossible. Her hips rocked forward, seeking a deeper penetration.

"Tell me," he whispered, his warm breath laced with brandy. "Tell me you want me inside you."

Judith bit her lower lip. She wouldn't say it. She wouldn't!

He moved his fingers, sliding his thumb over her moist flesh. "Tell me."

She responded to his harsh whisper, to the demand of his hand on her flesh, to the desire clawing at her loins. There was no hope for her. She needed this. "I want you," she said, slipping her arms around his shoulders. "Please."

"That's right, my sweet queen," he said, pressing his smiling lips against her neck. "And how can I deny you?"

Lumps. The sofa in Devlin McCain's parlor was nothing but a series of boulders stuffed into scratchy burlap. Kate rolled to her side, pulling the mosquito netting down from the back of the sofa. She tugged it back into place, forming a low canopy over her head. For all the money they were paying the man, she should have taken his bedroom as McCain had suggested. Still, she had a stubborn streak as wide as the Atlantic running through her, as her father had often said, and at times, it got the better of her.

She wanted to show Devlin McCain she wasn't a flimsy piece of fluff who needed a bed. Rosebud indeed. She would show him she was just as strong as he was.

The muffled roar of voices and laughter and music from the casino below filtered through the planks of the floor. She slammed her fist into the pillow Devlin McCain had provided her. Was her father faring any better on that narrow cot in the storeroom downstairs? A gentleman to the core, her father had also rejected Devlin McCain's offer to use his room.

It was pointless lying here. She wasn't going to get any sleep tonight. She tossed back the white cotton blanket and mosquito netting. The knots in her back eased as she stood and stretched. In the moonlight streaming through the open windows, she could see the deep creases in her ivory linen gown. She hated sleeping in her clothes, but she had no intention of slipping into her nightgown. Not with a casino below. Not with Devlin McCain so near.

A woman couldn't trust a man like that. Not a man who seemed more animal than human. A man who could look at her with those silvery blue eyes and conjure that powerful heat inside her. Then, with an awful suspicion, came another thought: perhaps it was someone else she couldn't trust. Perhaps herself?

Nonsense. She did not find Devlin McCain the least bit attractive, she assured herself. She would never find the barbarian attractive.

Across the room a dark shadow marked the door leading to Devlin McCain's bedroom. The man wasn't even using it. That bed was in there going to waste, while she had a bed of rocks and McCain caroused in his casino. Well, better a bed of rocks than a bed where that man had slept.

Thin white cotton drapes fluttered in the evening breeze drifting through the open windows. Except for the sofa, a small table at one end of that miserable piece of furniture, two spindly armchairs nearby, and a desk on the opposite wall, the room was bare, and scrupulously clean. The scent of lemon oil and beeswax lingered here.

There were no photographs on the whitewashed walls, no paintings, nothing to give a glimpse into the man. Except the small library he had made in one corner of the room.

The moonlight guided her to the desk near the opposite wall. Using the matches she found in a wooden box beside the base of the brass oil lamp on the desk, she lit the lamp. A soft, flickering light flowed over the books filling the shelves that reached halfway across the two adjoining walls. When she had first noticed the library, she had been surprised. Now, looking at the titles on his shelves, she was nothing less than astonished.

Most of the leather-bound volumes looked worn, but clean. Not a trace of dust existed anywhere. She glanced through the titles, which were barely legible on some of the spines, looking for something that might take her mind off the disturbing American. Yet what she found made her wonder all the more about Devlin McCain.

Poetry, plays, the classics of literature as well as contemporary authors like Twain, James, Maupassant, and Zola filled his shelves. And there was more: books on mythology, philosophy, history, mathematics. Books a scholar might possess. On the shelves of a man like Devlin McCain.

"Philosophy. What are you doing with a book like this, Devlin McCain?" she whispered, lifting a copy of Sir Thomas Browne's *Lectures on the Philosophy of the Human Mind* from the shelf.

"Am I breaking the rules?"

Kate pivoted on her heel, turning to face the door leading to the back stairwell, and the man standing on the threshold. Noise from the casino careened up the stairwell and tumbled into the room. Devlin McCain stood with his hand upon the door handle, a small bundle under his left arm. He was staring at her as though he wanted to slip his hands around her neck and strangle her.

The look in his eyes instantly sparked her defenses, making her voice sharper than she intended it to be when she spoke. "I didn't hear you come in."

He entered the room and closed the door behind him, shutting out the clatter from the casino. She could sense his anger as he approached her, see it as the lamplight streamed over the taut lines of his face. Yet there was something more in his expression. What? A shadow of vulnerability?

He took the book from her hands and turned it faceup, staring at the leather cover a long moment before he spoke. "Is philosophy something that only rich young men in college are allowed to read, Miss Whitmore?"

She stiffened at his tone. Did the man think she was some type of snobbish boor? "Of course not. I was surprised, that's all."

He slipped the book back on the shelf as though he didn't want her touching it. "Surprised I can read?"

She stared up at his profile, mesmerized by the odd mixture of emotions she saw in his face: anger coupled with aching vulnerability. Yes, vulnerable, like a young boy facing ridicule. Looking up at him, she found herself wanting to touch him, to smooth away the lines carved into his handsome face. Why should the urge be so strong to touch him? "I'm surprised by your choices."

"I discovered books a long time ago." He drew his finger reverently down the leather spine. "Knowledge, Miss Whitmore, is something no one can take away from you. No matter what. Even the poorest man can journey far and wide if he can read."

Simple philosophy from this man. How utterly surprising. How utterly appealing. He turned and looked down at her, the look in his eyes challenging her to dispute him. He didn't like her, that was clear.

What wasn't clear was the reason she found that knowledge so devastating. After all, she didn't like him. Not in the least. She shouldn't care what his opinion of her might be. But she did. Good heavens, she did.

His expression shifted as he stared down at her, the anger lifting, curiosity filling his eyes. "Your glasses."

Kate lifted her hand to her face, feeling for the thin wire frames. They were gone, leaving her hopelessly exposed. "What about them?"

"You don't need them. Do you?"

"What an odd thing to say." She turned away from him, hiding from his perceptive silver-blue eyes. "Why on earth would I wear glasses I don't need?" she said, heading for the table by the sofa where she had left her glasses.

"I wonder."

He followed her; she could feel him close behind her, feel his eyes on her. When she reached for the glasses, he covered her hand with his. The sudden contact triggered a response in her, a spark that shot along every nerve.

"Mr. McCain!" She snatched her hand away from his.

Devlin lifted her glasses, holding them up to his eyes. A slow smile curved his lips as he peered at her through the small lenses. "Just like looking through a windowpane."

"Give them here." She held her palm faceup between them.

"Why on earth would a woman wear glasses she doesn't need?" he asked, parroting her words, laying the glasses in her palm.

Kate quickly donned the glasses. Yet she couldn't hide behind those small lenses. Not any longer. Not with this man. "I do need them."

"To keep people from looking too closely? Or should I say, to keep men from looking too closely?"

She moved away from him, seeking the cool breeze drifting through the windows. The glasses were part of her armor. Beauty had long ago become a curse rather than a blessing. And beauty coupled with wealth made a lethal combination. What man could see beyond a beautiful face? What man could see beyond the glitter of gold?

"You wouldn't understand."

"Because I'm an uneducated buffoon who should be wearing animal skins and carrying a club?"

"A quick judgment, I admit." Kate rested the sides of her clenched fists on the windowsill. "But accurate, I believe."

Pinpoints of gaslights streamed out from the city, spreading upward along the hills, reflecting like fairy lights in the bay. The first night they had arrived in Rio, Kate had spent the entire evening on the deck of the ship, looking at the city, imagining the mystery waiting for them.

She wished she could go back to that night. She wished she had never met this man, because she had the terrible feeling her life would never be the same again. She had an image of being dragged from a safe little burrow and forced to live in sunlight, the light so bright it would blind her.

"What are you afraid of?"

Kate flinched at the sound of that deep, gravelly voice. He stood behind her, disturbingly close. For a moment she wondered how he could move across the squeaky floor so quietly, but that question fled, chased from her mind by the rush of emotions he kindled inside her: anger, frustration, humiliation, and something else. Something warm and fragile and frightening.

"You are mistaken, Mr. McCain. I am not afraid."

"Yes, you are."

The scent of him filled her senses, a tangy aroma she would always associate with the image of sunlight glistening against smooth, male skin. Her own skin tingled with the memory.

He ran the palms of his hands upward along her arms, so close she could feel the heat of him. Yet he didn't touch her. He only made her wish for that warm touch. And somehow, that was worse.

And then he did touch her, a soft tug at the base of her braid where it rested against the small of her back. The white satin ribbon restraining her braid yielded to his marauding fingers. He slipped his long fingers into her hair, sliding upward, releasing the tight coils.

"What are you doing?" she asked, leaning away from him. But she couldn't lean far enough to escape him. Any farther and she would be plummeting from the window.

He worked his fingers through her hair, fanning the thick strands, grazing her back, her shoulder blades. "I want to see what all of this golden hair looks like hanging loose in the moonlight," he said, his lips brushing the top of her ear.

Warm breath. Firm lips. The soft graze quickened her blood until the pulse beating in the tips of her breasts throbbed in a delicious ache.

"Do you always satisfy your curiosity?" she asked, clutching at her hair, colliding with his hand at the nape of her neck. She jerked back her hand. He brushed the tiny curls at the nape of her neck.

"Do you always deny your curiosity?" He pressed his warm palm to the side of her neck, long fingers spreading, brushing the soft underside of her chin, the smooth line of her collarbone.

"Of course not." Her voice sounded husky to her own ears. "I seek out mysteries, Mr. McCain. Archaeology is, after all, the study of . . . it's the . . ."

He turned her with just a whisper of pressure against her neck. Moonlight poured across his face, smooth silver molding the features of an ancient god; Vulcan tossed from Olympus, forced to wander the earth with mortals who paled in his strength and beauty. In his eyes she saw questions. But they didn't frighten her as much as the answers she saw there.

"You're afraid people will see only your beauty. So you hide." He cupped her face in his hands, such warm, strong hands.

How could he know? How could this man understand?

He pierced her soul with his eyes, shredding all of her defenses, until she felt naked before him. It was at once exciting and frightening to know this man could strip her bare.

The breeze lifted her unbound hair, the strands glowing in the moonlight as they brushed his arm. He smiled. *Beguiling*. If she had ever wondered at the meaning of that word, she wondered no longer; his smile embraced her with warmth, with promise.

He tilted her head as he drew closer, his fingers a soft brush of warmth across her cheek. Had she ever guessed he could be so gentle?

"You are beautiful, Katherine Whitmore. So very beautiful."

She tried to escape him, but she was trapped between his body and the window casement. Face and form, without mind or soul; that was all he saw with those compelling eyes. She couldn't delude herself into believing he saw more.

He pressed his lips to the corner of her mouth. She lifted her hands to push him away, but her fingers curled against his shoulders, his heat radiating through his clothes to warm her.

She shouldn't let him do this. No, she absolutely should not. He moved his head, opening his lips over hers.

Heat. Pure, blessed heat flowed from him into her, filling her. He slipped his arms around her, embracing her, pressing her breasts against his hard chest.

And oh, it felt wonderful, being held like this, as though he intended to absorb her into him; feeling his lips move against hers, tasting his hunger, his incredible hunger for her. Somehow her arms were around his shoulders, holding him. Somehow her fingers had tangled in his hair, his soft, silky hair.

He wanted her. Naïveté couldn't spare her that knowledge. And inside her, a primitive flame kindled in this fire storm of his heat, burning her with a need she had never before known. He would consume her with his fire. And she would welcome the destruction.

"Breathe," he whispered, his lips brushing hers. "It's all right to breathe, sweetheart."

She pulled back in the cradle of his arms, staring up at him, shocked by her own response, dizzy from . . . lack of breath. She would admit nothing else.

He was smiling, sensual lips curved and parted, silvery blue eyes half closed with the desire she could feel pumping through his big body. That same desire flowed through her own veins like liquid fire, refusing any attempt at denial. She felt shaken, exposed as she had never been before.

"My father hired you to guide us through the jungle, Mr. McCain," she said, pushing against his chest. "Not to seduce his daughter. Kindly remember your place."

He stiffened, his hands growing tense on the sides of her waist. "I almost forgot." He stepped back from her, all the warmth draining from his face, the moonlight turning the strong lines of his features into carved marble. Cold. Unyielding. "I'm the hired help."

She glanced away from that cold expression, a lump of regret twisting like jagged ice in her chest. "That's right. And paid handsomely, I might add. You would do well not to forget yourself in the future, Mr. McCain." And she must never forget herself again with this man.

Again came his smile, only this time instead of beguiling charm, it held stunning venom. "I got the feeling I wasn't the only one doing a little forgetting, Professor."

She pressed her fingertips to her lips. The man had no right, no right at all to make her feel this way—cheap, wanton, like one of his girls dancing on the stage below. This time she heard his footsteps as he moved away from her, a sharp, angry sound against the wood. She glanced over her shoulder, watching as he retrieved a bundle from the sofa.

"We'll be leaving in an hour. Put these on," he said, offering her the small, dark bundle.

She had to come to him to accept his offering. She closed the distance quickly, keeping her head held high. "Our ship doesn't leave until two tomorrow afternoon." She snatched the bundle from his hands, careful not to touch him, as careful as she would be with an open flame. She unraveled the bundle, revealing a long black gown and a headpiece. "This is a nun's habit."

He smiled, though there was only contempt in the curving of those finely molded lips. "Until we leave Pará for the Amazon, you are Sister Elizabeth. Your father is Father Dodson."

"And you?"

He bowed his head. "Father Reilly, at your service."

"That should make heaven shudder."

"I've chartered a boat to take Father Dodson and his flock to Pará," he said, ignoring her call to arms. "Get dressed, and put everything you need in one bag. We'll be traveling light from here on out."

Kate held the habit to her breasts as she watched him march across the room. He opened the door leading to the gallery above the casino, admitting a rush of laughter and music and voices. He left, closing the door with a soft click. Yet the sound slammed against her ears.

Through the jungle with that man. Day and night with that man. Would he try his little game of seduction again? And if he did, what then? But she knew he wouldn't. She knew her rejection had been complete. She had seen the hurt in his eyes. She had seen the anger, more complete than in the moment after she had slapped him this afternoon.

No. Devlin McCain was finished with her. And for some horrible reason, she found no comfort in that knowledge.

Chapter Five

Devlin gripped the gallery railing and stared down into his casino. People crammed the lower floor, mainly men, dockworkers and sailors, their nationalities as varied as the different ships that traveled to Rio. The few women, all Europeans, milling among the gamblers were out for a night's wages: money in exchange for a quick rutting in the alley beside the Paradise, or a longer, more involved tumble in the brothel across the street. Devlin didn't mind, as long as they played fair. They were just doing what they had to do to survive. And he knew all about survival.

Although men sat playing cards at every one of the 15 round tables scattered across the scarred oak planks, roulette was queen here. Men stood shoulder to shoulder around the perimeter of each of the three long tables, trying to coax fickle lady luck into making them kings.

Tobacco smoke hung in a low cloud over the room. It twisted in pungent gray plumes around the brass oil lamps suspended from the ceiling, trapping the odor of spilled beer and sweat. A garbage heap, Devlin thought. And he was just one more piece of trash. He clenched the smooth oak railing beneath his hands, his knuckles blanching white.

That kiss had been a mistake. A big mistake. Because now he knew she was just as curious as he was. And although she was as innocent as a babe, he sensed the hunger in her, hunger for the mystery. It was as if she had been reaching out to him, silently, needing him. And he had found no will to resist her.

It was a kiss. Only a kiss. Nothing more. And he had kissed more women than he could remember. Still, he knew with a certainty that came from instinct that he would long remember Katherine Whitmore.

If only it hadn't felt so right with her. That one moment, when he had held her in his arms, he had felt he was holding sunshine, so warm was she, so filled with light. But then had come dark reality.

Katherine Whitmore had wealth, social position, and beauty that could capture a king. By touching her, by tasting the sweetness he could never have, all he had managed to do was dredge up all the hurt inside him, all the humiliation that had accumulated over the years.

Did he want too much? Was it beyond his right to feel clean? Beyond his right to retain some small measure of dignity? Or was that privilege allowed only to those who had been gifted with a father and a mother?

And Katherine Whitmore, was it beyond his right to hold her in his arms? Still, he knew the answer. He might steal a kiss or two. He might steal even more. But Katherine Whitmore would never be his, not really his. She would never belong with a mongrel, a bastard who had been abandoned by his own mother.

The nuns had told him he had been left on the front steps of the orphanage when he was two, with nothing more than a note tucked into the blanket bundled around him and the name Devlin McCain scrawled across the paper. For years he had looked for answers. Even now, it was hard to understand what a two-year-old child could have done to warrant being abandoned.

At twelve he had left the orphanage, determined to find his mother, or at least learn what had happened to her. In time he had come to realize his mother had been a prostitute working the city. Yet he had failed to find any trace of her. And now it hurt to realize he didn't even remember his mother's face.

Could money buy dignity? In the world he knew, money could buy anything. Yet he knew money couldn't buy his way into Katherine Whitmore's world. That took more than money, more than he would ever have.

Damn her! Damn the fresh rose scent of her. Damn those huge blue eyes that whispered *take me* while she pushed him away with both hands. And what was the truth? What did the lady want?

Katherine Whitmore was quickly becoming a mystery to him, a beautiful woman who hid her looks, a fiery siren one moment, an icy schoolmarm the next. Intriguing contradictions. Enticing possibilities.

Weeks ahead of them, months, and that woman would be there, within his grasp. And still a world apart.

"What's wrong, Devlin, my lad?"

Devlin turned at the sound of Barnaby's voice. The little man was strutting toward him, his chin held high, as it always was, a grin curving his lips.

"You're looking like a soul just turned down for heaven."

Devlin straightened, his hands aching from the pressure he had exerted on the wooden rail. "How about a man about to walk through hell's front door?"

Barnaby's smile grew wider, deep lines flaring out from his blue eyes. There were times when the little man seemed no more than a child, and times when he seemed older than time itself. "Walking through hell's front door with an angel at your side."

Devlin let his breath slide between his teeth. "If she's an angel, I hope I'm never headed for heaven." He shook his head, smiling down at his little friend. "'Course, I don't expect there's much chance of that happening."

Barnaby pursed his lips. "Pity, your not liking her much. It's a long journey we're headed on. And I'm thinking the two of you would travel lighter if you were to take a shining to each other."

"And I'm wondering just how I'm going to keep from taking a shining to her."

"Would that be so bad? She's lovely. A rare gem. I'm thinking what a handsome couple you'd make."

"Sure. Hell, we're perfect for each other." Devlin stared down into his casino. "I can just hear her friends at tea." He affected a very correct British accent as he continued. "Katherine dear, is it true he once owned a casino? You say he has no parents, does that make him a bastard? I don't suppose he married you because you're rich, did he, dear?"

"Maybe she wouldn't care, Devlin."

"Yeah. And maybe I'm really a crown prince kidnapped at birth." He laughed, trying to shake off the feeling of hopelessness that had gripped him. "I don't need the kind of grief that comes with that kind of woman. I intend to keep my distance."

Yet Devlin thought of that one moment when he had held her, that one moment when he had felt her filling him with light and warmth. God help him, he wanted to feel that again.

The vibration of the engines started at the soles of Kate's feet and rattled through her until her teeth clattered. This was not exactly what she had expected. She stared into the small cabin. It was barely larger than a narrow closet, with two narrow berths, one above the other, each draped with a thin, yellow blanket that she suspected had once been white.

At least the cabin was hers, she thought, grasping for some positive thought. The others would all be sharing cabins.

The scent of ripe fish and stale bodies hovered in the cabin, penetrating her nostrils with every breath, prickling her stomach. She never fared well on ships, even large, comfortable ships like the one they had taken across the Atlantic. But the ship McCain had hired to take them to Pará was neither large nor comfortable, and it wheezed through the water as though it might die at any moment.

"Good God, McCain, we could be bitten by rats on this tub," Robert Melville said.

"We don't need to hear your complaints." Although Edwin kept his voice low, the underlying anger was unmistakable.

Robert glanced from his father to Devlin McCain, his expression more that of a sulky child of ten than a man of 28. "This might fit your style, McCain, but I see no reason why we didn't wait for the steamer. You can't really expect us to spend a fortnight on this garbage scow."

Kate could smell the thick scent of whiskey drifting from young Melville. She had known this man all her life; they had been playmates on those occasions when her father stayed in London between expeditions. There were moments when she wondered how the mischievous little boy she had known had managed to grow into a pompous, arrogant boar. Right now, she wanted to slap his face. He had no right to talk to anyone in that condescending manner. "We are fortunate Mr. McCain was able to find a ship on such short notice."

Robert snorted. "Fortunate? We should feel fortunate to be on this miserable excuse for a ship?"

Although Kate loved Edwin Melville as part of her family, she could not feel any love for the man she had once thought of as her best friend. Rumors had long ago seeped through London society that gambling and drink and wicked women had stolen Robert's soul. "Unlike some members of this expedition, Mr. McCain is invaluable. Without him I doubt we should reach Avallon."

Robert clicked his tongue against his teeth. "Really, Katie, always the champion of the poor and downtrodden. In another minute you'll be launching into one of your speeches in defense of the beggar children in the East End, or improvement of the working conditions in the factories, or—what was your latest cause, Katie? Protection of the poor defenseless fox from the bloodthirsty hunters? I seem to remember hearing of some uproar you caused last year by snatching the Earl of Dartmouth's fox from the jaws of his hounds. That must have been rather spectacular."

"I released the poor creature the evening before the hunt." Kate drew a deep breath, trying to control her rising temper. From the corner of her eye she could see McCain watching her. Yet she had no idea what he was thinking. "Robert, if I were you I should mind my tongue."

Robert rolled his eyes. "I can't believe you are all willing to spend a fortnight on this stinking barge."

"Under the circumstances, I'm afraid we have little choice." Although Austin was smiling, his voice low and calm as he spoke, there was a subtle current of anger in him as he looked at Robert. "It would be dangerous to take the steamer as we had planned."

"It would be dangerous to continue in this floating disaster. At any minute I fear we will be called to man the lifeboats." Robert paused, raising his brows theatrically. "Did anyone notice if there *were* any lifeboats?"

"If you like, I'll put you in a yawl and send you back to shore."

McCain had spoken, his voice barely rising above a whisper. Yet the gravelly tones riveted all who stood in the hallway; Robert, Edwin, Austin, Frederick, Barnaby, and Kate all turned to give Mr. McCain their complete attention.

Kate stared at McCain. He stood with his shoulder braced against the wall just outside her cabin, his arms crossed over his chest, one knee cocked at an angle. He looked predatory, filled with latent power, like a jaguar watching his prey through half-closed eyes. Intensely masculine. Dangerous. Mesmerizing.

There was no denying it: the man fascinated her.

She must stop this madness. She must stop wondering what it would be like to be held by Devlin McCain once more, to feel his lips touch hers. Oh yes, she must definitely forget all about that kiss and the way he had made her feel. Passion without love and respect was nothing short of degrading.

Robert drew himself upward as though he were trying to match McCain's height. He fell short by several inches.

Why would Robert come on this trip? Kate wondered. Why leave the soft, gilded life he led in London for the hardened danger of the jungle? It must have been Edwin's idea. And there was only one reason for it: Edwin still hoped she would accept Robert's proposal of marriage.

The muscles in Robert's throat tightened, and his Adam's apple bobbed before he spoke. "Who do you think you are to speak to me in this manner? You have no right."

"When he hired me to lead this little group, Mr. Whitmore gave me the right." McCain looked straight at Robert as he spoke. "If you want to continue on this expedition, you'll do as I say."

"I daresay." Twin spots of color rose in Robert's pale cheeks. He looked around as though seeking an ally. Yet he found none. No one would question McCain's command.

"Perhaps you need to think about this trip, Robert," Frederick said, his voice as gentle as if he were speaking to a child. "This is nothing more than a prelude to what awaits us in the jungle."

Robert opened his mouth as though he intended to speak, but he didn't. Instead he turned and hurried down the corridor, retreating into his own cabin. The loud slam of his door echoed in the narrow passageway.

Edwin stared after his son for a long moment before turning to face McCain. "Allow me to apologize for my son. I'll talk with him. It won't happen again."

McCain nodded, his face revealing nothing of his thoughts. Edwin walked down the passageway toward his son's cabin, his shoulders drawn forward, his head bowed. Kate looked at the man who had always been so proud and felt a horrible anger for the son who had broken him. After saying good night, Frederick, Barnaby, and Austin continued down the passageway, finding the cabins Devlin had secured for them.

McCain stayed in the passageway, staring at her, light from the grimy oil lamp overhead stroking one side of his face, slipping into his hair, discovering the chestnut highlights hidden deep amid the ebony strands. There was expectation in his stormy gray eyes—a man poised for battle.

Did he expect her to react as Robert had? Did he really think she was a spoiled, complaining child? The realization made her angry and determined, determined to show this man she was every bit as capable as he was.

She pulled the black headpiece from her head, hesitating only a moment before laying it across the yellow blanket. She sensed him watching her. She knew he expected her to turn around and start ranting about the accommodations. Well, she would show him she was made of stronger stuff. After molding her lips into a smile, she turned to face him.

"I think we shall all be quite comfortable, Mr. McCain," she said, lying through her teeth.

A frown etched shallow lines into his brow. He traced the curve of her smile with his gaze as though he were remembering the shape, the taste, the way her lips had moved beneath his. Was that what he was thinking? Was he remembering the kiss they had shared?

Through the stale air, Kate caught a whisper of an intriguing scent: McCain's skin heated by the humid air. She breathed deeply, the exotic spice curling around her, tugging her in some unexpected way, drawing on her until she had to fight the urge to move closer to this man. She turned and tried to pull open the porthole. Perhaps a little bit of air might help. The porthole wouldn't budge.

A warm hand covered hers. She glanced up, straight into Devlin McCain's silvery blue eyes. He seemed a giant in the little cabin, bending his head to keep from bumping the wooden beam running along the center of the ceiling. He was quiet, looking down at her, the anger washed from his features, in its place a smooth, unreadable mask.

She stared up into his face, wishing she could read his thoughts. What had he seen in her own face hours ago? What had led him to kiss her? Was she looking at him the same way now? Would he kiss her again? Heaven help her, but she wanted to kiss him again. If only to prove it wasn't as devastating as she remembered.

And then he did something unexpected—he smiled. A generous smile that surrounded her, that held her and bathed her in warmth, a smile that spoke of acceptance and more.

The heat was immediate, a slow burn that seared through her limbs, leaving her trembling. She slipped her hand from beneath his, certain he could feel the sudden agitation he had wreaked on her body. His smile grew wider, confirming her fears.

"Let me." He yanked on the handle of the porthole.

With a groan the cover opened, allowing a cool breeze to rush into the little space. She pulled air deeply into her lungs. Yet it was his fragrance that filled her, his sharp male essence that played havoc with her senses.

"Is there anything else you need?" he asked, his lips still curved into that compelling smile.

She needed some distance from this man. She needed to keep in mind just who and what Devlin McCain was. He certainly wasn't the type of man she admired. He didn't respect women. No doubt he seduced women just for the sport of it.

No, she certainly should not be standing here, gazing up into those beautiful eyes of his. She should not be thinking about his kiss. And, above all else, she should not be hoping he might kiss her again. She was not some fiddle-headed, simple-minded fool. She would not fall under the spell of this man's primitive brand of charm.

"No, thank you," she said, appalled at the breathless sound of her voice.

He lowered his eyes, his gaze sliding along the curve of her lips. Kate held her breath, waiting. If he took her in his arms, what would she do? But she knew. Oh yes, she knew. And the answer was both exciting and humiliating.

He lifted his eyes, the silvery blue depths turbulent with emotions. Once again she glimpsed the vulnerable boy hiding inside this hardened man. Once again she fought the urge to touch him.

"Good night, Miss Whitmore." He turned on his heel, leaving her before she had the chance to respond.

"Good night," she whispered, listening to the steady march of his footsteps on the wooden floor.

Kate gripped the edge of the porthole and stared out at the evening sky. She picked out a star as her father had long ago taught her to do, one bright diamond shimmering in the indigo sky. Silently she made a wish, as she had countless times as a child. She would need every ounce of good luck to keep from making a fool of herself with that man. Somehow she would learn to resist him. She had to.

Devlin rested his hands on the smooth oak railing of the little steamship. The cool breeze washed his warm cheeks with the salty tang of the sea. Beneath him the deck vibrated with the engines driving them through the Atlantic. He was only just beginning to realize how little he knew about Katherine Whitmore.

He hadn't expected her to defend him. He had expected the spoiled little aristocrat to pound her feet and weep over the ugly little cabin.

He closed his eyes, seeing her face once more as she had stood in that stinking cabin. There had been a smile on her face, a small, brave smile that was trying hard to cover her dread, a smile that had severed all of his defenses. She looked like a porcelain doll, fragile in her beauty. Yet she had a streak of determination running down her spine like steel.

He found himself thinking about that one moment he had held her, the way a green boy dwells on his first kiss, conjuring every detail—the scent of her warm skin, the shape of her firm breasts pressed against his chest, the startled look in her huge, blue eyes. Desire twisted like a knife in his belly. *Better think about something else.*

He tossed back his head, breathing in the salty air. He barely knew the woman. What was it about her that made him want to lock her in his arms and hold her forever? He had known beautiful women before, plenty of them, women every bit as alluring as Katherine Whitmore.

The funny thing was, he couldn't remember the faces of the women he had bedded, not in detail. Their images were faded, like chalk pictures in the rain. The women he had allowed into his life had all been passing through; no one had remained more than a few days, a few weeks at a time. And he had wanted it that way. He still did. Didn't he?

He stared into the water, moonlight skipping across the tops of the rolling waves, a fleeting touch of silver. He wanted more from life than an affair that flared hot and passionate, then burned out in a heartbeat. That kind of passion left nothing but ashes behind. He wanted more. He needed more.

He wanted someone to love. He wanted someone to love him. A woman who wanted a home, a life together. He wanted his own place, somewhere clean, where he could breathe the air and not choke on the stench of smoke and whiskey. He wanted children. And he was only fooling himself if he believed Katherine Whitmore would ever want those things with him.

She lived in a different world than he did. She was accustomed to gentlemen, men who kept their proper distance. He had taken her by surprise, that much he knew.

In some way she found him interesting. He was different. He ignited a fire in her; that much she couldn't hide. But, no matter what he wanted to see in those beautiful eyes of hers, it would never be more than lust. He had to remember that. He had to remember the lady would never have a place for him in her life. If he forgot, if he allowed himself to fall for her, he would be torn into pieces.

The door leading to the deck opened and closed behind him. Devlin glanced over his shoulder, his jaw growing tight when he saw the man stepping onto the deck. He didn't want to talk to anyone, especially Lord Austin Sinclair. The man reminded him of everything Devlin wasn't.

"Would you care for a cheroot?" Austin asked as he moved to stand at the railing beside Devlin.

Devlin glanced down at the gold cigar case the man was holding and shook his head.

Austin closed the case and slipped it into his coat pocket. He struck a match on the rough wood, the flame illuminating his features as he held it to the tip of his cigar: wide brow, high cheekbones, and a thin, straight nose. A British aristocrat who was also rich and good-looking. And what was there between Katherine Whitmore and this shining English marquess? Suddenly, Devlin wasn't sure he wanted to know.

Austin puffed, igniting the rolled tobacco, releasing a fragrant cloud of smoke into the breeze. After a moment, he spoke. "Young Melville is a spoiled child masquerading as a man. He wouldn't be here if Edwin and Frederick weren't such good friends. I hope you won't let him bother you."

"I can handle Melville."

"Yes, I'm sure you can."

Devlin glanced at the man, looking for some sign of sarcasm in the blue-gray eyes that gave him the odd impression of looking into a mirror. He saw only friendship in Austin's eyes, a warmth that couldn't be counterfeited. Still, Devlin didn't want to be friends with this man.

"I'm glad you changed your mind, Mr. McCain. I think with you, we will make it to Avallon."

"You really believe in this fable?"

"You don't?"

"I believe in the money I'm being paid to take this little group on this mythical quest. And that's all I believe in."

Austin stared for a moment at the smoldering tip of his narrow cigar, a frown drawing together his black brows.

"Perhaps you will find more to believe in on this quest than you ever thought possible."

There was a strange note of melancholy in his voice, but Devlin was beyond wondering about this British aristocrat. He didn't want to know these people. They too were only passing through his life. It was better for him not to think in terms of friendship with anyone. And it would be nothing short of disaster to think of anything more with one beautiful English rosebud.

Austin stared at the door where Devlin McCain had disappeared. In two weeks they would reach Pará. The riverboat and supplies were waiting for them to start their journey. This journey to Avallon would not be easy, for any of them. It was possible they might not succeed at all. Still, he wouldn't think of failure; the consequences were unthinkable.

The Southern Cross blazed above him, shimmering dots of fire searing through black velvet. Staring up at the stars, Austin cast his thoughts to the lies that had brought him here, the lies that would lead him into the jungle. Deceit was new to him. He did not wear it well.

He drew the cool evening breeze into his lungs and tried to banish the doubts sinking like thick, pointed blades into his heart. There was no choice left to him. He would follow his instructions carefully, even though his soul rebelled.

Chapter Six

Two weeks later, Pará, Brazil

Devlin walked along the main deck of the riverboat Frederick Whitmore had chartered for their trip to Santarém, checking the supplies Whitmore had commissioned for the expedition. The *Rio Bella* had three decks in all, two decks stacked one on top of the other above the main deck like layers on a cake, all frosted white, with lacy patterns decorating the top of the supporting posts of each tier. The stern-wheeler could hold 50 first-class passengers. And the man walking beside him had hired the entire boat.

"Do you think there is anything we've forgotten?" Frederick asked.

Devlin paused beside a stack of wooden crates that rose to his chin, *Canned peaches* stamped across the side of each one. There were enough supplies crammed onto the main deck to outfit a small army for several months. "I didn't notice a bathtub."

"A bathtub?" Frederick stared at him a moment, his dark brown eyes reflecting first confusion, and then the humor Devlin had learned to expect from this man. "You are, of course, roasting me. I suppose you think we've collected far too much for this expedition."

"Only if you're planning to take a regiment with you up the Amazon." Devlin noticed Katherine Whitmore descending the stairs leading from the hurricane deck. Dressed in white linen, with the setting sun glinting on her golden hair, she seemed otherworldly, a mystical goddess descending from her throne. Devlin realized he was staring and forced his attention to a crate of tinned milk to his left. "We'll sort it out on the way to Santarém. I'll tell the captain to get under way."

"So soon?" Kate paused on the bottom stair, her slender hand resting on the carved newel post.

She still looked pale, Devlin thought, the dark smudges under her huge, blue eyes telling the story of nights gone without sleep, the loose fit of her gown a testament to the weight she had lost. The woman had been seasick nearly every day for the past two weeks. And she hadn't complained once. In fact, the little professor had done her best to hide her sickness from everyone. And Devlin had not been able to help her, had not been able to hold her as he ached to do.

Even now, he wanted to lift her in his arms and cradle her against his chest. And each time he thought of her, each time he realized the growing strength of his own feelings, he felt as though he were standing at the edge of a high cliff, the ground crumbling beneath his feet.

Never had he felt so protective. Never had a woman grabbed hold of his thoughts, his imagination. Day and night, the woman haunted him. He had stayed as far away from her as that little steamer had allowed. And still, he couldn't escape her, or the spell she was weaving around him. Disaster, to feel this way about her.

"Have you had a change of heart, Miss Whitmore?" Devlin turned to face her. "Are you considering staying in Pará?"

That determined little chin of hers came up. "No, I have not considered staying behind, Mr. McCain." She looked at her father, pointedly dismissing Devlin. "I'll tell the others we will be leaving as soon as possible."

Devlin watched her leave. He wanted to go after her, to grab her and shake her and tell her to stay put until he could find that damn fabled city for her. He wanted her to run, because he had nowhere to hide from her and the feelings she awakened inside him.

"I notice she has stopped wearing those annoying little spectacles of hers," Frederick said. "I suspect you had something to do with that."

"I called her bluff."

Frederick chuckled. "Yes, I rather expected you would be capable of doing that the first day I met you."

Devlin looked down at him, surprised at the smile on the other man's face, amazed Frederick Whitmore would want him anywhere near his daughter. Perhaps Frederick didn't realize the strong attraction his daughter held for Devlin. Perhaps he didn't realize that each time Devlin saw her, it was all he could do to keep from touching her. "I don't understand why you're allowing her to go on this expedition. You must realize how dangerous it'll be for her out there."

"Yes, I realize the danger. And I must tell you, Katie is the most precious thing in the world to me. To lose her would be . . . I would not care to live." Frederick drew a deep breath. "But if I were to forbid her to go, what would I be telling her?"

"You'd be telling her that you love her, that you want to keep her safe from harm."

Frederick nodded. "Perhaps. Tell me, would you expect me to tell my grown son he could not travel on this expedition, if he were healthy and capable?"

Devlin saw where the conversation was leading. "If I could, I'd keep all of you from going into that hell. I know too well how easy it is to die out there."

"You evade my question, Devlin," Frederick said, smiling up at him. "I believe the truth is, you want Katie to stay behind because you feel women should be protected, that they should be wrapped in tissue paper and placed high on some imaginary shelf, where nothing can touch them."

Devlin shook his head. "Believe me, Frederick, I don't think your daughter is a porcelain doll. But—"

"But you don't think she is strong enough to make this journey." Frederick shook his head. "She's a determined young woman, intelligent, strong willed, capable. You won't be able to convince her to stay behind. If you try, she will only come to dislike you." He studied Devlin a moment, a speculative glint in his eyes, a smile on his lips. "I think you may just discover she is stronger than the lot of us."

He had already discovered too much about the lady. He wanted to think of her as spoiled, as flighty, but he couldn't. "There's a thousand ways to die out there."

"Yes. And we have chosen the very best man to help keep the entire expedition safe."

The muscles in Devlin's shoulders tensed. "I didn't do a very good job of keeping my partner safe."

Frederick shoved aside Devlin's words with a wave of his hand. "I have complete faith in you, Mr. McCain."

God, he wanted to keep them safe, but he was only a man. And he knew how quickly death could come, as quickly as a dart tipped with curare. One moment he had been talking to Gerald, the next, Gerald was dying on the floor of the canoe, and Devlin was paddling like hell to get away from the Indians who had materialized onshore.

Devlin was quiet a moment, holding Frederick's gentle gaze, wishing there was something he could say to change his mind, to chase this kind man and his distracting daughter back to England. Yet he knew it was beyond his power to stop them.

"Have you had a chance to read my book and the copy I made of Randolph's journal?"

Devlin nodded. Since Frederick had given them to him to read, Devlin had gone through both books several times. "They make interesting reading."

"I had rather hoped you might begin to see why it's so important we find Avallon."

"I learned a long time ago to believe only in what I could see." Devlin stared at the base of the curving staircase, empty now. Yet in his mind, the image of one determined young woman lingered, just as she haunted his dreams.

Kate sank to the settee in her stateroom. She rested her elbow on the rosewood arm and dropped her forehead into her open hand. Her accommodations on board the riverboat were spacious, with an adjoining dressing room and bathroom, a virtual palace after the closet of the steamer.

The floor was not vibrating under her feet, as it had for the past two weeks. And for once, her stomach was not creeping up into her throat. But, oh, how she dreaded the thought of going back out on the water. Still, she wasn't about to give Devlin McCain the satisfaction of knowing of her weakness.

She glanced up as someone knocked on the door. It was probably her father, or perhaps Barnaby, coming to see how she was faring. In the past two weeks, she and Barnaby had become friends. She enjoyed listening to the tales of Irish folklore he was so fond of telling. Still, at the moment, she didn't want to talk to anyone.

She dragged herself from the settee and squared her shoulders, prepared to send her visitor away with a smile. She opened the door, her smile vanishing when she saw Devlin McCain. "You! What are you doing here?"

A muscle at the corner of his mouth twitched. "I didn't realize I needed permission to approach your cabin."

"I'm sorry, I didn't mean to sound so brusque, but you startled me." He always startled her. In the time since they had left Rio, she had often caught herself daydreaming about the man, reliving every detail of that one moment he had held her in his arms. Not just once a day, but it seemed all day she thought about him.

"I brought you this," he said, offering her a small metal tin. He continued as she took it from his hand. "It's a native tea, a local remedy for bellies that've curled in at the edges. Just brew some of it the next time you feel a little sea-sick."

Heat crept into her cheeks. She had been miserable aboard the steamer, but she had hoped no one had noticed. "I didn't know it showed."

"You aren't usually green around the edges, Miss Whitmore. Starchy, but not green."

His voice was richly masculine. He had spoken so little to her in the past two weeks, she had almost forgotten how the deep, gravelly tone of his voice could make her skin tingle. Behind him the sun was dipping toward the horizon, the last rays reaching out to brush gold across his cheek, to tease the chestnut highlights from his black hair, the shaggy mane nearly brushing his wide shoulders.

The first few buttons of his white cotton shirt were open, revealing a healthy expanse of sun-darkened skin and black curls. She tried not to stare. She tried not to wonder how it might feel to touch him, to feel that warm-looking skin and those intriguing curls under her fingertips.

Curiosity. That was all she felt. Nothing more, she assured herself, trying to draw air into her constricted lungs.

She glanced up into his face and found him smiling at her. The look in his eyes made her wonder if he could read her thoughts. Right now that would be a disaster, because all she seemed to think about was how very much she wanted him to kiss her again.

What was he doing to her? She wasn't the type of woman who allowed emotion to rule her. And yet with this man, she didn't seem to do anything but feel.

He stood for a moment, looking down at her as though he were committing each feature of her face to memory.

Quite unexpectedly, he lifted his hand to her face, cupping her cheek in his palm, touching her as though she were as delicate as a rose blossom.

"I'm glad you stopped wearing those ugly little glasses, Kate. Your eyes are far too lovely to hide."

It was the first time he had ever used her given name. She liked the sound of it, a rough caress spoken in his husky voice. He slid his thumb over the curve of her lower lip. In his silvery blue eyes she saw a haunting light, a longing for . . . for what? she wondered.

He slid his thumb back across her lip. His touch reached deep within her. He triggered a thick, voluptuous flow of desire that started low in her belly and spread upward until her breasts grew heavy and ripe, until her limbs felt deliciously languid, until she leaned toward him like a rose seeking the heat of the sun.

He lowered his head. His breath spilled across her cheek in an inviting stream of warmth. She parted her lips, waiting, craving the touch of his lips. He paused, his gaze sliding over her lips. He seemed to struggle for just a moment, and then he was frowning, dropping his hand, moving back from her as though she were poison.

"You can still change your mind, Professor. Go back to London."

With those few words he snapped the spell he had so delicately woven around her. "Thank you for the tea, Mr. McCain. But you can keep your advice to yourself."

"Yeah, the only thing you need from me is a little help getting through the jungle." He shook his head, releasing his breath in a long sigh. "I just hope you have enough starch to get through the nightmare that lies ahead."

Without another word, he turned and marched down the deck. She closed the door and rested her brow against the cool wood. She would show that man she was every bit as capable of surviving this trip as he was. Yet she shivered when she thought of what might await them in the jungle.

*   *   *

The private riverboat *Styx* sat at the wharf in Pará. In the elegant salon, Leighton Van Horne stood at the open French doors leading to the hurricane deck, staring through his telescope. Judith watched him, knowing it wasn't stars that had captured his attention.

"So the lady has a soft spot for gamblers," he whispered. "Feast your lovely brown eyes on this, my queen."

Judith took the long, narrow brass telescope from his hand and lifted it to her eye. Through the lens she saw a dark-haired man and a blonde woman standing a few hundred yards away on the deck of a white stern-wheeler. The woman stood with her face lifted to the man, his hand resting on her cheek.

Judith turned the lens, bringing the man into clearer focus, catching her breath when she at last saw him clearly. Handsome did not begin to describe him. And the way he was looking at the woman, as though she were something precious and rare, triggered a wave of longing deep inside Judith.

"Do you think he's handsome?"

Was she so transparent to this man? She lowered the telescope as Devlin McCain walked away from Katherine Whitmore. He hadn't even kissed her. And from what Judith had seen, the woman had been inviting a kiss, and more. "I suppose some women might find him attractive."

Leighton tilted back his head and laughed. "Maybe I'll let you have him. Would you like that, my queen? Would you like to have your very own slave?"

A slave. Was that what she had become?

"We could have him fitted with a gold collar. You could keep him at my place in Cornwall, lead him around with a golden chain."

Images crept into her mind of the dark-haired man she had glimpsed through the lens, his strong male body naked except for a gold collar around his neck, on his knees before her, awaiting her every command.

"You could break him, train him. Just think of all the ways he could pleasure you."

"Stop it," she said, turning away from Leighton and the disturbing cravings he had conjured inside her.

"Ah, my sweet, beautiful Judith." He rested his hands on her shoulders. "You have had only a sip of the wine. I will show you how to savor it."

Judith closed her eyes. She wanted to pray, but she knew she was beyond salvation. Just as she knew, if given the chance, she would have that beautiful, dark-haired man on his knees before her.

"Leighton, let's go back to London. I'm frightened." *Frightened of what I shall become if I don't escape your spell.* "The jungle, it's too dangerous."

He rubbed his thumbs against the taut muscles of her shoulders. "But the danger makes it all the more intriguing."

"What are you after?" she asked, glancing over her shoulder. "What could you hope to find in this city that could be worth our lives?"

Leighton smiled. "The answer to a mystery."

"You would risk your life, and mine, for a game?" she whispered, pulling away from his hands. "You are searching for a city in the jungle that in all logic does not exist, risking our lives, and you aren't even sure what you are looking for."

"Oh, but the city does exist. I know it does. You see, I've read all of Frederick Whitmore's theories." He rested his hip against the back of a winged chair and traced a rose in the green silk brocade with his fingertip. "And I believe the riches in that city are beyond compare."

Devlin sat with the other members of the expedition at the round table that had been placed on deck for dinner. Moths and other insects gathered in fluttering clouds around the oil lamps that hung from the roof on either end of the table, close enough to lend light, far enough to keep the insects away from the diners. The red-and-white striped awning, which could be lowered to enclose the entire side, was drawn and rolled close to the roof, allowing the passengers a view of the river glittering in the moonlight.

As a boy in New Orleans, Devlin had often gone to the docks to watch the big riverboats roll into the city. This boat was every bit as luxurious as the best he had ever seen. At 12 he had taken one of these tall, lacy-looking boats up the Mississippi. He had worked as a roustabout for his passage, sleeping on the lower deck between bales of cotton and kegs of rum, but not this trip. This time he had a suite of rooms.

So this was the way the rich made a trip up the Amazon, Devlin thought, glancing across the table to where Katherine Whitmore sat beside Lord Austin Sinclair.

Kate was smiling at Sinclair, nodding her head at something he had said to her, something so low Devlin hadn't heard what it was. He felt a tightening in his chest as he watched them. Jealousy. Plain and simple.

Jealousy. A stupid emotion if Devlin ever knew of one, especially when it was directed toward that English rosebud.

"It is a logical explanation of the myths," Frederick said, wagging his empty fork at Edwin Melville. "Egypt, Greece, Rome, the Mayans, the Incas, the Celts, all had similar myths. The gods these people worshiped, the legends they passed on through generations, all arose from their exposure to the Atlanteans."

"A lot of poppycock," Edwin said, slicing a piece of roasted chicken.

"You don't believe there is a lost city of Atlantis secluded in the heart of Brazil?" Devlin asked.

"Unfortunately, my dear friend has been chasing a rainbow for years." Edwin swirled the piece of chicken at the end of his fork through the white-wine sauce on his plate. "I have come on this journey as a service to him, to verify his claim."

"To prove I'm wrong, you mean."

"I believe it's possible that Connor Randolph's journal is nothing more than a collection of notes he was gathering for a novel he was planning to write."

"That's stretching it a bit, Edwin," Frederick said, slanting his friend a wry glance.

Devlin lifted his wineglass to his lips, tasting the warm white wine, tracing with his gaze the inset of white lace dipping from Kate's chin to an enticing point just between her breasts. He had noticed she never wore bustles or corsets. Her clothes were simple, elegant, draping the natural flow of her slender curves. As far as women's clothes went, they were practical for this climate. But they were playing hell with his imagination.

"You can't dismiss the deep-sea soundings made by the British ship the *Challenger*," Kate said. "The captain and his crew mapped an area in the Atlantic that corresponds to the sunken continent of Atlantis. The American ship, the *Dolphin*, reproduced the same results."

"It proves nothing." Edwin pressed his linen napkin to his lips. "An underwater mountain range, nothing more."

"How do you explain the fact that we find the same arts and sciences, religious beliefs, customs, traditions, plants, animals, as well as myths and legends in ancient people on both sides of the Atlantic?" Kate asked. "Some of the American Indians, the Dakota and Sioux for instance, share similar customs with the Tartars of Russia, as well as the Mayans and Egyptians. How do you explain that?"

"It's quite obvious." Edwin took a sip of his wine. "They were derived independently."

"Now that is a stretch of the imagination." Frederick tipped his wineglass in a salute to his friend.

"We must acknowledge the fact that Atlantis once connected both sides of the Atlantic Ocean," Kate said, warming to the subject, her face taking on the glow of her enthusiasm, her eyes sparkling in the lamplight. "If we are to find a plausible explanation for the similarities among widely dispersed cultures, we must accept the fact that Atlanteans colonized

Egypt and Ireland, Spain, South America, Central America, as well as the United States."

Devlin stared at this enchantress, feeling the pull of her spell. He felt as though something wild was trying to break free inside him, something savage that clawed at his vitals whenever he thought about the woman sitting across from him in the white linen dress. And he couldn't stop thinking about her.

"More whiskey," Robert Melville said, lifting his glass for a steward to fill.

"Go easy," Edwin whispered, leaning toward his son, who sat to his right.

"A few years ago people believed the legends of the buried cities of Pompeii and Herculaneum were nothing more than myths," Austin said.

"If you look into the history of Ireland, you'll find traces of the Atlanteans," Frederick said. "The annals tell of the island being settled before the deluge, settled by a civilized race from the East. At that time, Atlantis was east of Ireland."

"I've read a good bit of the folklore, and I'm thinking there is much in what Frederick has to say," Barnaby said.

Frederick nodded. "In the *Book of Invasions of Ireland*, we're told of the Tuatha-de-Dananns, people who were descendants of a nation that was destroyed by a great deluge."

"The Tuatha-de-Dananns. I've read the myths." Devlin twisted the stem of his wineglass between his fingers, the lamplight reflecting like sunlight in the crystal. "They were people skilled in the arts of Druidism and magic."

"Aye, the good king Nuadha who was fitted with a silver arm after he lost his in battle," Barnaby said. "Spells that could bring the dead back to life."

"You believe these people really existed, and they came from Atlantis?" Devlin asked Frederick.

"I believe there is some truth in every legend, a kernel, so to speak, like the pit of this fruit." Frederick lifted a papaya from the bowl in the center of the table. "Time and ignorance have caused the fruit of exaggeration to grow around that pit." He shoved his knife into the heart of the papaya. Juice dripped onto his plate as he parted the yellow-orange flesh and revealed the seeds inside. "If you pierce those layers of ignorance, you will find the truth hidden at its center."

"People manipulate the truth to suit their own understanding," Devlin said.

"Exactly. For example, it is clear these people had the ability to fashion a mechanical arm out of silver, that much I believe." Frederick scrubbed at his damp fingers with his napkin. "And I believe it is quite possible these people originated in Atlantis."

Edwin made a low groan deep in his throat. "Frederick, you would have us all descendants from Atlantis. Myths. Gods. Goddesses. Nothing but smoke."

"The ancient Celtic gods and the Druid gods, are very similar," Kate said.

Devlin looked at her over the rim of his glass. A goddess of summer, with sunlight forever in her hair, and eyes the color of a cloudless morning sky. He felt his blood grow warm in the presence of this summer goddess.

"More similar still are the gods worshipped by the cult of Osiris in Egypt. They are far too alike for coincidence. They must have had a similar origin." Kate looked directly at Devlin as she finished speaking, as though she could feel his gaze. Their eyes met and held for a moment before she glanced down at her plate. He watched the blush rise to stain her cheeks, wishing he could feel the rosy heat beneath his lips.

The breeze was growing cool, as it usually did in the evenings in this part of the country. Sweltering in the daylight hours, 20 degrees cooler at night. Yet the breeze did nothing to cool the heat inside Devlin, a heat burning more intensely than the sun.

Robert Melville's right arm brushed Devlin's left. "Got your sights set a little high, don't you, McCain?" Melville

whispered, his whiskey-soaked breath assaulting Devlin's
nostrils.

Devlin carefully molded his features into an expressionless mask as he glanced at Melville. He was accustomed
to hiding his emotions; it came with his profession as a
gambler. Yet the smug look on Melville's face told Devlin
he had not always been so successful in hiding his need for
Katherine Whitmore. He decided to ignore the man, and the
sudden urge he had for planting his fist in the middle of his
smiling face.

"How could a civilization that advanced exist in Atlantis
while the rest of the world was barely crawling out of caves?"
Edwin asked of Frederick. "Were these people dropped from
heaven? Perhaps they came here from another planet."

"Perhaps." Frederick grinned at his friend.

Edwin rolled his eyes. "Really, now."

"Look at Europe and America at the time of discovery,"
Austin said. "The natives thought Columbus was a god.
It is possible that people with advanced skills, perhaps in
medicine and science, would be looked upon as divine. What
we consider today as commonplace would take on the guise
of myth if we were suddenly thrust back three thousand
years."

"If these people were so advanced, why did they disappear?" Devlin poked at a piece of roasted potato on his plate.
"Wouldn't there still be descendants, as there are descendants
of ancient Egypt?"

"And well there could be." Frederick paused with his water
glass near his lips. "I have a theory that somewhere there are
still living colonies of Atlanteans."

"Now, that would be interesting to see," Devlin said.

"Why, Mr. McCain, does this mean you are no longer a
skeptic?" Kate asked.

"I found out a long time ago, Miss Whitmore, fairy tales
never come true." Yet, for the life of him, Devlin wasn't sure
why he was beginning to believe in this fable. Perhaps there
was still a little boy inside him who wanted to believe in

magic, a little boy destined to have his heart broken.

"This is not a fairy tale, Mr. McCain," she said, her fingers growing tense on her wineglass. "My father is a scholar, not a weaver of fairy tales."

"Now, Katie," Frederick said, patting her arm. "He's not trying to ridicule us, only to voice some questions."

Kate glanced down at her plate, her lips tugging into a narrow line, a sign of her fight to control her temper. Maybe he should have kissed her a few hours ago when he had the chance, Devlin thought. She had wanted him to kiss her; he wasn't blind, and he wasn't inexperienced. He could tell when a woman was feeling the warm ripple of desire course through her. And he knew his refusal was one of the reasons she was so vexed with him.

So why hadn't he? Why hadn't he taken her in his arms? He ached to hold her. But the simple truth was, a few stolen kisses would never be enough. Not with this woman.

And if she did let it go beyond a few kisses, if she did allow her natural curiosity and her awakening desire to overrule her common sense, then what? Would he be a fool if he believed Katherine Whitmore would ever want him for more than a moment's pleasure? Could a woman like Katherine Whitmore fall in love with a man like him?

"So tell us, Sinclair," Robert said. "When are you and Katie going to make it official?"

Robert might have thrown a live cobra onto the table. Conversation halted. Kate stared at Robert, as did the rest of the little group gathered at the round dinner table. Devlin felt a tightening in his chest as he watched Kate and waited for the answer he wasn't sure he wanted to hear.

"I beg your pardon." Austin set his wineglass on the white linen beside his plate. His expression revealed only a mild curiosity.

Robert laughed. "Come on, old boy. You can tell us. When are you going to announce you've won the lady's hand?"

"Robert, you don't know what you're talking about," Kate said.

"You mean you haven't accepted the good marquess?" Robert lifted his glass and drained the last of his whiskey. He thumped his glass on the table and gestured for a steward to refill it. One of the three white-uniformed black men attending the table quickly responded, pouring amber whiskey from a crystal decanter into the glass. "Better not let him get away, Katie. He'll be a duke one day."

"That will be enough, Robert," Edwin said.

"Poor father. He was so hoping you would succumb to my considerable charm." Robert shook his head. "Don't think that's going to happen."

"Not in this lifetime," Kate murmured, her eyes growing narrow as she stared at Robert.

"How you wound me," Robert said, pressing his hand to his heart. "And to think of all the Whitmore millions going to Sinclair. You don't need them much, do you, old boy? Or is that the reason you've come on this little trip? To seal the deal?"

Devlin didn't wait for Austin to reply. "I think you've had enough to drink, and more than enough to say."

Robert smiled. "Didn't want to hear the truth, did you, old boy?"

Devlin rose from the table. "I can see you need some help getting to your cabin." He took Robert's arm and dragged him to his feet, Melville's chair tumbling backward, crashing on the wooden deck. "We wouldn't want you to trip and hurt yourself on the way."

The smile slipped from Robert's lips, his expression turning to one of fear as he stared up at McCain. "I'm going, McCain. I don't need your help."

Devlin watched Robert stagger down the deck and enter his stateroom. He could feel the others watching him. Were they also condemning him for what they would call his boorish behavior? Water rushed over the paddle wheel, the steady splash mingling with the rumble of the engines, filling a silence that seemed to stretch for miles.

It didn't matter what these people thought of him and his lack of social graces, Devlin thought, sinking into his chair. No matter how friendly they seemed, he knew he was only the hired help.

Frederick cleared his throat before he launched once more into his favorite subject, sharing his insights on Atlantis. Devlin looked at Kate. Gone was the self-confident mask. Color had risen high on her cheeks, and she looked for all the world as though she wanted desperately to run away and hide. Never had he wanted to hold her more than at that moment.

Austin slipped his hand over Kate's, her hand a fist on the white table linen. He leaned toward her and whispered something near her ear, something that made her smile and look up at the handsome young aristocrat. They were right for each other, any fool could see it, Devlin thought. He glanced down into his wine, watching the lamplight shimmer in the pale liquid, feeling a sharp pain twist in his chest, and knowing it was only the first thrust of a pain he would come to know far too well.

Chapter Seven

Kate rested her sketchbook on the railing at the stern of the ship. One of her jobs on this trip was to provide sketches for the book her father would write outlining this expedition. She needed to concentrate on work. She needed to divert her thoughts from Devlin McCain.

The paddle of the big stern-wheeler churned below her, kicking up plumes of dark water that turned to glittering silver in the moonlight. On either side of the wide river, the forest soared in dark, twisted shapes, ancient sentinels guarding the gates to land untouched by man. In the distance she could see the lights of another riverboat, the only sign of civilization in a wilderness of shadows and moonlight. A great mystery waited in those shadows. And all she could think about was a man.

Above the splash of water tumbling over the paddles, she could hear the others, their conversation drifting to her on the cool evening breeze. She had left the men to their after-dinner brandy and their polite arguments. It was too disquieting, being near Devlin McCain. She could read nothing in his face, while he seemed to reach into her very soul with his eyes.

Work, think of work. She opened the tapestry cover of her sketchbook and flipped through the pages. Sugarloaf Mountain, the bay of Rio, native huts along the Amazon near Pará with their thatched roofs overhanging open porches; respectable work filled up the first few pages of her sketchbook. But something quite different lurked on the pages near the back of her book.

She should sketch the river and the trees; she shouldn't be flipping through these pages. Yet she was. She hesitated a moment before lifting a page and exposing her secrets to the moonlight. Images of Devlin McCain spilled across the white parchment. His face—smiling, frowning, thoughtful—the sharp lines of his profile. And there were others, sketched from memory, including one very detailed sketch of Devlin McCain stepping from his bath.

Could any artist capture the rare beauty of the man? She hadn't. But how could she capture that light in his eyes? How could she force charcoal and paper to come alive with power and grace? And how could she forget being held in his arms? She hadn't. She wondered if she ever would.

She glanced up at the stars. They seemed so close, so bright, as though she could reach up and capture one. Perhaps if she picked one special star, perhaps if she made one special wish, a wish to purge Devlin McCain from her thoughts, she might be able to.

"Wishing on a star?"

She pivoted on her heel at the sound of Devlin McCain's voice. He stood no more than three feet away. And he was smiling. Her heart stumbled; she felt it bump against the wall of her chest before it careened into a headlong gallop. "How do you manage to do that? Sneak up on a person without making a sound?"

"Maybe you were just too involved in making a wish to notice me."

She wished to heaven she could do anything but notice

him. "I suppose you think it's silly, making wishes on the stars."

"I've got nothing against wishes." He rested his hands on the railing and turned his face toward the creamy flow of moonlight. "As long as you aren't too disappointed when they don't come true."

She studied his profile, tracing the lines of his face, a face that seemed older than his years. Was he always like this, hard and callous? Was there ever a time he had looked up at the stars and believed his wish would come true? "Is there anything you believe in, Mr. McCain?"

"I believe in the sun coming up every morning and going down every night. I believe in playing fair, and keeping one eye open all the time for those who don't."

He turned, resting his hip against the railing, facing her. Moonlight caressed his features, stroking him with delicate fingers. He had such warm skin. She curled her fingers against her sketchbook, fighting the infuriating urge to touch him.

"And there are a few other things I believe in."

The look in his eyes made her breath catch in her throat. So full of heat, so full of sensual promise, those beautiful eyes looked as though he wanted to hold her, kiss her, touch her in ways she could only imagine possible.

"I believe in the smooth curve of your cheek," he said, sliding the back of his fingers over her cheek, a gentle stroke of warmth that set her legs to trembling like a willow in a summer storm. "The softness of your lips."

"Oh," she whispered, a curious tingle vibrating deep in her belly. "Mr. McCain, are you always so brazen with women?"

"Brazen?" Tiny lines crinkled at the corners of his eyes as his smile grew wide. "And here I thought I was being the quintessential gentleman."

"Gentlemen do not discuss such things in the presence of a lady." And a lady did not crave a man's touch, she reminded herself.

"Well, you'll have to excuse me. I haven't spent much time in the company of ladies."

Kate suspected any woman who spent much time with this man would soon find she was no longer a lady. He was the type of man all mothers warned their daughters about: sensual, indecently handsome, filled with dark passions. Pagan. Savage. Magnetic. The type of man who made a woman wonder what it might be like to taste the forbidden, to feel the heat of the fires she sensed smoldering inside him. And she had little doubt that a woman would be burned in his fire.

"Working on the sketches for your father's new book?"

Only when he leaned forward to take a look at her book did she realize the danger she was in; she slammed the cover closed, the sudden puff of air ruffling his long hair.

He cocked one black brow as he looked down at her. "Got something to hide?"

Too much to hide and nowhere to run. "I don't like people looking at my work before it's ready, that's all."

He leaned against one of the posts supporting the upper deck and grinned at her. "You're very good."

"How do you know?" she asked, clutching the sketchbook to her chest, her face flaring with heat at the thought of the sketches she had made of Devlin McCain. "Have you been snooping around my things?"

All the friendliness faded from his face. He lowered his thick, black lashes until his eyes were shimmering slits of silver in the moonlight. "I don't have the habit of going through other people's belongings, Miss Whitmore."

"I didn't mean to imply—"

"Didn't you?" He turned away from her and looked out across the water. A muscle throbbed in his cheek as he clenched and unclenched his jaw. "Your father gave me a copy of his book, *Atlantis: Ancient Roads Traveled.* That's where I saw your work."

"I'm terribly sorry, Mr. McCain. I apologize for insulting you. I spoke without thought. If I . . . I really . . . I'm so sorry." She hugged her sketchbook closer, feeling the frantic pounding of her heart against the cover.

He glanced at her, and she saw in his eyes the hurt she had inflicted by her careless words. How vulnerable he seemed, as vulnerable as she felt.

"Please forgive me. I know you wouldn't do anything dishonest. But, for some misbegotten reason, you have the most disconcerting way of catching me off guard as no one else can. I'm not usually this . . . this easily aroused to heated emotions, I assure you."

"Heated emotions." The smile returned to his lips, a slow, sensual slide that sparked memories of the way those lips had moved against hers. With the memories came the warmth only he had ever been able to kindle inside her. "Sounds intriguing."

"There is nothing intriguing about it."

"No?" He moved away from the post.

She stepped back as he approached. "I find it tiresome. We will be together for weeks to come, Mr. McCain, and I would expect . . ." She hesitated as her heel hit the wall.

"What?" he asked, bracing his hands on the wall on either side of her head.

His warmth reached out to surround her, the tangy scent of his skin invading her every breath. She raised the sketchbook as a shield against him. "I would expect you to try to get along with me."

"I am." He leaned his chest against the book; warm linen and the resilience of finely molded muscles pressed against the back of her fingers. "So you say no one else can arouse such heated emotions. Now what do you suppose that means?"

"It means you can be the most infuriating man." He leaned so close she could feel his long legs brush her skirt. She flattened her back against the wall, trying to escape the compelling warmth of his body. All of her defenses were melting, dissolving in his heat.

"I've never met anyone like you," he whispered, brushing his lips against her temple.

And she had never in her life met anyone like Devlin

McCain. Without words the man spoke to her, whispered of mystery and pleasure in a language she was only just beginning to understand. She clenched the sketchbook, feeling her pulse throb in her fingertips, the solid heat of his chest against the back of her hands. "You mustn't, I'm—"

"You're enchanting." He pressed his lips to her brow. "I think about you all the time, day and night."

"Please don't. I'm . . ." *Drowning. Drowning in the scent of your skin, drowning in the heat of your body.*

He slid his hands across her shoulders, his heat soaking through her clothes, spreading like warm butter. "I want to hold you. God, I want to hold you."

She felt her shoulders shifting, rolling toward him, as though controlled by strings. If she didn't do something soon, she would be lost, she would be tumbling into his arms, begging for his kisses. "Is this the way you play fair?" she whispered, pushing against his chest.

He looked down into her eyes, moonlight carving the outline of his head and shoulders from the darkness, leaving his face in shadows. Yet his eyes burned through the darkness, his silvery blue gaze burned straight into her soul. "What am I doing to break the rules?"

"You're trying to seduce me, Mr. McCain. You're trying to catch me unawares, when I have placed my trust in you. When my father has placed his trust in you. When everyone on this expedition is depending on you."

He eased away from her as though every movement brought him pain. She listened to the sound of his breath, a long pull of air before his sigh escaped his parted lips and touched her cheek with warmth.

"I guess it's my turn to apologize, Miss Whitmore. I should've known better than to step beyond my bounds. It won't happen again."

She sagged against the wall, watching him walk away, fighting the urge to beg him to come back to her. She lifted her sketchbook and pressed her lips to the rough tapestry, a poor substitute for his soft lips.

Heaven help her, how was she going to resist the temptation of Devlin McCain?

She stumbled to the railing and glanced up at the stars. But she didn't make a wish. For, at the moment, she was frightened of what that wish would be.

The breeze slid through Kate's open porthole in a delicious thread of cool air. Yet it was little more than a ripple in the stagnant heat of the room. She turned in bed, her nightgown twisting around her legs, clinging to her damp skin.

"That man," she murmured, tugging at her gown, freeing her legs from the tangled white cotton. If not for Devlin McCain, she would be sleeping comfortably on deck, nestled in one of those fishnet hammocks like everyone else. But *he* was out there. And she didn't intend to be anywhere near Mr. Devlin McCain.

Never in her life had she met anyone more arrogant, more barbaric, more . . . fascinating. Sighing, she pressed her cheek deeper into her pillow.

"Forget him," she whispered.

What was that noise? A soft click. The sound of the door to her cabin closing? She turned her head, staring at the door leading to the long main cabin which ran down the center of the boat. She held her breath and listened, straining her eyes to see in the darkness. Only a faint glow of moonlight shone through the open porthole.

Was that the steady throb of the engines she heard? Wood creaked. The hair on the back of her arms prickled. Had that shadow near the door moved?

"Who is it?" she whispered.

Into her mind flashed the image of Devlin McCain. He was a man who took what he wanted. Her skin tingled. He would have no scruples against coming to a woman in the middle of the night. He would slip into her bed. He would take her into his arms and . . .

That shadow did move. She sensed a presence near the bed, and her instincts told her it was not Devlin McCain.

She gathered the sheet to her neck.

"I say, who is—" Her words ended in a gasp as a man's hand slammed against her mouth, forcing her back against the pillows. She clawed at his bare arm, her hands sliding against his sweat-drenched skin.

"You no scream, senhorita." He leaned over her, the stench of whiskey and unwashed skin assaulting her senses.

He thrust the cold edge of a blade against her neck just below her chin. She fell still, her breath turning to frost in her throat.

"You no make trouble."

With his hand on her mouth, he pushed back her head, exposing her neck. She fought the terror rising inside her, sensing the wrong move would end her life.

He drew the knife slowly across her neck, the blade grazing her flesh, the pain burning like a red-hot coal dragged across her skin. Fear rose inside her like a huge, wild beast, tearing at her with sharp, jagged claws. She bit her lower lip, trying in vain to catch the whimper that escaped her tight throat.

"You no make noise, you no make trouble. Or I kill you." Blood trickled down her throat. "You understand?"

She nodded.

He tugged on her arm, dragging her from the bed, his fingers pinching her nerves. Her knees threatened to buckle; she had to fight to keep from falling. Somehow she had to grab hold of her runaway wits. "What do you want?"

He lifted the knife in his right hand to the glow of moonlight flowing through the porthole. "You draw me map to city."

The city. Her mind churned as he pushed her toward the writing desk on the far side of the stateroom. After he had the map, would he kill her then? It seemed likely. The only chance she would have was to escape him.

He shoved her into the seat behind the desk. She blinked against the light as he lit the small oil lamp on the desk. The yellow light flickered behind the emerald-colored globe, casting light on his features, deepening the scar that cut across his face from his left ear to the corner of his mouth, making his dark eyes recede into his head until it seemed she was staring into empty sockets. He was a *mameluco,* a mixture of Indian and Portuguese blood. She recognized him as one of the men her father had hired in Pará as a bearer.

He smiled, revealing yellowed teeth, and lifted the knife. In the light she could see the dark red stain on the edge of the blade. Her blood. The same blood she felt sliding in a warm trickle down her throat. The fear inside her rose once more, threatening to overwhelm her. She bit her lower lip to keep from screaming.

"Map," he said, pressing the flat edge of the blade against her cheek. Slowly he drew the knife away, smiling down at her. "You draw. You make no trouble for José."

Be calm, she told herself as she pulled a sheet of paper from the top drawer, the white parchment trembling in her fingers.

She lifted the lid from the ink pot. There had to be a way to escape, she thought, staring into the indigo ink. The man was not much taller than she was, and slender, but strong. Perhaps she could take him off guard. She grasped the ink pot. In the next instant she tossed the contents into José's eyes. He gasped, clasping a hand to his face.

Her chair tumbled to the floor with a loud crash as she lurched toward the door leading to the deck. She screamed, allowing her terror to rush past her lips in a piercing sound, knowing she must alert the others.

Above the sound of her own screams, she heard shouts from outside, deep, rumbling shouts that blended with José's groans. By the time she reached the door, it was swinging open. She stumbled across the threshold, colliding with something as solid as oak. But this something was covered in warm skin and soft curls, and smelled of sandalwood and the tantalizing musk of sleep-drenched male skin. She knew that fragrance. She pressed her face against his skin, breathing his scent deep into her lungs.

Suddenly there were arms around her. Strong arms, locking her against a powerful male body. She felt safe, so safe. Her knees were giving way beneath her; there was no hope for it. Others were pushing past her, running into the cabin. She heard more shouts, the crash of a door hitting the wall. And Devlin was scooping her up into his arms.

"Kate, are you hurt?" Devlin asked, cradling her against his bare chest as though she weighed no more than a kitten.

She leaned back in his arms and stared up into his face, a beautiful face carved with bold lines and curves, an ancient pagan prince. He was frowning, staring at her neck. He looked upset. He looked positively panicked.

"My God," he whispered.

He started running, clutching her in his embrace, the thick muscles of his chest shifting against her breast, his arms taut around her shoulders, beneath her knees.

When he laid her on the bed, she groaned. She didn't want to leave his arms. She was safe in his arms. But he didn't leave. No, he was leaning over her, stroking the hair back from her face. His hand was so warm, his touch so gentle. And then he was easing open the buttons of her nightgown, peeling the blood-drenched cotton from her skin.

She shouldn't let him do that. Should she? It wasn't wise. No, it wasn't at all wise. "You mustn't," she said, covering his hand with hers.

He looked as though he were in pain, as though he were the one who had been sliced like a ripe papaya. "How badly did he hurt you?" He stripped the cover from one of her pillows. He dabbed at her neck with the edge of the embroidered cotton. "Did he try . . ." His face tightened. "Did he touch you? I swear to God, I'll kill him with my bare hands if he touched you."

She swallowed hard, fighting the sudden rush of tears gathering in her eyes. "He cut me." She started trembling, the fear, the horrible fear washing over her. Why now? Why was she falling apart now? She reached for Devlin, gripping his upper arm, absorbing his strength beneath her palm. "He wanted the map. Nothing else."

Devlin closed his eyes, a soft sigh slipping from his lips.
"It's all right, sweetheart." He slid his arms around her and
held her, cradling the back of her head in his hand, rocking
her as though she were a baby. "It's all right. You're safe.
Thank God, you're safe."

He whispered softly, pledging to keep her safe. Yes, nothing could hurt her while she was in his arms. She would
not cry, she thought, clenching her eyes shut, listening to
the rough tenderness of his voice. She would not cry. She
swallowed, her neck flaring with pain at the movement.

She wanted to show Devlin she was strong. She couldn't
fall apart like a broken doll. And yet she couldn't stop her
tears; they slipped between her lashes in steady streams, her
body shaking, Devlin McCain's chest growing slick beneath
her cheek.

"I'm sorry. I don't usually cry, but I can't seem to stop."

"It's all right, sweetheart." He brushed his lips against her
temple. "There's nothing wrong with shedding a few tears."

She turned her head, sliding her cheek against his shoulder,
his skin warm velvet beneath her skin. She wanted to wrap
herself in his warmth, stay in his arms forever.

Footsteps pounded on the floor of her room. Through the
thick film of tears in her eyes, she looked past the curve of
Devlin's shoulder to see her father rushing toward her, his
white shirt half tucked into his trousers, the shirttail flapping
as he ran.

"Katie!"

Devlin released her, laying her back against the pillow.
With a reluctance that came from more emotions than she
cared to acknowledge, she released the death grip she still
held on his arm. He backed away as her father sank to the
edge of the bed.

"Katie, are you all right?" Frederick asked, taking her
hand. "Good Lord. Your neck."

Kate dragged her gaze from Devlin's face. Good heavens,
what McCain must think of her, crying, clinging to him like
a frightened child. She swiped at the humiliating moisture on

her cheeks. "It's nothing more than a scratch."

"Katie, are you sure? You look—"

"Worse than I feel." She must take command of her emotions. She must pull together her scattered wits. "He was after the map," she said, appalled at the shrill sound of her voice. "Have you caught him?"

"Yes, we have him in the main cabin." Frederick rested his palm against her damp cheek. "You nearly blinded him with that ink pot."

"Remind me never to have an argument with you when you're anywhere near a pen or an ink pot."

She risked a glance at Devlin McCain as he spoke. He was still watching her, frowning, as though he didn't like what he saw. Unfortunately, she liked what she saw, far too much.

He seemed to come to her from another time and place, from a realm of swords and conquests, when knights battled for fair ladies. He stood before her wearing nothing except a pair of dark blue trousers. Flickering lamplight stroked the side of his face, his shoulder, his chest, forging an intriguing tapestry of shadow and light against the smooth skin she had so recently touched. His luxurious mane of hair was tousled, tumbling in a thick, black wave over his brow. He had such soft hair, so thick, so silky to the touch.

How could she be thinking about his hair at a time like this? "Father, if you wouldn't mind, perhaps you could bring me my medicine box."

"Oh, my, yes," he said, coming to his feet. "Of course."

Devlin stayed where he was, frowning down at her, while her father rushed into the adjoining bathroom. "So it seems you have all your starch back, Miss Whitmore."

"I'm quite fine." Kate forced herself to hold his steady gaze, forced herself to ignore the nagging trembling of her limbs. "Thank you so much for your help."

He shook his head. "Hasn't this been enough to tell you to go home, little girl? You should be on the first steamer back to England."

"I'm twenty-six years old, Mr. McCain. Far too old to be addressed as a little girl."

"Yeah, ancient by any standards."

She felt like crying all over again. Not from fear this time, but from humiliation. "I regret if I have given you the impression I am the type of person who will fold at the first sign of trouble. I apologize for this watery display. I assure you, I am unaccustomed to hysterics, and I shall do better in the future."

He looked as though he intended to say something more, but at that moment her father came dashing back into the room, carrying the wooden medicine chest Kate always carried with her on trips. Devlin left without a word, marching away from her in long strides. She stared after him, wishing she could take back every tear, wanting for the first time in her life to punch someone in the nose.

Somehow she would show Mr. Devlin McCain she was strong and independent. She would show him she didn't need his strong arm to lean on.

"Katie, where is the, ah, is the cut very bad?"

She glanced up at her father's pale face. He never could stand the sight of blood. "Let me," she said, taking the bottle of alcohol and moist wad of cotton from her father's trembling hands. "You sit down before you faint."

Frederick sank to the edge of the bed, turning his head away from her as she started to clean the wound beneath her chin. The alcohol seeped into her torn flesh like liquid fire. She clenched her jaw against the pain, thinking of Devlin McCain and how his handsome face might look with a broken nose.

Ten round tables were planted in a single line down the center of the main cabin. One of the three brass-and-crystal chandeliers had been lit, the oil lamps carving a wavering pyramid of light in the dark shadows of the long room. Devlin paused outside Kate's stateroom, staring at the scene being played in the spotlight, thinking of the woman who had nearly made this play a tragedy.

Her tears were still moist against his skin, the tears she had been embarrassed to shed. He had known grown men who would have been shivering on their knees after what she had gone through, and that woman was embarrassed she had shed a few tears. She had kept her head, used her wits, and managed to stay alive.

God, when he had seen the blood on her throat, when he had thought she might be dying—his body trembled with remembered fear. And he was supposed to keep her safe. *Nice job, Devlin.*

He stared at the man who had taken a knife to Kate's lovely skin, the man who had terrorized her, the man who had made her cry. At that moment he knew a hatred so powerful, it was all he could do to keep from ripping the man apart limb by limb.

José sat in a chair directly under the light with his hands tied behind his back. His face was stained, the black ink taking the shape of a grotesque black butterfly, the wings spreading out across his eyes, the tail sweeping down his nose.

Austin stood beside José, his bare foot propped on a wooden chair, his arms crossed on his raised knee as he questioned him. Edwin and Barnaby stood on the opposite side of Austin, staring down at the bound man. Each man looked as angry as Devlin felt.

"Tell us who hired you," Austin said.

José shrugged his shoulders. "I tell you nothing."

Devlin stepped into the pyramid of light. José looked up. When he saw Devlin, his eyes grew wide, the whites stark against the black stain. He strained back in his chair as though he could sense the raw fury emanating from every pore of Devlin's body. José's knife was on the table, Kate's blood a dark stain on the steel blade.

Devlin gripped the arms of the chair in which José was sitting. He leaned over the man, smiling at the look of fear in José's eyes. "Do you feel helpless, José? As helpless as Katherine Whitmore felt when you put a knife to her throat?"

"I didn't mean no harm," José said, his voice a harsh whisper. "I didn't mean to hurt her."

Devlin reached behind José. Without taking his eyes from the dark, frightened eyes of the other man, he gripped the smooth wooden handle of the knife. He lifted it, testing the weight of the blade. Slowly he brought the knife around until he held it suspended before José's eyes. The man whimpered and leaned back in the chair.

"*Por favor, senhor!*"

Devlin turned the blade, letting the steel capture the light, his chest constricting as he stared at Kate's blood. "What kind of man takes a knife to a helpless woman?"

"Senhor, I no mean no harm. I only scare senhorita."

Devlin looked past the blade to José's face; fear twisted the man's features, tears sliding past the black stain on his cheeks, catching the lamplight. Smiling, Devlin lowered the blade, pressing the edge against José's throat. He heard the sharp intake of breath that came from Edwin Melville, the soft whisper of his name that sounded like a plea from Barnaby's lips.

"Now tell me," Devlin said. "What kind of man cuts a woman's throat?"

José swallowed hard, the roll of his Adam's apple causing the blade to nick his throat, drawing a whimper from his trembling lips.

"You didn't answer me." Devlin brushed the edge of the blade across José's throat, grazing the skin with the razor-sharp steel, leaving a fine line of scarlet in its wake.

José sucked air between his sobs, tears spilling down his cheeks. "Don't let him hurt me, Senhor Sinclair. *Por favor*, have mercy!"

"Devlin," Austin said, his voice deep and calm. "I think—"

"Leave if you haven't the stomach for this, Sinclair." Devlin shot Austin a sharp look. "This isn't your civilized England. That goes for you too, Mr. Melville."

Edwin stroked the luxurious length of his drooping mustache. "The bastard deserves whatever you do to him."

For a moment Austin held Devlin's gaze; then a small smile curved his lips and the frown faded from his brow. Devlin felt at that moment the man could look into his mind, read his every thought. "He's all yours, Devlin."

"*Madre de Dios!*"

"I'm waiting, José," Devlin said. "Tell me what kind of man cuts a woman's throat?"

Great, rolling tears spilled down José's cheeks. "Don't hurt me, senhor."

Devlin thought of Kate, of the tears drying on his chest, of her blood staining the soft, white cotton of her nightgown. "I guess you don't know." He straightened as he spoke. He lifted the knife, staring at the bloody blade before looking down at the man who had taken this knife to Kate's throat. "Well, I'll tell you."

With a flick of his wrist, Devlin released the knife. It shot straight down between José's thighs, penetrating the wooden chair with a sharp thud.

José wailed. A stench rose in the room as his bowels emptied. A soft gasp came from the other men as they all stood staring down at the knife quivering between José's thighs, at the narrow band of scarlet seeping through his dirty trousers where the blade had nicked his scrotum.

"The only man who would cut a woman's throat is a man without balls," Devlin said. "Now, you're going to tell us what we want to know. Aren't you, José."

José nodded, his body convulsing with sobs. "A man, he come to me, in Pará, American."

"What was his name?" Austin asked.

José shook his head. "Don't know. He a big *hombre*, dark, ugly."

Edwin and Barnaby continued questioning José, but he refused to change his story, describing the American, confessing he was the only one on board involved.

Austin looked to Devlin, a whisper of a smile on his lips. "I think he's telling the truth."

Devlin nodded. He stared at the door leading to Kate's

stateroom. He wanted to go to her, he wanted to take her in his arms, he wanted to feel her soft breath against his skin, hold her through the night.

"I think I'll look in on Katherine," Austin said.

Devlin watched Austin cross the room and knock at Kate's door before he was invited inside. In his mind he imagined the smile she was giving the Englishman, imagined Austin taking her hand and kissing her fingertips; his imagination spawned a very real pain in his chest. Devlin turned away and found Barnaby watching him, a knowing look in his dark blue eyes.

Devlin turned and left the room. It was bad enough feeling like a lovesick schoolboy. It was worse to know he couldn't hide his feelings.

Chapter Eight

The sunlight beating down on the Amazon was brighter than any Kate had ever seen. It was white in intensity, and so hot she imagined she could see steam rising from the golden brown water. Hotter than any sun had ever been in England. Hotter than the Nile. And it enveloped her, that steamy air, so thick she could feel it rub against her skin like a hot, wet towel.

"You believe King Arthur was an Atlantean." Edwin's voice rose above the steady chug of the engines.

Kate glanced to where her father sat with Edwin at the dinner table, which this morning was strewn with journals, maps, books, and papers.

"I believe it is possible."

"Poppycock!"

"Let me show you something in my book tying together the legends of Britain with those of Atlantis," Frederick said, grabbing a red, leather-bound book from a pile of books to his right. He began riffling through the papers and books on the table, as though searching for something. "Where are those blasted glasses?"

"On your forehead, Father."

"Oh, yes, so they are," Frederick said, patting his brow. He slid his glasses into place on the bridge of his slim nose and smiled at Kate. "Thank you, dear. Now Edwin, I shall show you—"

"The next thing you will be telling me is you believe descendants from Atlantis are walking the streets of London today."

"Why, yes, I think it is quite possible."

"There are times when I worry about you, Frederick."

In their argument they didn't seem to notice the heat, although she could see the perspiration beading on Edwin's wide brow. They were all gathered on deck, too hot to be inside, everyone except Robert. She suspected Robert was below deck, playing poker with the crew as he had for the past three days.

She leaned back in the deck chair, her white linen shirt sticking to her damp skin, tiny trickles of perspiration sliding down her sides. This was just the beginning, she reminded herself. They had only traveled three days on this river.

Three days and Devlin McCain hadn't said more than three words to her. He hadn't come near her since the night he had held her in his arms while she spilled tears against his chest. She cringed when she wondered what he must think of her. She felt ill when she realized she cared what he thought of her.

This morning she had donned a pair of the trousers she had designed for this trip. After her voyage up the Nile, after struggling in the heat with petticoats and long skirts, Kate had decided she would never travel on an expedition that way again.

The trousers were made of cotton, pleated at the waist, dark blue and white threads forming a herringbone pattern. At breakfast, Austin had paid her a compliment on her appearance. Devlin McCain hadn't given her more than a glance.

"Atlantis never existed," Edwin said, catching Kate's attention. "Plato made up the story of the island nation to make his point about his ideal Republic. Even Aristotle rejected Plato's story as fiction."

"Atlantis is fact, not fiction. Plato says several times the story of Atlantis is indeed fact, a fragmentary account of a continent that existed."

"All right, I will give you this. Plato's story of Atlantis is a wonderful piece of fiction."

"Just look at the ancient deluge myths. If you believe most myths are based on some kernel of fact, then . . ."

Kate had heard the arguments a thousand times. At least Edwin had never laughed at her father. Too many others had. Kate had come to realize those skeptics needed proof to believe Atlantis once existed. And they would have it. Devlin McCain would get them through the jungle. They would find Avallon.

She glanced to where Mr. McCain sat playing chess with Austin near the bow of the boat. Barnaby sat on a stool beside the table, watching the chess match as though it were a world-class exhibition. Devlin was leaning back against the white wooden deck chair, his long legs stretched out before him, looking impossibly cool in his white cotton shirt and sand-colored breeches, dark brown boots rising to just below his knees.

Devlin seemed unconcerned with the game, looking through half-closed eyes at the board, like a sleepy lion. Austin looked more intense, dressed in a white shirt and trousers, sitting with his elbows braced against his thighs, his chin resting on the back of his clasped hands. So different, these two. Elegant charm. Earthy masculinity.

Who was winning? she wondered. The gentleman, or the rogue? But she knew who would win; Austin Sinclair was a master at chess. No doubt he was beating Mr. McCain soundly. An odd sense of discomfort twisted in her chest at the realization that Mr. McCain was in over his head.

Now, why should that bother her? Why was she sitting here hoping Devlin McCain would win? It was better not to think of Mr. McCain at all, she thought, directing her gaze to the shore.

Thick, green forest rose from the water's edge to tower 100 feet above the ground. Trees Kate had never before seen grew with thousands of palms, some vaselike in form, others tall and slender, with pendant clusters of reddish fruit and long fronds stretching out over the water. She should try to capture this in a sketch. She should try to concentrate on work, try to think of anything other than one confusing man.

Her fingers left moist smudges on the paper as she turned the pages of her sketchbook. She glanced at the sketches of Devlin McCain. She turned her head and looked at the two men locked in civilized battle.

Devlin's black hair stirred with the breeze, a thick wave falling over his brow. His shirt was open at the neck, his sleeves rolled up to his elbows, exposing his skin to the breeze. Her skin prickled, and she wondered what it might be like to strip away her clothes, to feel the breeze on her bare skin.

Had McCain stripped himself bare those months he had lived with the Indians? It would suit him, enhance the raw, savage beauty of him. In her mind she stripped away the layers of his clothes, seeing him as she had first glimpsed him, feeling heat burn deep inside her. She felt restless, her body craving something she couldn't define.

Devlin leaned forward. He turned his head, his silvery blue eyes looking directly into hers. Perspiration slid between her breasts, which felt constrained by the linen camisole clinging to her skin. Her skin tingled. Her every nerve came alive, throbbing with anticipation. She tried to breathe, but the air was suddenly too hot, too thick.

Devlin frowned, his eyes growing narrow before he glanced away from her. Kate stared down at the sketches in her lap. Devlin McCain could dismiss her with a glance, while she burned with memories of the way his lips had moved against hers, of the way his body had embraced hers, so hard, so warm, so filled with promise.

This horrible fascination could lead to no good. She knew exactly what she wanted from life, and it had nothing to do with getting entangled with a man, any man. Especially a man like Devlin McCain. A man who thought of her as a rosebud who needed to be kept in a nice, safe English garden.

Still, it didn't matter what she wanted. It was painfully clear Devlin McCain wasn't interested in her.

Devlin stared at the board, but for the life of him he couldn't remember his next move. Katherine Whitmore had wiped his mind of everything but one thought. And it had nothing to do with chess. Did she have any idea what she could do to a man by looking at him that way, as though she were stripping away his clothes, as though she wanted to . . .

"She's intriguing, isn't she?" Austin said.

Devlin glanced up from the board. The smile on Austin's face made him wonder if the man could read minds, but if he could read minds there should be malice in that smile, not that open warmth Devlin saw. Apparently the man didn't realize Devlin had been fighting his primitive instincts for days. Apparently Austin Sinclair didn't realize Devlin wanted to take the man's future wife in his arms and devour her. Or maybe Austin was so sure of himself, he couldn't feel jealousy.

"Look at her. In this heat she looks as cool and lovely as a dewy rosebud. And those trousers." Austin released his breath in a long sigh between his teeth. "I don't suppose she has any idea how provocative they are."

"They're practical." And the way that soft cotton outlined her long legs was driving him mad. Devlin glanced back down at the board. It was still his turn, wasn't it?

"You would never know a few nights ago someone had taken a blade to her throat."

Barnaby nodded. "She's got backbone, that one."

"I don't think I've heard her complain once about anything," Austin said.

Devlin wished she would complain. He wished she were some spoiled, flighty little piece of fluff he could exile from his mind. But she wasn't. She was strong and determined and too damn desirable.

Devlin breathed deeply, craving the scent of her skin, catching only a pungent blend of smoke trailing from the riverboat and humus drifting from the shore.

One thought of Katherine Whitmore and his blood burned. One look at her and something wild stirred inside him, his mind filled with erotic images, his muscles tensed, and it was all he could do to keep his hands off her. And she belonged to Lord Gallant, or soon would. The worst part about it was, he liked Sinclair. But it didn't stop Devlin from wanting to plant a fist in the center of that smiling, aristocratic face of his.

Devlin stared at the chessboard and tried to rein in the sudden aggression he felt toward this man. He forced all other thoughts from his mind. Now, what was he going to do about Austin's marauding bishop? Knight to . . .

"I'm thinking Dev can't be appreciating the lady's qualities," Barnaby said. "They didn't exactly get off on the right foot, so to speak."

So much for not thinking about her. Frowning, Devlin glanced at the little man sitting at his right. His coppery hair was tousled by the breeze, and he was wearing that wide smile that always made Devlin think of a leprechaun up to mischief. "The woman shouldn't be on this trip."

"You're not the kind of man who believes women should all stay at home and knit baby booties, are you?" Austin asked.

Devlin leaned back in his chair and stared past Austin to the shoreline. Nestled between the rolling, caramel-colored water and the dense emerald green of the forest, a wide stretch of beach baked in the sun, heat rising in shimmering waves from the pale sand. Long, dark shapes lay in the sunlight, like pieces of driftwood—the *jacare,* the huge, black alligators of the Amazon. As the boat churned by, one of the reptiles opened his mouth as though he were warning the intruders to leave his territory, the loud hissing sound slicing the air.

Devlin thought of Kate, of her smooth, ivory skin, of the delicious rose scent of her. And he thought of all the dangers awaiting her, the insects that would ravish her sweet skin, the animals, the savages. Yes, he wanted to keep her safe. And if that made him some kind of caveman, well, then he should damn well be carrying a club. "I guess I don't understand why a woman would want to walk through hell."

Austin shoved his hand into his hair, pushing back an ebony lock from his brow. "For the same reason the rest of us are on this expedition: to be there when a mystery is solved."

Devlin stared down at the chessboard. "You're risking your life for a quest of dreams."

"And what is it you're risking your life for, Devlin?" Austin asked. "If it isn't for a dream?"

Devlin glanced to where Katherine Whitmore sat looking out across the water, her sketchbook propped open on her lap. Tiny tendrils of hair had escaped the single braid draped over her shoulder to curl around her face and the nape of her neck. Austin was right; they were each trying to capture a dream. Only for Devlin, his dream was merely Austin Sinclair's reality. He looked down at the chessboard, and the logic of his strategy became clear. In two moves he had Austin in check.

Devlin felt Kate approach before he saw her. She stirred the air as she drew near, a cool whisper of an English garden, brushing his cheek with the light fragrance of roses. Without glancing up at the woman who stood beside the table, Devlin moved his knight, capturing Austin's throne. His joy blossomed and faded in the span of a heartbeat. At the moment of triumph, with a realization that seemed to drain the life from him, Devlin knew the other man had already won the only prize in the world worth fighting for.

"You won," Kate said, staring down at the chessboard.

Devlin looked up from the mahogany-and-mother-of-pearl

inlaid board. She looked shocked. Apparently the lady found it hard to believe he could possibly outwit Lord Gallant. "Close your mouth, Miss Whitmore, a bug might fly inside."

She bit her lower lip, her cheeks coloring a dusky rose. "I'm only surprised, Mr. McCain, because I have never met a better player than Austin."

"It appears I've met my match." Austin leaned back in his chair, smiling across the table at his opponent.

Austin glanced from Devlin to Kate, and Devlin had the uncomfortable feeling Austin knew exactly how Devlin felt about her. Still, it wouldn't take a mind reader to see the tension between them, Devlin thought. The air crackled with it. Strange though, it didn't seem to bother Lord Gallant.

"Aye, but they're evenly matched," Barnaby said, smiling up at Kate. "I'd be saying on any given day the game might fall to one or the other."

Was the little man talking about Austin or Kate? Devlin wondered.

The steamboat lifted her voice in the early morning breeze, singing like a huge bird in sight of its nest. Kate hurried to the railing near the bow. Devlin, Austin, and Barnaby followed her. Soon, Edwin and Frederick left their argument to join them at the railing.

Hills stretched to the south, flat, as though God had wielded a machete across them, topped with a crown of green trees and vegetation. Ahead of them the black waters of the Tapajoz met—but did not mingle with—the golden brown waters of the Amazon. White sand beaches dotted with tall javary palms led the way to Santarém.

Kate leaned forward, lifting her face to the breeze, breathing in the damp air. It would be heaven to set her feet on solid ground, if just for a few hours.

"I thought we might visit the church while Mr. McCain takes that man to the magistrate." She turned to face her father. "I'm anxious to see the cross von Martius sent from Munich." The naturalist had nearly lost his life in a wreck off Santarém in 1819. As thanks for his deliverance, he had sent a full-length figure of Christ upon the cross, made of gilded iron.

"I'm afraid you'll have to skip the sight-seeing this trip, Professor," Devlin said. "Lord Sinclair and I are going to take the yawl in to shore; the rest of you will stay on board."

So deep was that voice, rough and sensual, it commanded a response in her, a quickening of her blood. It appalled her to know she didn't even have to see the man to feel the heat he ignited inside her.

Kate pivoted to face McCain. He was standing a few feet away, his shoulder propped against one of the pillars supporting the upper deck, his arms folded over his chest, looking far too handsome, far too arrogant, far too certain of his own male power.

"Mr. McCain, I don't see what harm can be had by spending a few hours in the city."

"You have a short memory, Miss Whitmore."

"If we stay together, I should think—"

"You are staying on board."

It was an order—not a request, not a suggestion, but a blatant order. If he hadn't been looking at her as though she were some foolish child, if he didn't have the uncanny ability to strip away all of her social pretenses, she might have been able to keep a rein on her anger. As it was, she felt as though she might explode.

"In case you forgot, let me remind you, Mr. McCain, my father is your employer. You are not in a position to give me orders."

Devlin's expression shifted, the look of arrogance dissolving into a fury that made Kate take a step back. He moved toward her, closing the six feet of empty deck in two strides, halting when only inches separated them.

He towered over her. He stood so close she could feel the heat of his skin. So close his scent filled her every breath— sandalwood mingled with the exotic fragrance of damp, male skin heated by the tropical sun. There it was again, that delicious heat flaring low inside her, that phantom emotion she couldn't name rising to steal the strength from her limbs.

"We need to get something straight, Professor. Here and now. Your father hired me to lead this expedition, and that's what I'm trying to do. But if you think you can do a better job, just say so. And I'll take the first steamship back to Pará."

"I understand the need for discipline, Mr. McCain. But I do not expect to be bullied."

"If you want courtly manners, you've come to the wrong place. I'm willing to try to slip this little group through hell without the devil noticing. But that's going to be impossible if everyone thinks they can do just exactly what they damn well want to do."

Kate became aware of the others standing nearby. A spoiled child, no better than Robert Melville, that was how she must appear to them. And she had allowed the volatile emotions this man evoked inside her to goad her into this position. She would lose this argument no matter what she did.

"Thank you for making your position so clear, Mr. McCain."

"And what's it going to be, Miss Whitmore?"

Although she felt like shriveling into a small, inconspicuous ball, she forced her back to stiffen. "You have been hired to do a job, Mr. McCain. I shall not keep you from doing it."

He turned away from her, dismissing her without another word. She stared after him as he marched down the deck, feeling heat simmer in her cheeks, wondering when she had last felt this humiliated. But she knew; it was the last time she and Devlin McCain had exchanged more than a few words.

Sunlight streamed through the skylight overhead, shimmering on the seven gold crests lining the smooth stone walls of the council chamber in Avallon, the ancient emblems for each council member. Long ago their ancestors had escaped the great cataclysm. Displaced scientists in a primitive world, they had created the shield of pagan cults to disguise the knowledge they took for granted, the knowledge that was dangerous in that simple world. Beneath the cloak of ancient rituals, they had continued their exploration of science and nature.

In time even their rituals could not shield them from the superstition and fear of the primitive tribes surrounding them. The ancestors of those gathered in this council chamber had come to this mountaintop, escaping persecution as witches and wizards, embracing the freedom to expand their knowledge, to explore the mysteries of nature.

Rhys sat beside his wife at the round mahogany table, waiting for judgment on his petition. It occurred to him that after the passing of 6,000 years, his people still had not escaped all of their ancient rituals. They still believed in rites of passage for those who would seek a place in the Inner Circle, and some tests were far more primitive than others.

Rhys glanced from one council member to the next as the judgment was spoken by each. He saw sympathy in their eyes, even as they voted against his son. Three for. Three against. It was left to the leader of the Central Council, his grandmother, to decide the issue.

Deirdre stared down at her folded hands. Rhys watched the rise of her narrow shoulders as she drew a deep breath, as though she were drawing strength from the sunlight shimmering all around her. She looked as fragile as a sparrow. Yet Rhys knew she had the heart of a hawk.

She lifted her dark blue eyes and focused on her grandson. Rhys knew the words she would say before they were spoken.

"We have read the report sent by the watcher," Deirdre said, never taking her eyes from Rhys. "We have carefully considered the added danger this unknown Outworlder presents in his desire to attain the map to this city. But the danger to the people of Avallon must take precedence."

Beneath the table, Brianna tightened her grip on his hand. Silently he tried to reassure her, stroking his thumb over her taut knuckles, sensing her fear. Once again he thought of the son they might lose. He fought to keep the waves of pain from his heart and his mind.

"No member of the Whitmore party will be allowed to enter the city until the council is certain of the nature of these strangers," Deirdre said. "It is our judgment the added danger does not warrant cancellation of the test. According to the report, the Whitmore party left Pará three days ago. They should arrive in Santarém late this morning. The watcher will keep us informed. If the danger becomes too great, the test will be ended."

"It is possible damage could be done before our knowledge." Rhys kept his voice calm, even though he wanted to scream at these people. "Someone could be injured or killed."

"From all reports, the Whitmore party was aware of the risks before they started on this journey to find our city." Deirdre glanced down at her folded hands. "We can only hope your son is capable of preventing disaster."

"It is much to ask of one man."

"There is an alternative." Deirdre glanced up to meet her grandson's eyes. "The test can be ended."

The people of Avallon were all tested, in one way or another, from the time of their birth, to determine their skills, their intellect, to help guide them on the proper path they would take in life. Yet this was the first time for such a test as their son would endure. Never before had a situation such as this occurred.

"Of course, that would mean another test would have to be devised. It would take several months to arrange, perhaps a year."

"This has all taken too long as it is," Rhys said.

"Without a test, your son would be allowed to live in Avallon only as an Outworlder. For the remainder of his life he would be denied access to the Inner Circle." Deirdre was quiet a moment, holding Rhys in her steady gaze. "You hold his future in your hands. Have you faith enough in the young man to allow him this chance to take his proper place in our society?"

Although his fear for his son pleaded with him to end the test, Rhys knew he could not. "We agree to the council's decision."

Rhys and Brianna were expected to leave the council chambers without argument. This was more difficult for Brianna. Rhys felt the overwhelming urge within her, the need to fight for her son, the same need he was keeping under rein. He took her arm and quickly led her out of the chambers. His eyes narrowed against the bright light as they emerged from the council building into the sunshine.

Like the other structures in the city, the council building was made of natural stone carved from the sides of the mountain. It blended with the surroundings, as his people had long ago learned to blend with the Outworlders. Bankers, magistrates, nobility, businessmen, advisors to kings and politicians, the people of Avallon possessed places in society all over the world, as they had always done.

"Those people are living in the Dark Ages."

Rhys looked down at the woman walking beside him, noting the mutinous thrust of her small chin. Her pale green silk tunic was belted at her waist by a wide band of gold, a waist still incredibly small even after giving birth to his three children. And her legs were long and shapely beneath the close-fitting white silk trousers.

He knew her mind as well as he knew the sweet curves and lines of her body. She blamed herself for what had happened to their son. She blamed herself for this mission he must now accomplish before he could return to them. And nothing Rhys could say would change her mind.

"Why don't they simply fit our son up in armor and ask him to go slay a dragon."

"I understand it's difficult to find a dragon ready for a good fight these days."

Although he could see her fighting it, one corner of her

lips betrayed her smile. "Don't try to coax me out of my foul mood, because I'm not going to let you." She paused on the stone walkway beneath the shelter of one of the trees that lined the street. "Let's end it. Let's bring our son home. Let's tell these people we don't give one fig for their medieval quest."

Rhys stared at the long, two-story building that stood across the street, one of their development centers. A park stretched from one side of the building, a low stone wall surrounding a large expanse of emerald green grass. Trees rose from the lawn, knitting a living canopy over the boys and girls who were playing below, throwing balls, building with blocks of wood, chasing after each other. They ranged from five to 12 years old, their laughter singing on the breeze in spite of the fact that they were all blindfolded with a strip of black cloth. It was part of their training, to develop their senses. The training for children of Avallon began before they could walk.

"What would you say to our son when he realized he must forever live as an Outworlder in the place of his birth? Would you tell him we condemned him because we feared he was not strong enough to complete this test?"

She hesitated a moment, looking down at the black stones beneath her feet. "I've lived here most of my life and I still don't completely understand this place or these people. You guard your secrets well, my love."

A hard hand squeezed his heart when he thought of the wonders he must forever keep from her; the secrets of the Inner Circle; the secrets that could be disasters if ever discovered by the Outworld; the secrets kept by a chosen few of Avallon. "If I could, I would reveal the world to you. But upon my oath, I cannot."

"I know." She glanced up at him, a smile curving her lips. "And I know how difficult it can be living as an outsider in this place of mysteries. I don't want to deny our son his future."

"Have faith in him, my love." Rhys slipped his arms

around her. Faith in their son. Only faith would carry them through this time of trial.

Kate rested her hands on the railing. Below, the yawl carrying McCain, Austin, and the man who had held a knife to her throat was pulling away from the riverboat, headed toward the city of Santarém. Rows of one- and two-story whitewashed buildings spread upward from the white sand beach, flanking streets that would be pretty, if there were any trees. As it was, the entire city shimmered in the heat.

"Look there, Katie," Frederick said, pointing toward a cluster of palm-thatched huts huddled near the beach. "The *Aldeia,* the original Indian settlement, existing right along with the modern city. A suburb, so to speak. Devlin said that's where he and Austin would secure the canoes and paddlers we need."

"I wish we could explore." Kate pulled her gaze from Devlin McCain to the remains of a fort perched on a rocky hill near the shore. There were washerwomen on the beach, colorful clothes stretched out on the sand and hanging from lines, bathers enjoying the cool water. "I feel like a prisoner."

"Now Katie, Mr. McCain is right. There's no need for us to take the added risk of going ashore."

Devlin McCain's harsh words echoed in her ears. Perhaps he was right, but she didn't have to like it. The man was nothing less than infuriating.

Many crafts were coming and going all around them: cattle barges, trading canoes, and fishing boats. One boat, a white steamboat anchored a hundred yards downstream, caught Kate's attention. On the deck she could see a couple near the railing, a dark-haired woman standing beside a tall man with silvery blond hair. Sunlight reflected on the brass telescope the woman was holding. Kate glanced back to shore, wondering what had captured the lady's attention.

Judith stood beside Leighton at the railing of the *Styx,* staring through a telescope, watching as Devlin McCain and another tall, dark-haired man escorted Leighton's man from the boat at the landing. McCain moved with the confident grace of a predator. He towered above the men and women swarming around him, the peasants who crowded the dock, trying to peddle their wares to the riverboat passengers, holding up baskets of fruit, brightly plumed parrots, monkeys, snakes, anything they thought the English and Americans might buy.

As McCain slipped from her field of vision, Judith wondered what it would be like to tame him. She wondered if she would have the chance. "It looks as though your little friend failed." She handed Leighton the telescope.

"Have you so little faith in me, my queen?"

Leighton rested his chin on the eyepiece and smiled at her. The breeze caught his hair, tossing it back from his face. He seemed too beautiful to be of this world: an angel's face hiding a devil's soul.

"Remember this. I always get what I want."

Judith felt the hair at her nape tingle as she looked up into Leighton's cold, blue eyes. He wanted that mythical city in the jungle. And he would kill anyone who got in his way, including Devlin McCain.

Chapter Nine

Kate shifted on the narrow seat of the canoe, wishing she could stretch her legs, her knees grazing Devlin McCain's back. He didn't even glance at her. Perhaps because it had happened often in the past few hours. Perhaps because he couldn't stand the sight of her. With that realization came an unexpected rush of pain, like the burn of acid drizzling over her heart.

It didn't matter what he thought of her, she assured herself, trying to ignore the ache centered in her chest. It didn't matter. It didn't!

Although they had engaged two Indian paddlers for each of the four canoes they had acquired in Santarém, Devlin McCain was not content to sit idle. He applied his paddle in rhythm with the other paddlers, dipping into the black waters of the Tapajoz over and over again, lapping the water softly against the side of the canoe. His quick, efficient movements set the muscles in his back flexing beneath the white cotton of his shirt, so damp, so clinging, defining every powerful curve and line. A haunting rhythm. A dance of power and grace in time with the music of the rippling water.

With each breath she caught the intriguing scent of his moist skin. The heat of his body radiated against her legs, a taunting reminder of how warm it had felt to be held in his arms, and how cold it was to be held in his contempt. It was enough to make her shiver in the heat of the dwindling day.

"Devlin, we should turn off the main channel just up ahead," Frederick said.

Devlin lifted his paddle, the flat itauba wood dripping as he rested the grip across his thigh. From beneath the brim of his dark brown hat, he looked past Kate to where her father sat beneath the small, arched cabin of thatched palms near the stern of the boat. "Are you sure? It doesn't look much like a major tributary."

"I know, but I believe it is the one we're looking for." Frederick leaned forward, crossing his arms on his knees. "According to Randolph's map, that wedge-shaped hill marks the entrance. I believe that is the landmark we're looking for, wouldn't you agree, Katie?"

Kate lifted her hand to the brim of her pith helmet, shielding her eyes from the bright sunlight, her shirt sticking to her arm, her shoulder, her back. A thick film of moisture covered her body. Her scalp was drenched under her hat, her braid damp and sticky against the nape of her neck. A few yards ahead stood a wedge-shaped clay hill marking the entrance to what appeared to be no more than a stream. "Yes, I think it is."

McCain turned back without looking at her, as though she weren't even there. She wanted to scream. She wanted to grab his wide shoulders and turn him toward her. She wanted to plunge both hands into the thick, black mane curling around his collar and force him to look at her, really look at her. What did he see with those beautiful, silvery blue eyes when he looked at her? Why did it matter so much?

What was wrong with her? Why was this man able to stir her emotions so violently? Unable to understand her own feelings, she dragged her gaze from the intriguing play of muscles beneath Devlin McCain's damp shirt and stared toward the opposite shore, trying to purge the terrible restlessness within her.

The land to the west was no more than a dark line on the horizon. The sun was sinking toward that line, tossing scarlet and gold across the few tufts of white clouds dotting the blue sky. This was only the beginning, she reminded herself. Weeks stretched out before them. Somehow she must learn to ignore the confusing emotions Devlin McCain conjured inside her. She had no choice.

As they left the main channel of the Tapajoz, they entered another world. Trees soared on either side of the narrow river: palms of different shapes and sizes, laurel, rosewood, mahogany, cedar, and hundreds more she couldn't recognize. All lifted their branches toward the sun, drinking the golden light greedily, entwining their leaves overhead into an emerald canopy, allowing only a glimmer of sunlight to slip from their grasp. High in the trees she could see faces peering down at them as they rolled past, monkeys curious about these human intruders.

She stared in awe, stared as though she were seeing the forest of creation. Cordlike vines crawled upward along thick trunks of trees. Orchids dripped in great clusters of violet and white and pink from the trees, plump pendants swinging with the sultry breeze that dispersed their fragrance, swaying no more than 20 feet above the water. It was as if they were the first human beings ever to pass this way.

For miles she stared, a child lost in a fairy-tale land, looking from left to right, following the fluttery flight of a swarm of blue butterflies, catching a glimpse of a toucan. But as they traveled farther, Kate began to feel the uncomfortable pressure brought on by drinking far too much tea earlier in the day.

"Mr. McCain, do you suppose we will be making camp soon?"

"We still have a few hours of daylight," he said without glancing at her, his voice unduly gruff.

"Oh, I see." She shifted on the seat. She looked back at her father, wondering if he might be in the same uncomfortable position. He was lying back on the cushions beneath his green canopy, sound asleep. It seemed she had two choices: agony or humiliation. She stared at Devlin McCain's broad back, wondering what he might say of her plight. She would wait.

She stared at the forest, trying to take her mind from her troubles. A large blue-and-green macaw glided from a tree branch overhead, landing on a long frond of a miriti palm to peck at a cluster of reddish fruit. The jungle was alive with noises: chattering monkeys, screeching birds, rustling leaves, and the constant swish of water.

Biting her lower lip, she glanced down at the water flowing against the side of the canoe. There was no hope for it. If they didn't stop soon, she would be humiliated in a different way. "I wonder, do you suppose we might stop for a few moments?"

Devlin glanced over his shoulder, frowning at her. "Are you ill?"

She shook her head. "No. Not exactly."

He studied her, his frown slowly dissolving into a knowing smile. "Too much tea?"

Kate felt the heat rise in her cheeks. "I won't take long. If we could just stop for a few moments."

"Hmmm, don't suppose you're equipped just to go over the side of the canoe."

Kate stiffened. "No, Mr. McCain, I am not." Is that what the others had done? She wondered if that was what Devlin McCain would do should the need strike him. She supposed he would show her no respect in the matter.

"I didn't guess those trousers came with all the necessary equipment." He turned away from her.

"And what is that supposed to imply?"

He glanced over his shoulder. A shaft of sunlight streaked through the canopy of leaves overhead, slicing through the shadows, surrounding him with a shimmering golden light.

Once again, ancient fables of magical men high upon mist-shrouded mountains drifted into her mind. She clasped her hands in her lap to keep from touching him.

"You can dress like a man, Miss Whitmore, but underneath you're still a woman. And a woman has no business trekking through the jungle."

The canoe slipped through the sunlight back into the shadows. "I might not be equipped to take care of my bodily functions over the side of a canoe, Mr. McCain, but that certainly does not mean I have no right to be here."

"A woman like you should be sitting in the shade, on the front porch of a big house, with a baby in her arms."

"Men like you are the reason women are still considered second-class citizens, too weak and soft of mind to be more than a man's property. But we are more. We are just as intelligent and capable as those children of God who have been given that equipment you seem to be so very proud of."

He turned to more fully face her, his hard side pressing against her knees. "In that other world, Miss Whitmore, the world where people have been civilized for a few hundred years, you can preach your talk of equality. But here, we're down to the basics. Only the strongest survive."

"You forget, Mr. McCain, women survived the Stone Age right alongside the men."

"Yeah." He tipped back his hat, his eyes filling with a mischievous light, his lips curving into a smile. "You think you're ready to crawl into an animal skin and start wielding a club?"

"Mr. McCain, right now you should be very grateful I do not have a club in my hands."

He laughed, a deep, rumbling sound that made her fight the smile threatening her lips. "Is it safe to turn my back on you?"

"Only if you intend to direct this canoe to that strip of sand up ahead."

Still smiling, he nodded before he turned back around and shouted an order to the paddler in the front of the canoe.

The river grew wider here, the trees farther apart, allowing sunlight to strike the wide white sand beach.

Kate was out of the canoe the moment it touched the sandy shore. Her feet sank into the soft sand as she rushed toward the great wall of emerald rising a few hundred yards from the river. Intent on her mission, she didn't notice Devlin following her until she reached the edge of the forest.

Kate paused and turned to face him. "Mr. McCain, you can't mean to follow me."

"Don't worry, I'll keep my back turned."

"Why, I've never heard anything so preposterous in my life." She planted her hands on her hips and glared up at him. "You will not follow me."

Devlin lifted his hat and dragged the back of his wrist across his brow before settling it back on his damp, black mane. "Miss Whitmore, I'm only trying to keep you safe."

A trickle of moisture dripped down his neck and slipped into the glistening, black curls revealed by his partially open shirt. Who would keep her safe from him? she wondered. "I don't need your protection to handle my affairs."

He shook his head. "You're one stubborn female."

"I simply do not intend to . . ." She hesitated, watching as he drew the long, wicked-looking knife from the brown leather sheath he wore strapped to his hips. The blade captured the light, glittering, sparking memories inside her. She lifted her hand to the rough scab beneath her chin. "What are you going to do with that?"

"Relax, Professor, you haven't become a big enough pain in the behind for me to slit your throat."

"How flattering."

He turned the knife, offering her the handle. "Take this with you."

"I don't need that."

"Take it."

The intense look in his eyes made the tiny hairs tingle at the nape of her neck. She glanced at the thick vegetation behind her. From every description of the forest she had ever read came the terror stories echoing in her mind. A knife might not be a bad idea after all.

"Very well, if it will make you feel better." She took the knife from his hand, his warm fingers grazing hers, the smooth wood warm from his skin.

"Don't go more than a few feet."

Kate glanced to where the others were landing their canoes near the far end of the beach. "But I have to—"

"Don't worry, no one will be able to see anything."

"I'll make sure of that, Mr. McCain." She found an opening in the tangle of vines and stepped from the sunlight into the forest.

The darkness seemed a tangible thing, a frightening creature that could reach out and swallow her. She felt cold suddenly, the film of moisture covering her skin chilling in this dark void. She stared upward, seeking the light. A few hundred feet above her, the afternoon rays of the sun glinted against a woven canopy of leaves and vines.

As her eyes became accustomed to this darkness, she became aware of the great tangle of vegetation surrounding her. Tree trunks rose like pillars in an elaborate green and gray labyrinth. Roots grew in buttresses from the trees. Vines crawled over everything, some as thick as a tree trunk, others hanging in festoons over her head. Foliage everywhere, like mist, a heavy green mist that filled her nostrils and left a tang on her tongue.

Insignificant. She was nothing in this thick, green world. And she had only crossed the threshold. She had to fight the urge to turn and run back to the light.

"Take a good look over your head, Miss Whitmore."

Kate jumped at the sound of Devlin McCain's voice. She turned and stared back the way she had entered, seeing only the curve of his shoulder past a palm leaf.

"Make sure there aren't any snakes in the branches. They like to drop down on their prey."

Kate's gaze snapped upward, her eyes straining to see clearly through the gloom. Had she seen movement on the branch of that mahogany tree? She took a step, nearly colliding with a spiny palm stem, snagging long, slender filaments of a spider's web. The knife dropped from her hand in her haste to wipe the sticky strands from her hair.

"And be careful where you're stepping. Fire ants make their nests in the ground."

Kate bent to retrieve the knife, staring down at the ground, wondering what possible defense the weapon would be against marauding ants. She turned in a circle, her skin prickling. The forest seemed to be growing all around her, the vines, the trees, closing in on her. It seemed to be draining the life from her. Fear coiled around her chest, squeezing until she could scarcely breathe.

This was nonsense. She needed to take care of her business and get out of here. Quickly. She unbuckled her belt, slipped down her trousers, and parted the center of her drawers.

"Don't get too close to any leaves, Miss Whitmore. They might be covered with black ticks. The nasty little demons love to crawl into a person's private parts."

Caught in an awkward crouch near the ground, Kate shivered. She closed her eyes and willed nature to hurry. When she was finished, with the last button fastened on her trousers, she rushed out of the darkness and collided with Devlin McCain's broad back.

"Sorry," she whispered, backing away from him.

He tipped back his hat and smiled. "You did check to make sure you didn't pick up any ticks, didn't you?"

Kate shuddered. "I think I managed to avoid them," she said, handing him his knife.

He slipped the long blade of his knife into the sheath, studying her with those clear, penetrating eyes of his. She felt heat rise in her cheeks and wished she could control the telltale blush.

"You know, you can take one of the canoes tomorrow morning and be back in Santarém in time for dinner."

Kate clenched her trembling hands into tight balls at her sides. "You said all those things to frighten me, didn't you?"

"Do you think I said anything that wasn't true?"

She knew it was true, all of it. "I think you want to frighten me into—"

"Don't move."

Kate froze at the deadly tone in Devlin McCain's voice. "What is it?" But then she felt it, a soft brush against the side of her neck. Something was crawling across her skin!

"Kate, stay very still." Devlin drew near, his eyes narrowed into silvery slits, his face carved into a stern mask.

She felt the feathery legs cross her collarbone and slip inside the open collar of her shirt. A scream rose inside her, yet her throat tightened around it, choking the scream until it was no more than a whimper when it finally escaped her lips.

"That's right, sweetheart." Devlin unfastened the buttons of her shirt, slowly slipping the mother-of-pearl buttons through the damp white linen with barely a movement.

Her body trembled, the spasm rising with pure, undiluted fear.

"Don't move, sweetheart. Please, don't move. You'll be all right."

Delicate legs brushed the skin at the top of her camisole. Kate bit her lower lip, a pitiful mewling sound escaping her throat. She stared at Devlin, listening as he told her over and over again it would be all right, clinging to his presence as if he alone would pull her from the chilling pit of fear.

Slowly, Devlin peeled back her shirt. She lowered her gaze. Poised at the top of her camisole was a deadly brown spider, one long leg reaching out, testing the band of embroidered lace that trimmed the edge. Moisture beaded on her skin. Her breath halted in her lungs as she fought to remain still. If it bit her, she would die. Here in this godforsaken place.

With a flick of his fingers, Devlin sent the spider flying. Kate wobbled on her feet.

"Did it bite you?" he demanded, grabbing her upper arms.

His hold was fierce, yet oddly gentle, almost caressing. Had it bitten her? She couldn't be sure. She wanted to answer, but her tongue wouldn't obey. All that came out when she opened her lips was a humiliating sob. She was trembling all over.

With gentle fingers on her chin, he tilted her head, searching for any sign of a bite on her neck, her throat. He slipped his fingers into the top of her camisole, brushing the swell of her breast as he pulled the material away from her skin. Heat flared where a moment before fear had held her in a frozen claw.

She stared at the long, bronzed fingers pressed against her pale skin. In his quest, he had peeled back her camisole until the back of his fingers rested against the plump pillow of her breast, the damp cotton lawn of her camisole nearly transparent, clinging to her skin, revealing the rosy shadows of her nipples beneath. The sight of his hand against her flesh made her blood surge. The tips of her breasts grew taut and tingling, startling her. Yet she didn't move.

"I don't see any marks," he said, slipping his fingers from the top of her camisole.

Still, she couldn't move. Shock, perhaps. Or perhaps she wanted him to touch her again. He lifted his eyes, meeting her gaze. In his silvery blue eyes she saw relief and more. Did he care about her?

The sun flowed over her, heating her damp skin, caressing her thinly clad breasts. What would sunlight feel like against her bare skin? What would it feel like to have this man touch her again, without restraint? Man touching woman. Woman touching man. As they had since the beginning of time. Skin sliding smoothly against skin. What would it be like?

Beneath the brim of his dark brown hat, his eyes narrowed. The sensual curve of his lips parted, and he was so close, she could feel the warm sigh of his breath against her lips. She liked the smell of his breath. She loved the taste of his mouth. His hair stirred in the breeze, teasing her, tempting her to touch the silky mane.

Did he know what she was thinking? Did he know she wanted to feel his arms slide around her? Heaven help her, she wanted this man to kiss her. She wanted this man to lock her against his body, to press his hard chest against the horrible aching in her breasts.

And he knew. Oh yes, he knew. She could see the sudden awareness in his eyes, sense the hardening of his body, a response to her own sultry arousal. And she didn't care. She felt deliciously wicked.

"Kate," he whispered, resting his hand on her shoulder, brushing his fingers against the nape of her neck.

Kate trembled. She wanted to lean against him. But she couldn't move. It was all so new.

He lifted his thumb, brushing the curve of her jaw. "I don't want anything to happen to you."

Kiss me, she thought. *Please. Hold me in your arms and kiss me.*

With his eyes, he traced the curve of her lips. She parted them in invitation. He lowered his gaze to her breasts and she felt herself lifting, thrusting upward, wanton, supplicating. Even in her innocence she knew only he could ease the ache throbbing in her breasts.

He drew a deep breath and shook his head as though he were trying to clear his mind. "I must be crazy," he murmured, stepping back from her.

Crazy. Yes, she must be crazy. Good heavens, what was wrong with her? Humiliation washed over her, an icy flood that left her shivering.

"Take a canoe tomorrow morning. Go back to Santarém."

She pulled together the edges of her shirt and fastened her buttons as she spoke, struggling to keep her fingers from shaking. "I don't frighten that easily, Mr. McCain."

When she glanced up at Devlin, he was frowning, his expression fierce enough to scare a full-grown jaguar.

"There's something you should keep in mind, Professor. Hundreds of years of civilization only deposits a thin veneer of respectability on a human being. Underneath we're still the same people who lived in caves. And a place like this strips us bare of that veneer."

"For some of us, the veneer is thinner than for others."

"My thoughts exactly." Devlin smiled, a slight curving of his lips that left his eyes glittering with anger. "Be careful what games you play, Professor. I'm not one of your proper English gentlemen. You take one step too far, and there won't be any turning back."

Kate stared after him as he walked away from her, fighting the horrible urge to throw herself on the sand and cry. She had made a complete fool of herself, offering herself to that man with everything but words. She must be mad!

For a long time she stayed on the far side of the beach, under the shade of a single palm, watching the others, afraid someone might approach her. She didn't want to talk to anyone.

She watched as Devlin McCain took command of the men they had hired, directing them to make camp. Soon the strip of beach was alive with activity, men dragging the canoes well above the dark water, setting up tents, collecting wood for a cooking fire.

Devlin McCain was a natural born leader, taking control with ease. And if she weren't careful, McCain would take control of her.

In time she would have to join the others. In time she would have to face Devlin McCain and her own compelling desire. She stared at the canoes drying on the sand. A part of her wanted to run away, but not from the forest and its dangers. No, for her, one man was far more dangerous than anything waiting in the forest.

Kate sat on a camp stool just outside of her tent, staring down at the half-finished sketch she was drawing of the opposite shore. She refused to notice Devlin McCain as he emerged from his tent, not more than six feet away from hers. Devlin McCain intended to sleep so close to her she would be able to hear him turn in his sleep. Had he planted his tent there on purpose, to taunt her?

A flash of light flickered across Kate's eyes, dragging her gaze from her sketchbook. McCain was adjusting a shaving mirror he had attached with a leather thong to the front of his tent, turning the silvery surface in the steeply slanting rays of the sun. He was bare from the waist up, and completely oblivious to the fact that she was sitting in view. Apparently he had no intention of showing her the least regard a gentleman would afford a lady.

Well, that was fine with her, she decided, fighting the sudden surge of emotions inside of her. Anger was the only one she chose to recognize. She was a member of this expedition, to be treated as any other member.

A warm breeze stroked her face with the evocative fragrance of sandalwood. She couldn't stop the memories from forming in her mind: a man stepping from his bath, power radiating from a body carved with strong lines and curves.

A few minutes ago he had bathed in the river. He had slipped into the tangle of bushes and trees a few yards away before stripping off his clothes and stepping into the river. He had been out of sight, but with each soft ripple of water she had heard had come the images of water stroking his golden skin. His skin was still damp, his hair a tumble of waves, the wet strands curling against his wide shoulders.

Did he intend to shave before dinner? He had shaved each night before dinner on board the riverboat. She knew, because each afternoon his cheeks grew rough, making her wonder what it might be like to touch the black stubble, and each evening his cheeks were as smooth as they were every morning. Intriguing contrasts.

Through her lashes she watched as he swirled a brush in his shaving mug, the rim of white porcelain chipped on one side. With the tip of the brush he swirled white froth across his cheeks and down his neck, tilting his head back, his black hair skimming his bare shoulders. He pulled a folding straight-edged razor from his back pocket and opened it.

With her gaze, she traced the sunlight that curved along his arm and across his shoulder. Sharply carved muscles moved beneath smooth skin, hypnotizing her. Her palm tingled with the temptation to touch him, to feel the fascinating friction of his skin beneath her palm.

Slowly he scraped the soap and black whiskers from his cheeks, cleaning the blade on a towel that dangled from the waistband of his trousers. Strange, how intimate it seemed, watching him in this purely masculine task. Did wives watch their husbands in this manner?

"How are the sketches coming?"

Kate jumped at the sound of her father's voice. She glanced up, realizing he was standing beside her and she hadn't even noticed him approach.

"Sorry, I didn't mean to startle you." Frederick planted his camp stool in the sand beside her. "I've never known you to be so jumpy."

Devlin glanced to his side as he wiped soap from the blade of the razor, one black brow lifting in a silent question as he looked at her. She ignored him, glancing down at her sketchbook.

"Let me see how the sketches are coming," Frederick said, reaching for the open book.

Kate slammed the cover shut, catching her father's fingers. "Sorry," she whispered when he yelped.

"Something wrong?" Frederick asked, shaking his injured fingers.

"No, I just prefer not to show the sketches until they're ready."

Frederick frowned. "When did you start becoming shy about your work?"

Heat crept up her neck and into her cheeks, a blush she couldn't hide. She could feel McCain looking at her. She could only guess what he might be thinking. "I'm not very proud of the sketches I've made so far."

"Oh, I see." The tone in her father's voice told her he thought there was more than she was telling him.

She should destroy the sketches she had made of Devlin McCain, all of them. And yet she couldn't bring herself to tear those pages out of her book.

"I wouldn't do that, Devlin," Frederick said, looking past Kate. "You could take off an ear with that blade."

"I'll be careful."

Kate glanced up in time to see Devlin hack a lock of hair from his shaggy mane with his razor. She bit her lower lip as he dropped the silky tresses to the ground. He would have a mess of it if he weren't careful. Of course it didn't matter to her how he mutilated his looks, she assured herself.

"Katie always trims my hair when we're on expedition," Frederick said, patting Kate's shoulder.

Knowing what would come next, Kate felt her heart stumble. She glanced at her father, but before she could say a word of protest, Frederick was already sealing her fate.

"I'll get her scissors so she can play Delilah."

Kate stared down at her hands as her father slipped into her tent. How would she ever keep her hands steady enough to trim McCain's hair and not cut off one of her fingers?

She couldn't do it. She could not be that close to McCain. She could not feel his hair sliding between her shaky fingers. Could she? No, it was far too dangerous.

Still, he would butcher the thick mane if she didn't help. And it would seem terribly rude if she refused.

No. She simply could not do it. She should find some excuse, she thought, glancing up at Devlin.

His eyes betrayed what McCain thought of the idea of having her cut his hair. Looking at him, Kate had the distinct impression McCain would rather take a long swim with a pack of alligators than let her come near him. Well, that settled the matter, she thought, coming to her feet.

"I can manage, Miss Whitmore." Devlin turned back toward the mirror.

"What's wrong, Mr. McCain?" She dropped her sketchbook on the ground. "Afraid I really am Delilah?"

Devlin stared down at the blade he held in his hand, seeing his reflection captured in the well-honed steel, knowing he was a man who had just been condemned.

"I assure you I am quite capable of trimming a man's hair."

Devlin didn't have to look at her to know her chin was raised in that determined tilt she always had when she was about to go to battle. And he knew there was nothing short of shaving his head that would keep her from trimming his hair. When Frederick emerged with scissors in hand, Devlin walked to Kate's camp stool and sank to the canvas seat.

"Relax, Devlin, Katie has been doing this for years," Frederick said before he left to join Edwin and Austin near the river.

Kate stood for a moment, studying Devlin as though she were about to paint his portrait, scissors in one hand, a tortoise-shell comb in the other. The setting sun reached out to touch her, slipping light into her hair, the wayward curls escaping the thick braid that tumbled down her back, shimmering like polished gold around her face, tempting him to capture the silky strands between his fingers.

He closed his eyes, trying to block out her image. Yet with his eyes closed, his other senses came more fully into focus.

Her fingers slid through his hair, the pads of her finger-tips gliding against his scalp. Roses settled around him, like velvety petals raining over him, drenching him in her fragrance. And beneath the roses he caught a whisper of woman, damp skin, smooth skin, salty skin he wanted to taste. He swallowed hard.

She dragged the comb through his hair, over and over again, hard teeth massaging his scalp. With gentle fingers she worked the tangles free, soft tugs that both aroused and relaxed. Water dripped from his hair, falling on his shoulders and chest, sliding over his skin in a warm caress.

"I suppose I shall have to wait until evening to take my bath." The scissors clicked softly in her hand while her fingers pulled gently against his scalp.

He thought of how she would look wearing nothing but moonlight and water. He thought of how she would feel in his arms, her wet skin sliding against his, the velvety crests of her breasts brushing against his chest, the satin of her inner thighs slipping around his waist. A sharp blade of desire twisted in his loins. "No bath."

She paused, her fingers resting against his crown. "You took a bath. Why can't I?"

"You can. If you want to bathe before dark, and you want company."

"I see. I can have a bath if I decide to entertain the rest of the expedition."

"It's too dangerous to swim after dark. It's not all that safe swimming when it's light."

She was quiet, standing behind him, the warmth of her skin radiating against his bare back. Without looking at her, he could see in his mind the mutinous pout her lower lip always took when she was angry, the fire in her blue eyes, the blush rising to stain her cheeks. God, she was gorgeous when her emotions got riled.

"I'll have a tin of water heated and brought to your tent," he said, wanting to soothe the feathers he knew he had ruffled. "Will you settle for that?"

"I suppose I'll have to settle for that."

The scissors slid together with the smooth sound of steel against steel. Hair fell to his bare shoulders and chest, silky strands sliding across his sensitized skin. Into his mind crept images of a woman letting her hair tumble loose around her shoulders, the silky strands of gold sliding across his chest as she covered him with the sweet warmth of her bare skin.

"Are you always so concerned about your appearance, Mr. McCain?" she asked, her tone both accusing and curious.

"I learned a long time ago that a man is often judged by his appearance."

She hesitated, her fingers growing still against a lock of hair at his nape. "Is that why you shave each night before dinner?"

"Habit, I suppose."

"I see."

He could swear there was a trace of disappointment in her voice. Had she been hoping the only reason he shaved each night before dinner was because a certain English rosebud was on this trip? He had to admit it was the real reason he subjected his face to an extra scraping each night, but he would be damned before he let her know it. The woman already had enough power over him.

He heard her draw a deep breath, felt the soft tug of her fingers on the hair at his nape before the scissors slid together. Thick locks of hair tumbled down his back, fine filaments sticking to his damp skin.

Warm linen brushed his shoulder, the flesh beneath too soft to be her arm, too lush to be anything but the subtle graze of her breast against his skin. He felt a painful tightening in his loins. Damn, he couldn't remember the last time a woman could get him aroused so easily.

"You all but ruined your hair with that careless hacking of yours." She paused in front of him, her figure a dark shadow against his tightly clenched lids. "I've had to cut it to just below your earlobes."

"That's what I was aiming for." He glanced up at her. She was frowning, a deep crinkle between the light brown wings of her brows. "You like it long?"

His question seemed to catch her off guard. She slipped behind him and he heard the scissors and comb drop to the tarp just inside her tent.

"I assure you, Mr. McCain, it doesn't matter to me how you want to wear your hair." She swiped at his shoulders with her palms, lightly brushing the hair from his skin.

He sensed she was attracted to him, and that she didn't like it any better than he liked being attracted to her. They were wrong for each other, plain and simple. He arched his back when her fingers grazed his spine.

"Ticklish?" He could hear the smile in her voice.

"No." Being ticklish had nothing to do with the way he felt. He couldn't take this, not the soft, feathery caresses of her fingers against his skin, not when each touch made him think of her hands sliding across his flesh. He stood and glanced over his shoulder.

She was looking at him with that intriguing blend of innocence and passion of hers, as though he were the first man she had ever seen, the only man. He became too aware of the warmth of the sun touching his bare skin, too aware of the look in her eyes, as though she wanted to strip him bare and touch every inch of his body.

Sweet agony squeezed low in his belly. If he thought she had any idea what the look in her eyes invited, he'd take her in his arms. Yet, looking into her eyes, he saw the truth; God help him, she had no idea what she was doing to him.

"Thanks for the trim." He turned away from her. She had a way of whittling his will, chipping away his control, prying him wide open for disaster.

He headed for the river, knowing the warm water would have no effect on the fire she had ignited in his blood.

There was nowhere to hide. There was no escape from the torture of being near her. And he had the horrible certainty this pain inside him was going to get worse with each passing day.

Chapter Ten

It was lovely here, Kate thought, the evening air cool and free of mosquitoes. They would run into swarms of the little beasts soon enough, at least according to Devlin McCain. She had washed as best she could from a tin of warm water. Still, her skin felt cool and clean, and she was comfortable for the first time all day. At least comfortable on the outside. Inside she felt the turmoil of a thousand emotions, all colliding, like stones against flint, sparks splintering in all directions, making her edgy, restless.

A breeze whispered across the bonfire, swirling glowing red embers into the air; they drifted toward McCain, scattering on the pale sand, turning to ash before they reached him. Through her lashes Kate stared at the man sitting a few yards away, across the campsite from her, on the edge of the flickering firelight. He sat with his back against a log, the smooth wood looking like polished stone in the moonlight, his long legs stretched out on the sand in front of him. He was whittling a long piece of wood with a knife, using a much smaller blade than the one he carried strapped to his hips. What was he making? It looked like a flute.

Devlin McCain was alone with his thoughts, so alone she wondered if he even noticed the men sitting in a small group a few feet away from him, if he even heard a word of the loud discussion her father, Edwin, and Barnaby were having on Irish folklore and possible connections with Atlantis. And what was McCain thinking? Did he have any thoughts for a foolish English woman who couldn't seem to do anything but think of him?

"You're a thousand miles away."

Kate glanced at Austin. He was lounging on the blanket across from her, his elbow planted on the smooth gray wool, his cheek resting on his open hand. And he was smiling as though he had just confirmed a very interesting suspicion.

"I'm sorry, is it my move?" She glanced down at the chessboard that lay between them.

"It has been for the past five minutes."

"Oh," she whispered, feeling the heat rise in her cheeks. She stared at the board, trying to dredge up some logic from a mind that seemed only capable of the most primitive of notions. From her left she heard the soft shuffle of footsteps in the sand and glanced up to find Robert shambling toward her. That was all she needed.

"Are you sure you want to do that?" Austin asked as she moved her bishop to seize one of his pawns.

Right now she wasn't sure of anything. "I think so." She leaned back from the board, sitting on her heels.

Austin countered with his knight, taking her bishop, threatening her queen. "Check."

"Oh, Katie, darling. It doesn't look as though you're giving Lord Sinclair much of a challenge." Robert dropped to his knees on the blanket beside her. "Or are you?" He leaned closer. "Still holding out on the old boy?"

Kate turned her head. Robert reeked of whiskey, fresh on his breath, stale as it seeped through his pores and mingled with the ripe odor of his unwashed flesh. "You're going to kill yourself if you don't stop drinking."

Laughing, Robert fell back on his heels. "Oh, hell, we're all going to die of something. And there's enough somethings on this trip to kill every one of us."

"I wonder." Austin lifted one of Kate's captured pawns. He rolled the smooth mahogany piece in his long fingers, staring at Robert. "Why did you decide to come on this expedition?"

"I didn't have a choice, old boy. No choice at all." Robert struggled to pull a whiskey bottle from his coat pocket. He succeeded, dragging out the white satin lining of his pocket along with the bottle.

"It's getting late, Robert." Kate noticed the way the bottle shook in his unsteady hand. "Why don't you go to bed?"

"Yes, it is late, too late for second thoughts, just like old Faust," he said, his voice filled with a strange blend of melancholy and humor.

Robert pulled out the cork and took a long drink before he continued, resting his open palm on his thigh and leaning toward Austin as though he were imparting a secret. "Did you know Father is still hoping this trip will give me a chance to win Katie's hand? I could use the Whitmore millions, even if you can't. So if you haven't asked her to marry you, don't. For my sake, old boy. Maybe she'll get desperate in her old age."

His callousness sparked Kate's anger. "I suppose you've bled your father dry with your gambling?"

Robert nodded. "I've been a very naughty boy," he said, swaying toward her. "Very naughty. I've made friends with the devil, you know. And I'm afraid I've left poor old honorable Edwin on the steps of the poorhouse." His right shoulder pressed against her left shoulder. "Have you ever been naughty, Katie? I've always wondered if you're really as virtuous as you look. Still the vestal virgin?"

Kate glanced across the board to Austin. Firelight flickered against one side of his face. His expression was utterly still, like the waters of a deep lake on a breathless morning. He was staring at Robert, the only sign of his anger the pawn clenched in his fist.

"Go to bed, Robert." *Before you start an argument, or worse,* she thought.

"I saw you this afternoon with McCain, trimming his hair," Robert said, his voice a whispered slur in her ear. "Be careful, old girl. He's not one of us, you know. Bad sort, that one."

Outrage surged with the anger inside her. She turned and planted both hands on his chest, pushing him, knocking him back against the sand, where he sprawled like a rag doll. "You have no right to speak of Mr. McCain in that arrogant fashion."

"Look at this, you've made me spill my whiskey." Robert struggled to pull himself into a sitting position.

Austin stood and grabbed Robert's arm. In one smooth motion he hoisted the drunkard to his feet. "I think you've had enough."

Robert swayed as he tried to break free of Austin's hold. "Is that right?"

Austin smiled down at the man, his lips a slight curve in the black fringe of his beard. He didn't move; he didn't speak; he simply stared down at Robert, the firelight reflecting in eyes the color of polished silver. Kate sat transfixed, her gaze on Austin's face. An odd serenity seemed to flow from him; like a cool stream, it surrounded her, it filled her, draining her anger. And it seemed she was not alone.

"Yes, I think I would like to go to bed," Robert whispered. "Would you help me, Lord Sinclair? I'm not quite steady."

"Excuse me," Austin said, smiling down at Kate. "I won't be long."

She sat back on her heels and watched the two men cross the sand toward the tents, Austin tall and steady, Robert staggering at his side. Lord Sinclair truly was a splendid man. A woman could easily lose her heart to him, and yet . . . her gaze drifted across the campsite, seeking the dark form of Devlin McCain. He was watching her.

Even from a distance she felt the intensity of his gaze, the hunger in him. Like the flames dancing in the bonfire between them, it burned in his eyes. Something inside her responded to that look in his eyes, something that made her heart pound, her skin tingle, her body come alive in a way she was only beginning to understand.

He frowned, his lips drawing into a tight line before he glanced down to the piece of wood he held in his hand. She stared at him a moment longer, waiting for him to look at her, wishing he might put down that wood and come sit beside her, wanting . . . wanting . . .

No. It was better if he stayed away from her. Better if he stayed far, far away from her.

So alert were her nerves, every thread of her clothing seemed to stroke her skin with every breath she took. She felt the echo of her heartbeat in the tips of her breasts, felt it low in her belly, a slow, steady throb. Her body pulsed with need.

It was powerful, this attraction, this lust for that man. But there was danger in this restless urge inside her.

Kate stared down at the chessboard. She felt like a pawn, being pushed from square to square by a will not her own. And where would it lead? How would the game end?

Sometime after midnight, Devlin floated on his back, letting the river take him downstream, the warm water licking at his naked flesh. Branches and leaves arched above him, the trees on the opposite banks trying desperately to reach their mates from the other shore, falling short, a narrow shaft of dark sky slicing between them.

It was foolish to swim alone at night. He had told Kate as much. Although he had made a cursory check, there could still be piranha in the dark water. There could be *jacare* on the banks. At the moment he didn't care.

He rolled to his stomach and began swimming against the current, kicking hard, plunging his arms into the water. His body needed this, to be drained of strength, to be left so exhausted he could sleep.

Yet he knew there would be no peace in slumber. The dreams would come, as they had every night since the first day he had met Katherine Whitmore. The dreams that left him restless and weak. The dreams he both scorned and welcomed.

At least in dreams he was free to touch her the way he longed to touch her. At least in dreams he was free to strip away her clothes and hold her naked body in his arms. He had kissed her a thousand times. He had felt her arms slide around his bare shoulders. He had felt her holding him as though she would never let him go.

Only dreams.

But what was reality? Time and time again he caught her watching him, like a kitten awakening to discover she was a tigress. Still unsure of herself, uncertain of her prowess as a hunter. Yet hungry. And he was her prey.

Was it a game to her? Did she hope to make Lord Gallant jealous, so jealous he would propose? Or was there more?

He'd be a damn fool to believe there could be more. And yet he wanted to believe. He needed to believe she could feel something for him.

The breeze rippled across his skin as he waded toward the shore, raising gooseflesh. He tossed back his head, shaking the water from his hair, stretching his arms wide, resisting the urge to roar his frustration. He glanced toward the tents standing like pale pyramids at the far end of the beach. A lantern was glowing in her tent. From a distance he could see the outline of her body, sitting, her head bent. She was having trouble sleeping.

What would she do if he went to her? What would she do if he laid down with her, the soft sand cushioning their bodies? What would she do if he gave her what she'd innocently been seeking the past few weeks?

Images came to life in his mind. He imagined tearing the nightgown from her body, stroking her smooth skin with his hands, devouring every inch of her flesh with his lips, his teeth, his tongue.

Ah, the woman had him bewitched with her beauty, and her strength, and her smoldering sensuality. He wanted her. Not just for the moment. Not just to ease the pain in his loins. He wanted to hold her and protect her and keep her by his side forever.

Forever.

Foolish thoughts.

Better get the lady out of your blood, McCain. Only a fool would allow himself to be possessed by a woman beyond his reach. And yet, how could he prevent it? How? When she was there every day, her knees brushing his back, her soft voice lilting in his ears, her tantalizing fragrance intoxicating his senses. He had a horrible feeling he could do nothing to stop his own destruction.

As he reached the pile of clothes he had shed on the beach, he heard the first screams. Fear pierced his heart as keenly as a blade.

"Kate!"

He started running across the beach, running toward the piercing screams, kicking up sand in his wake. A shot. Another and another. Good God, what was happening?

The lantern cast her silhouette against the tan cloth of her tent. She was standing, her arms outstretched in front of her. Devlin nearly ripped the flap from the tent as he shoved it aside. She turned to face him as he rushed across the entrance, aiming a pistol at his chest. He froze, stooping in the low tent, staring into her wide, terrified eyes, feeling his life pass into her hands. In her fear, would she shoot?

"Devlin," she shouted, throwing herself against his chest, wrapping her arms around his waist.

"Kate," he whispered, closing his arms around her. He pressed his cheek to her hair, holding her close, breathing in her fragrance.

This was no dream, but a woman, warm and real, with only the thin cotton of her nightgown keeping him from the smooth skin he so longed to feel. But he could feel every curve of her body snuggled against his; the lush heat of her breasts seared his chest, the smooth curve of her belly cradled his loins, the soft lines of her thighs brushed his. He felt his muscles tighten, his blood pump painfully, and he fought for control. Yet he felt his body rise and tighten against her.

"You aren't wearing any clothes." She pulled back in his arms, staring up at him, the warm barrel of the gun nestling against the small of his back.

"Very perceptive." Devlin held her when she tried to back away from him. He was aware of the others gathering behind him, their frantic questions directed to his bare back. And his front, well, at the moment it was better not to display his front to anyone.

"What are you doing?" she asked as he started to sidestep toward her bed, which was no more than a tarpaulin and blankets thrown over the sand.

"I need a blanket."

He kept her in front of him, trying to hide the incriminating evidence of his arousal. Yet he had to release her as he bent to retrieve one of the blankets from her bed. As he stood, wrapping the soft blue cotton around his waist, he noticed she hadn't moved. She was standing a foot away, watching him, her eyes wide, her lips parted in shock.

This time he hadn't been able to hide the desire she always managed to awaken in him. No wonder the lady was quickly turning a lovely shade of pink.

"Katie, what happened?" Frederick asked, crowding into the little tent. "I thought I heard shots."

"There was something trying to get into my tent. I could hear it clawing, growling. So I shot."

Frederick looked up at Devlin, a frown pulling together his dark brows. "Devlin, what happened to your trousers?"

Devlin felt a prickle of heat in his cheeks. "I was swimming when I heard the shots."

"Swimming," Kate said. "At night."

"Yeah." Devlin squeezed his way past Frederick, ducking his head to leave the tent. He was in no mood to explain his actions to anyone.

Robert and Barnaby flanked the entrance to Kate's tent. They stepped aside to allow Devlin passage, their questions tumbling one after the other. He didn't try to answer. He marched to the back of the tent.

Austin Sinclair was already there, crouched beside the tent, examining the slashes in the heavy canvas. He looked up when Devlin drew near, moonlight falling full upon his face, illuminating the deep crease between his black brows.

"A jaguar, I think." Austin pointed to the deep paw prints in the soft sand.

Devlin, with Austin following behind him, followed the tracks across the sand to where they disappeared into the forest. "There's no blood." Devlin turned to face him. "Looks as though she missed."

"I'm glad," Kate said.

Both men turned at the sound of Kate's voice. She stood near the tent, hugging her arms to her waist. Her hair fell in a thick braid of gold to her waist, moonlight twisting around the coils as if trying to release the heavy tresses. Her bare feet peeked out from beneath her white cotton robe. She looked like a lost, little girl and Devlin had to consciously fight the urge to take her in his arms.

Kate stared down at her feet, squishing her toes into the sand. "I would hate to think of any animal wounded, in pain, with no hope but to suffer a slow, agonizing death."

Devlin watched as Austin moved toward Kate. He watched the other man brush his hand across her cheek, watched as she lifted her face to look into Austin's eyes. And he felt a pain twist in his chest, a sharp, jagged pain that came from wanting more than he could ever have.

"Has anyone seen Edwin?" Frederick asked.

Devlin glanced around the group of people gathered in the moonlight. Everyone had come to investigate, including the Indian paddlers and the men they had hired as bearers. But Edwin Melville's hawkish face was not among the ones he could see. Had he slept through all the commotion? Or had he been out when the jaguar had come to call? "Robert, was your father in your tent when you left?"

"No." Robert glanced around at the others, his expression growing tense. "No, he wasn't."

"The jaguar," Kate whispered, turning to face Devlin.

"You don't think he could have come to any harm?" Frederick asked.

Devlin glanced out across the campsite. The man in question was crossing the beach, headed for his tent. "I think he was out for a stroll. Look there, on the beach."

"Edwin!" Frederick shouted, rushing toward his friend. The others followed.

Edwin slipped his pipe from between his lips and glanced over his shoulder as though he were expecting to be ambushed from the rear; then he stared at the small group advancing on him. "I say, what is all this activity about?"

"A jaguar tried to get into Katie's tent." Frederick clasped his friend's arm. "We were worried you might have met up with him."

"A jaguar." Edwin's thick, gray brows rose. "Thank goodness, no. I just took a walk. That's all. Needed to stretch my legs a bit."

These people treated the Amazon jungle like Hyde Park, Devlin thought. "Mr. Melville, it isn't a good idea to go wandering around on your own, especially after dark."

Edwin tapped his lower lip with his pipe stem. "Yes, well, I shall keep that in mind."

Still, Devlin had the uneasy feeling the gentleman would take one of his solitary walks the next time the inspiration struck him.

After the others retired to their tents, Devlin returned to the stretch of beach where he had left his clothes. He felt too vibrant to sleep, too filled with need and pain. He was falling for that English rosebud, tumbling headfirst, straight into oblivion. And there wasn't a single thing he could do to prevent his fall.

With Kate's blanket still secured around his waist, he stood beside the river, staring into the dark water, listening to the night sounds of the jungle, more alive than during the day with the screech of birds, chatter of monkeys, and a low-throated growl from a distance. He hoped the big cat had been scared far away from the camp. He hoped the animal wouldn't need to be destroyed. This was the jaguar's territory; they were the intruders here.

He stiffened, sensing someone approach. And he knew without turning who it was.

"Did the jaguar steal your trousers, Mr. McCain?"

Devlin took a deep, steadying breath before he turned to face Katherine Whitmore. "I thought you'd gone back to bed."

She shrugged, her braid lifting with the motion, the golden strands shimmering in the moonlight. "I can't sleep."

Three feet of white sand separated them. He wanted to cross those few feet, to snatch her up into his arms, to lay her back against the soft sand and make her his. Yet he knew more than three feet of sand stood between them. And he knew he didn't possess the means to forge a bridge to reach her.

"I thought it was too dangerous to go swimming in the river after dark." She pointed with her bare toes at his clothes, sand drifting from her foot.

"It is too dangerous."

"For me, but not for you?"

"For anyone."

She rubbed her arms with her hands. "Mr. McCain, I really must insist you not take chances with your life in such a careless manner. It's not only those dreadful piranha to think about, but you could develop a cramp, or get caught up on one of those submerged logs we were trying to avoid all day, or . . . well, it simply isn't wise to go swimming alone at any time."

He smiled. "Worried about me?"

She glanced away, directing her gaze to the river. "After all the trouble we had in talking you into leading this expedition, I would hate to have something happen to you. Not only would it put us all in a terrible position, but I should feel somewhat responsible, since you didn't want to come in the first place."

"I've been looking after myself for a long time. No one forced me to come on this trek. No one is responsible for me."

She stared at the river, hugging her arms to her waist. Devlin watched her, fighting the desire pulsating inside him. He ached to hold her in his arms, to feel her softness pressed against him.

After a long moment, she lifted her gaze, meeting his eyes. "I don't want anything to happen to you, Devlin McCain."

Her words were spoken so softly, for a moment he thought he had imagined them. It had been a long time since anyone had cared a damn about what happened to him—his entire life. And here she was, looking at him with those huge, blue eyes, telling him she cared if he lived or died.

Something good opened up inside him, something far too fragile, something he could only glimpse with this woman. He knew at that moment he would hand over his life if it meant saving hers. And at that moment it was more clear than ever before that she was far too fine for a man like him, a man without a family, without a home, without a future.

No, Katherine Whitmore deserved more. She deserved a handsome young man who could make her a marchioness, a duchess one day, a man who could give her everything Devlin could not, a man who fit into her life the way Devlin could never dream of doing.

"Go to bed. Get some sleep. We have a long day ahead of us." *Endless,* he thought, remembering the soft brush of her knees against his back.

She hesitated, looking at him, her own longing naked in her eyes. He sensed her need; it surrounded him the way her fragrance drifted on the breeze and filled his senses. It tugged on him, teasing him, tempting him to snatch her up into his arms. She wanted him, at least for this moment.

If he touched her right now, he could have her, here on the sand. If he touched her, she would come into his arms, she would spread her lovely white thighs and draw him into the sacred haven of her body. His blood quickened and his body tightened in response to the promise in her eyes.

Devlin didn't move. He knew it was the jungle working its magic on her. It was the potent reality of knowing your life could end at any moment. It made you think of things you had never done, things you might regret in the morning. And he didn't want to be a regret in this woman's life.

He had to swallow hard before he could use his voice. "Go to bed, Kate." He turned his back to her. *Go. Leave me. Because if you don't run away right now, the game is up.*

He felt her draw near. He felt the soft brush of her fingers against his bare back. God, what did she think he was made of? Did she think she could hone her skills of seduction on him? Did she think she could experiment with him, tease him, sample the forbidden fruit, then run back to the safe arms of Austin Sinclair?

Rage rose within him, for everything he wanted, everything he had been denied all his life. Rage warred with the desire pumping through his veins, shredding his control. He pivoted on his heel. He threw one arm around her waist and dragged her against his chest. He caught a glimpse of her startled face before he closed his eyes, before he slammed his mouth against her soft lips.

He kissed her with none of the tenderness he wanted to give her. These feelings he felt were too vulnerable, too tender to allow her to see, allow her to trample. With one hand he tugged the blanket from his hips, exposing her to the raw heat of his need. She struggled in his arms, pushing against his shoulders as he thrust his hardened sex against her belly, as he plunged his tongue past the smooth seal of her lips, silently telling her what he wanted to do with her.

"Is this what you want from me, Kate?" he asked, his lips brushing hers.

He didn't give her a chance to respond. He slipped his hand into the hair at the nape of her neck, holding her still for this brutal reflection of the kiss he longed to give her. With the other hand he found her breast beneath the smooth cotton of her robe and gown, curving his fingers over the firm mound, squeezing her nipple between his thumb and forefinger.

He felt her gasp against his mouth, felt her arch, heard the sharp sob splintering in her throat. He knew he had shocked her. He knew she would hate him for it. And he knew he must let her go.

She leaned against him. She opened the clenched fists she held against his shoulders, sliding her palms across his shoulders, stroking his skin with a soft warmth before tangling her fingers in his hair. She opened to him, her lips fluttering beneath his, her tongue testing the tip of his.

Surrender.

Dear God, she was melting in his arms. And he had no power to release her.

He opened his mouth over hers, gentling his kiss, letting her taste the sweet flow of feeling shimmering inside him. He wanted her, needed her, more than anything he had ever needed in his life. She was home. She was life itself.

He slid his hand down her back and over the pouting curve of her buttock, lifting her into the saddle of his loins, showing her his need for her. She gasped against his lips, but she stayed, steady and trusting in his arms, as though absorbing each new sensation.

Desire for her grew into a physical pain, sharp and steely. He needed her more than he needed his next breath. Slowly, he slid the pad of his thumb over her nipple, wanting to feel the hard bud naked against his flesh, wanting to taste her, needing to show her how much he adored her.

Kate stretched against him, lifting her breasts, sliding her belly against his aroused flesh. He groaned against her lips, raw with need. Dreams of her could not compare to this moment, this sweet torment of feeling her heat slide against his skin, tasting the desire on her tongue. Yet he knew it was only desire she felt. Nothing more. And he needed so much more than she would ever be willing to give him.

He couldn't take her. Not like this. Not when he knew he could have her only for this moment, a moment she would come to regret.

He couldn't have her. Not now. Maybe never.

She moaned as he lifted his lips from hers. She reached for him when he stepped away. He couldn't look at her, not when he knew he had to deny her, deny his own aching need for her. Devlin turned his back to her, shutting out the sight of her face, her lips soft and parted, her eyes half closed, as though she were just awakening from a dream.

Dreams.

He had lived his life searching for a dream. He needed more. "Go to bed, Kate."

He felt her standing behind him; he sensed her hesitation, her confusion. He clenched his hands at his sides, fighting the urge to turn to her, knowing one look and he would be lost.

"You want me to go?" she whispered.

God, don't do this to me. He couldn't take this. He couldn't take the rejection he knew would follow the ecstasy. "I don't play games with rich little girls who want to toy with fire and walk away without getting hurt. You play with me, you're going to get burned."

"So you kissed me just to teach me a lesson."

Devlin drew a deep breath. To face her would be disaster. He wanted too much; he wanted to hold her; he wanted to kiss away the frown he could hear in her voice. And he wanted more, much more than she could ever give—a lifetime of kisses, a lifetime of having her by his side.

"That's right." He forced the tenderness from his voice, allowing only the harshness to show. "Now get to bed before I decide to take you up on your little offer, before you're flat on your pretty backside with me between your legs."

He heard her gasp. "Mr. McCain, I had no intention of . . . of . . ."

He closed his eyes, begging her silently to leave, knowing he had only so much will to resist this beguiling temptress.

"I shall not make the mistake of seeking your miserable company in the future."

She left without another word, leaving behind only a trace of roses in the cool night air. He drew a deep breath, collecting her fragrance like scattered rose petals.

It was better this way, he tried to convince himself. Better to have her think he was a bastard. Better to have those gorgeous blue eyes filled with loathing when she looked at him.

But it hurt. God, it hurt. He felt as though she had rammed a knife between his ribs, and each thought of her only served to twist that blade.

After a long time, he turned and stared at her tent. The lantern was dead. And he could only pray she had found some peace in sleep, the peace he knew would forever elude him.

He waded into the river, aware of the danger in the warm, dark water, and not caring if those dangers claimed his worthless life.

Kate tried to stop them, but she couldn't. Plump tears rolled from the corners of her eyes and slipped into the hair at her temples. She turned, pressing her damp cheek into her pillow. How horrible to dissolve into this creature she didn't recognize. How horrible to feel all of these emotions, all at once: desire, anger, frustration . . . lust.

Good heavens, was it lust that had her in this miserable turmoil? Had she been asking for . . . No! She had only wanted to feel his arms around her again; she had only wanted his kisses. Hadn't she? What he had said, it was base, it was perverse. And heaven help her, it was also true. Good heavens! If he hadn't stopped, she would be on the sand this very moment, with Devlin McCain locked in her arms, and her innocence no more than a memory.

She flicked her tongue over her lips, tasting him. She could smell his scent on her skin, and that scent sparked taunting memories—Devlin's arms around her, his lips moving against hers, the delicious feel of his potent male body thrusting against her belly.

The hunger was worse now than it had been before. It was as though every small scrap of knowledge heightened her craving for more, like twigs tossed on a smoldering flame, feeding its intensity, until it raged into a flaring inferno.

What was happening to her?

Her entire adult life she had scorned the artificial response men had to her face, to her form. What did she care if they thought she was beautiful? They only looked at the package and not at the contents. And so she had constructed a mask. She had decided to live her life as she pleased, never to become trapped in the silk-lined prisons men created for women.

And here she was, crying like a ninny because one man didn't want her. McCain didn't find her desirable, even when she was throwing herself at him with both hands.

She dabbed at her eyes with the edge of her pillowcase. This had to stop. This was madness. This was only some hideous response brought on by the heat, by the danger, by . . . the look in his silvery blue eyes, the way he moved, the sound of his voice, the scent of his skin.

Oh good heavens, she had to get a grip on her emotions. She would rather take a long walk over burning coals than make a fool of herself with that man again. She refused to be drawn into this horrible whirlpool of primitive emotions.

Chapter Eleven

Ignore him. Ignore him. Ignore him. In her mind Kate sang the chant over and over again, in rhythm with the paddles dipping into the water.

Ignore him. She didn't want to stare at the muscles flexing in Devlin McCain's broad back, the damp white cotton of his shirt stretching with each movement of his wide shoulders.

Ignore him. She didn't want to notice the way his black hair curled above his collar.

Ignore him. She didn't want to breathe, for each breath delivered the intriguing scent of sandalwood and man.

Ignore him. Ignore him. Ignore him.

Impossible. Easier to ignore the sun blazing down upon her. Easier to ignore the humid air that closed around her in a steamy embrace, until her clothes were drenched, until her skin prickled, until she wanted to scream. And it was worse knowing he could ignore her so easily. It had been 11 days since their encounter on the beach. Eleven days, and Devlin McCain had barely spared her a glance.

"I'm worried, Katie," Frederick said, leaning toward her. "We should have seen the connecting channel by now."

Kate glanced over her shoulder, feeling guilty, for she hadn't even been looking for the channel they were to take. "We haven't reached the waterfall yet."

"But we're close. You can hear it."

For the first time Kate noticed the distant whisper of rushing water. She turned to stare at the north shore. The forest grew thick here, rising from the water's edge in an impenetrable wall of green. According to Randolph's map, the splinter channel flowed around the waterfall, ascending gradually before rejoining the main river. If they didn't find the channel, it would mean dragging the canoes overland, along the shore. And from the looks of the shore, with the heavy vegetation and the slope, it would be dangerous, if not impossible.

The distant whisper of the water grew in intensity until the full-throated roar of the falls bellowed in the air. And still the splinter channel remained hidden. Water tumbled in a heavy cascade from the river overhead, plunging more than 60 feet into the lower stream, white foam churning at the base, kicking up a cool spray. Kate could feel the violent vibration of the churning current beneath her, the slap of water against the wooden bottom of the canoe.

At Devlin's command the men maneuvered the canoe close to shore. He turned, looking past Kate to where Frederick sat beneath the awning. "We'll turn around and take another look," he shouted, raising his voice above the rumble of the falls. "This time we'll stay closer to shore."

Devlin turned back around without glancing at her. Kate felt like sinking both hands into his hair and giving the silky strands a good, hard tug. She wanted to remind him she existed. She wanted to prove to him she indeed was not invisible. She wanted to inform him she didn't like being ignored. She did none of these things. Instead, she felt the humiliating sting of tears. Thank goodness for the mist from the waterfall. Thank goodness it concealed the sheen of tears in her eyes.

This wasn't like her. She never cried. She took pride in how well she could control her emotions. She shouldn't be thinking of Devlin McCain. She shouldn't be wondering what she had done to make him dislike her so intensely. But she couldn't seem to help herself.

They paddled so close to the shore they were forced to duck thick, hanging vines. With a start, Kate noticed a boa constrictor coiled on a low-hanging branch not ten feet in front of the canoe, his head as big around as her clenched fist. Their current course would take them right into the snake's path. Instinctively she reached for McCain, touching his back, recoiling when she felt him flinch. He couldn't even stand to have her touch him, she thought, feeling her throat tighten with an emotion she didn't want to identify.

He turned his head, showing her his frowning profile, refusing to look at her. "What is it?"

"There," Kate whispered, pointing to the snake.

Devlin turned back around and continued paddling as though he hadn't noticed the huge snake and the way it was looking at them. They were nearly even with the snake now, close enough to touch it, should she decide to reach over the side of the canoe, or the boa decide to poke his head a little forward. The serpent was staring at her, his red tongue flicking between the slit of his mouth.

"Aren't you going to do something about it?" she whispered.

"You expect me to shoot it?"

"I thought you might."

"If he tries to have you for lunch, then I'll shoot him. Otherwise, I see no reason to kill anything for just minding its own business."

There was logic in what McCain said. At another time she might have applauded his sentiments. At the moment, though, she was having a difficult time feeling comfortable with that logic and the snake that seemed far too curious about the humans within his reach. Only when they were out of range of that deadly reptile did she breathe again.

"What do you think?" Devlin glanced back at Frederick as they came alongside a narrow stream flowing into the river, the entrance half hidden in a tangle of branches and vines.

"It seems no one has passed this way in a very long time. Of course, it's been eighty years since Randolph made this journey."

Devlin pushed back his hat and dragged the back of his wrist across his brow. His shirt was sticking to his chest. Kate glanced down at her hands, wishing she hadn't noticed the dark shadow of black curls beneath the moist cotton.

"Someone could have cut their way through here last month, and it'd look like this," Devlin said.

Frederick looked back at the narrow stream. "I'm not sure if this is the channel. It could be, I just can't be sure. But I would say it's about the right location. Randolph spoke of a stone monolith marking the correct route. If this is the right channel, we should come across it within the first mile."

"All right." Devlin pulled the brim of his soft felt hat low on his brow. "Let's see where it takes us."

Once they hacked away the vines and branches covering the entrance, they began paddling up the narrow stream. It was like skimming over the ground, the channel less than four feet wide on either side of the canoe. The trees rose on either shore, joining their branches overhead, forming a long, green tunnel, fragrant with the scent of damp earth and leaves.

Here the sun was little more than a glimmer through the tangled branches and vines. A flock of birds—small and yellow, reminding Kate of canaries—swarmed from the trees, singing like a church choir as they flew over the canoes and disappeared into the trees.

"There, look there." Frederick grabbed Kate's shoulder.

Kate followed the direction he was pointing and saw a stone pillar rising six feet above the ground a few yards from the shore. Although vines had crept over most of the surface, a carving of an eagle with spread wings could still be seen near the top of the stone.

Frederick leaned over the side of the canoe and stared back at the canoes following them. "Edwin, look there," he shouted.

Although Edwin was traveling in the last canoe, Frederick's voice carried in the living tunnel. Edwin poked his head out of his cabin and stared at the monolith. After a long moment he turned to face his old friend. "An Indian tribe," he shouted, before sitting back under the green thatch roof.

"An Indian tribe," Frederick whispered, turning to face Kate. "The man simply refuses to see the obvious. How can he ignore Randolph's journal now? Doesn't this prove anything? How would Randolph have known about this channel if he hadn't come this way?"

"I suppose Mr. Melville would tell you Randolph might have come this way to research that book he never wrote." Devlin smiled as he glanced back at Frederick.

Frederick leaned forward, resting his elbows on his thighs and dropping his chin on his clasped hands. "And what about you, Devlin? Starting to believe?"

For a long moment, Devlin didn't respond; he sat staring at the stone monolith as they paddled past it, a wistful expression on his handsome face. Kate wished she knew what he was thinking. She wished she had the right to ask.

"I'd like to believe. It'd be nice to know some dreams come true."

At that moment it took all of her willpower to keep from touching him. He seemed so young, so vulnerable, so incredibly appealing. She wanted to slip her arms around him, hold him, and instead all she had the right to do was look at him. As if he sensed her watching him, Devlin glanced at her.

It was the first time in 11 days he had actually looked straight at her, the first time in 11 days she had looked directly into those silvery blue eyes. They were as beautiful as she remembered, filled with a haunting light that made her wish she could look into his eyes every moment of every day for the rest of her life, a light that dimmed as he looked at her, his expression growing hard and closed before he turned away from her once more.

Kate felt staggered, as though he had slammed his fist into her jaw. She turned and stared at the thick forest, wishing she might hide in the emerald green maze. But how could she hide from her own treacherous emotions?

Judith drew her handkerchief down her neck, swabbing the perspiration from her skin, dabbing inside her open collar. The small piece of linen with its trim of embroidered lace was of little use. She had never felt so hot, so scratchy, so miserable in her life. How could the air possibly be this moist and not be raining? And there had certainly been enough rain in the last 11 days, too much rain, too much heat, too much worry.

She stared at the waterfall tumbling a few hundred yards in front of them, wishing they could order the men to paddle right underneath the cool cascade. "Leighton, you don't think we'll have to climb to the top, do you? I simply don't see how we could manage."

He turned, a frown marring the smooth perfection of his face. "If our friends have made the climb, then we shall." He hesitated, staring at the nearby shore, a smile lifting the tense lines from his face. "It looks as though our friends have taken a different path."

Judith looked in the direction he was staring. A stream emptied into the river a few feet ahead, the entrance recently opened, vines and branches revealing the fresh scars of sharp blades. And tied to one vine, hanging a few feet above the water, was a white strip of cloth. It hadn't surprised her to discover Leighton had planted more than one snake among McCain and his companions. It seemed his confederate was making sure they had a clear trail to follow.

She stared at the strip of white cloth fluttering in the breeze. What would Leighton do when he caught up with the Whitmore party? Would he really kill everyone?

An image of Devlin McCain blossomed in her mind. Since the first day she had glimpsed his handsome face, he had haunted her day and night. The thought of him lying bloody at Leighton's feet made her shiver in the steamy air.

The campsite was small, a narrow strip of white sand beach and a clearing they had hacked out of the jungle. Not big enough. Not nearly big enough to hide from Kate and her English marquess. Devlin tossed an armful of brush on the cooking fire. He couldn't resist a peek in her direction.

She was sitting cross-legged on the sand a few yards away with Austin Sinclair, but then she was usually with Lord Gallant. And why not? Devlin thought. She was going to marry the man. He felt his chest tighten with a longing he could not deny. God, he wished he were anywhere but here.

"Making fishing poles, it looks to me." Barnaby poked at the kindling, coaxing the twigs and pieces of driftwood to catch the flames. Smoke drifted in a pungent wave of gray toward the canopy of green leaves overhead. "I'm thinking they're more friends than lovers."

Devlin frowned down at the little man. "No reason why they can't be both."

Barnaby grinned, the corners of his eyes crinkling. "I was thinking you might have reason to be hoping they were only friends."

"And what if I did, Barnaby? What if I did?" Devlin stared down into the awakening flames. "I don't have anything the lady needs."

"The lady might have other ideas."

"Yeah." Devlin glanced over his shoulder to where Kate and Austin were sitting side by side on the sand. "But those ideas have nothing to do with thoughts of happily ever after."

"Devlin, I need a moment of your time," Frederick said, striding from his tent. "I have something important I'd like to discuss with you. Excuse us a moment, Barnaby."

Frederick took Devlin's arm and led the way to a driftwood log near the water, glancing around the campsite as though he wanted to make sure they wouldn't be disturbed.

No one was around. Edwin was strolling on the beach, still too stubborn to stay in camp. "A man can't be a dog on a leash," he had told Devlin. Robert was dozing under a palm tree on the opposite side of the campsite, unconscious from the whiskey he had been drinking all day. And Kate was too busy with Austin to notice anything else.

Devlin sat beside the older man on the log and watched as Frederick drew a piece of paper from his trouser pocket.

"I drew this for you this afternoon." Frederick unfolded the white parchment. "It's a copy of Randolph's map."

Devlin took the single sheet of white paper and stared down at the carefully drawn lines and symbols. "I thought you didn't want anyone to have this."

"I didn't want it to fall into the wrong hands. But if something happens to me, I want you to be able to help Kate find the city." He smiled as he patted Devlin's shoulder. "I trust you to do that."

Devlin could sense warm, genuine affection in this man's smile. And he felt the same for Frederick, a sense of acceptance, a feeling of belonging, like family.

Dangerous, these emotions. A man could get too attached to these people. Devlin had to remember there would come a time when he would watch them walk out of his life. He stared down at the map, committing it to memory, planning to destroy it later.

From behind them, the sound of Kate's laughter sparkled on the damp air. Devlin turned and found her walking beside Austin Sinclair. Her smile was sunlight in the gloomy shadows, as warm as summer and shining for one man—Austin Sinclair. Devlin ached inside with the need to feel the light of that smile shimmer around him.

"Care to join us?" Austin held out his makeshift fishing poles, four long pieces of bamboo strung with narrow lines. "We're out to catch dinner."

"Not me, I've no luck with fishing," Frederick said. "Perhaps you would like to try your hand, Devlin?"

Kate didn't look as though she wanted his company. In fact, she was staring at her father as though she would like to strangle him for issuing the invitation. She needn't worry. The last thing in the world Devlin wanted was to be a chaperon for Kate and Lord Gallant. "No. You go ahead. But be careful. There are piranha in the water as well as more edible fish."

"And how will we know which are which, Mr. McCain?" Kate asked.

A winter chill set in when she looked down at him, all of her warmth blanketed beneath cold contempt. "The piranha will be the ones trying to have you for dinner, Professor."

"How very amusing."

"Are you sure you wouldn't—" Austin began.

"Come along." Kate tugged on Austin's arm. "We'll be out of light soon. Twilight is sinfully short in the tropics. The mosquitoes will be out and chase us under our nets."

"Have them build a nice big fire for us," Austin said, glancing over his shoulder as Kate tugged him toward the river. "We'll need it to fry all of our fish."

Devlin watched them walk along the narrow beach until they disappeared behind a stand of palm trees. They looked comfortable, smiling, enjoying the time they shared together.

A lifetime. Austin and Kate would share a lifetime together. Devlin felt his throat tighten with emotion as scenes drifted through his mind: a man and woman waking in each other's arms, sitting together in front of a Christmas tree, standing in an embrace, watching their baby sleep. Only, in the dreamscape of his mind, he was the man he saw sharing Katherine Whitmore's future, not Lord Austin Sinclair.

Treacherous things, dreams. They made you believe you could actually pluck a star from the heavens.

"Like brother and sister, those two."

Devlin glanced at Kate's father. There was a look in the gentleman's eyes that made Devlin wonder if he had once again allowed emotion to write a painful story across his face.

"They're well matched." He glanced down at the map. He didn't want to talk about Kate and Austin. He didn't want to think about them. "It looks as though we'll meet up with the main channel in a few days. Four or five, depending on how accurate this map is."

"I suppose in a way they are well matched," Frederick said, watching Devlin, ignoring his attempt to change the subject. "But I wonder if something isn't missing. A spark, perhaps?"

Lust, Devlin thought. Perhaps the woman felt love for one man and lust for another. "Sparks die. It takes something more solid to build a lifetime together."

"And you think they have it?"

Devlin breathed deeply, pulling the heavy aroma of humus deep into his lungs, catching a whiff of the coffee Barnaby was brewing. "I don't think it's any of my business."

"I suppose I have no right to—" Frederick hesitated at the sound of Kate's scream. "My God! Devlin, what do you . . ."

Devlin was already on his feet and running down the beach, his heart pounding wildly against the wall of his chest, his thoughts tumbling one after the other. When he broke the line of palms, he saw her. She was sitting on the beach, leaning back on her forearms, her legs stretched against the white sand. Even from 50 feet away he could see the look of pain on her face.

Austin was kneeling beside her. The left leg of her trousers was split, and he sat clutching her bare calf just below her knee. He didn't look up when Devlin dropped to his knees on the sand beside Kate.

"What happened?" Devlin asked.

She looked up at him, her eyes wide, dazed. "Snake. It bit me."

Devlin felt a blow against his chest, fear hitting him with the force of a prizefighter's fist. "What did it look like?" He tore open the buckle of his belt.

"Grayish brown, I think. It just lunged at me from the woods."

A fer-de-lance or jararaca. Vipers. Deadly.

Devlin tugged the belt from his waist and fastened it around her thigh, dragging a moan from her lips when he stretched it until it was tight around her skin. "Easy, sweetheart," he whispered, smoothing his hand across her temple. "Austin, let me see the wound."

Austin didn't seem to hear; he was staring at the hand he held clenched to Kate's leg, his expression intense, as though he were trying to draw the venom from her with the force of his will. Devlin pulled his knife from the sheath and grabbed Austin's hand. His skin was hot from the pressure he was exerting on the wound.

"Austin, I have to draw out the venom."

Austin glanced up as though he only just realized Devlin was there. "Yes." He sat back on his heels, releasing his grip on Kate's leg. "You do what you must."

The imprint of long fingers marred Kate's smooth skin, and in the center, where Austin's palm had rested, her blood trickled from twin puncture marks. "This is going to hurt, Kate. Take a deep breath."

"It was poisonous, wasn't it?" she whispered.

He had little doubt it was poisonous. And he knew there was little he could do to keep her from dying. Again came that sharp, invisible blow to his chest. God, she couldn't die! "Just take a deep breath, Kate."

Kate gripped Austin's hand as Devlin slit her skin, cutting a line from puncture wound to puncture wound. He felt the tension in her body, heard her sharp intake of breath as he sucked blood and venom from her wound.

Dully, Devlin heard others moving around them, their voices pounding with the blood roaring in his ears. He heard Frederick's anxious voice rise above the others, and Austin's reply, his voice deep and firm and calm. He worked methodically sucking at the wound, tasting her blood, spitting out what he prayed would be enough of the venom to save her life.

Chapter Twelve

Kate sipped from the tin cup Devlin had given her, crinkling her nose at the smell. Whiskey. She had never developed a taste for it, or any hard liquor. Still, this cup of the stuff didn't taste nearly as bad as the last cup Devlin had coaxed her to drain. He had told her it would help lessen the pain, and the pain in her leg did seem to be fading. How many cups had she had? Two. No, three. Yes, three cups of whiskey. Her tent was warm, stuffy actually, with her father and Devlin crowding under the canvas with her.

"I feel numb." She fell back against her pillow, laughing, feeling strangely giddy. "Perhaps I've had just a drop too much whiskey."

Devlin looked up from the damp mass of sticky leaves he had applied to her calf, a look of intense pain sweeping across his features. He held her gaze a moment before he lowered his eyes and continued fussing with the poultice. Yet she had seen fear in his eyes, fear and a profound sadness that sent a ripple of panic through her veins.

178

"It isn't just the whiskey, is it?" she asked, trying to keep her voice steady. "I'm dying."

"Now, Katie, you mustn't talk like that." Frederick leaned closer, taking her left hand in both of his. He was kneeling beside her bed, as was Devlin. Seeing them both on their knees made it all worse somehow. "You're going to be fine. Just fine."

The lantern in her tent cast flickering light across her father's face, glittering on the unshed tears in his eyes. Not again. The poor man had watched his wife die, and now she was dying. Oh, she just couldn't bear to see his pain. "Please, Father. Why don't you go out and get some air."

"Katie, I . . . Oh, Katie." He bowed his head over her hand. "I never should have allowed you to come."

She lifted her hand, wanting to press her fingertips against his lips. But his face was so unsteady above her. "Hush now," she whispered, missing his lips, pressing her fingertips to his chin. "I'm here because I wanted to be here. Now, you just wait outside. Everything is going to be fine." Was she slurring her words? Was that from the venom too?

Frederick rose to his feet, keeping his head bowed in the low tent. For a long moment he stood staring down at her, the tears she had seen in his eyes slipping down his cheeks. He looked so heartbroken, and there was nothing she could do for him.

"Go on, now. And don't worry."

He turned and left her alone, alone with Devlin McCain. She was worried for a moment, afraid Devlin might want to leave, to escape this death vigil. Oh, how hard it was to face one's own death. She wanted Devlin with her. "You won't leave, will you?"

Devlin glanced up at her, his eyes reflecting a flicker of surprise. "No, I'm not going anywhere."

"I hear you playing your flute at night sometimes."

He touched the flute that peeked out from the top of his boot. "I'm sorry, I didn't mean to disturb you."

"You didn't. I enjoyed your playing."

He lifted another fat leaf from a calabash sitting on the ground beside him. It dripped a milky white substance as he placed it on her leg. She watched him, noting the way his hands trembled. "I don't know much about you."

He looked up from his ministering, his right hand resting on the leaves above her wound. "There's not much to know."

The flickering lantern light etched his face from the shadows. He looked tired, angry, a deep, seething rage bubbling just below the surface. She wanted to touch his face, to ease the lines of tension that bracketed his full lips, to smooth the single, deep crevice between his black brows with her fingertips. Would he draw away from her if she touched him? "Where were you born?" she asked, clenching the cup, afraid to take the chance.

"I'm not sure. New Orleans, I guess." He glanced down at the damp leaves. "I was left in an orphanage in New Orleans when I was two."

Abandoned at two. Poor darling. Poor, beautiful Devlin. "Was your mother ill?"

He hesitated a moment before he spoke. "I don't know."

"She must have been. Why else would she abandon a beautiful little boy?"

He kept his eyes lowered. "I suppose she had her reasons."

"I never knew my mother. I killed her, you know. She died giving me life."

He looked up at her, that crevice between his brows growing deeper. "You can't blame yourself for her death."

"No, I know I shouldn't. But sometimes I can't help it. They loved each other so much. I've seen him sometimes, at night, in his study, my father, weeping, staring up at my mother's portrait. It doesn't seem fair, does it? He should lose her, and only get me in the bargain."

"He loves you, Kate."

"Yes, I know he does. I'm all that's left of her, you see. Me and memories." She lifted the cup to her lips, bumping the rim against her teeth when she tried to take a sip, spilling the whiskey down her chin. She was losing control, and she felt drowsy, as though her life were being drained slowly into a deep, dark oblivion. Was this the first sign of death? "And now he's going to lose me. Poor Father."

Devlin moved to her side and took the cup from her hand. With his fingertips he smoothed the liquor from her chin, catching the dribble that ran down her neck, stroking her skin with a tenderness that stole her breath. It had been so long since he had touched her, and he had been so curt with her in the past few days, she had started to wonder if she had imagined the tenderness she had glimpsed inside this man.

"I wish I had more time. There's so much I've never done."

He slid his fingers along the curve of her jaw, a smooth stroke, a gentle slide of his skin against hers. He was frowning, his jaw held in a tight clench, as though he were fighting something inside him.

If she had time would she ever be able to capture this man on canvas? *Portrait of a pagan god*. She could imagine his portrait hanging on the wall of her bedroom in London. But she would never see London again, and she would never get the chance to paint this man.

Strange that there was no pain, just a slow drain of her being. It was hard to focus her eyes; Devlin's image blurred, and she so wanted to see him clearly. His was the image she would take to her grave. "Would you kiss me, Mr. McCain?"

He seemed startled, and for a moment she thought he might refuse this last request. And she knew it would be her last request in this life, for she could feel the darkness reaching for her. "Please."

"Kate," he whispered.

Light shimmered in his eyes. Were there tears there, in his eyes? Tears sparkling like diamonds in the twilight sky? But no, she must be wrong. Devlin McCain would never cry.

His warm breath stroked her cheek, and then she felt his lips against hers, opening, sliding so gently. She savored the scent of his skin, smoldering sandalwood and man. It had been a lifetime since he had kissed her. Too long. Why had she waited? Why had she fought against this attraction?

He slipped his arms around her and held her close, so close she could feel the steady throb of his heart beating against her breast. She felt as though she were being pulled into a dark void, as though her life were draining from her body. She fought the darkness. She wanted to stay here, with Devlin.

Something warm and wet fell against the crest of her cheek. What was it? She tried to slip her arms around his shoulders, but her muscles refused to obey. She wanted to hold him. She wanted to . . . but it was too late.

The darkness was dragging her down into oblivion. The darkness . . .

Devlin felt her lips grow still beneath his, felt the soft exhale of her last breath against his cheek. "Kate," he whispered, drawing back to look at the woman lying lifeless in his arms. Dear God, she couldn't be dead!

And yet he had known she would die. He had known from the beginning there was no hope of fighting the deadly venom.

"Oh God, Kate," he whispered, clasping her to his chest, willing her to absorb his own life's force, his tears falling to tangle in the golden sheen of her hair.

God, he couldn't stand this. And yet his heart kept pumping, throbbing against her still body. His life would continue even after his soul had died, he thought, laying her back against the pillow. He smoothed the hair from her brow, the wayward curls teasing his fingers.

She had been so full of life. And now she lay with her long, dark lashes still against the crest of her cheeks, her lips parted, her skin pale in the lamplight. Still beautiful, but empty now. Gone was the fire. Gone the stubborn will. Gone the woman he loved.

Love. Had he loved her? He had fought against it. But right now, at this moment, he knew all of his efforts had been futile. Yes, he had loved her. He loved her still. Tomorrow. The next day. The next year. Every year until he died, he would still love this woman.

With a soft brush of his lips, he kissed her closed eyes, the tip of her nose, and finally her lips. "Good-bye, my love," he whispered as he drew a soft blue cotton blanket over her face.

With his fingertips he wiped the tears from his cheeks. He took a deep breath before he left her side. The faint glow of sunlight was fading, the air growing chilled, as though nature was mourning Kate's passing.

Frederick was waiting, standing with his back to the tent. On the sand near the campfire, Edwin, Robert, and Barnaby sat, each staring at Devlin, each waiting for the words that would end this vigil. Through his own grief, Devlin wondered where Austin Sinclair was. The man had stayed with Kate briefly, had pressed her to drink a headache powder, before leaving her. Had she thought of Austin in those last moments, wondered why he was not by her side?

Frederick turned when he heard Devlin approach. In the glow of the camp fire, Devlin could see the tears shimmering in his dark blue eyes.

"She's gone, isn't she?" Frederick said, his voice choked with tears, barely rising above a whisper. "Katie's gone."

Gone! Once again Devlin felt the pain slam into his chest. He didn't try to use his voice; he only nodded, knowing there were no words to console this man who had lost his daughter.

Frederick crossed his arms across his chest, his shoulders rolling forward with the impact of his grief. "Katie," he whispered. "My beautiful little girl."

Devlin rested his hand on Frederick's arm. There was nothing he could say, but he wanted to give comfort.

"Frederick!" Austin shouted, running from the shadows near the far end of the campsite. "I've found it."

Devlin turned to watch Austin approach. He was running, carrying a three-foot piece of vine in his hand. And he was smiling, laughing as he drew near. Devlin curled his hands into fists. Right now it would feel very good to smash Austin Sinclair's aristocratic nose.

Frederick looked at him as though Austin had gone mad. "Austin, Katie has—"

"Look at this," Austin said, holding out a gray piece of vine. "Katherine's snake. It even has a piece of her trousers on it."

Devlin snatched the piece of vine from Austin's hand. About an inch in diameter, the vine was forked into two sharp points at one end. One point still held a small scrap of buff-colored cotton. Could it be possible?

"Kate must have stepped on it and caused it to lunge upward," Austin said.

Devlin dropped the vine and rushed back into the tent, with Frederick on his heels. Kate was lying just as he had left her, the blue blanket covering her face. With his heart pounding at the base of his throat, he knelt beside her and pulled back the blanket.

God, please, please let her live. He hesitated a moment, not wanting to shatter the fragile hope inside him. When he pressed his fingers against the pulse point in her neck, she sighed and nuzzled her face against her pillow like a sleepy kitten.

"Dear merciful God," Frederick whispered.

Alive! Relief flooded his veins, leaving Devlin trembling. He started to gather her in his arms, but stopped. He wanted to hold her. God, how he wanted to hold her. Yet he had to face reality. She was alive, but she was still beyond his reach. Still, he couldn't keep from touching her, from brushing his fingers across her warm cheek. Kate hiccoughed softly.

"She's drunk," Devlin said, rising to his feet, a smile tugging at his lips. He turned to face Frederick. "I have a feeling the lady's going to have one hell of a headache tomorrow morning."

"Thank God," Frederick said, his voice dissolving into trembling laughter.

She was seasick. With each awakening nerve Kate became more convinced of it. A dozen demons were pounding drums in her head. And her stomach—oh, she didn't want to think of her stomach. And for some reason her leg ached.

Careful not to move, she pried open her eyes. A man was sitting on the tarpaulin beside her. She could see the curve of his shoulder beneath white linen, his black hair curling just above his collar.

Wisps of memory teased her. Had Devlin McCain held her last night? Had he kissed her? Or were the memories only part of another haunting dream? A snake. There had been a snake. And she had died in Devlin McCain's arms. Hadn't she?

"Well, Sleeping Beauty, it's about time you awakened."

Kate tried to focus her blurry eyes on the face suddenly suspended above her, staring up into silvery blue eyes. "Mr. McCain."

"Hmmm, perhaps you aren't awake after all."

As her vision cleared, his face became more distinct; she noticed the neat, black beard surrounding the smiling lips. "Austin," she whispered, touching his arm with her hand. He was too solid and warm to be an illusion. "Am I alive?"

He lifted her hand to his warm lips, his beard a soft caress against her skin. "Very much alive."

"But how? The snake wasn't poisonous?"

Austin laughed, a soft, indulgent rumble filled with his own relief. "The snake wasn't a snake." He turned and lifted something from the ground beside him. "Here's what pricked you."

"But I don't understand." Kate stared at the long piece of dark gray vine he held out for her inspection. "I'm certain I saw a snake."

"The way this leapt at you, I'm sure it looked like a snake."

Kate shook her head, regretting the impulsive movement immediately. "Why do I feel as though I've been on a rough sea for a week?" she asked, pressing her palms to her throbbing temples.

"Probably because of all the whiskey I fed you last night, Miss Whitmore."

Kate's heart bumped into her ribs at the sound of Devlin McCain's gravelly voice. She looked past Austin to where McCain was standing in the entrance of her tent. Although he blocked most of the light with his big body, she could see his face. Yet she couldn't for the life of her tell what he was thinking. His face was expressionless, the finely chiseled features revealing nothing of what she needed to know. All those memories from the night before fluttered in her mind, like a cloud of misty butterflies, teasing her with elusive glimpses of what might have happened.

She remembered being held by this man. She remembered the gentle touch of his hand on her face, the spicy taste of his lips against hers. And there had been tears in his eyes. Had it all been a dream? Looking at him now she was certain it must have been nothing more than an illusion.

"This should help straighten out her crinkles," Devlin said, handing Austin a tin cup wrapped in a white linen towel. "Be careful, Professor, it's hot."

"Thank you," she said as Austin handed her the cup. Steam rose from the light brown liquid, bathing her cheeks with a sweet aroma laced with mint. "I'm sorry to have caused such a fuss yesterday. I don't understand how I could have possibly mistaken a vine for a snake."

"You were walking over some pretty heavy brush," Austin said. "It would be easy to mistake that vine for a snake."

"I'm certain I saw it." Kate stared down into the cup. "At least, I think I saw it."

"At a time like that your mind can play tricks on you." Austin smoothed back a lock of hair that had tumbled over her cheek.

"If it'd been a snake, Professor, you'd be dead right now." Without another word, Devlin turned and left her tent.

"I wonder what I've done to make him dislike me so," she whispered, watching him walk away, speaking her thoughts before she could catch herself.

"I don't think he dislikes you."

She glanced up at Austin and found him studying her, gentle gray eyes looking deep into her soul, seeing all of her secrets. She stared down into her cup, embarrassed by the emotions she couldn't hide.

Why should she feel this terrible hurt simply because one man didn't like her? A man she knew thought her starchy and unfeminine and completely unattractive. "What Devlin McCain thinks of me is of no great significance to me, I assure you."

"No? I thought you found him interesting."

"I find him infuriating." Kate held the cup between her hands, the linen wrapped around the tin warm against her palms. "He's arrogant and rude . . . and . . . and barbaric. Why, the man would be right at home living in a cave."

"I wonder if I should be any different if I had never known the love of my family. If I had been on my own since I was twelve."

"You're two very different men."

"With two very different backgrounds." He rested his arm on his raised knee and stared out the opening of her tent.

Kate followed his gaze. A few yards away, Devlin was standing with his hands braced on his slim hips, supervising the loading of the canoes. He looked commanding, as though he ruled legions, as though cities fell beneath his sword. And just looking at him made her heart lurch, her pulse sprint into a dizzying pace.

"Too often people are judged by appearances," Austin said, keeping his gaze on Devlin. "Take a man like Mr. McCain. Because he runs a casino, his character is judged to be suspect. Perhaps even criminal. Yet I've found him to be honest in every regard. Intelligent. Worthy of respect."

"He's all sharp edges." Kate sipped from the cup Devlin had brought her, the tea tasting of mint and something that reminded her of chamomile. "Like a porcupine, ready to spear anyone who tries to get close."

Austin smiled down at her. "Look past the armor. I think you might see Mr. McCain has his own dreams, just like the rest of us."

Kate stared down into her tea. "You always look for the good side of people; that trait, I'm certain, will bring you nothing but disappointment, if not trouble."

"It's true, Kate, there are people in this world who can't be trusted. People who will try to steal your soul. Some of them look like angels."

The haunting sadness in his voice brought her gaze up to his face. Yet he wasn't looking at her. He was staring out the narrow entrance of her tent, staring as though he were looking at things she couldn't see. And she wondered who he saw in that distant stare. An angel who had tried to steal his soul?

She watched Devlin McCain walk along the beach, away from her. She didn't want to think of him, or the dreams he might have. Because it was far too dangerous to think of Mr. Devlin McCain. For the first time in her life, her own soul was tempted by this dark angel, in this dark paradise.

Chapter Thirteen

"Sunlight." After five days of traveling the narrow splinter channel, five days of living in a dark green tunnel, Kate could see a bright streak of sunlight up ahead, a shimmering light at the source of the stream. Every stroke of the paddles brought them closer to that light. "I was beginning to wonder if I would ever see sunlight again."

"I was beginning to wonder if we would ever rejoin the main channel." Frederick leaned toward his daughter, who sat in front of him in the narrow canoe. "But, I must say, it's very good to see sunlight again. Don't care much for the life of a mole."

The soft, sighing voice of the falls echoed in the green tunnel, a distant siren's call that seemed to come from all directions. Rays of the sun poured through the narrow shaft of foliage above the main channel, seemingly brighter than any sunlight Kate had ever seen, so bright it set the damp air aglow with gold. Just a few more yards and they would break free of the dark green shadows.

She leaned forward, seeking that sunlight like a vine seeking nourishment, silently urging the paddlers to quicken their pace, to draw them closer and closer to that sunlight. Yet it was the heat of Devlin McCain's skin she felt against her cheeks, the tangy scent of him she absorbed with every breath.

The sunlight faded into a blur. The thick, green forest rising all around them, the distant falls, the chatter of monkeys and birds, all dissolved, insignificant compared to this one man. Devlin McCain commanded her every attention. The shift of muscles in his back, the damp, black hair curling just below his ears, the heady fragrance of salty male skin filled her universe.

It was getting worse. This horrible attraction she felt for McCain seemed to feed on the heat smoldering in the air. It was growing. It was consuming her.

The man dominated her every thought. Waking. Sleeping. Day. Night. He was there, bewitching her with those silvery blue eyes, tempting her every passion with every move of his splendid body.

And the memories. She couldn't escape the memories of his lips against hers, of his arms holding her, of his body burning against hers. Heaven help her, she wanted more. Nothing short of destruction, that was all she would get from this horrifying attraction if she didn't learn to get a grip on her own emotions. She must learn to overcome this.

A sudden jolt pitched the canoe. Kate hit the side with her hip. They had entered the main channel. Water rushed beneath the canoe. It splashed over the sides, slapping Kate's face, drenching her clothes. The current snatched them in a powerful grasp. It dragged the fragile vessel downstream.

The canoe careened sideways. The deep-throated roar of the falls growled in the distance. Kate clutched the sides of the canoe. Fear awakened inside her, snatching her heart, thumping painfully against the wall of her chest.

She stared at Devlin as though she were drowning and he was her only lifeline. He fought against the current, slicing his paddle over and over again into the swiftly flowing water.

Slowly the nose of the canoe inched forward until they were once again facing upstream.

"We'll be all right." Frederick grasped Kate's upper arm. "These men know what they're doing."

"Of course they do," Kate said, glancing over her shoulder.

Five days of following the twists and turns of the narrow splinter channel and they were only a few hundred yards above the falls that roared near the entrance. So close she could see the churning white water of the rapids above the falls. So close she could feel the mist which rose in a shimmering cloud that captured the sunlight and drifted on the breeze. Too close to allow any sense of calm.

Twilight was fleeting in the Amazon. Kate knew the sun would soon slip from their grasp. After paddling all day, she wondered if the men could endure this struggle against the current much longer. And what would happen should they fail?

She grabbed a paddle from the floor of the canoe. Water sprayed over the side, splashing her face, stinging her eyes. The falls roared in her ears, laughing at the struggle of these puny mortals.

"Katie, be careful!"

The current snatched at the paddle, trying to wrest it from Kate's grasp. She shifted, rising in her seat, digging her paddle into the river. The canoe pitched as she leaned into the stroke. She had the sensation of weightlessness, of being lifted and tossed, the canoe sliding out from beneath her, the river rushing to grab her.

"Katie!"

Her father's voice reached her over the roar of the falls as the turbulent water dragged her under. She fought the current, breaking the surface of the water in time to see Devlin dive over the side of the canoe after her.

She swam against the powerful pull, sinking her arms into the water over and over again, kicking hard. The river sucked the strength from her body, draining her until she could scarcely move her arms and legs, dragging her under.

Water flooded her nostrils as the current slapped at her with punishing blows. She fought, but her arms and legs felt heavy, like lead weights pulling her deeper into the dark river. In her mind she had a fleeting image of her lifeless body, reduced to nothing more than food for the creatures in this savage land.

Strong arms closed around, pushing her upward. *Devlin.* They broke the surface of the water together, Devlin with his arms cinched around her waist. Kate coughed water from her lungs and sucked at the air. She knew one moment of hope before she realized the rapids had them both in a tight embrace.

The river churned like a witch's cauldron, slinging arrows of water into their faces, tossing them, pitching them, trying to break them apart. Devlin held fast to her waist.

The great roar of the falls drowned the sound of their own hearts. Kate looked up into the mist; a shaft of darkening sky, an arc of shimmering color painted by the dying sun, and then they were sailing under the rainbow.

For one brief moment she felt as though she were flying, soaring upward through the mist. She felt Devlin's arms yanked from her waist. She called his name, her voice swallowed in the roar of the water. And then she was falling, plummeting into the void.

Kate grabbed a thick vine, crushing the leaves in her hands as she dragged herself from the water. She collapsed on her side, resting her cheek on her upturned palm. She dragged air into her burning lungs, the tangle of vines digging into her side. The falls roared in her ears, mist settling on her exposed cheek and hand. Her body felt fragile, her muscles stretched and sore. Yet she had survived.

"Devlin," she whispered, lifting her head when she felt a hand touch her shoulder.

It was nearly dark now, a golden glow all that remained of the sun. Yet it was enough to fully illuminate the man bending over her. That man was not Devlin McCain.

Black hair, cut short and round, falling in a shallow fringe over a narrow brow, skin the color of reddish brown clay, features flattened, fierce, prehistoric. And he was naked, except for a thin strip of animal hide tied around his thick waist. In one hand he held a crude spear. With the other he reached for her. A scream rose inside her; it caught in her tight throat. Only a whimper escaped.

She scooted back on the corded vines. She bumped something solid, another man. Turning her head, she looked up at the others. There were seven of them, staring down at her, reaching down for her.

"No!" Again, no more than a whimper.

She batted away brown hands. Yet there were too many of them. They dragged her to her feet and shoved her toward the forest, brandishing their spears as though they had every intention of killing her if she didn't obey.

Devlin! Where was he? Dear God, where was he?

She stared through tears at the dark river. Foam topped the churning water at the base of the falls; farther out, the surface was carved into deep, rolling waves by the swift current. As the men forced her into the forest, she saw a hat on the shore, Devlin's dark brown hat. Yet she caught no other sign of Devlin McCain.

A horrifying thought crystallized out of the cold flow of fear streaming through her mind. What if Devlin hadn't survived the fall? What if he were hurt, wounded and alone in this wilderness?

"My friend needs help." She turned to the man walking directly behind her, speaking the words slowly in the lingua geral, a corrupted form of the Tupi language, which the Jesuits had spread throughout the Amazon. "Do you understand? My friend is—"

The man bared his teeth and jabbed at her with the blunt end of his spear.

"Please, he might be hurt."

Waving his spear, he shouted at her in a language she

didn't understand. But his meaning couldn't be missed. She turned away and followed the others. How could she hope to help Devlin when she couldn't help herself? She could only pray he was all right.

Vines slapped at her, tearing her trousers, her blouse, scraping her skin. The men were bare, yet they weren't hampered by the thick vegetation, moving with the ease of animals, finding a path where she could see none. After a hike that seemed hours, but in reality was only a few minutes, her captors pushed aside a barrier of brush and vines, an opening of some sort that they dragged her through.

A village spread out behind that barrier, more than twenty crude, palm-thatched huts scattered around a central clearing, surrounded on three sides by a six-foot-high wall built of posts and leaves strapped together by vines. The fourth side opened to a narrow beach, firelight from the huge bonfire that roared in the center of the compound reflecting on the dark water of one of the narrow tributaries splintering off of the main channel. The odor of the place nearly staggered her— rotting food, unwashed bodies, human waste.

The savages pushed her, forced her into the center of the clearing. They were shouting now, a raucous chant of triumphant hunters, a sound that chilled her blood.

A group of women who were clustered around the fire all looked in her direction, but none drew near. They stared, curious, perhaps a little frightened. Three large birds about the size of wild turkeys sizzled in the fire, feathers crackling in the flames.

Her captors were thumping their chests, chanting, shouting. Kate spun around in a circle, body trembling, legs threatening to buckle beneath her. She had never fainted in her life. She couldn't faint now. She stared, trying to absorb it all. She might have tumbled over the falls into another century, the savage beginning of mankind.

Men rolled from their hammocks, crawled from their huts, all as naked as her captors, and none showing the reticence of the women. Like jackals moving in for the kill, they approached her, jabbering in that guttural tongue, gesturing with their long arms.

They were about her height, yet burly, and they were looking at her as though she were on the dinner menu. Perhaps she was, she thought, looking at the cooking fire and the charred bodies of the birds.

They started circling her—over 30 strong—quick brown hands poking at her, snatching her braid, tugging at her shirt, grabbing her breasts. Kate slapped away the hands, pushed against the broad, naked chests as they drew closer, a new fear sparking panic inside her. They wanted her, but it wasn't for dinner.

"Get away! Stay back!" She pushed, she slapped away the hands, fighting her own crippling panic. It was a nightmare, the worst she could ever imagine.

Suddenly they were backing away, dropping their hands, forming an aisle of sorts. Kate glanced around her, panting, nearly paralyzed by fear. A man strode down that aisle of sweating savages. He looked like the others, except that the belt around his large waist was more ornate, bright plumes of macaw and toucan tied from the narrow leather thong, the feathers brushing his naked belly as he strutted toward her.

Kate backed away as he drew near. There was something even more menacing in this man, leader of the others, something even more primitive. Hands hit her back, her shoulders, pushing her toward the advancing savage.

Trapped. She swallowed the whimper rising in her throat. She forced her back to straighten as he drew near. She forced her gaze to stay steady with his. "You are obviously the leader here." Once again she tried the lingua geral. "I come as a friend."

Raising his arms, he shouted. She stumbled back, sucking in her breath. The man smiled and looked around at his followers, obviously pleased with himself. His followers muttered their approval.

Kate felt her cheeks flush with shame, her mind rebelling at how easily this man had cowered her. This was what they wanted, to frighten her, to weaken her, to turn her into a scared little animal. She would show them she could not easily be conquered. Still, it took every ounce of courage just to remain standing when he started moving toward her.

She slapped away his hand when he reached for her braid. He looked startled. "Stay away from me."

Laughter rippled through the men who had formed a circle around them. The headman snarled, raising both hands at his sides, turning like a rooster fluffing his feathers, ready for a fight. He stared at the other men, and the laughter died.

Fear formed a knot in Kate's stomach. She was prepared to fight him, fight him and the others with every last drop of strength. She held her clenched fists in front of her, watching him, ready to strike.

As he began to circle, she had to turn to keep him in front of her. Hands grabbed her shoulders, tugged her braid, distracting her. She turned for only a heartbeat, hitting the hands that grabbed for her. In that heartbeat the headman attacked. He grabbed her braid, wrapping the long coil around his arm.

Shouts, laughter. The headman swung her around by her hair, lifting her until only her toes touched the ground, jabbering to his followers. Kate kicked her feet and thrust out with her clenched fists, connecting with nothing but air. He shook her, like a cat shaking a helpless mouse, sparks of pain flaring from her scalp. The others moved in, grabbing her wrists, her ankles, stretching her arms and legs wide. She bucked wildly in their grasp, screaming, losing all control over the panic raging inside her.

Hands grabbed her breasts, her thighs, squeezing, prodding. She felt the material of her shirt give way under those hands, buttons flying in all directions, her camisole shredded in their hands. And then she·felt rough hands on her skin. Dear God, this could not happen! She could not allow this to happen.

As quickly as the attack began, it ended. The men released her. She collapsed on the ground, falling to her knees. Their voices rose in a chorus around her, sobbing, childlike, fearful now.

She pushed the loose strands of hair from her face. Through her tears she saw some of the men kneeling beside her, rocking back and forth, keening softly, staring toward the river as though they had seen a ghost. A few were escaping the compound, scurrying for the entrance.

Through the dull roar of blood in her ears came the voice of a flute, the notes rippling on the evening air. It sounded familiar. It sounded like Vivaldi. And then she saw what had frightened these savages.

Chapter Fourteen

A man was rising from the water, a wooden flute lifted to his lips; Poseidon rising from the sea, revealing himself to his mortal subjects. Kate stared, unable to look away from him. Water dripped from his thick, black hair, streamed across his bare shoulders. Rivulets of water streamed down his broad chest catching in crisp, black curls. With each step, more and more of the dark water dropped away from him, revealing slim hips, long muscular legs. Naked. Majestic.

Kate stared as though this man were truly a pagan god risen from the dark waters to shine and shimmer in the firelight, golden skin, ebony hair, sleek, glistening. And all around her savages were on their hands and knees in the dirt, bobbing their heads, paying homage in low, keening chants to Devlin McCain.

All except the headman. He stood a few feet away from her, staring at Devlin, hatred molding his thick features.

"Kate, come to me." Devlin lifted his arm in a dramatic gesture, as though he could draw her to him with a sweep of his hand.

Kate rose to her feet and started walking toward him, as if in a trance, as if he really could command her with a wave of his hand. He was safety. He was sanity in this savage world. And all she wanted was to feel his arms around her.

A few feet before she could reach Devlin, a hard hand clamped on her upper arm. The headman stood beside her. He held her, his fingers sharp talons biting into her flesh. He shouted at Devlin, then thumped his chest.

A deep murmur passed through the Indians on the ground. Kate understood his meaning without understanding his words. It was a challenge. The headman intended to fight to keep her, fight until one man was dead.

"Let go of me." She tried to break free, but his grip was like a steel band.

She looked at Devlin. He was moving toward her, his face carved into taut lines, his eyes narrowed, firelight reflecting in the silvery slits. Power flowed in every move, and she could feel his rage radiating from him, pulsing against her chest like a summer storm. He glowed in the firelight, shimmered with that power and rage. The headman's hand flexed on her arm. He released her. He stepped away from her to meet Devlin.

The headman was a foot shorter than Devlin, but broad and muscular, a wild boar facing a jaguar. One of the others handed the headman a spear. Devlin pulled his knife from the sheath he had strapped to his naked hips, the blade as long as Kate's forearm, the steel capturing the firelight as though it were coming alive—Excalibur drawn from the stone.

On the edge of the water, they circled one another. The headman shouted and threw out his chest. Devlin growled deep in his throat, primal, frightening. Kate pressed her clasped hands to her lips. She wanted to believe this was all a dream, some horrible nightmare. She wanted to believe she would awaken in her tent, longing for Devlin, as she longed for him every night. But she knew it was all too real.

The headman made the first move, lunging with his spear, the stone point directed with deadly accuracy at Devlin's broad chest. Devlin sprang to the side and brought his knife along the headman's side, slicing a scarlet path across his ribs. Devlin could have killed in that move. He had chosen instead to wound.

"Don't, Devlin," Kate whispered. Devlin couldn't show the man mercy. He couldn't, because that savage would take any advantage to kill him.

The other men moved toward the combatants. They knelt in the dirt, forming two lines between the fire and the water, staring at their headman and this pale god, containing them between their swaying bodies, between the fire and the water.

Devlin maneuvered clear of the shorter man again and again, nicking him with the blade of his knife, drawing soft gasps from the crowd with each slice of the blade. With each cut the headman roared, his rage and frustration soaring. The others chanted softly, rocking back and forth on their heels, swaying in time to the rhythm of their voices.

Tongues of flames flared upward behind Devlin and the savage, scarlet and gold light flickering on their skin. It was at once real and illusory. Mythical. A fight of good and evil. And who would win?

The headman thrust wildly at Devlin. With one smooth move, Devlin stepped aside. He brought the blade arcing downward, slicing the spear, leaving the headman with nothing but a blunt stub in his hand. The headman looked down at his mutilated spear, then turned to face Devlin. Baring his teeth, thumping his chest, he refused to surrender. And Devlin refused to kill him.

"No!" Kate shouted as she watched Devlin sheathe his knife.

Devlin glanced in her direction. The headman roared. He charged, wrapping his powerful arms around Devlin's waist. Devlin tossed back his head in agony as the headman lifted him from the ground, squeezing his waist, trying to break his back.

Kate screamed. She ran toward Devlin, crashing into the barrier of Indians. They pushed her, shoved her down into the dirt outside of their barricade.

Devlin brought both hands down at the back of the headman's neck, over and over again. The headman staggered under the blows, but held tight to his prey. He carried Devlin into the river. Locked in combat, they sank below the dark, rippling water.

Kate came to her feet. She stared at the river, the flames reflected in the dark water. The Indians chanted louder and louder, rocking violently on their heels. On the far bank she noticed movement, several long, dark logs coming to life, lifting on short legs and darting toward the water. Alligators!

Devlin and the headman broke the surface of the water, both gasping for air. Kate saw them clearly. The headman had his arm around Devlin's neck. He was choking the life from him. "Devlin!" she shouted as they sank below the dark surface.

Something slapped the water. She saw a flash of charcoal in the reflected flames, the flick of a long tail, an alligator moving in for the kill. "My God," she whispered, pressing her hand to her racing heart, straining to see through the darkness.

She stumbled to the edge of the river. The water churned as if boiling, lapping at her feet.

The men broke the surface of the water. Horrible screams ripped through the air. Scarlet shone in the flames flickering across the water, spreading across the ripples like a flag unfurling in the wind. One last scream, and then nothing but the splashing of the struggle.

Kate stared at the bloody water. Devlin couldn't be gone. Dear God, he couldn't be gone. *Please spare him. Please*.

The seconds collected into an eternity. Blood drained from her limbs. Blackness closed around her. She couldn't faint.

Not now. Dear God, not now! She had to help Devlin.
But how?

The water stirred. A man waded toward shore. A tall man
with pale skin staggered from the dark water.

"Devlin." Kate thought she had screamed his name, but the
sound emerging from her lips was no more than a whisper.

The Indians parted as he approached. They pressed their
faces to the dirt, whimpering as if they feared Devlin would
strike them dead if they should glance into his eyes. She
wanted to run into his arms, but she couldn't move.

"Kate," Devlin whispered, opening his arms.

As he reached for her, she tumbled into his arms. He
locked her against him, his strong arms closing around her,
shielding her from the savage world surrounding them.

She pressed her cheek to his chest, listening to the strong
beat of his heart, a sharp, tangy scent filling her nostrils.
Through the blood throbbing in her head, she heard him
whispering her name, over and over again, as if it were a
prayer.

"Are you all right?" He pulled back to look down into
her face.

She nodded. "How did you find me?"

"I followed you through the jungle. There were too many
of them to come barging through the front door, so I tried a
different approach."

"I thought he was going to kill you."

"Yeah, I had the same thought." He looked over her head
at the Indians; they were moving toward them, closing in,
forming a circle around them. "And it doesn't look as though
we're out of it yet."

"What are we going to do?" she asked, cinching her arms
around his waist.

Devlin slipped his knife from the sheath, the heavy steel
comforting in his grasp. He lifted the long knife, turning the
blade in the firelight, the polished metal reflecting gold and
scarlet. He only hoped they would come at him one at a time.
Otherwise, he and Kate didn't stand a chance.

The Indians dropped to their knees, murmuring, their voices blending in a chorus of fear. Although the dialect was different from what he knew, Devlin understood their language.

"They're the Kuraya." As he listened to their chanting voices, he began to smile, then laugh. Kate looked up at him, her blue eyes wide. "No, I'm not crazy," he said, answering her silent question.

"What is it?"

"It seems our friends think I'm a god. Do you believe that?"

"Yes," Kate whispered, closing her eyes.

The tone of her voice sent a warm current of longing rippling through him. She snuggled against him as though she drew comfort from his body. And he drew his own comfort from having her near. Her clothes teased his bare skin, a gentle scrape of warm cotton with every breath she took. Ignoring the chanting natives, he indulged his own longing, holding her, pressing his cheek to her soft hair.

"Will they let us go?" she whispered, her words muffled against his chest.

"There's nowhere for us to go tonight." He smoothed loose curls back from her cheek.

"We have to stay here?" she asked, looking up at him.

The firelight flickered against her face, so lovely, so frightened. He stroked her soft cheek with the back of his fingers, wishing he could stroke away her fear. "I won't let anything happen to you, Kate. Will you trust me?"

She glanced at the natives, who were on their knees, rocking back and forth on their heels, chanting in soft cries. Devlin could feel her hands tense against his back as she looked up at him. "Of course I trust you. If there is anyone who can get us out of this alive, it's you, Devlin McCain."

The strength of her faith stunned him. No one had ever believed in him before. No one. And he would do everything in his power to justify that faith.

He looked at the natives. With a few words he had them on their feet. They were more than happy to provide a hut and food and anything the god of the river wanted.

Kate clenched Devlin's arm as the natives ushered them to one of the crude huts, which Devlin suspected had once belonged to the headman. Conical in shape, the hut seemed an effigy of a volcano done in leaves and wood and vines, with several hammocks hanging from posts along the walls to poles planted near the center of the hut.

A small fire was burning, gray smoke curling toward the hole in the roof at the center of the hut. After they had all entered, one of the Indians started shouting at the women and children inside the hut, sending the four women scampering through the low entrance, each carrying or dragging a small, screaming child with her. Kate glanced up at Devlin. She looked as bewildered as Alice must have looked on her trip through the looking glass.

"The headman's wives and children," Devlin said, answering her questioning look.

"But where will they go?"

"To a relative's hut." He stroked the slender hand that clutched his arm. "They'll be all right."

Her hand relaxed, then convulsed on his arm. She was staring at something in the corner of the hut: small, brown objects, round and shriveled, with tufts of black hair sticking out from the tops.

"Oh, my good heavens!" Kate turned away from the brown balls piled a foot high in the far corner of the hut. "Heads." She pressed her cheek against Devlin's upper arm. "They're heads!"

"They take the heads to imprison the souls of their enemies." Devlin stroked her shoulder. "You've seen mummies, haven't you?"

She nodded without looking up at him. He could feel her terror, sense the horrible internal fight she was having to control her fear.

"They aren't any worse than mummies. You aren't frightened of mummies, are you?"

She drew her teeth over her lower lip. "No."

"Sit with me." He sank to the packed dirt floor with his back to the fire and the shrunken heads, tugging on her hand.

She followed him, sitting close, her thigh brushing his, her shoulder slipping behind his. Her breasts grazed his side, her soft breath warmed his shoulder, and it was all he could do to keep from pulling her into his arms.

The Indians delivered bowls filled with baked *makashera,* a type of sweet potato, calabashes filled with *kashiri,* a strong native beer, and three charred *mutums,* wild turkeys, two of which Devlin gave back to be shared with the others. When it became clear the devoted Indians intended to stay and watch their new god eat, Devlin sent them away with a terse command. They scrambled out of the hut, tripping over each other, leaving him alone with Kate.

She sat cross-legged beside him, her hands tightly clasped in her lap, staring down at the blackened bird, which lay on a palm leaf on the ground in front of Devlin. In the firelight, her cheeks were pale, and he could see she was trembling.

"Kate." He wanted to hold her, but he knew he couldn't. Because if he took her in his arms, if he felt the heat of her melting against his body, he might not be able to contain the lust inside him, rumbling deep within him, fighting like a great wild beast to break free. "It's all right, sweetheart. You're safe now."

"I thought they were cannibals at first. Then I realized what they wanted to do with me. If you hadn't come . . ." Her voice trailed into a tightly clenched breath.

"They won't touch you again, I swear." He cupped her cheek in his palm, her skin like cool marble to his touch.

"I've never felt so helpless."

"That's because there isn't a pen or pot of ink for miles," he said, hoping he might coax a smile.

She drew her lower lip between her teeth and he could see her struggle with her emotions. "I wanted to be strong. I've always admired strength. But I was so frightened."

With his fingers beneath her chin, he tilted her head. When she looked at him, there were tears shimmering in her eyes. "Do you want to know a secret?"

She nodded and a single tear slipped from the corner of her eye. He slid his thumb over her cheek, catching the glistening teardrop.

"I was scared half out of my skin." Frightened he wouldn't get to her in time. Frightened they would rape her, as they raped any woman they captured. He had witnessed it once, an entire tribe of 30 men taking the six women they had brought back from a raid.

"You were frightened?" She seemed shocked at the thought.

"My heart was pounding like a drum. Didn't you hear it?"

She smiled. "You're teasing me."

Ah, how he loved her smile. "Maybe a little."

He traced the curve of her smile with his thumb, feeling her warm breath against his skin, recalling the feel of those lips beneath his, the taste of her mouth, the way she felt snuggled against his naked body.

He wanted to take her in his arms now. He wanted to hold her, kiss her, ignite a fire between them, a fire to sear away the painful memories. God, how he wanted her.

He sensed a sudden stillness in her. She was watching him, holding her breath, waiting. Did she think he would try to rape her, like the others had?

Silently he cursed the desire pumping through his veins, so hot and thick it consumed him. She didn't need what he had to offer. Not now. Not ever. He turned away from her, hiding the hard evidence of his desire. "You need to eat something."

"Will you hold me?"

No. He couldn't hold her. Holding her now would be nothing short of disaster. "You'll feel better once you've eaten." He sank his knife into the turkey. Although charred on the outside, the bird was nearly raw inside.

"Please. Hold me, just for a little while."

The plea was so soft, so filled with need. He glanced over his shoulder. A mistake.

She was sitting with her arms crossed over her breasts, her hands clasping her slender shoulders. Firelight shimmered in the tears clouding her huge, blue eyes. And she was trembling. The need to comfort her outweighed everything, including his own pain. "Kate," he whispered, slipping his arm around her back.

She surged against him, throwing her arms around his neck as if she were being chased by demons, as if she could take refuge in his embrace. He drew her onto his lap, cradling her in his arms, rubbing his open palm up and down her back. He tried to ignore the ache in his loins. Yet she felt so good in his arms, so enticing.

Roses still lingered in her hair. The intoxicating fragrance of her skin, damp, salty, filled his senses, scraped his resistance until he was raw. The heat of her, soft warmth, inviting warmth, intoxicating warmth. God, how he wanted to lose himself in that warmth. He clenched his jaw.

"I feel safe in your arms," she whispered, her lips brushing his bare shoulder.

She trusted him. She trusted him with the innocence of a child. And if she knew how powerfully the lust burned inside him, she would never be sitting here in his arms.

She moved her head, pressing her lips to the base of his neck. Devlin stared up through the opening in the hut, following the trail of smoke as it drifted into the air, as it caught the breeze and dissolved into the darkness. He was dissolving into darkness, into the thick, dark passion swirling inside him.

"Your skin smells different," she whispered, nuzzling her lips against his neck, her breath scalding his skin.

Devlin swallowed hard before he could use his voice. "It's barbasco juice."

"Barbasco juice?" she asked, sliding her hands along his shoulders.

"It's a bush." Did she have any idea what she was doing to him? "Some of the Indian tribes use it to kill fish. Alligators hate the smell of it."

"Clever. Though I have to admit, I like the sandalwood better."

She had noticed the scent of his soap. He smiled and slid his hand over the back of her head, smoothing the tousled silk of her hair, stroking the tangled remains of her braid. She snuggled closer, rubbing her thigh against the throbbing length of his need, the need for her he couldn't hide. She had to feel it; it was like a bone ramming into her thigh.

He would shock her, frighten her. She would draw away from him. She would look at him in disgust. Yet she made no move to leave the shelter of his arms.

"Tell me, why don't you like me?" Her voice barely rose above the soft crackle of the fire.

The woman had no idea, no idea at all. She didn't realize just looking at her stirred emotions in him, both fragile and violent. Love. Lust. Anger. Desire. Aching desire to hold her, to love her, to ease the lust throbbing like an open wound inside him. And anger because he could never have her. Vibrant, flaring anger because he wasn't good enough, not nearly good enough for her. How could he expect her to understand? He didn't understand.

"Is it because you think I'm starchy? Is that why you don't like me?"

He slid his palm over the curve of her shoulder. She moved beneath his touch, pressing closer to him, the lush heat of her firm breasts searing his naked chest through the tattered cotton of her shirt. "Is that what you believe, Kate? That I don't like you?"

Without looking up at him, she nodded, her smooth cheek sliding against his shoulder. "You avoid me. Sometimes I think you would like to toss me over the side of the canoe because you can't stand the sight of me."

He drew a deep breath. "Maybe I like the sight of you too much."

He felt her draw a breath and hold it. She pulled back in his arms. She stared at him with clear blue eyes, and he knew at that moment she could look right through him, as though his body were nothing but glass containing the churning tempest of his emotions.

Color crept into her cheeks, a soft rose staining the smooth ivory. A smile slid along her lips and lit her eyes. She parted her lips. She looked as though she were about to speak. He prayed she wouldn't. He dreaded the words, knowing he had exposed himself completely.

A loud shout at the entrance to the hut saved him from the humiliation. One of the men was asking for permission to enter, something the Indians rarely did. Only his status as resident god permitted him this favor. Devlin gave his permission, and the man entered, followed by three women.

The women were young, barely in their teens. They were smiling at him, giggling, black eyes shimmering with laughter, long, black hair falling like inky shadows over bare shoulders, full breasts firm and erect, the dark nipples pert and tempting. And he knew before the man told him why they were here that if he wanted them, the girls were his.

It had been a lifetime since he had felt a woman's thighs wrap around his waist. His body was hard and aching beneath Kate's thigh, his every nerve scraped raw by weeks of being near this woman. He looked at the three women as the man offered them for Devlin's pleasure. He glanced down at the woman in his arms, and he knew only Kate could feed the hunger in his belly and in his heart.

Kate was watching him, a frown crinkling the smooth skin between the light brown wings of her brows, her eyes narrowed to blue slits. Perhaps she didn't understand the language, but he had the feeling she understood what was being offered. And she wasn't at all happy about it.

"Your offering is generous." Devlin used the language of the Kuraya, choosing his words carefully. "The women are ripe and tempting fruit. But tonight I want only my woman."

The women murmured a protest, staring at Kate with jealous eyes. The man looked at Kate, smiling, nodding his head as though he understood. When he turned to leave, the women refused to follow until the man was shouting at them, waving his arms and threatening to beat them. That sent them scampering from the hut.

"He was giving them to you, wasn't he," Kate said when they were alone.

"It's considered good manners."

"I see."

Kate wiggled off his lap. The sensation made him wince with pain. He couldn't contain the groan rushing up his throat. She glanced in his direction, catching a glimpse of his aroused flesh before he could shift his thigh and shield his tortured sex.

She sat a few feet away, propping her back against one of the hammock posts, stretching her long legs out in front of her. "So women are considered nothing more than objects to be given away at a man's whim."

"Women are valuable in their culture. They're used to secure alliances through marriage, to seal peace agreements, to—"

"Women are a commodity. To be dealt with as a man sees fit."

Devlin sighed. "This isn't a civilized culture, Kate."

She stared down at her hands, lacing together her fingers. "I'm not so certain our culture is much different. Women are given in marriage, often arranged to secure alliances between families. A woman has few rights, none if she marries. We are not allowed to vote, to hold a decent job, to be anything but decorations in a man's home. No, I don't think our culture has made great strides where it concerns women. Men still treat women like objects."

"All men?"

She glanced at him. "Most men."

"And Austin Sinclair?" He hadn't meant to ask the question, and now that it was out of his mouth he wished he could snatch back the words. And yet he needed to know. "Is he different than most men?"

"Yes." She glanced down at her hands, drawing her fingers apart, sliding her palms together. "He treats me like a human being. He's very special."

And do you love him? It was the question he most wanted to ask. The question he most needed to know. The question he couldn't bring himself to voice. He stared down at the charred bird and told himself it didn't matter. Even if she didn't love Austin Sinclair, she was still beyond his reach.

He sliced the turkey, choosing only the cooked pieces. When he turned to hand them to her he found her studying him, watching him as though he were a rare breed of animal on public display.

"I never thanked you for rescuing me," she said, smiling up at him.

"There's no need to thank me for anything. I'm just doing what you hired me to do."

"Seems to me, going over a waterfall is beyond the call of duty." She lowered her eyes, her gaze drifting over him.

If she hadn't noticed he was stark naked before, she did now. And she wasn't embarrassed by it. In fact, she seemed blatantly curious. And that curiosity made him far too aware of his own nakedness, of his own vulnerability where she was concerned. Heat crept into his cheeks.

"I had to strip to smear on the barbasco." He sounded like a schoolboy explaining himself to the headmistress.

"I don't mind." She accepted the slices of turkey he offered, grazing his hand with her fingers. "Right now, Mr. McCain, you are wearing bright, shining armor."

He glanced away from her. At the moment he saw too much in those blue eyes, everything he had ever wanted to see. But he knew it wouldn't last beyond the fringe of the jungle. "Don't make me into anything I'm not."

"I see. You're still no one's hero, is that it?"

"That's right."

"Well, Mr. McCain, I'm afraid you will have to live with being my hero."

Devlin stared at the charred bird, looking at the raw meat, pale and bloody. *Her hero.* It wouldn't last. In London she would see him for what he really was: common white trash.

"Did you do as the natives do when you lived with them? I mean, did you go around in the altogether?"

"After you're in the jungle awhile, it makes sense to wear as little as they do. You stay wet all the time in clothes, your skin gets raw."

She leaned back against one of the hammock posts, nibbling the turkey. As he watched, she licked the juice sliding down the side of her hand, catching the drops on the tip of her pink tongue, like a kitten lapping cream. "And did you accept their offers of feminine companionship?"

He nodded. "I suppose that makes me some kind of monster."

"No, I suppose that makes you a man taking his pleasure where he can find it."

She didn't seem to notice the way the torn edges of her shirt gaped open, revealing the tattered white lace of her camisole, the curves of her breasts. The firelight flickered against her skin, stroked it like golden fingers, curving, caressing. He imagined if she breathed deeply the torn edges would part, revealing the rosy tips of her breasts through the silk of her camisole. And would her nipples be hard?

A sharp blade of desire twisted in his belly. He caught himself staring at her and glanced away, directing his gaze to the calabash of beer beside him.

"Was that Vivaldi you were playing when you came out of the water?"

"Yeah." He took a drink of *kashiri,* which was sweetened with sugarcane and pineapple juice. "I wanted to make a big impression on them. Some tribes worship insanity." And right now the lady was driving him insane.

"Did you teach yourself to play?"

"No." He hacked the leg off the turkey and began scraping the burned skin from the flesh, remembering the music lessons, wanting to forget.

"Where did you learn?"

"Does it matter?"

"I've known you for weeks, and I still know almost nothing about you."

"Why do you want to know about me?"

She looked at him over the rim of her calabash of *kashiri.* "I thought we might be friends," she said, before taking a sip.

Friends. How could he be her friend when just being near her was tearing him into shreds? How could he be her friend when he wanted so much more?

"This is good." She took another delicate sip of *kashiri.*

"The women bake pancakes of sweet potatoes, *kara,* and *madioca.* When the cakes are nice and hard and blackened, they chew them and spit them into a large jar. That's what ferments the stuff."

"Oh." She crinkled her nose as she swirled the milky liquid around in her calabash. "Still, it isn't at all bad." She looked at him, a clear, appraising stare, a look that tore away pretense. "And I would still like to hear about your musical career."

"My musical career." He stared down at the burnt pieces of flesh in his hand. Well, why not tell her? Once she heard about him, she would forget all about her notion of being friends. Once she knew about him she wouldn't want to be within a mile of him. It was better to shatter any illusion of heroes in shining armor right now.

"A woman gave me lessons. When I was fourteen, she took me out of her stables and gave me a room in her fine Fifth Avenue mansion. She gave me clothes and taught me proper table manners and how to play chess and behave like a gentleman. She was a widow, but young, no more than thirty-three, I guess. She never told me."

He drew the blade slowly across the blackened flesh. "I thought she was lonely. She didn't have children. I thought she was adopting me, this beautiful woman, with her clean-smelling clothes and fancy house." He had been amazed she wanted him. For the first time in his life, someone had wanted to give him a home. Pity it had all been an illusion.

He twisted the knife in his hand, catching the firelight, letting the gold and scarlet light ripple along the steel. "One night, a few months after I'd been living in her house, she came to my bedroom. She was wearing this dark red silk robe. It moved around her as she walked toward me, giving me glimpses of her legs, long and white. She was naked under that robe." He drew a deep breath, fighting the pain that came with the memories. Even after all these years he couldn't escape the pain of humiliation.

"I remember she said: 'Don't be afraid of me.' She showed me what she wanted. She taught me how to pleasure her. And I did. But I didn't know what she really wanted." He stared at the blade, wishing he could carve the memories from his mind. "For months she came to me every night."

"Did you love her?"

"I adored her. So when she asked me to pleasure one of her friends, I did it, that night and every night she brought someone to my room. Sometimes she would watch, sometimes she would join us. I did everything she wanted, deaf and blind to everything but that woman." He had been so grateful she had chosen him, so grateful she loved him. So incredibly naive.

Kate was quiet, but he felt her gaze on him. He should stop now, without telling her all of it, without letting her know how far he had been drawn into the web. But he wanted her to know the truth. He wanted her to see the man beneath the veneer.

"I never knew what day I was born. But she decided I should choose one day as my birthday, and we'd celebrate. I'd been with her nearly a year. So I chose that day in May, the first day she had taken a stableboy into her house, the sixteenth. When the day came, we celebrated with a big cake. She bought me a gold pocket watch that played 'Fur Elise' when you opened the cover. I'd never been so happy in my life."

He jabbed at the ground between his spread feet, sinking the tip of the knife into the dirt. "That night, she brought a man to my room. She told me if I loved her, I would do what her friend asked of me."

Beside him he heard Kate move, heard the soft exhale of her breath. He could feel the tension in her body. And he knew he was slowly shedding all of that nice shining armor she had fashioned for him.

"I never knew things like that could happen. I never realized boys could be used like women. I remember looking at her, seeing her smooth, white skin in the gaslight. I remember her voice, urging me to kneel on the bed, to get down on my hands and knees on the bed. And I remember the moment I realized she didn't love me. She was using me. When that man touched my arm, I lashed out at him. I ran past him, and I kept running."

He stared down at the dirt encrusting the tip of his knife. He tried to breathe, but he couldn't. The air was closing in around him, pressing against him like a slab of marble. He tried to convince himself it didn't matter what Kate thought of him.

And still she stared. He could feel her gaze without looking at her. Silent. And in the constricting folds of that silence, he waited for her condemnation, waited for the words that would fall like a blade across his neck.

"Don't ever blame yourself for her sins."

He glanced over his shoulder and looked at her, his heart not believing what his ears had heard. He saw tenderness in her eyes, compassion in her face.

"And please, don't look at me like that. As though you're astonished I could understand, as though you expect me to shun you for what happened when you were a boy. I hope, when you know me better, you will see I'm not that shallow."

He moved toward her, a subtle movement of his shoulders that he halted almost as soon as it began. He struggled with the need to hold her and the need to protect her from the violence of his own hunger for this woman.

He turned away from her. He rose and shoved his knife into the sheath, a swift, angry motion of muscles.

"No one will bother you tonight, Kate." He didn't look at her as he spoke. He couldn't. She was far too tempting. "On this you have my word. Tomorrow, we'll start hiking upriver. I'll get you back to your father, I promise you."

Kate watched Devlin leave. She sank back against the pole, her breath locked in her throat. Her skin burned, as though she had stood too long naked in the bright light of the sun.

He would keep her safe. She was sure of it. Devlin would protect her from the Indians. He would shield her from the desire she knew smoldered inside him. The desire she had felt in the taut muscles of his arms as he had held her. The desire she had felt like a burning sword against her thigh. Yet she wasn't sure she wanted to be safe, at least not from one compelling pagan god.

He could have taken her tonight. He could have made love to her, and there would have been no one to blame but herself. She would have done anything to keep Devlin from making love with those beautiful women the savage had offered him. She would have made love with him, here in this horrible little hovel. If he had laid one finger on her, she would have melted in his embrace.

And he had been a gentleman.

She felt as though her skin had grown too tight to contain the emotions surging inside her. What was wrong with her? She should be happy he had not taken advantage of her. She should be relieved. She should not be sitting here contemplating going after him. Yet she was.

Chapter Fifteen

The only people on the face of the earth. It was easy to believe, Kate thought, following Devlin through the thick tangle of forest. With each step, her boot-clad feet squished against the vines and ferns and rotting leaves covering the ground. In a few places mud oozed up between the heavy ground cover.

Rain pounded against the canopy of leaves overhead, penetrating, falling in a warm deluge that soaked her to the skin. Wouldn't any sensible person try to get out of the rain? she wondered, staring at Devlin's back. They would in England, but here nothing stopped for the deluge. Perhaps because it was as common as fog in England, more common, falling at odd times every day.

The drenched white cotton of Devlin's shirt stretched across his back as he wielded his long knife, hacking away vines and brush, reaping a tangy scent that filled the moist air, air so thick she could scarcely draw it into her burning lungs. He had dressed soon after leaving the village this morning, and she was certain the clothes were a concession to her presence,

one she felt like telling him he could forego. She really didn't
object to his nudity. Here it didn't seem at all out of place,
but natural, proper even. That was it, the proper attire for a
stroll through the jungle.

She wiped the back of her hand across her wet brow. Her
clothes were clinging to her, scraping her skin with every
move she made. Only her pride kept her from begging for
a few minutes rest, a few minutes shelter from the storm.
Only her pride kept her legs moving, legs that had turned to
rubber hours ago.

One, two, three, four. Silently she repeated the cadence
over and over again, lifting one foot, then the next. Light-
ning flashed against the emerald canopy overhead, casting
a tangled pattern of silver across Devlin. Thunder rumbled.
Yet Devlin didn't seem to notice the tempest.

One, two, three, four. Their trek had started at daybreak,
when they left the Kuraya village. And they had been walking forever, following a stream of the river, winding upward
toward the crest of the falls, at times climbing on all fours
along the steep terrain.

One, two, three—She bumped into Devlin's back. "Sorry.
I didn't realize you had stopped."

He pushed back his hat, water streaming from the brim as
he looked down at her, his dark brows pulled together into a
frown. "Why didn't you say you were about to collapse?"

Now that she had stopped, her legs were trembling so
badly she had to fight to keep from collapsing into a pool of
gelatin at Devlin's feet. She tried to force her back to stiffen
and discovered a kink in her spine. "I'm fine."

"I can see you are." He cinched his arm around her waist.

"You don't need to carry me." She slipped her arms around
his shoulders as he lifted her, taking her weight against his
side. "I can make it on my own."

"I don't think I've ever met anyone more stubborn than
you, Professor."

"I'm not stubborn." She closed her eyes, relaxing in his
hold.

With one arm he carried her close against his side. With the other, he hacked his way through the forest. Each step he took vibrated upward through his body into hers. The muscles in his chest shifted against her breasts, strong, vibrant. The curve of his neck brushed her lips, damp, salty. The scent of his skin teased her every breath, musk, spicy.

Man and woman. *The only people left on the face of the earth,* she thought, holding him closer, taking shelter in his embrace.

After an hour that seemed a lifetime, the rain halted, as if a valve had been closed by the hand of God. Sunlight slanted through the tress overhead, painting gold streaks against air so moist it wrapped around her in a heavy cloak. Her skin prickled, chafing against her clothes. And still Devlin marched through the forest. Did the man never tire?

Devlin paused when they reached a wide part of the stream; here was its source. The stream plunged from the river above them, tumbling over the rocky cliff, cascading into a pool before winding down through the jungle and back to the river below the falls. An entire day of marching and they were only halfway to the crest of the falls.

"Try not to fall in." Devlin lowered her to the narrow strip of sand beside the pool.

"Can't I have a bath?" she asked, staring into the clear depths, feeling the inviting spray of mist from the little waterfalls against her cheeks.

"Later."

"Oh, there's work that needs doing." She struggled to stand, a marionette with broken strings.

Two strong hands on her shoulders eased her back on her heels. She looked up and found him smiling at her, his eyes filled with a haunting tenderness. Devastating. Did he have any idea how devastating that smile could be? She wanted to touch that smile, feel his lips curving beneath her fingers.

"Rest a little while I make camp."

She sat staring after him, watching his every move. He was like a jaguar, all fluid power and grace. He cleared away the brush and vines, tossing them in a pile near the stream.

Sunlight streaked through the leaves overhead, shimmering on the bubbling water beside her. She dipped her hands in the cool water of the pool and splashed her face, her neck, letting the water stream down her neck and between her breasts. Lovely. So cool. Perhaps he wouldn't notice if she stripped off her blouse, she thought, pulling the damp linen from her trousers. It was tempting, yet some small shred of propriety refused her the liberty.

After tugging open the laces Devlin had made of vine to keep the edges of her blouse fastened, she lifted handfuls of water beneath her torn camisole, bathing her naked breasts, splashing water under her arms, behind her neck. Still, the water did little to revive her strained muscles.

She slid to the sand, lying on her side, resting her head on her arm. She should help him. She would help him, just as soon as she caught her wind. A few minutes rest, that was all. Her eyelids fluttered against her cheeks. She would rest for just a few minutes.

Sound asleep, Devlin thought, glancing back to where Kate was lying on the sand. And he well understood her exhaustion. He felt drained, and he was accustomed to the heat and humidity. He hadn't meant to push her, but the fewer nights they spent alone in the jungle, the better for everyone.

He cut four pieces of bamboo and pounded them into the sandy ground with a flat rock, lashing the longest pieces—which stood about six feet high—together in front, placing the two shorter pieces—each about four feet high—in the rear, forming a triangle. He joined the pieces with sticks and vines and covered the structure with long banana leaves. After covering the ground under the structure with banana leaves, he went to Kate.

Sleeping like a babe, he thought, brushing a damp strand of hair from her cheek. She stirred beneath his touch, nuzzling her lips into his palm, her breath a warm stream across his wrist. His throat tightened with emotion. Hunger throbbed in his veins, a hot, spiraling hunger for this woman. He wanted her in his arms. He wanted to taste her, to feel her flesh close around his, to devour every inch of her.

You will have to live with being my hero. Her words echoed in his mind. She trusted him. She was depending on him to get her back to her father. Frederick Whitmore's smiling face loomed in his memory. Trust. Faith. Devlin couldn't betray them.

He gathered her in his arms, intending to hide her in the shelter while he hunted for their dinner. She felt fragile, small, and delicate in his arms. A rosebud in the jungle. A rosebud he would keep safe no matter what happened.

The sweet scent of freshly cut leaves greeted him as he entered the small shelter. She curled against him, turning her face into his shoulder, grasping one edge of his open shirt in her hand when he laid her down on the fragrant green leaves. Gently he removed her hand from his shirt. She moaned in protest, her lips forming a tempting pout.

He felt all of his good intentions unraveling inside him, picked apart by the sharp talons of his need for her. He stroked her cheek. He moved toward her, drawn by the hunger inside him, lowering his head until he felt her breath against his lips. It would be so easy to seduce her into giving him what he needed. So easy to betray them both.

He sat back on his heels, drawing deep drafts of air into his lungs. Her clothes were soaked, white cotton sticking to her skin, molding the curves of her breasts, her nipples rosy shadows beneath the thin cloth. Through the torn edges of her shirt he could see the red marks at the top of her camisole where the damp cloth had chafed her smooth skin. If she didn't get out of those wet clothes she would have a rash by morning.

"Kate." He stroked the hair back from her temple. "Wake up, sweetheart."

She moaned and turned her head.

He should leave her now. A rash was nothing compared to the pain he felt twisting inside him. He started to back away, but he thought of how her skin would be swollen and sore in the morning.

"Damn."

Quickly he slipped off her boots and socks. His hands were trembling as he unfastened the buttons of her trousers. And still she didn't awaken.

"Of all the miserable luck." He stripped off her shirt and camisole, trying not to look at the lush curves. Trapped in this place with the one woman he wanted more than any in his life. This close and not able to have her. "Of all the miserable, rotten luck."

He peeled away her trousers. Lace-trimmed drawers with little rosebuds adorning the bands, the linen warm against his hands. "God help us both." He tossed banana leaves over her. After gathering her wet clothes in his arms, he escaped the hut as though a tribe of headhunters were on his heels.

Kate turned and stretched, her cheek sliding against something cool and smooth, a sweet fragrance filling her awakening senses. "Devlin," she whispered, sliding her hand across the smooth mattress beneath her, reaching for him, finding herself alone.

She had only been dreaming, she thought, opening her eyes. Dreaming of his strong arms holding her.

She sat up, blinking the sleep from her eyes, trying to gain her bearings. She was in a small hut, and there was light coming from outside, the flickering light of a fire shimmering through the small entrance, close enough to warm her, golden light pulsing against her bare breasts.

"Oh, my heavens!" she whispered, crossing her arms over her breasts.

Through the entrance she saw Devlin McCain. Light radiated from the fire, forming a circle of gold, a circle of warmth in the chilly jungle night. Devlin was sitting cross-legged near the center of that circle, dressed only in his trousers.

Firelight stroked his face, his shoulders, his chest, his bare skin glowing with light and vitality.

He held a stick over the fire, the flames lapping at a plump fish. Across from him, beside the fire, two sticks had been driven into the sandy soil. A vine was stretched between the two sticks, and tossed across that vine, beside his shirt, were her trousers, her shirt, camisole, and lace-trimmed drawers.

"Hungry?" he asked, without glancing in her direction.

Scattered around her were big banana leaves. She clutched one to her breasts, held another across her belly, and peeked out of the hut. "Mr. McCain, my clothes."

He glanced in her direction, a smile curving his lips when he saw her. "I once knew a woman who did a dance with fans in San Francisco. She sure knew how to tease a man. Every night she'd have the whole place shouting for her to drop 'em."

Heat seared her cheeks. "Mr. McCain, will you please bring me my clothes?"

"No thoughts of going native?" Amusement colored the deep, gravelly tones of his voice.

"None at all."

"All right."

He dropped the fish on a palm frond before taking her clothes off the line and tossing each garment over his arm. When he came to her drawers, he glanced back at her, a wide, mischievous grin on his lips. "Now, Professor, I'd never have guessed you were hiding lace and rosebuds under your breeches."

She watched as he slid his thumb over a pink rosebud adorning the band of lace on the cuff of one leg, a slow caress, as if the rosebud were a living thing. Something happened inside her, a sudden tightening in the tips of her breasts.

"Wearing trousers makes me no less a woman, Mr. McCain." Kate took a step back into the shadows as he approached, but there was nowhere to hide. He glanced down at her, his gaze dipping to where she held the banana leaf flush against her breasts, the pressure of her hand causing her flesh to swell above the dark green strip.

"I can see you're every inch a woman, Miss Whitmore."

"Oh," she whispered.

He dropped her clothes on the banana leaves just inside the hut, brushing her arm with his bare shoulder. The heat was immediate, a flash of fire that stole her breath. She stiffened and pressed back against the hut so quickly she nearly wrecked the fragile dwelling.

He glanced down at her and smiled. "Don't worry, Professor. I've never forced a woman to do anything against her will."

She stared at him as he walked toward the fire. No, he would never force her to do anything against her will. But what would happen if he realized she had no will when it came to him?

As she dressed she noticed her clothes smelled of river water and smoke. He had washed them.

"Oh, my heavens," she whispered, feeling horribly exposed and at the same time shamefully excited. He had undressed her. He had seen her nude body, touched her, washed her drawers. She drew a shaky breath, her body trembling with the intimate images flashing in her mind. How in the world would she face him? For a long time she stood in the shadows of the hut, gathering every ounce of courage to walk into the golden light of the fire.

"About time." He stood and came toward her as she left the shelter. "I was beginning to think you were hiding in there."

"I was trying to get some of the tangles from my hair," she said, accepting the long, narrow plate he was offering.

"Looks like you didn't have much luck."

The man didn't have to tell her she looked like a wretch. She knew it. "Kind of you to notice."

He laughed as he moved back to a place on the fringe of the firelight where he sat on the sand and leaned against the trunk of a tall palm. She sat on the carpet of banana and palm

Join the Historical Romance Book Club — and GET 4 FREE* BOOKS NOW!

A $23.96 Value!

Yes! I want to subscribe to the Historical Romance Book Club.

Please send me my **4 FREE* BOOKS.** I have enclosed $2.00 for shipping/handling. Each month I'll receive the four newest Historical Romance selections to preview for 10 days. If I decide to keep them, I will pay the Special Members Only discounted price of just $4.24 each, a total of $16.96, plus $2.00 shipping/handling ($23.55 US in Canada). This is a **SAVINGS OF AT LEAST $5.00** off the bookstore price. There is no minimum number of books I must buy, and I may cancel the program at any time. In any case, the **4 FREE* BOOKS** are mine to keep.

*In Canada, add $5.00 shipping/handling per order for the first shipment. For all future shipments to Canada, the cost of membership is $23.55 US, which includes shipping and handling. (All payments must be made in US dollars.)

NAME: _____

ADDRESS: _____

CITY: _____ **STATE:** _____

COUNTRY: _____ **ZIP:** _____

TELEPHONE: _____

E-MAIL: _____

SIGNATURE: _____

If under 18, Parent or Guardian must sign. Terms, prices, and conditions subject to change. Subscription subject to acceptance. Dorchester Publishing reserves the right to reject any order or cancel any subscription.

The Best in Historical Romance!
Get Four Books Totally FREE*!

A $23.96 Value! FREE!

leaves Devlin had spread across the ground, close enough to the fire to feel its warmth against her cheeks.

She balanced the plate he had carved from a dried palm on her crossed legs and faced the flames, feeling too embarrassed to face him, too embarrassed to eat. Yet one taste of the roasted fish awakened her appetite. She discovered she was ravenous and the meal was wonderful: tender whitefish, crunchy hearts of palm, slices of ripe, juicy papaya, so sweet she licked every last drop from her fingertips.

"There's more, if you're still hungry."

She glanced back at him and smiled. He held his knife in one hand, a piece of wood he had been whittling in the other. "Maybe a few more slices of fruit."

After putting aside his knife and the wood he was shaping, he came to his feet, grabbing a papaya from the small stack of fruit he had piled on a palm frond near the base of the tree. She watched him approach, tilting back her head as he drew near, staring up at this man who towered above her. He seemed taller here in the jungle, more powerful than he had in the confines of civilization, as if he drew his strength from the savage wilderness surrounding them.

Sitting on his heels beside her, he sliced the fruit, dropping succulent slices onto her plate, juice sliding down the sides of his hands. She ran the tip of her tongue over her lips, tasting a trace of juice, fighting an almost uncontrollable urge to capture the sparkling orange droplets on his skin. She imagined taking hold of his arm, pressing her lips to his hand, sliding her tongue along his wrist, tasting the sweet, salty taste of his skin.

Wicked, dangerous thoughts. Heavens, she shouldn't be having such thoughts.

"Enough?"

"Yes." Quite enough. Too much. Far too much daydreaming. "Thank you. Everything was wonderful."

He stood and tossed the remains of the papaya into the fire, sending sparks flying into the air. "Anything tastes good when you're hungry."

Hungry. Yes, she was hungry, for things she ought never to taste.

Was it this place? The isolation, the complete dependency she had on him, was that the reason she was so infatuated with the man? Infatuated, what a mild word for what she felt for him. Bewitched. Enchanted. Mesmerized. All too mild for what she felt for this man.

He walked to the stream and rinsed his hands before settling once more against the palm.

"I apologize for not helping."

"I'm just doing what you hired me to do." He picked up a piece of wood from the sand beside him.

An obligation. She was nothing more than an obligation. As she watched, he continued whittling as though he didn't have a fear in the world, at home in this savage place. He had saved her life, he had risked his own life, battled a savage for her, and all because of an obligation. Nothing more.

From the treetops came deep-throated barks. Kate jumped, spilling a few pieces of papaya on the leaves beside her.

"Night-howling monkeys," Devlin said, smiling at her. "Harmless."

"Harmless," she repeated, resisting the urge to run to him, to huddle at his feet and press against his leg like a frightened child. "My father is probably out there, hiking through the jungle, looking for us." She tossed the fruit she had spilled into the fire.

Devlin nodded without looking up from his work. "I doubt he'd sit still while you're lost. I'd guess we'll meet up with them in two or three days. Depending on how much progress we both make."

"I hope they're all right."

"I wouldn't worry. They're better equipped than we are."

Were they? Somehow she doubted they were better equipped than Devlin McCain. How many of the men she knew could survive in the jungle with only a knife and his wits? Not many. It occurred to her that there was no one she would rather be with in this savage paradise. And he was with her because of money.

Her appetite gone, she walked to the stream, tossed the remaining fruit into the water, and rinsed the plate and her hands. Moonlight flowed through the trees, casting her image on the water, where it was swept away by the current. She felt like plunging into the stream, allowing the cool current to sweep away the horrible turmoil inside her.

Never in her life had she tried to attract a man. And now, when she most wanted to make a man think she was special, she was utterly, completely at a loss.

"Your bath will have to wait until morning."

She glanced over her shoulder and found him watching her, his expression unreadable. "Yes, I'm afraid it will."

She stood, shaking the cool water from her hands. She dropped the plate on the ground beside him, then glanced around the small campsite, looking for something, anything to take her mind off Devlin McCain. Nothing, not a book, or a game, or any diversion. But then, she had been trying in vain for the past few weeks to keep her mind off Devlin McCain, and she had failed miserably.

"Here, this should help."

She glanced over her shoulder, wondering if he had read her mind. He was holding out a piece of wood for her to take. As she drew near she noticed the wood had been shaped into a wide-toothed comb. She took the comb from his fingers and stared down at the finely carved rosewood; the handle was even curved to fit easily into her palm. Staring down at the thoughtful gift, she felt the horrible bite of tears in her eyes. Mr. McCain did his job well. He could make her feel he actually cared about her.

"Thank you," she whispered, turning away from him.

She sank to the carpet of leaves near the fire and fought the foolish emotions swirling inside her. What did it matter if he thought of her only as an obligation? She grabbed a handful of her hair and started slashing at the tangled tresses with the comb. It was better this way. A business arrangement.

No threats to her heart. No romantic entanglements to ruin her plans. Much better this way. The comb caught in the thick tangle of gold, tugging her scalp, dragging a groan from her lips.

"If you aren't careful, we'll be cutting that comb out."

From the corner of her eye she saw him move toward her, a casual flow of raw, masculine power in each long stride.

"Let me." He knelt beside her and lifted the tangle of hair from her hand.

She caught herself taking a deep breath, trying to capture the intriguing essence of his skin. "Perhaps we should just use your knife and hack it all off."

"Now that would be a crime." He sat on the ground behind her, the heat of his body, warmer than the fire, radiating deliciously against her back.

"You like my hair?"

With gentle fingers and a wealth of patience he began untangling the comb. "I like your hair."

She smiled, gathering that small compliment the way he was gathering her hair in his hands, as if it were precious and fragile and beautiful. She had always disdained women who sought after compliments. And now look at her. Strange, how he had turned her inside out and upside down.

He worked the wide teeth of the comb through the tangles, starting at the bottom, working his way upward. Soft tugs, nothing harsh, nothing painful, long fingers easing their way through the tangles, exerting a rhythmic pressure against her scalp. Soon the thick strands dangled freely in his hands, and still he combed the heavy cascade of gold.

Kate closed her eyes, surrendering to the luxury of having his hands in her hair. She could just feel his knees sheltering her hips, inches away from her. Cushioned between his warm body and the fire, she wanted to stretch, like a kitten in the sun.

"Sunshine." Devlin lifted her hair, allowing the strands to capture the firelight. He followed the tumble of gold as it spilled through his fingers, watching the play of light in the golden filaments. "You have sunshine in your hair."

She tilted back her head. Her eyes were closed and she was smiling, a satisfied curve of lush, pink lips. Devlin drew the comb down through the luxurious cascade of gold, the silky strands coming alive in his hands, reaching out for him, stroking his bare chest. His muscles tightened in response.

Within him desire stirred, the passion for her that was always there, throbbing like an open wound. He lifted a handful of gold, brushed the smooth silk against his cheek, breathed in the rose fragrance of her. He wanted to wrap that golden skein around his shoulders, press his lips to the hidden warmth of her neck. "Like a fairy princess."

She glanced at him over her shoulder, her sunshine hair framing her beautiful face, thick, dark lashes raising just enough to give him a glimpse of the blue sky of summer in her eyes. "Mr. McCain, I never would have guessed there was a romantic hiding beneath that gruff exterior."

"I guess we all have something to hide."

"Yes, and yet you leave me so few secrets."

"I'm not sure I understand what you mean."

She turned toward the fire, shielding her face in the tumble of her hair. "You have a way about you, Mr. McCain. A way of stripping a person bare. Sometimes I think you can read my mind. I find it . . . disconcerting."

Devlin stroked her hair, the strands following the comb, clinging to his hand. There were times when he could read her. He knew women well enough to recognize desire when he saw it.

Slowly, he drew the comb from her crown to the ends of her hair, stroking her back, her waist, her hips, through the curtain of gold. She arched in response, drawing back her shoulders, lifting her hips.

Desire. She shimmered with it. He could see it in the way she moved, the way she looked at him when she didn't think he would notice. He could smell it on her skin, that warm, sultry fragrance of feminine arousal. Yet he could sense nothing more. None of the depth of feeling he craved from her.

"Why did you come to Brazil?"

"I met a man who said we could make a fortune in Brazil, panning for gold." He continued combing her hair, knowing he should stop. Yet it felt too good, the golden strands sliding through his fingers, shimmering strands of silk warming his skin. "I didn't have anything to lose, so I bought a ticket and came along for the ride."

"The British Council told us your partner died in the jungle."

Devlin's jaw tightened when he thought of the investigation into Gerald's death, the condemning glances cast in his direction even after he had been officially cleared of any wrongdoing. "What else did they tell you?"

"Only that he was killed by a poisoned dart."

"He was killed on the way back to Pará. Three days before we reached civilization."

"I'm sorry for insisting you come back into the jungle. I know how difficult it must be."

"No one put a gun to my head. You don't have anything to feel sorry about." He lifted a handful of her hair, breathing in the scent of roses. A man could get all tangled in the silky strands, and never want to find a way to escape.

"Are you going to stay? In Brazil, I mean."

"No. I'm going to take that fat check you're paying me for this little excursion and buy a piece of lush California land."

She straightened, drawing away from him. "I don't think you need to comb my hair anymore, Mr. McCain." She tugged her hair from his grasp and pulled it over her shoulder as she spoke. "You've done a fine job of untangling it."

He frowned, sensing her barely restrained anger. Just what the hell had he done? "My pleasure."

"If you'll excuse me, I think I'd like to go to bed now." She came to her feet and marched to the shelter, pausing at the entrance. Without looking at him, she continued. "I hope you realize I do not require you to sleep in the open. I understand we must share the shelter. Good night."

Devlin stared at the entrance of the little hut. She had disappeared into the shadows, but he could hear her, hear each movement of her body against the banana leaves.

So she thought he could read her mind. Well, right now he was drawing a blank in the mind-reading department. She was angry—furious, unless he missed his guess. But for the life of him, he hadn't any idea why.

He tossed an armful of dried palm fronds and vines on the fire, watching the sparks fling upward toward the dark sky. For a long time he sat beside the fire, listening to the night sounds, the tumble of water over the rocks, the screech of birds and monkeys, the rustle of a woman turning on soft, fragrant leaves. When he thought she was asleep, he entered the little hut.

Kate was lying on her side, her head resting on her arm, one knee thrust upward toward her pert little nose. A woodland nymph, sleeping in her forest nest. Firelight flickered through the entrance, stroking her skin with gold.

For a long time he stood at the entrance watching her sleep, imagining what it would be like to hold her, to wake her with kisses. In time, when he could keep exhaustion at bay no longer, he lay beside her, turning on his side with his back to her, giving her as much room as he could in the snug hut.

He closed his eyes and tried not to think of her lying warm and inviting just a few inches away. He was just drifting into a welcome slumber when he felt a slender arm slide around his waist. A vibrant warmth snuggled against his back, soft breasts burning him through his shirt. The unmistakable press of feminine thighs brushed against his.

She slid her hand across his chest as she brushed her lips against his neck, the soft touch stealing his breath. His heart crawled into his throat. Her soft fingers grazed the waistband of his trousers; there they came to rest. Exhaustion was no refuge from the sudden searing flames licking at his loins.

"Kate," he whispered, unsure of what he would do if she answered him. He couldn't remember the last time he was

in bed with a woman and didn't know what to do with her.
It was damn unsettling.

A warm sigh against his neck was her only response. She
was asleep.

Sleep. God help him, he wasn't going to get much of it
tonight.

Chapter Sixteen

Kate stretched her arms wide in the warm summer sun. The apple orchard spread out in all directions, and the fruit was huge and ripe, hanging from the thick trees, bending boughs until they were about to break. She was hungry, so very hungry. The apples surrounded her, reaching out for her, their rich fragrance heated by the summer sun, beckoning her.

Hunger beat inside her like the deep chiming of a church bell on Sunday morning. And the apples stirred in the breeze, great, shining orbs of scarlet. The taste of cider streaked across her tongue. Hunger filled her, consumed her.

One apple dipped lower as she drew near, deep scarlet, plump, ripe amid dark green leaves. She lifted her hand, reaching for that shiny fruit. Yet as she touched it, the scarlet began to dissolve, sticky, moist, dripping on her hand, sliding down her outstretched arm. The apple turned on the branch, the round fruit changing in her grasp, molding into the head of a serpent, white fangs dripping blood.

Kate came awake with a start, a sudden jolt of fear that sucked the air from her lungs, that jerked every muscle and sent her heart careening into the wall of her chest. She lay for a moment, gathering her senses, trying to shake free of the fear.

Only a dream. A dream brought on by hunger and fear and the snake that had bitten her. No, it was a vine, Austin had said. *And I'm still alive to prove his words.*

It was dark. Through the entrance of the hut she could see the fire still burning, red and gold flames lapping upward toward the dark sky. She reached for Devlin, her hand sliding over the cool leaves that had cushioned his body. He was gone.

She needed to see him. She needed to know she wasn't alone. She stumbled out of the shelter, searching for him. The campsite was deserted. Devlin would never abandon her, she thought, fighting the nagging fear that chilled her like a cold December wind sweeping across the moors.

"Devlin, where are you?" she whispered, moving toward the blessed light of the fire, glancing around as though she expected the devil to leap out at her. Firelight flickered against the shutters of the forest, unable to penetrate the dense shadows.

"Devlin!" Again her voice was no more than a whisper. Why was she whispering? There was no one to disturb, no evil being to awaken, she assured herself, glancing around the campsite. And yet she couldn't bring herself to raise her voice. She didn't want anyone or anything to notice her.

Devlin's clothes lay on the sand by the stream, his knife, still cradled in the sheath, on top of the neat pile. She ventured toward the stream, walking on the balls of her feet. Something moved near the waterfalls. She sank to her knees, crouching low, making herself as small as she could, and peered through the darkness.

Devlin stood beneath the waterfalls, his palms pressed flat against the rocks, his head bowed. The moon poured silver into the water tumbling over the rocks, the sparkling light cascading over his shoulders, down the curve of his back, tumbling into the pool, bubbling all around him, greedily lapping at his naked hips.

Kate tried drawing air into her lungs, but it caught in her throat. Here, in his element, the raw beauty of nature a backdrop to the savage perfection of this man, he stole her breath. Looking at him kindled heat deep within her, a heat that chased away the last traces of icy fear.

She moved closer, taking refuge behind a clump of bushes growing near the stream. She should leave him, allow him some privacy. It wasn't right, this spying on the man. Yet when she thought of returning alone to that cold hut, of denying herself the beauty of this moment, all thoughts of propriety dissolved into insignificance.

He tilted back his head, lifting his face to the deluge. His arms were taut, the muscles in his shoulders stretched and corded with strain, his hands pressing into the stone. He seemed in pain, in agony. She could feel it, and with that feeling came an overwhelming need to comfort him.

She stood. It was then that she noticed the shadow moving in the water, the sinewy, dark shape moving toward Devlin. In the moonlight she could see the blunt head of the anaconda, the long, undulating body.

"Devlin!" she screamed, but it was too late. As Devlin turned toward her, the serpent coiled around his legs. She saw the startled look on Devlin's face, heard his low groan before the snake knocked him off his feet, throwing up a great plume of silvery water.

"Devlin!"

He broke the surface of the water, lunging upward, struggling in the grasp of the snake. He had his hands around the constrictor's huge head, but the snake was coiling once more, wrapping around Devlin's chest. A horrible scream—her own—split the air.

Kate turned from the horrifying scene. She ran back to where Devlin had shed his clothes. She slipped the knife from the sheath in one smooth motion, the steel glittering in the moonlight, and then she was running, splashing through the water, headed for Devlin.

She reached them as the snake was dragging Devlin under. She saw the look of pain on Devlin's face, heard the breath whooshing from his lungs.

"No!" she screamed, sinking the blade into the snake's body once, twice.

Devlin reached toward her. "The knife," he murmured, his voice dying with his dissolving breath.

She turned the heavy blade, thrusting the handle into Devlin's hand. The serpent lashed out with his tail, striking her chest. Pain flared in her and she reeled, plunging backward into the water. Water filled her nose, burning like acid. She broke the surface of the water, coughing. Beside her the water roiled. In the moonlight she saw a scarlet stream drift like a banner in the current.

She pressed both hands to the sides of her head and screamed, sheer terror washing over her. Devlin rose from the water, the snake slipping away from him like the darkness sliding away from the rising sun. He stood gasping for breath, his shoulders curled forward, his chest rising and falling with each ragged breath.

"Thank God you're all right."

He moved his lips, yet nothing escaped but the horrible, ragged sound of his breath.

"Devlin? You are all right, aren't you?"

He groaned, his legs buckling. She caught him, steadying him with one arm tight around his waist, one hand braced against his shoulder.

"I don't know what you were thinking," she said, her voice sharp from her fear for him. She dragged his arm over her shoulders. "Bathing alone in the dark. For heaven's sake, you should have more sense."

He didn't respond, except for that thready sound of air wheezing in and out of his lungs. Broken ribs. Punctured lungs. Good heavens, what would she do if he were badly injured? He made it as far as the fire before he collapsed, taking them both down to the carpet of banana and palm leaves.

"Devlin!" She grabbed his shoulders, trying to roll him to his back. If his ribs were broken, his own weight would drive the fractured pieces into his lungs or his heart.

A long exhale of breath escaped his parted lips as she shifted him. He flopped on his back, one arm outstretched. The firelight illuminated the dark red lashes around his waist and chest.

Fear coiled around her heart, squeezing until her chest ached. With trembling fingers she traced the ridge of each rib, feeling for jagged edges. "You can't die on me, Devlin McCain. You can't!"

Gradually the throbbing of blood in Devlin's temples faded. As his senses began to sharpen, he became aware of soft strokes brushed against his ribs, gentle, warm fingertips drawn across his skin. He opened his eyes. His vision cleared to reveal the sight of Kate leaning over him.

The firelight flickered against her face, a gentle pulse of gold against ivory satin. She looked concerned, fiercely determined, her brows drawn into a frown, her soft lips pulled into a tight line.

The damp white cotton of her shirt molded her breasts. Rosy tips pressed in hard little buds against the sheer cloth. Ivory skin gleamed through the tattered edges of the garment. Bewitching. She was so close, if he lifted his head he could press his face against her soft breasts. Ah, she was far too tempting. He tried to breathe, slow and steady, but his lungs wouldn't obey, too taut to accept more than a trickle of air.

She glanced up, as if she sensed him staring at her.

"Thank God," she whispered, cupping his cheeks in her hands. "Are you all right?"

Her breasts grazed his chest, her warm skin radiating against his naked flesh, luring him. He tried not to think of his need for her, the love he felt, the lust surging inside him.

"Are you in pain?"

God, he was in pain, but he wasn't sure she would understand his suffering. And he knew there was nothing either one of them could do about it. "I'm fine. Just had the wind knocked out of me."

"Are you sure? Your ribs, do you think any are broken?"

He bit his lower lip as she brushed her soft hand over his ribs. "I don't think anything is broken."

"When I saw that snake . . . I thought . . . couldn't you wait until morning to bathe?" She sank back on her heels. "What were you thinking?"

"I guess I forgot the first rule of survival. Never let your guard down."

"Please don't ever do that again. Please don't take chances with your life." She leaned forward, her damp hair tumbling across his chest. "Promise me you won't take chances with your life. Promise me!"

Devlin brushed his fingers over the curve of her cheek. There were tears in her eyes, tears clinging to the thick fringe of her dark lashes. "I promise."

She slipped her arms around his neck and sank against him. "I don't know what I would do if something happened to you."

He held her, her tears scalding his shoulder, her body trembling against him. It had been his burning need for her that had driven him into the cool water of the stream, his need that had almost cost them both their lives.

"I'm sorry, Kate." He slid his hand through her hair, smoothing the golden tangles.

"So am I. I didn't mean to sound so cross. I don't mean to be crying." She took a deep, shuddering breath. "I never cry. But I guess you won't believe that. I always seem to be crying on your shoulder."

"I don't mind."

"You don't?"

"But I'd rather see you smile. You have a pretty smile, Professor." Her lips moved against his shoulder, and he hoped what he felt was her smile.

"I never thought I was a coward, and yet I feel so inadequate. I feel as though I've fallen through a rabbit hole and ended up in another century. I feel as though I should be wearing animal skins and carrying a club."

"You've held up just fine, Professor. You've nothing to be ashamed of." He stroked her shoulder, the curve of bone delicate beneath his hand. "A man couldn't ask for a better traveling companion."

"Really?" She lifted her head to look into his eyes.

"Really." He saw her smile before she buried her cheek against his neck.

"You were right about this place." She smoothed her hand across his shoulder. "It strips away everything but the basic human needs. It makes you think about dying, and how precious life really is. It makes you think about time, and how we all take it for granted. You know, there's always tomorrow, always time to do those things you mean to do."

He held her tighter, pressing his lips to her temple. A fragile trace of roses teased his senses. He had always lived from moment to moment, a man without a home, just doing what he had to do to survive, living on scraps of memories and dreams. And here he was, holding everything he could ever dream of, thinking of tomorrow and the day after and every day of his life.

"Are you sure you're all right?" She slid her hand down his ribs as she spoke, spreading heat across his skin. And the heat kindled flames inside him.

He closed his eyes, fighting the desire that flared within him. "Yeah, I'm fine."

"Devlin," she whispered, her lips against his neck. The heat of her sigh entered his blood like a stream of fire. "I like feeling your arms around me. I always feel safe in your arms."

Devlin closed his eyes. Safe. He should tell her to go back to the hut. He shouldn't hold her, not another moment. He wanted to warn her. He wasn't safe; he was dangerous, too filled with need, too filled with lust.

"I don't want to die without ever having known what it's like to make love with you," she whispered against his skin.

Seductive words, stoking the heat blazing within him. Dangerous words.

She kissed his neck, soft, moist kisses. Devlin's breath caught in the tangle of emotions in his chest. She explored his body, her hand sliding across his chest, testing the curls beneath her fingers. His body responded without thought, his muscles tensing beneath her hand, blood rushing, heat escalating, scorching the denials he knew he should speak.

"You don't have to love me, Devlin. I won't ask for promises, I swear." She pressed her lips beneath his ear and flicked the tip of her tongue against his sensitive skin, raising gooseflesh along his shoulder. "But I want to know. I need to know. Please, don't let me die without ever knowing the mystery."

"Don't." He grabbed her shoulders. He sat up, dragging her with him. She didn't resist his hold, sitting beside him, her hip against his, her lips parted, her eyes darkened by the desire he could feel throbbing inside her. "You have to stop this."

"I see." She closed her eyes. "You don't want me."

"God, Kate." He tightened his hands on her shoulders. "I want you more than I've ever wanted anything in my life."

She looked up at him, her blue eyes reflecting her confusion. "Then why won't you make love with me?"

"I don't want you to do anything you're going to regret. And if you start this, I'm not sure I can stop."

"The only regret I'll have is if you turn me away." She smiled, a trembling curve of her lips that was at once shy and seductive. "I'm not a child, Devlin. I'm a woman who wants to know what it feels like to truly be one. Show me. Teach me."

He watched as she tugged the laces of her shirt, her fingers trembling, parting the linen, giving him a tantalizing glimpse of smooth, ivory skin. Behind her the fire blazed, forming a golden nimbus around her head, an angel offering him a taste of heaven.

He dropped his hands. "Tomorrow, you'll—"

She pressed her fingertips to his lips. "No talk of tomorrow. There is no tomorrow. Only today. Only this moment. Let's live for each day, Devlin. Let's devour each moment, every moment we're given."

She slipped the shirt from her shoulders. The wet silk of her tattered camisole revealed the curves of her breasts, the pink nipples that were already drawn into tight little buds.

Devlin swallowed hard, trying to find the words to stop her as she grabbed the bottom of her camisole and drew it upward over her head, baring her breasts to the firelight and his eyes. He watched her breasts rise and fall with her breath, the nipples soft rose against ivory. Heat flared inside him, melting the bars confining the awakening beast of his desire. "So beautiful."

At the soft touch of her hand on his cheek, he glanced up into her eyes. She was smiling, and in her eyes he saw the clear reflection of his own need—to be accepted, to be loved.

"When I was young, men told me I was beautiful and it frightened me. But tonight, and every night since I met you, I've been frightened you wouldn't think I was at least pretty, or in some small way desirable."

For too long he had denied himself the aching sweetness of loving her. "Kate," Devlin whispered, taking her into his arms, pulling her across his lap.

She slipped one arm around his back, the other around his neck, the silken skin of her breasts searing his bare chest. "Let's forget about the world outside of this savage paradise. There's only you in my world, Devlin. Please, make me feel beautiful, make me feel wanted. If only for this one night."

Devlin smoothed the hair back from her cheek, slipped his fingers into the thick, golden mane behind her ear, drenching his skin in the humid heat near her scalp. "I've wanted you since the first moment you came charging into my life."

She smiled. "Then take me, Devlin. Take me the way a man takes a woman he can't live without. Make me believe this fantasy."

Fantasy. Is that what she was offering him? A dream, an illusion of everything he had ever wanted in his life? And would it all vanish with the first light of day, dissolve in the ruthless reality of the sun?

"Devlin," she whispered, pressing against the nape of his neck with her hand, urging him down to her waiting lips. "Make love to me."

Fantasy. Reality. It didn't matter. He loved her, and he had the chance to show her how much he cared, the chance to show her how good it could be if they were together. And he would take the chance, risk his heart for the one chance to love her. She parted her lips beneath his, her soft sigh warming his cheek. He took what she offered, drinking sunshine from her lips, saturating his soul with her light.

"Breathe," he whispered when he realized she had been holding her breath since he started kissing her. "You'll turn blue if you don't breathe. And I've never seen a blue rosebud, have you?"

She shook her head, silky strands of hair stroking his arm. "You must think I'm terribly naive, but I've never kissed anyone like this."

Her innocence pierced his soul in ways her passion had only grazed. "I think you're enchanting." He kissed her, brushing his lips over hers. "Breathe. Remember to breathe."

"Breathe," she whispered, tugging on his nape, reaching up to press her lips more fully against his.

He traced the curve of her lips with the tip of his tongue, defining the shape and texture in his memory. He slipped inside to taste the sweetness of her mouth, storing each detail as though he would never have the chance to kiss her again. For no matter how much he wanted to deny it, tomorrow would come.

"Your skin," she whispered, pulling back in his arms. She stroked his cheek, as though marveling at the texture of his beard. "So rough."

He turned his head, sliding his lips into the cup of her palm. "I'll shave."

"No." She grabbed his upper arm when he started to lift her from his lap. "I like the feel, the differences between man and woman. You're rough where I'm smooth. You're hard where I'm soft. I want to feel it all, Devlin."

He closed his eyes, and Kate watched the play of his Adam's apple as he swallowed hard. She felt the rigid thrust of his male member against her back, and she knew she wanted to touch him there too, she wanted to explore all of him. But she couldn't ask him for that liberty, not now, not yet.

"It's like sipping fire, kissing you." She slid her hand from his smooth shoulder to one dark, male nipple, the hard nub peeking at her through a thick pelt of crisp, black curls covering warm skin. So many different textures, each part of him a revelation, a celebration of masculinity. "Kiss me, Devlin. Let me taste your fire."

And his kiss was another revelation, hard where a moment before it had been soft. This kiss was urgent, his lips sliding across hers, sucking on her lips, his tongue thrusting into her mouth as though he wanted to devour her, as though he wanted to draw her into his body. And she opened to his harsh demands, meeting him, drinking his fire, feeding her own hunger, a hunger that sent her heart careening against her ribs, a hunger that grew inside her, replacing everything but the need for this man.

"Kate, my beautiful Kate," he whispered, sliding his lips down her neck.

Devlin wanted to taste her, all of her, every delicious inch of her. Breasts, plump, round, lifting to him, offering the ripe fruit of her nipples. Firelight licking her skin. He brushed his cheek against one high peak, his beard bringing the blush blooming in her skin. She moaned and tossed her head from side to side, grasping his arm, her fingers sliding against his bare skin.

With his tongue he tasted her, lapping at her nipples, first one and then the other, devouring her, until she was whimpering, until she was arching, wordlessly demanding more.

Never in his life had he hungered like this, had he wanted to consume a woman completely. Never in his life had he wanted to give every fiber of his being.

"Easy." He stroked her side, feeling her tremble at his touch. Nice and slow, as though they had all the tomorrows in the world. That was how he wanted to initiate her into this realm of pleasure. That was the gift he wanted to give her as he took the gift of her innocence.

"Let's see what you've been hiding beneath these breeches," he said, slipping the buttons free of the buff-colored cotton.

"Only a woman," she murmured, her lips curving into a shy smile. "Like any you've known."

"Like none I've ever known." She sighed and reached for him as he laid her on the soft banana leaves, a tangy fragrance escaping the green carpet. She lifted her hips as he slid her trousers over the curve of her buttocks.

He had undressed women countless times. Black silk, red satin, nothing was more provocative than these white linen drawers with the little pink rosebuds. Through the delicate cloth he glimpsed a triangle of dark golden curls, a tempting nest waiting to be filled.

He tugged free the light blue ribbon at the top of her drawers. He had never imagined innocence could be so seductive. Slowly he stripped away the damp, white linen, sliding the drawers from her hips.

In the tiny cup of her navel, he pressed a kiss, the smooth skin of her belly growing tense beneath his swirling tongue, seductive curls soft against his cheek. Ah, here he lingered. He breathed deeply, drawing the hot musk of her perfume into his lungs. Sultry arousal. Sweet, searing arousal piercing his soul.

"I'm shaking, Kate. Like a boy."

Kate stroked his black hair, intrigued by the sight of him nestled between her thighs. Not a boy. Not this man. A pagan god, she thought, an immortal claiming a mortal woman. And the way he looked at her, she felt a goddess.

She watched as he followed the slow slide of the linen he was stripping away, brushing the inside of her thighs with kisses, with the quick, hot flick of his tongue. Unexpected, no matter how many times the damp tip of his tongue touched her; each time sent a new, fiery arrow of sensation shooting along her nerves. And the brush of his hair, like black silk sliding against her skin.

And then she felt him turn his head, felt the touch of his lips against the damp curls crowning her thighs, the folds of flesh beneath. She would hold back nothing. She would embrace every nuance. She would taste this, savor this, the unfolding of the mystery. Her body tightened, throbbing like the strings of a violin stroked by a master, the music rising inside her, escaping her lips in low, shuddering notes.

Ah, Devlin, you know all of this so well.

Her soft moans sang like music in Devlin's ears. She rose and strained beneath him, the tension rising in her as he drank the dew from the secret folds of her woman's flower. He found the tight bud where he knew the sensation would flare and throb. With his lips and his teeth and his tongue he coaxed that intriguing little bud, holding Kate when she would push away from the scalding sensations.

"Stay with me, love, trust me," he whispered against the sultry curls. "Let me show you how good it can feel."

"Show me Devlin, show me everything."

Trust, complete and unflinching. He trembled at her surrender. He loved her until she cried out, until he felt her body stiffen and shudder and sparkle with the gloriousness of feminine release.

"I've waited so long." He rested his cheek against her belly, sliding his hand upward along the curve of her hip. "It seems I've wanted you a lifetime."

"From the first time I saw you," she murmured, reaching for him as he moved upward, covering her with his body, "I've imagined this."

Desire curled into a knot in Devlin's groin, a pain that throbbed and pulsed within him. He smoothed the hair back

from her cheek, her blush warm against his palm. Her thick
lashes fluttered against her cheeks, yet she didn't lift them,
as though she were too shy to look at him.

"Look at me, love." He needed to see her eyes, he needed
to see into her soul, he needed to know if there was a place
for him there.

She opened her eyes, the shimmering blue depths filled
with wonder and confusion. When he slid his hand over her
belly, she sighed. He covered the soft curls at the joining
of her thighs with his hand, seeking her entrance with one
finger. Sleek, smoldering flesh closed around him as he
entered the virginal sheath. The pain twisted inside him,
the hungry beast of his desire demanding he devour that
hot, tight flesh.

"Tell me to stop Kate, tell me you've changed your mind,
and I'll leave you." *Even if I leave the best part of me
behind.*

"No," she said, grabbing his arms. "Don't leave me."

He pushed into her, feeling the fragile barrier of her
maidenhead, the shock of his penetration drawing her hips
upward. Wood crackled in the fire beside them, surrendering
to the flames. "There's no turning back once it's done."

She ran the tip of her tongue over her lips, leaving a
tempting sheen. "No regrets."

Would there be? Should he stop? But he knew their fates
had been sealed. "Kate."

His husky whisper reached deep inside her, her name a
prayer on his lips. He kissed her softly, a slow slide of
his lips, his warm breath brushing her skin. Kate pressed
her lips against his, drawing the fragrance from his skin.
Salt and musk, intriguing, elusive tastes and scents, like
the sea mist in Cornwall, like the newly planted fields after
a spring rain. Her scent on his skin. Her essence on his
skin.

Shattering.

She knew no fear with him, only expectation, only exquisite pleasure. And his hands on her, his body pressed against

her breasts, her belly, her thighs, his heat warming her, his
fingers sliding into her, withdrawing, slowly stretching her
to receive him, teaching her the rhythm, her body lifting to
meet him.

"You know all of this," she whispered against his lips.
"You know all of this so well."

Then there was no thought, only sensation, only the
splintering of her heart and her soul, and the joining of
man with woman as he entered her, as he filled her until
she thought she would shatter and die.

Yet she did not die. She came alive, more fully alive than
ever in her life, every nerve awakening, soaring on the wings
of this fire he conjured within her. And she rose to meet him,
to dance to his rhythm, to watch the firelight blaze against his
skin as the fire blazed between them.

When the moment of release came, it consumed her in the
roaring blaze he had ignited inside her. She arched against
him, her body shuddering, clasping him with her arms and
her legs, with every muscle in her body. He tossed back his
head, firelight streaming upward along the column of his
neck, dancing on muscles corded and strained. He shuddered
against her. A low moan escaped him as he too surrendered
to the conflagration burning between them.

A deep sigh slipped from his parted lips as he eased against
her. He pressed his open lips to her shoulder in a hot caress,
his chest settling against her breasts, his heart a hard pulse
against her heart. She slipped her arms around his shoulders,
holding him, without thought, without care.

In time—an eternity—her senses cleared and sharpened,
the shattered pieces of her mind gathered slowly, until
thought once again became possible. Against her shoulder she felt the hot pulse of Devlin's breath searing
her skin, the shaky movements of his chest rising and
falling in ragged gasps against her breasts. Deep within
her body she felt him touching her. Still joined. Foreign. Compelling. Frightening. She stiffened with the
fear.

He lifted away, bracing his weight on his forearms, looking down into her face, his eyes darkened to a smoky blue. "Are you all right?"

Her throat tightened around the words she might have spoken.

"I've hurt you. I should have—"

She pressed her fingertips to his lips. "You didn't hurt me. I just didn't expect to feel so . . ." *connected to you, as if my soul had merged with your soul, as if my heart beat to the same rhythm as your heart, until there was only one heart beating.*

Dear God, she didn't want this, not this all-consuming passion. It was too demanding, too frightening. It jeopardized every thought she had ever had about the way she would live her life.

He looked vulnerable suddenly, this giant of a man who could defy savage nature with his bare hands. "Kate, I've never felt this way with any woman. I never realized—"

"No, please. No words." She saw commitment in his eyes, love in his eyes. "Please, don't say anything. I don't want words." *I don't want commitment. I don't want to think of the future beyond this savage Eden.*

He rolled to his side, taking her with him, cradling her in his arms as though she were rare and precious to him. Behind him, flames greedily devoured the wood in the campfire, the last remaining pieces surrendering with creaks and groans.

The sky was coming to life, growing lighter, indigo fading to silvery blue. Yet it seemed she was already bathed in the rays of the sun, his heat surrounding her in shimmering warmth. And she didn't ever want to leave.

Good heavens, why had she done this? Why had she opened herself so completely to this man?

"Hold me." She buried her face against his neck. "Let me sleep in your arms."

He brushed his lips against her hair. "Forever, my love."

Kate bit her lower lip and tried not to think of anything beyond this moment.

Chapter Seventeen

Kate opened her eyes to the golden glow of early morning. The cool air was growing warm; in her mind she could see the sun inching upward in the sky. Yet the warmth of the man pressing against her back rivaled old Sol.

With each breath Devlin took, his chest brushed her back, silky, black curls teasing her skin, each sultry exhale fluttering the tiny curls at the nape of her neck. Hair-roughened thighs cushioned the backs of her thighs, and she could feel his loins nestled against the soft pillow of her buttocks.

The jungle was awakening around them; a macaw screeched on a limb above their snug little hut, and somewhere in the distant emerald shadows a jaguar roared. Kate shivered and pressed closer to Devlin.

She felt surrounded by him, held like this, with one strong arm resting across her waist, his palm turned upward, a whisper from her bare breast. And it felt the most natural thing in the world to awaken like this.

She stared at his open palm, tracing his long heart line with her gaze, recalling the feel of his callused hand on her body, stroking her, inflaming her. If she pushed forward, just a fraction of an inch . . . As the thought formed, her body responded, filling his hand with her breast. Long, golden fingers curved against her white skin, and the sight triggered a tightening low in her belly.

The soft, rosy flower of her breast curled into a tight bud against his palm, releasing a delicious stream of heat into her blood. She sighed, covering his hand with hers, pressing more fully against him.

Like a cat in a beam of sunshine, she arched against him, wanting to feel the slide of his skin against hers, needing the silky rasp of black curls, the smoldering heat of golden skin—his curls, his heat, his skin. Only Devlin McCain.

Was she insane for feeling these things, for wanting him this way? This need went against her every principle, her every goal in life. This need frightened her. This need threatened her.

And yet she could no more deny this overwhelming desire for him than she could deny her body nourishment to sustain life. She refused to think of anything but her need for him, refused to allow reason and thought and logic to intrude on this wonderful feeling.

Even while he slept, his body responded to hers. He snuggled closer, his arm tensing around her, locking her against his body. He shifted his thighs against hers, black curls a rough caress against her smooth legs. She felt the blood surge in his loins, felt the rise of velvety flesh against her buttocks, felt him growing thick and rigid and ready to give her pleasure. She felt her body respond, a sweet flow of welcoming moisture. And she felt the very moment he awakened.

Hunger dragged Devlin from his dreams. A hunger throbbing in his flesh. A hunger pulsing in every inch of his body. A soft slide of silken warmth against his skin scraped his naked need, enraging the hunger clawing inside him.

He opened his eyes and found Kate peeking at him over the curve of her soft, white shoulder, a single question in her blue eyes: *Will you make love to me, Devlin?* He heard her words without seeing her lips move, without hearing her voice.

For a moment he couldn't breathe, excitement and desire stealing the air from his lungs. She wanted him. Now, in the light of morning, his beautiful Kate wanted him. It was beyond his dreams.

"Yes," he whispered, answering her silent question. "God, yes."

He moved his hips, sliding the hard length of his arousal between her thighs. Soft curls stroked him, the lush, damp heat of her welcomed him. He sighed against her neck. He pressed his open mouth against her nape, flicking his tongue against her skin, tasting the tantalizing fragrance of her hot skin, perceiving the scent of her arousal. It pulled on him, that earthy scent, tugging on his vitals, until he was pumping his hips against her, sliding back and forth across the soft, moist folds of her body, feeling her need for him in every slick stroke.

"Devlin." She moaned and arched her neck, her hand tensing on his naked hip.

He stared down at her breasts, bobbing softly with the rhythm of his hips rocking back and forth against her buttocks. The taut little nipples beckoned him.

"Look at you." He cupped the firm, white globes in his hands. "So beautiful." He squeezed the rosy tips, smiling against her neck when he felt her stiffen and moan and push back with her hips to meet his next thrust.

Kate welcomed every movement of his body. *The only people on the face of the earth.* The only man she would ever feel this with, she thought, surrendering to the sublime sensations he summoned from her soul. There could be no other after Devlin McCain.

He slid his hand down her ribs, across her belly. She knew what he had in mind, and trembled in delicious anticipation. With his fingertips he found that part of her that still remained a mystery—to her, not to him. He knew of these mysteries. He reigned supreme as master of these mysteries. As the bright, shimmering sensation spiraled upward from that incredibly small cluster of nerves, she arched against his hand, his name escaping her lips in a whimper. Oh, yes, he knew.

Devlin felt her reaching for him, trying to capture him. He turned her toward him, slipping his thigh between her thighs. He kissed her side, ran his tongue over the swell of her breast and pressed his lips to her flushed nipple.

"Inside me, please. I need you inside me."

Her words made him tremble. She closed her hand around him and led him to her entrance. He took her nipple deep into his mouth as she took him deep into the honeyed core of her feminine sheath.

Nothing had ever felt like this, he realized, sucking hard on her breast. Nothing like the pure joy of being joined with this woman.

Making love—words, before this woman—an act of coupling, before this woman. Ah, but with this woman, the words had meaning—a joining of bodies and souls, a fulfillment of dreams and hopes and wishes. She was home to him. She was life to him.

His name escaped her lips as he felt her climax shimmer around him, as he felt her body tug and squeeze and coax him to join her. But he resisted. He wanted to give her more, give her so much pleasure she couldn't imagine a world without him beside her.

He turned her in his arms, covering her with his body. Her hair formed a glittering pool of gold around her face, her skin pale ivory against the emerald leaves beneath her. For all of the tomorrows he might never have, he loved her.

He watched the wonder on her face as the pleasure rose and crested inside her over and over again, until she was pleading with him to join her, until her hands tensed on his arms and he could no longer resist. He joined her then in one last, dazzling explosion of light and heat, giving himself to her, as he had never given himself to another soul.

A sweet fragrance seeped into Kate's awakening senses. How long had she slept? she wondered, blinking the sleep from her eyes.

Orchids cushioned her cheek; they spread out beneath her, forming a soft, fragrant bed, cradling her with delicate petals. Orchids covered her, pink and white and scarlet blossoms kissing her naked arms, her breasts, her legs, each breath she took brushing velvet petals against her skin.

He had made a bed of orchids for her. Inhaling their exotic fragrance, she closed her eyes. Had she really slept in Devlin's arms? Had she really made love with him this morning? This was a dream, and she didn't want to awaken. She didn't want to face reality. Not yet.

She sensed the moment he entered the hut; she felt his shadow move across her face. Memories awakened, bringing the blood rushing to her cheeks. He had touched her, every inch of her, with his hands and his lips and his tongue. How could she face the man who knew her more intimately than she knew herself?

"I brought you some breakfast, sleepyhead."

The warmth of his skin brushed her arm as he drew near. She clenched her eyes tightly, feigning sleep, needing time to adjust to her newly fashioned state of womanhood.

"It won't do you any good." He brushed his fingertips across her cheek. "I know you're awake."

"Am I?" Kate peeked through her lashes. He was kneeling beside her, dressed in his shirt and trousers, making her feel all the more naked. And he had never looked more handsome, the harsh lines of his face softened by his warm, generous smile, making him look younger, more approachable than he had ever looked in the past. "I thought I might still be dreaming."

Orchids tumbled from her side as she sat up. She crossed her arms over her breasts, cradling orchids to her naked skin, glancing around for something to wear.

"I don't seem to have any clothes." She remembered as she spoke that he had hung her clothes on the line by the fire last night.

Last night, after she had asked him to make love to her, after he had so exquisitely obliged. Good heavens, things had changed forever. And she was only just beginning to feel the effect of those changes.

He lowered his eyes, his gaze sliding over the bouquet she held against her naked breasts, her skin rising shamelessly in pale mounds above her crossed arms. He lowered his gaze to the riot of scarlet and white and pink blossoms nestled on her lap. When he looked into her eyes, she saw the flicker of flames in the silvery blue depths. And inside, she felt the glow of answering fires.

"If you're thinking about turning shy, I have to warn you, it's far too late for that, Professor."

She glanced down at the orchids nestled in her lap, the golden curls he had touched so intimately peeking through the petals. Wanton, wicked, shameful, she should feel all of those things. But she didn't. No, she had enjoyed every second of every embrace, every kiss, every touch of his body. Oh dear, she really was a far cry from a proper English lady. "The truth is, I don't feel shy. I suppose I should, but I don't."

He lifted a lock of her unbound hair and slid the silky strands through his fingers. "Maybe because it's so natural between us. Like the sky embracing the morning sun."

Like the sky embracing the morning sun. Yet she knew the morning sky would give way to evening, and the sun would slip from its grasp.

"Maybe because you know I love you. I do love you, Kate."

Her heart stirred at his words; she felt it flutter against her chest. She stared down at the orchids on her lap, avoiding his eyes. She knew what she would see in those eyes: a future that could never be.

"The orchids are beautiful, thank you. I've never been given orchids before. I think they're exotic, don't you? So soft and delicate." She knew she was babbling. She always babbled when she was nervous. "The fragrance elusive, sweet."

He tugged gently on her hair. She glanced up, meeting the honest intensity in his eyes. "What happened last night, this morning—"

"Were the single most exciting moments in my entire life." She sensed he wanted to talk of the future. It was the last thing she wanted to discuss. "My father told me making love was an experience I shouldn't miss."

Devlin's black brows lifted. "Your father told you about making love?"

She nodded. "He's always been frank with me. When I became curious, as I suppose all young people become curious, he answered all of my questions." *But he never told me it would be devastating. He never warned me I could lose myself. He never told me I would feel as though I belonged to the man who had touched me this way.* Suddenly, she felt horribly exposed. "My clothes, do you think they're dry?"

He quickly unfastened his shirt. Golden brown fingers flicked down white cotton, conjuring the image of those long fingers curved around her breast. She watched the play of muscles in his chest, his shoulders, the intriguing dance of steel bands beneath taut, golden skin as he stripped off his shirt.

She wanted to touch him. It was all she could do to keep from touching that golden skin. It was staggering to realize the hunger to have him inside her was worse now than ever before.

He slipped the shirt around her shoulders, the cotton warm from his skin, fragrant with the spicy scent of his body. "I see you're still not willing to go native."

She was far too willing to do anything with this man. She moistened her lips. "No, I suppose I'm not."

He lowered his gaze to her lips. He tightened his grip on the shirt, gathering the edges beneath her chin. With a slow tug, he drew her toward him. Would he draw her into his arms, kiss her lips, lay her down on the soft, sweet petals? Her body trembled, responding to the promise in his eyes, a slow burn of liquid heat low in her belly, a searing sensation centered in the tips of her breasts. One touch and she was ready to join with him once more.

She turned her head, afraid of this power he had over her. If she weren't careful, she would be lost, totally, completely, absorbed into his life. She felt his hands tighten, then drop away from the shirt. When she looked up he had turned his head away from her, giving her some privacy.

She slipped her arms into the sleeves and buttoned every button. Yet feeling his shirt slide against her bare skin, inhaling the intriguing scent clinging to the soft cotton, did little to ease her discomfort. "Thank you."

He turned to face her, sitting with one knee raised. She sat on her heels, her hair tumbling in a lavish cascade of gold around her shoulders, his shirt covering her from her chin to her knees. Yet it didn't matter. She couldn't hide from him; he knew every curve of her body.

He glanced down at the tip of his bare foot, poking at a white orchid with his toes. "We'll probably meet up with your father today, tomorrow at the latest."

The world would expand once more. No longer would they be alone in the universe. A hard hand squeezed her heart at that realization.

"Kate, I'm not sure how to say this, I'm not even sure I have the right to—"

"You mentioned breakfast. I'm starving."

He glanced up, meeting her eyes. "We need to talk, Kate. We need to—"

She pressed her fingertips against his lips. "Don't you know, it's not permitted to have a serious discussion before breakfast."

"Bad breach of etiquette?" he asked, his lips moving against her fingertips.

"The worst."

He sighed, his soft breath warming her fingers. He pressed his lips to her fingertips and she snatched back her hand. If he was surprised by her abrupt withdrawal, he didn't show it. He merely smiled, a gentle, indulgent smile that spoke of warmth and love and all the things that terrified her.

"Breakfast is served, milady." He lifted a plate heaped with strips of papaya and round slices of banana from the bed of orchids at his side.

Prolonging the inevitable, Kate thought, taking the narrow wooden plate from his hand, that was all she was doing. But she wanted to prolong this time with him, if only for a few more minutes. Reality would come soon enough, crashing through the carefully built walls of this sanctuary, crushing both of them.

"Have you ever been to California?" He toyed with a slice of papaya on the plate that sat on the ground by his side. "To the rich, rolling hills and valleys near San Francisco?"

"I've been to San Francisco, but never beyond the city limits."

"I worked on a horse ranch south of the city one year when I was seventeen. It's beautiful along the coast, the air crisp with the tang of the sea, waves crashing against the rocks, fog lingering in the morning, curling around the cypress trees, turning everything into a land where even a cynic can believe in fairy tales."

His words conjured images in her mind, of a man and woman standing arm in arm in the first light of dawn, a soft breeze in their faces, watching the sky fade from indigo to silver to gold. She could feel him watching her, feel him willing her to look at him. Yet she couldn't.

"Just inland, there's a valley, lush and green, a perfect place to make a home, to raise a family."

Kate stared down at her plate. *Please don't do this. Please don't make me think of tomorrow.*

Devlin watched her closely. She was drawing away from him, physically sitting back on her heels. And within her, was she drawing back as well?

He could play it safe. He could throw in his cards without risking humiliation. And win nothing. Or he could risk every shred of his pride for one chance to have her for the rest of his life. Suddenly there was no choice.

"I love you, Kate." He knelt before her, a sweet scent rising from the orchids crushed beneath his weight. He took her plate and set it on the ground beside her. He took her hand; her fingers curled tightly into her palm.

"I want to build a home for you. I want to live the rest of my life with you." Gently he eased open her fist and pressed his lips to her damp palm. He hesitated a moment before laying all of his cards on the table. "Marry me, Kate. Come live with me for all of our days."

She whimpered deep in her throat. She slid her hand from his grasp. Instead of asking her to marry him, he might have just slapped her for the pain he saw in her eyes.

"I thought we were going to live for today," she whispered. "Must we talk of the future?"

Devlin felt his blood settle in his veins. The soft glow of hope inside him turned cold, frozen by the rejection he saw in her eyes. "What did this mean to you? Anything? Did I mean anything to you? Anything besides a man with the proper equipment to scratch that itch between your legs?"

She gasped. "How dare you talk to me like that, as though I were a . . ." She caught her lower lip between her teeth, tears glittering in her eyes. "Devlin, please try to understand."

Understand. God, he understood far too well. He was a mongrel trying to find a place beside her fire. He should have known better. He should have kept his distance.

The pain went deeper than he expected, digging into the old wounds until his soul bled. Dreams, why had he ever believed in them? Why had he ever opened himself up to this pain?

She touched his arm, her hand trembling against his skin. "Please don't be angry with me."

He was angry. Furious. He wanted to smash something with his bare hands. He wanted to toss back his head and roar his frustration, his anger, his pain.

Yet could he really blame her for rejecting his offer? Could he blame her for choosing to stay in her comfortable little world of wealth and privilege?

He looked into the summer blue of her eyes, misty now with unshed tears. In all the anger swirling inside him, through all the layers of humiliation and pain, one reality remained, shining like a single point of light in the darkness—he still loved her. Knowing how she felt about him, knowing she had used him for her own purposes, hadn't changed his own feelings. He loved her as much as before. He had a horrible feeling he always would.

"You're right, I shouldn't be angry. Hell, you told me last night what you wanted. You tried to tell me today. Fear had you thinking about all the things you might miss. And I was convenient."

She closed her eyes. "I never wanted to hurt you."

He followed a tear as it slipped from beneath the fringe of her dark lashes and slid along the curve of her cheek. "Hey, I thought you never cried." He cupped her cheek in his hand. He slid the pad of his thumb upward, capturing the glistening droplet of her tear as it reached the corner of her lips. "Don't cry, sweetheart."

"Devlin." She threw her arms around his shoulders. "I'm sorry."

Hot tears flowed against his bare shoulder as she trembled in his arms. "It's all right."

"Please, don't hate me."

"How could I ever hate you?" He rubbed his cheek against the warm silk of her hair, breathing in her fragrance. Emotions crowded his chest, pulsing there, pressing against his heart until he was sure he felt it shatter. He held her closer, wishing for things beyond his reach, wondering if he would ever again feel whole.

They hiked through the morning and afternoon, cutting a path upward along the slope of the hill leading to the crest of the falls. Kate followed Devlin, watching him swing his long knife, cutting his way through the thick vegetation, wishing she could fight through the doubts tangling her mind.

She stood at a crossroads in her life, and she wasn't sure which way to turn. What he offered was so contrary to everything she knew, everything she had always thought she wanted. She couldn't marry him. And yet how could she let him walk out of her life?

By late afternoon they had not found her father's camp, and Kate was secretly relieved. She wasn't ready to face the others yet. Not with her turmoil.

Long after they had eaten a dinner of fish and papaya, they sat beside each other watching the fire. Kate ran the comb Devlin had made for her through her hair, the heavy strands still damp from her bath. Although she had hinted for him to join her, he had been content to allow her to bathe alone, sitting on the shore with his back to the water, silently guarding her. He had been silent most of the day, withdrawn from her.

A breeze stirred the fire, lifting glowing embers into the air. She glanced through her lashes at Devlin. He was lying on his side, staring at the fire as though he could read a story there, one elbow planted on the ground, his cheek resting in his upturned palm.

The golden light of the fire flickered against his features, impressing his image upon her memory. When she was old and gray and thinking back to the different path she might have taken, she wanted memories of this man, she wanted memories so vivid, so poignant, they would sustain her all of her days.

"It's late." She stood and looked down at him.

"Sleep well."

She watched him as he kept his gaze on the fire. "Aren't you coming to bed?"

He shook his head.

Perhaps he didn't understand. Perhaps he didn't know how much she wanted to hold him in her arms, how much she craved the taste of his lips, the touch of his hands. "We'll meet up with the others tomorrow." They had seen the glow of their campfire a short distance upriver, an hour away, no farther. "Tonight might be the last night we can be alone."

He looked up at her, his eyes reflecting the firelight and a haunting sadness that made her want to cup his face between her hands and kiss him until she erased all the darkness from his soul. "Last night was our last night together, Kate."

She felt as though he had struck her, a sudden blow that drove the air from her lungs and sent the blood swimming behind her eyes. "But I thought we might hold each other."

"Hold each other. For how long? Tonight?"

"Devlin, why can't we share the time we have together?"

"One last memory, is that what you want from me, Kate?" A muscle worked in his cheek as he clenched his jaw. "I'm sorry, but I have all the memories I can manage to live with."

She glanced away from him, staring at the dark wall of the forest rising behind her. He would accept nothing less than everything. He couldn't content himself with today, with the few moments they might share. He wanted her heart, her soul, her life. He wanted to take her away from everything she had ever loved.

"Good night." She marched toward the hut.

"Good night, my love."

The deep, gravelly tone of his voice held a wealth of emotion. She hesitated, fighting the urge to run to him, to throw herself into his arms.

She couldn't give herself to him. Not as wholly and completely as he demanded. It would end tomorrow or the next day or the next week, she reasoned, forcing her feet to move, to carry her away from Devlin.

Perhaps it was better it end tonight. Perhaps, eventually, she could convince her heart it was better this way.

Chapter Eighteen

The night was finally over. Funny, it seemed longer than any night Devlin had ever known. He rested his chin on his raised knee and stared into the charred remains of the fire. The morning breeze drifted across the blackened pieces of wood, coaxing scarlet to glow deep in the heart of burnt wood and ashes, a glow that faded and died. The scent of charcoal filled his nostrils as he drew a deep breath into his lungs, leaving a bitter streak upon his tongue.

They should get started soon. The others were close. Yet he didn't have the will to move. He was tired, weary to the bone, as though all of the life had been drained from him, leaving nothing but a shell behind. Last night he had slept little more than a few hours. And each time he had drifted to sleep, dreams of Kate had tormented him.

He glanced across the camp to the little hut where Kate slept. Sunlight peeked through the leaves overhead, sprinkling golden light on the dark green leaves of the shelter he had made for her.

One last night together. How tempting her invitation had

been. More than once he had left his bed by the fire during the endless night. More than once he had gone to the entrance of that hut, had stared inside at the woman who lay sleeping, firelight slipping inside the cozy hut to stroke her face.

Inside him a terrible hunger gnawed at his vitals. He wanted to lie with her, to take her into his arms, to sink into her welcoming warmth. He could give her everything she wanted. He could have only a glimmer of what he needed.

He closed his eyes. *Forget her. Let go of the memories. Let go of the dreams.*

He wouldn't be used again. He couldn't allow himself to believe in love when there was nothing for him but lust. False hopes and dreams had almost destroyed him once, when he was no more than a callow boy. He had fewer defenses now, little to save him from Kate. If he didn't find a way to protect himself, she would destroy him, shred every last piece of his pride. He couldn't let that happen. It was better to end it now.

"Good morning."

Devlin lifted his head, his drowsy senses jolting into awareness at the soft sound of Kate's voice. She stood a few feet away, looking for all the world like a lost waif, her hair tumbling in golden waves over her shoulders, her feet bare, her clothes tattered. Too beautiful. Far too tempting. God help him.

He stared into the blackened remains of the fire and tried to kill the desire raging like a wild beast inside him. "If you're hungry, there's fruit left from last night. We don't have time for more than that."

"I see. You're extremely anxious to meet up with the others."

It was an accusation. From the corner of his eye he could see her, standing with her hands clasped at her waist, her chin tilted, the indignant schoolmarm. "I would bet your father is half out of his mind with worry."

She glanced away from him, staring down at her bare toes,

the prim schoolmarm fading into a woman who wasn't at all sure of herself.

He clenched his hands into fists on his thighs. He would not go to her. He would not take her in his arms. Because if he did, he would be lost.

"It seems I haven't been thinking much of others these days," she said. "It seems I really don't know—"

A twig snapped nearby. Devlin reached for his knife, drawing the blade from the sheath on his hips, coming to his feet in the same moment as the intruders emerged from the forest.

Two Indians in loincloths, followed by two white men. In the sunlight filtering through the trees, Devlin recognized the two men he had fought in Kate's hotel room in Rio.

One of them, the shorter of the two, was smiling as he moved toward him. The other, the great, hulking bear called Jocko, stood staring at Devlin from beneath shaggy, dark brows, as though the thing he wanted most from life was to break Devlin's back. Both of them were dressed in some type of uniform: buff-colored trousers, buff-colored shirts with epaulets and brass buttons, the material stained with sweat.

"That knife ain't gonna do you no good." Frankie pointed a pistol at Devlin's chest.

Devlin squeezed the handle of his knife, knowing he could take down one, maybe two before they killed him. But there were four of them.

"We got a score to settle, you and me, but Mr. Van Horne wants to talk to youse both." Frankie smiled, revealing bits of tobacco stuck in his yellowed teeth. "Now, if you wanna go ahead and be a hero, I'll have a good reason to shoot."

"Devlin," Kate whispered, her voice drawn taut with tension. "Don't. Please don't."

Devlin glanced at Kate, seeing the fear in her eyes, knowing there was nothing he could do, at least not now.

With every step, Kate fought the trembling in her legs, the fear that shimmied along her every nerve and left her shivering. Devlin touched her, a warm slide of his palm against her shoulder. He smiled when she glanced to where he walked beside her.

Power and strength; even now, when he stood unarmed among their enemies, he radiated the sublime confidence of a man who could survive any ordeal. She took comfort in that strength. She absorbed it, like a tender plant drinking the rays of the sun, growing stronger, strong enough to fight her own crippling fear.

It had been Van Horne's campfire she had noticed the night before. An hour through the jungle brought them to the man's camp. Leaving the shadows of the jungle, Kate blinked against the sunlight streaming through the holes in the emerald canopy overhead.

A fleet of 16 canoes sat on the narrow beach, wooden hulls dark strips against the white sand. Nearby, 20 Indians, all dressed in loincloths, sat gossiping in a circle on the sand. They glanced up as Devlin and Kate were marched into the clearing etched out of the jungle.

Two tents, similar to the ones Kate and the others were using on the expedition, flanked a white tent that was easily twice the size of the others. A banner of scarlet and dark blue fluttered in the breeze from the center pole of the main tent, lending an odd, medieval cast to the camp.

From one side of the tent, a red-and-blue striped canopy stretched to poles driven into the sandy soil, shading the man and woman who sat beneath. Quite a pair, these two, a king and queen enjoying an afternoon in their garden. Two Indians dressed in blue-and-scarlet livery stood beside the royal couple, waving palm fronds in a fanning motion, stirring the warm air, the fragrance of orange blossom incense filling Kate's senses.

"Ah, so you've finally arrived." The man stood, rising from his tapestry-backed chair.

Kate balled her hands into fists at her sides as the man drew near. She faced their tall, slender captor with her head held high, embracing her anger like a shield against the fear that threatened her.

Van Horne smiled, pale blue eyes fixed on her, a wide curve of finely molded lips in a face that might have inspired Michelangelo to paint his archangel. His hair ruffled in the breeze, straight, silken strands of gilt brushing the shoulders of his white silk shirt. He was remarkably handsome—beautiful really, Kate thought. Yet in spite of his smile, in spite of the perfection of his features, there was ugliness here, a look in his pale blue eyes, a coldness, the arrogance of a bloodless tyrant who took pleasure in his conquests.

"How I've looked forward to meeting you, Miss Whitmore, and you, Mr. McCain. Allow me to introduce myself. I'm Leighton Van Horne."

When he reached for her hand, Kate held her fists close to her sides.

Van Horne laughed softly. "I had hoped we might enjoy a cordial visit."

"You're a kidnapper, a thief." Devlin squeezed her arm, a silent warning her anger refused to obey. "I see no reason to be cordial to you. Just as I see no reason to be cordial to a snake."

Leighton's lips slowly curved into a smile, yet his eyes betrayed another emotion. Rage flamed like the fires of hell in his pale blue eyes. "There are a few things we all must learn, Miss Whitmore."

As she stood in the storm of Leighton's silent rage, the furious pounding of her heart inched upward in her chest. Demonic eyes set in an angelic face. Kate sensed the man was capable of murder, and she knew she had taken one step too far.

"Frankie, take out your pistol and kill Mr. McCain."

"No!" Kate glanced at the squat man standing beside this tall, fair-haired devil. Frankie was smiling, anxious to carry out any lesson Van Horne might intend to teach.

"Nice going, Professor." Devlin flexed his fingers around her arm before dropping his hand.

Frankie chuckled as he withdrew his pistol from a brown leather holster belted at his waist.

"He's done nothing to you." Kate held Van Horne's icy gaze. "I'm the one who made you angry."

"Lessons." Van Horne waved his hand elegantly to dismiss her argument.

"Leighton, please." The soft plea came from Leighton's companion. The woman was standing, staring at Devlin, large, dark brown eyes wide with fear.

"I'm sorry, my queen," Leighton said, glancing over his shoulder. "I must deny you this time. Frankie, put a bullet through Mr. McCain's heart."

"With pleasure, boss." Frankie smiled widely as he pointed the pistol at Devlin's chest.

Devlin tensed beside Kate, ready to lunge forward into the gunman. He wouldn't make it. He was too far away. Devlin would be dead before he reached the gun.

A metallic click, the chamber sliding into place. Kate moved without thought, throwing herself against Devlin's chest, shielding him with her body.

"No!" Devlin shouted, his voice overlapping a woman's scream as he wrapped his arms around Kate.

Distantly Kate realized the shrill screech had come from the dark-haired woman behind Van Horne.

Devlin pivoted, putting his back to the gun. Kate fought to pull him out of the line of fire, but everything was happening too quickly.

Devlin toppled her, dragging her with him toward the ground, protecting her with his body. The gun exploded. Devlin jerked against her.

Pain shot through Kate's hip as she hit the ground. Devlin's body fell across her, forcing the air from her lungs.

Above them, parakeets shrieked and swarmed from the trees in a wave of green and yellow. The excited murmurs of the Indians mingled with the blood pounding in Kate's ears.

Wisps of thought pierced the fog of fear clouding Kate's brain. She was alive. She hadn't been shot. But Devlin lay still, covering her with his body, his deadweight pressing her into the sandy soil.

"Devlin!"

Slowly, Devlin raised his head, frowning as he looked down into her face. "Are you all right?"

She nodded. "Are you?"

"Just what the hell did you think you were doing?" Devlin demanded, the look of concern in his silvery blue eyes changing into anger.

"Saving your life, Mr. McCain," Leighton said. "It seems Miss Whitmore is very fond of you. Fond enough to risk her life for you."

Kate glanced past Devlin to where Leighton stood with his hand wrapped around Frankie's wrist, forcing the pistol toward the ground, gray smoke trailing from the tip of the black barrel. The dark-haired woman stood beside Leighton, her eyes closed, her smooth cheeks bleached of color.

"Now, Miss Whitmore, perhaps you will join us for a cup of tea," Leighton said, smiling down at her. "Or haven't you learned the wisdom of cooperating with me?"

Kate bit her lower lip, fighting the angry words she longed to sling at this man.

Devlin must have seen the mutiny in her eyes. He spoke before she had a chance to betray them both. "How could we resist such a gracious invitation." He stood and helped Kate to her feet.

"Oh, but I'm being rude." Van Horne turned to face the lovely woman at his side. "Lady Judith Chatham, allow me to introduce Katherine Whitmore and Devlin McCain."

"Lady Judith." Devlin smiled and took her hand.

As Kate watched, the color returned to Judith's cheeks as though she were blossoming in the light of Devlin's smile. And his smile was so warm, so generous, so appreciative of this woman's charms. Kate had an almost uncontrollable urge to slap that smile right off of his lips.

"Please, do be seated." Leighton gestured to the tapestry-backed chairs under the canopy, red and blue roses stitched against a dark green background.

Kate gripped Devlin's arm as she walked past Van Horne.

Strength and bravery; she desperately wanted both. But Leighton Van Horne made her skin prickle with apprehension. It was like being trapped in a room with a cobra, sensing he would strike anytime he chose, knowing you were powerless against his venom.

"We met once before, Miss Whitmore," Leighton said, falling into step beside Kate, Lady Judith on his arm.

"I'm afraid I don't remember."

"Last year. I attended a lecture your father presented at the British Museum. 'Ancient Myths of England and the Atlantis Connection,' that was the topic, as I recall. I've read all of your father's books." Leighton gestured for Kate to take a seat in one of the five chairs under the canopy. "His theories are fascinating."

"I'm sure he would be flattered to know you think so kindly of his theories." Devlin held one of the chairs for her before he settled into the chair beside her, a small folding table separating them.

Leighton laughed as though he were enjoying a private joke. "Joaquin, tea for my guests." He waved his hand toward a young Portuguese boy who sat cross-legged on the carpet beside Leighton's chair, dressed in the same livery as the Indians. The boy sprang to his feet and disappeared around the side of the tent.

Across from Devlin sat Lady Judith, studying him as though she were committing his every feature to memory. She seemed fascinated with the man. The woman couldn't have been any more obvious if she wore a sign around her neck: *I want you, Devlin McCain*. Kate glanced at Devlin, wondering what he thought of the lady's obvious infatuation. He was watching Van Horne, his expression revealing nothing.

"You look very familiar to me, Mr. McCain." Leighton stared at Devlin. "I wonder if we've ever met before."

"I doubt we travel in the same circles."

Leighton laughed softly. "I travel where it pleases me."

"What is it you hope to gain, Mr. Van Horne?" Devlin

crossed his long legs and leaned back in the chair. "Why is Avallon so important that you would risk your life on this quest through the jungle?"

"Do I detect a note of cynicism, Mr. McCain?" Leighton pressed his fingertips together, forming a steeple beneath his chin. "Yes, I can see you have doubts Avallon even exists, and yet you have come on this dangerous quest. Perhaps I should ask you why. But then, we know, don't we? Money, that time-honored persuader."

Kate clenched her hands, her fingernails digging into her palms. Didn't Van Horne notice the way his woman was looking at Devlin? And if he did come to notice, would he have Devlin shot out of jealousy? She stared at the other woman, willing her to leave Devlin McCain alone. Judith glanced at her, then lowered her eyes as if embarrassed to be caught in such open adulation of Devlin McCain.

A rattle of china heralded the boy's return. He carried a silver tray—laden with a silver tea set, cups and saucers, and a plate heaped with thin slices of pound cake—that seemed too heavy for arms no bigger around than Devlin's wrist. After setting the tray on a folding table between Van Horne and Lady Judith, the boy began to serve, asking Kate and Devlin what they would like in their tea, strutting like a pompous rooster in his attempt to mimic an English butler.

Devlin glanced down to the Persian rug that was spread across the rough ground. Sunlight slanted beneath the canopy, streaking across threads of scarlet and varying shades of blue that formed the intricate patterns in the carpet. The rug and the furnishings were opulent and impractical. This was the way a sultan would travel through the jungle, he thought.

Devlin accepted a delicate cup and saucer from the boy. "From the looks of things, I'd say you already have money. So what is it, Van Horne? What are you after?"

Leighton lifted his spoon from his cup of tea, watching the drops of creamy liquid slide from the silver back into the ivory cup. "Ah, there is more to this world than money,

Mr. McCain. Think of what might be waiting for us in that lost city, the mysteries we might discover."

Devlin stared at the gold necklace around Lady Judith's neck, ornately carved, a relic of Egypt, perhaps. "And treasures you might be able to carry home."

"Yes, the treasures." Leighton smiled at Devlin over the rim of his cup, a twisting of lips that left his eyes as cold as the devil's heart.

Devlin sipped his tea, the hot liquid soothing his parched throat. Across from him, Lady Judith Chatham sat staring down at her tightly clenched hands. Her dark hair was swept back from her heart-shaped face and caught in an elegant roll at her nape. Dressed in a gown of mint green linen, she looked like a lovely lily in this virulent garden. Beautiful. Delicate. How did a woman like that end up with a man like Van Horne? "You're risking a lot for a fairy tale."

Leighton shook his head. "I'm surprised the lovely Miss Whitmore hasn't convinced you to believe in fairy tales."

Devlin glanced into his cup, a muscle working in his cheek as he clenched and unclenched his jaw. The lady had made him believe all right, if not in Avallon, then in his own private fairy tale. A mistake he didn't plan to repeat.

Leighton set his cup and saucer on the table beside him. "Joaquin, fetch my writing case for Miss Whitmore."

The boy dashed inside the tent, returning a few moments later with a leather case. He took Kate's cup and saucer, placing them on the small folding table between her chair and Devlin's before he opened the case and placed it on her lap.

"Now, I'm sure you won't mind drawing a map to Avallon for me, Miss Whitmore," Leighton said. "I know we're close and I'm growing weary of following your little group. I hate taking the risk of losing you in the jungle."

"How do I know you'll let us go if I give you the map?"

"Do you have a choice?" Leighton leaned back in his chair and smiled his devil's smile. "You know I'll kill Mr. McCain if you don't cooperate."

"And if you murder him, I'll never give you the map."

"So you think you have me at a stalemate, do you?" Leighton slid his palms together, smiling as he held Kate's gaze. "It can take a long time to kill a man, Miss Whitmore. Frankie is an expert at the sport. He can peel the skin from a man without killing him. At least, not right away."

Devlin saw the fear in Kate's eyes when she looked at him, the silent questions. And he was fresh out of answers. If she didn't give Van Horne the map, Devlin was sure he would face that slow, ugly death. If she gave him the map, Van Horne might decide to kill him quickly. Either way, his life expectancy didn't extend beyond the next few hours. And Kate. What did the bastard intend to do with her?

"I guarantee in the end you will give me the map, and Mr. McCain will know agony before he dies. Do you think you can watch while his blood slowly drains from his raw, exposed flesh?"

Kate glanced down to the open writing case on her lap. "No."

"I didn't think so. Now, be a good girl and draw the map for me."

How would Van Horne know if she gave him the proper directions? Devlin wondered. And yet he felt certain Van Horne would know. He had sat across the table from too many gamblers not to know when a man was holding a royal flush. He glanced at the empty chair on Kate's right, a premonition of disaster scraping his nerves like nails drawn across a blackboard. He had to find a weak spot in their defenses. He had to get Kate away from this bastard. And fast.

"There is really no point in trying to deceive me, Miss Whitmore." Leighton gestured toward Frankie. The stout man nodded and started lumbering toward the tent. "You see, I'm holding more than one trump card."

Devlin watched Frankie disappear into the main tent, his muscles growing tense. A few moments later, Frankie emerged from the tent. He wasn't alone.

Chapter Nineteen

"Father!" Kate lunged from her chair, spilling the writing case, indigo ink spreading in a dark stain across the scarlet-and-blue carpet. As her father limped toward her, she rushed to meet him.

"Katie." Frederick caught his daughter in his arms. "I was so worried about you."

"Are you hurt?"

"My feet are filled with pins and needles from being tied, that's all." Frederick glanced over Kate's head to where Devlin was sitting. "Devlin, I'm glad to see you're all right. The others are here too. They came upon us the first night we went searching for you. No one's been hurt. At least, not yet."

"And I'm sure your daughter wants to keep it that way," Leighton said. "Joaquin, Miss Whitmore needs fresh paper and ink."

The boy scooped the writing case from the carpet and scampered around the corner of the tent. Kate's stomach drew up into a tight knot as she watched Van Horne take a folded sheet of paper from a pocket in his white linen trousers.

"Your father has already been gracious enough to draw a map to Avallon." Leighton held the folded parchment between his thumb and forefinger. "If your map is different, I will execute a member of your party."

Kate looked up at her father. "Did you give him the real map?"

Frederick frowned. "I didn't think it would be wise not to. But . . ."

"What?"

Frederick rubbed his chin, his dark brows pulling together over his troubled brown eyes. "I might have missed a few things."

"We shall soon see." Leighton gestured with the map toward the chair across from him. "Please, Miss Whitmore, I grow weary of this delay."

Kate sat on the edge of the chair across from Van Horne. Her father sank into the chair to her right. How exact need the maps be? And if they were the same, would any of them walk away from Leighton Van Horne alive? She glanced at Devlin, seeking some reassurance. He was staring down at the empty cup he held in his hands, barring her from his thoughts.

When Joaquin returned with another writing case, Kate took up the task of drawing a map to Avallon, aware she might hold Devlin McCain's life in her shaky hands. Quickly she etched the path that would lead to Avallon. When she was done, Joaquin took the map and delivered it to his master.

Kate sat with her hands clenched in her lap, watching Leighton Van Horne compare the two maps. He glanced at her, his blue eyes as bleak as ice floating in the Thames. Her breath caught in the tangle of fear crowding her throat.

Very slowly Van Horne's lips curved into a smile. "Well done, Miss Whitmore."

Kate released her pent-up breath, her muscles relaxing, trembling from her effort to keep her emotions under rein.

"But I'm afraid you were right all along. I intend to kill all of you." Leighton rose to his feet, a king rising from his throne. "Frankie, start with Mr. McCain."

"No!" Kate shouted, springing to her feet.

Frankie drew his pistol from his holster. She ran for him, her gaze fixed on that deadly, black pistol.

"Kate, get down!" Devlin shouted.

She glanced toward Devlin. Her father seized her from behind, wrapping one arm around her waist, grabbing her arm, keeping her from the line of fire. The chamber clicked into place. She screamed, staring at Devlin, knowing in another heartbeat a bullet would slam into his chest. She had to stop this!

Devlin's arm shot back and came forward so quickly Kate barely saw the missile he fired at Frankie. She heard a thud, coupled with a low groan. She glanced up in time to see Frankie crumpling toward the ground, blood spilling from a gash on his brow, Devlin's china teacup on the ground at his feet.

The gun discharged as Frankie hit the ground. The bullet slammed into the leg of Kate's chair, splintering the wood, the chair collapsing on one side.

"Jocko!"

A strangled cry brought Kate's gaze around to Leighton Van Horne. Devlin had his hands around the man's neck. Leighton's blue eyes bulged wide with fear, scarlet stained his cheeks, horrible gurgling sounds escaped his parted lips along with a single stream of saliva.

Jocko lumbered toward them, drawing a pistol from a holster at his thick waist. Kate glanced back to the pistol in Frankie's hand.

"The gun!" She pulled against the hold her father still had around her waist. "I have to get the gun."

"Yes, yes, of course," Frederick said, releasing her. He lunged forward, reaching for Frankie's gun at the same time Kate did, slamming into her shoulder, knocking her off balance.

Kate fell against the overturned chair, banging her knee on the carved rosewood. Pain flared as she careened onto the carpet, landing on her bruised hip. She rolled to her side, holding her throbbing knee, staring in horror as Jocko brought the butt of his pistol down across the back of Devlin's head.

A moan slipped from Devlin's lips. He slumped forward, into Leighton Van Horne's arms. Muttering an oath, Leighton thrust forward, sending Devlin tumbling to the carpet.

Frederick snatched the pistol from Frankie's limp hand and turned. But it was too late. Before he could raise the gun, two Indians had his arms, wrenching the pistol from his grasp, taking him prisoner.

As Kate struggled to her feet, Judith sank to her knees beside Devlin's still form. She cradled his head in her lap. "Mr. McCain," she whispered, touching his cheek.

"Devlin." Kate staggered to his side. She dropped to her knees, wincing as she hit the carpet.

Judith stroked Devlin's face, touching his lips, his cheeks, slipping her hand into his hair. Jealousy congealed inside Kate, drawing into a thick lump in her chest, pressing painfully against her heart. "Take your hands off him!"

Startled, Judith withdrew her hand from under Devlin's head, revealing a moist sheen of blood on her fingers. "My goodness," she whispered.

"Devlin!" Kate pressed her hand over his heart.

"I'll make him regret the day he was born," Leighton said, glaring down at Devlin. "He'll beg for death before I'm finished with him."

"He's already dead, Leighton." Judith looked up at him.

"God, no," Frederick whispered.

Beneath Kate's hand she felt the steady throb of Devlin's heart. She stared at the woman across from her, wondering what game she was playing. Judith met her gaze, and in her dark brown eyes Kate saw a warning, and a plea.

"I'm sorry, Miss Whitmore, I know how much Mr. McCain meant to you." Judith took hold of Kate's forearm, slender fingers gripping tightly. "I know you would have done anything to save his life."

Kate followed Judith's lead, not knowing where it would take her, sensing it was a chance to save Devlin. "Yes, anything."

"The bastard," Leighton said, rubbing his throat.

Judith gently eased Devlin's head from her lap and came to her feet. "Leighton, I think you should kill these people quickly."

Kate stared at the woman. She felt as though she had just stepped off the ledge of a high cliff. For one moment she had imagined the woman was on their side.

"Think of the hardships they would suffer if you left them here without supplies, without rifles." Judith rested her hand on Leighton's arm. "You should kill them now, quickly, painlessly."

"Painlessly?" Leighton glared at Kate. "And what have they done to deserve my mercy?"

"But think of what you would be doing to them if you abandoned them here, in this wilderness." Judith brushed her fingers back and forth across the bruises on his neck, scarlet lines left by Devlin's fingers. "Why, I'm afraid it would be a horrible death, at the hands of savages, or wild animals, or starvation. It's unthinkable to leave them here alive."

"Yes, it would be horrible." Leighton stared for a long moment at Kate, his pale eyes venomous, his lips a demon's smile. "What a splendid idea you have given me, my queen." He grabbed Judith's hand and kissed her fingertips. "We will leave them here, without a rifle, a canoe, or a piece of bread."

"But Leighton, you can't. Think of—"

He silenced her with a raise of his hand, a king that had issued his decree. Judith glanced down, catching Kate's gaze, amusement and triumph in those dark eyes. Unless Kate missed her guess, the Lady Judith Chatham had just tricked Van Horne into doing exactly what she wanted him to do. They would have a chance to survive. A small chance, but a chance nonetheless. Kate glanced down at Devlin, praying he would stay still until these people were gone.

"Jocko, get that trash out of my sight." Leighton swept his hand toward Devlin.

Kate glanced up as Jocko moved toward Devlin. "Don't touch him!"

Jocko didn't hesitate. He clamped one huge hand on Kate's shoulder and pushed her away from Devlin as though she were no more than a fragile willow in the path of a giant. She stared in mute horror as Jocko tossed Devlin over his shoulder. One loud sigh, one moan, and Devlin would truly be a dead man.

Nothing. Not a soft sigh escaped Devlin's parted lips. Kate scrambled to her feet. She followed on Jocko's heels as the big man carried Devlin across the campsite. He walked a few yards into the jungle before dumping Devlin onto the vines covering the ground. A soft moan, deep and masculine, exploded like gunfire in Kate's ears.

Jocko froze above Devlin, cocking his head as he stared down at the unconscious man. Kate moaned deep in her throat, drawing Jocko's attention. "You've killed the only man I've ever loved."

Jocko frowned, the heavy folds of his brow nearly obscuring his small eyes.

"Leave us. Go!" She sank to her knees beside Devlin, moaning as deeply as she could, praying Jocko was slow-witted enough to believe the noise he had heard had come from her and not from a "dead man."

"Devlin, oh, my darling," she wailed, leaning over Devlin's body, hiding the soft rise and fall of his chest from Jocko's mean little eyes.

The crackle of twigs breaking under the big man's feet as he returned to camp was a symphony to Kate's ears. She glanced over her shoulder as Jocko left the path and headed back to his master. Gently, as if he were made of delicate glass, as if he might shatter at any movement, she lifted Devlin's head and shoulders, cradling him on her lap.

Through the spindly fronds of a young palm, she watched as Jocko marched the others of her party from the main tent, each of them with their hands still bound. Austin looked around as he emerged from the tent, searching the campsite, his gaze fixing on the entrance of the jungle path.

He couldn't see her; the foliage was too dense. Yet he seemed to look straight through the dense, green cover. There was a sadness in his eyes, a deep soulful sadness, as if he were mourning, as if he had lost someone dear to his heart. One of the Indians prodded him in the back with a rifle.

Austin turned, an aggressive move that made his guard jump back and clutch his rifle.

"Don't!" she whispered, praying Austin wouldn't do anything rash.

Frederick stepped between Austin and the man holding the rifle. He said something to Austin, who nodded and turned away from the guard. They marched to where the others were standing at the edge of the river. She could see Leighton Van Horne on the far side of the campsite, giving orders, the Indians scurrying at his command.

She looked down at the man lying unconscious on her lap. "You're going to be all right," she whispered, stroking his cheek, her voice no more than a sigh on the breeze. "You have to be all right. You promised to take me to Avallon, remember? And you are a man who keeps his promises."

She smoothed the damp hair back from his brow, the silky strands curling around her fingers as though they had a life of their own. A single tear fell from her eye to puddle on his cheek, glistening in the narrow stream of sunlight that streaked through the leaves overhead to find Devlin.

"I never cry." She pressed her lips to that glistening droplet, tasting the salt of his skin mingled with her tear. "At least I didn't before I met you. You've turned me into someone I don't recognize. Do you know that? Do you know, I wanted to break that woman's arms when she touched you?"

She cupped his cheek and brushed the corner of his mouth with her thumb. "Jealousy. What a horrible emotion. Useless. Harmful. Stupid. And all because of you."

He turned his head, a sigh escaping his lips, his warm breath brushing the soft skin of her wrist, and deep within her she felt the flicker of flame. "Ah, Devlin, I have a horrible feeling you're going to haunt me until I take my last breath."

A twig cracked nearby. Kate glanced over her shoulder, fear for Devlin flooding her like a torrent of Arctic water. Had Jocko returned to check on them? No, the figure Kate saw moving toward her was the small, delicate figure of Lady Judith Chatham.

"How is he?" Judith kept her voice low.

"Alive because of your kindness."

Judith closed her eyes, a ragged sigh escaping her lips. She took a moment to collect herself before she spoke. "I brought you this." She slipped the leather sheath containing Devlin's knife from the folds of her skirt. "I'll hide it here, in case Leighton or one of his men comes to check on you before we leave." She slipped the knife and sheath into a tangle of vines a few feet away, concealing the weapon from view. "Leighton has agreed to leave behind a few of your belongings, the tents, your trunks."

"You convinced him to do that?"

She nodded. "He's been through your belongings, so he knows there aren't any weapons, nothing to really help. He's doing it as a concession to me, a grand gesture to show how generous he can be. I'm sure he feels leaving behind a few comforts will only prolong your suffering in the end."

"He enjoys giving pain."

Judith nodded. "I wish you well." She looked as though she wanted to say more. Instead, she turned to leave.

"Wait," Kate said, her voice rising just above a whisper.

Judith hesitated before she turned to face Kate. She looked uncertain, like a young girl facing a parent's censure.

"Thank you seems so inadequate for what you've done."

Judith shook her head. "Please know, I have no choice but to stay with Leighton. He has made certain I can never leave." She stood for a moment staring down at Devlin, longing naked in her sad, brown eyes. "You're a very fortunate woman, Miss Whitmore. I would give my soul to have a man like Devlin McCain look at me the way he looks at you. Take good care of him."

Judith turned and rushed back along the rugged path. The steamy air turned cold in her wake, so cold it froze Kate deep inside. "She's in love with you," she whispered, sliding her fingers across Devlin's cool cheek.

Someday Devlin would marry. He would find a woman like Judith, a woman who would give everything she owned just to be by his side, a woman who would have his children, grow old with him.

Devlin's words echoed in her memory, each one a blade slicing her heart: *Marry me, Kate. Come live with me for all of our days.*

"It would never work." She traced the curve of Devlin's lips with her fingertip, his breath a warm whisper against her skin. "We're too different, you and I. We want different things from life." Tears slid unchecked down her cheeks. "You wouldn't be happy in my world, and I wouldn't be happy in yours. We both know it. And yet, how am I going to live without you, Devlin McCain?"

Devlin.

The voice came from a distance, filtering through layers of darkness, brushing Devlin's mind. Someone was calling him. Someone needed him. Kate. He had to go to her, something was wrong, she needed help. But he was so tired, and the pain hovered there in the darkness, pressing upon him like a slab of granite. Too thick. He couldn't claw his way out of the darkness.

Devlin.

Her voice came again, a thread of shimmering silver slicing through the inky layers of darkness and pain.

Please wake up, darling.

Her voice was a beacon, a bright, silvery beacon. He had to reach for that light. If he didn't capture that light, he would never leave the darkness. He would never see Kate's face again.

Devlin, please don't leave me.

In his mind, Devlin reached for that shimmering strand of silver. As he touched it, the light expanded, silver tumbling over him, filling him. Light flowed through his veins, warm, glowing silver seeping into his pores, saturating the pain, until he was nothing but shimmering silver light.

Sunlight. He felt the warmth of sunlight on his face, saw the glow of sunlight teasing his closed lids. When he opened his eyes, he stared up through a shaft in the dense cover of leaves, the clear blue of the sky, the golden glow of sunlight flooding his dazed vision. Someone moved, a face blocked the sunlight, a golden nimbus framing the face of an angel.

"Thank God," Kate whispered, cupping his cheek in her hand.

When he parted his lips to speak, she pressed her fingertips against his lower lip.

"No more than a whisper. If they hear you . . ." She swallowed hard, as though she couldn't force the words from her throat. "No more than a whisper."

At the moment he wasn't capable of more than a whisper. "What did you hit me with this time, Professor?"

"I didn't. Do you remember what happened? Do you remember Van Horne?"

"Where is he?"

"Still in camp. A few yards away."

Devlin drew a deep breath and tried to sit up. Her slender hand on his shoulder was enough to overpower him. He fell back against her lap, panting from the exertion.

"Don't be a hero, Mr. McCain. You'll only end up getting yourself killed."

"I'm nobody's hero." He couldn't fight the lead weights dragging at his eyelids, pulling them shut. "Remember?"

"I remember too much." She stroked his temple, a soft brush of warmth.

"I'll never forget," he whispered, before succumbing to the siren call of unconsciousness.

For more than an hour, Kate stared through the slivers of foliage, catching glimpses of what was happening in the camp, while Devlin slept in her arms. After Van Horne's elaborate campsite was dismantled and loaded on his fleet of canoes, he sauntered toward the men assembled on the beach. Kate held her breath, a feeling of impending doom closing around her, thicker than the hot, humid air.

Van Horne said something to her father and the other men, but he was too far away for her to catch his words. And then he was raising his arm, giving a signal to his men. At his command the Indians pushed four canoes into the water, allowing the vessels Devlin had acquired in Santarém to catch the current. Van Horne's laughter carried on the warm breeze as the canoes were swept out of sight. Waving farewell, he boarded his own canoe and led his small fleet upriver.

With his hands still bound behind his back, Austin started running toward the jungle path, her father following him. The others remained by the river, staring into the dark, churning water as though they were attending their own funerals.

Austin disappeared from view. A few moments later he reappeared, moving steadily on the jungle path, light and fleet, barely disturbing the vines beneath his feet. He paused a few feet away, staring at Devlin, a look of anguish on his features, and something else. Guilt?

"This shouldn't have happened," he whispered, moving toward Kate, his gaze fixed on Devlin's face.

"Austin, he's—"

"Alive." Devlin opened his eyes.

Austin's entire body sagged with the sudden relief Kate could see on his face.

"Alive?" Frederick said, coming up behind Austin. "I don't understand."

"Lady Judith was on our side." Kate stroked Devlin's cheek, his day-old beard rasping her palm. "She pretended he was dead."

Devlin dragged himself to a sitting position, clasping both hands to the sides of his head. "I'm getting damn tired of people thumping me over the head."

"This is one time you can be thankful for a thick skull." Frederick patted Devlin's shoulder, laughing at the doubtful look Devlin gave him. "I'll tell the others. They'll be relieved to know you're alive."

"Katherine, can you release the rope from my wrists?" Austin asked, as Frederick hurried down the jungle path.

Kate quickly retrieved the long knife Judith had hidden. The razor-sharp blade sliced through the rough hemp of Austin's bonds, revealing the ugly red marks on his wrists. He grimaced as he rubbed the raw skin. "How did you manage to hide that knife?"

"Lady Judith. We owe her our lives. She managed to manipulate Van Horne into abandoning us in the wilderness." Kate glanced over her shoulder at Devlin; he was watching her, his expression shuttered. A single strand of sunlight, all that slipped past the canopy of leaves, embraced him, spilling in a golden caress across his features.

"What's a woman like that doing with Van Horne?" Devlin asked, rising to his feet, swaying unsteadily.

Kate darted toward him, but the look in his eyes brought her up short. Good heavens, he didn't want her to touch him.

"From what I've heard in London, Van Horne has a penchant for ensnaring the aristocracy, or anyone who suits his fancy," Austin said. "I suspect Lady Judith was vulnerable."

"You know her?" Devlin ran a hand through his tousled mane, exploring the lump at the back of his head.

"We met briefly a few years ago, before she was married."

"And Van Horne?"

"I've seen him at several gatherings," Austin said, a frown etched deeply between his black brows.

From the expression on his face, Kate had the impression there was something Austin wasn't saying, something that worried him.

Austin glanced down at his raw wrists. "Since he moves in the highest circles in London, it's hard not to run into him."

"The highest circles," Devlin murmured, his gaze resting on Kate, his pain clear in his silvery blue eyes.

She took a step, moving toward Devlin, wanting to throw her arms around him. But it wasn't possible. A chasm had opened between them, a chasm filled with the jagged pieces of broken dreams. She knew she could bridge that chasm. She didn't know who she would become if she did.

"I was worried about you," she said, looking up into his eyes. Where once she had looked into his eyes and glimpsed a soul filled with the brilliance of love, she now saw only the surface beauty of his eyes, the varying shades of gray and blue, like storm clouds surrounded by the deep indigo of an evening sky. "Are you going to be all right?"

"I'm fine, Miss Whitmore."

So cold, so formal. He had withdrawn from her, completely, irrevocably, and she didn't blame him. She wished she could apologize, but she could find no words to apologize for how deeply she had wounded him.

"Your head," she whispered, wanting desperately to touch him, fearing he might back away from her.

"Hard enough to take a few knocks. Don't worry about me, Professor, I can take care of myself."

Without another word he walked away from her. She stared after him, watching each fluid movement of his powerful body, remembering, knowing she must forget the feel of his arms around her, the taste of his lips, the exquisite sensation of having him move inside her. She must forget the memories she had tucked away so carefully for safekeeping, the memories that felt like splintered shards of glass inside her.

Chapter Twenty

Pity. He had seen pity in her eyes, Devlin thought as he marched from the jungle. An aristocrat staring at a ragged beggar, that was what he had seen in her eyes. For too many years he had seen that look in people's eyes when they glanced at the young boy in shabby clothes.

And now, to see it in Kate's beautiful eyes . . . God, he wouldn't have it. He couldn't stomach her pity. His muscles tightened; he could feel the pulse throb in his neck, the strain of containing his emotions. He felt raw and bruised and ready to tear something apart with his bare hands.

He stepped from the shadows of the jungle path into the bright sunlight flooding the clearing. The blazing light blinded his throbbing eyes, freezing him in a column of gold. He blinked against the light, looking around the campsite, wondering how deep Van Horne had dug the pit in which he'd tossed them.

Frederick and Edwin stood by the river, arguing, their voices carrying on the thick, moist air. Barnaby stood beside Frederick, watching the two men like a referee in a fight ring. Robert Melville sat under a palm tree a few yards away from his father, sitting with his head back against the trunk, watching the two men with a look of amusement on his face. The Indian paddlers he had hired in Santarém sat in a close circle on the far side of the deserted campsite, heads bowed, voices a low murmur. No doubt debating how to desert them.

"We are this close." Frederick lifted his hands to indicate a foot of space between them. "I can't believe you want to turn back."

Edwin shook his head. "And what if we run into Van Horne again? He'll kill us all this time."

"We've come too far to give up now." Frederick pulled his handkerchief from his pocket and began mopping his brow as he continued. "Another two weeks at the most, and we'll be there."

"If we put together a raft, we can float down the bloody river. We have a chance if we turn around."

"I really believe we can—"

"Saints preserve," Barnaby said when he saw Devlin. "It's good to have you back with us, lad."

"There he is," Robert said as Devlin drew near. "Our fearless leader, risen from the dead."

Robert's sarcastic tone teased the anger Devlin was trying so desperately to control. He turned slowly, aiming his gaze at the young man.

"So tell us, oh great jungle prince," Robert said, blind to the rage simmering just beneath Devlin's calm surface. "How are you going to get us out of this hell?"

Devlin smiled, a slight twisting of his lips. He had known men like Robert all his life: born of wealth and privilege, filled with the arrogance of a spoiled child, certain of their elevated station in life. Little boys masquerading as men. "We could always try what the Indians do."

Robert frowned, the first signs of unease showing in his face. "And what is that?"

"Appease the river-god." Devlin stalked the other man.

Robert moistened his lips. He glanced behind Devlin to his father before craning his neck to look up at the man towering above him. "And just how do they do that?"

Devlin rested his hand on the rough trunk of the palm and leaned over the sitting man, blocking the sunlight slanting through the leaves overhead, shrouding Robert in his shadow. "They choose a sacrifice, someone useless to the tribe. After they bind his hands and feet, they toss him into the river and watch him drown." Although Devlin had never heard of such a ceremony, the idea appealed to him at the moment.

Robert sat with his back pressed against the tree trunk, staring up at Devlin, beads of sweat breaking out above his upper lip. "If we were in London, McCain, I'd . . ." He flicked his tongue over his lips. "Someone should teach you how to talk to your betters."

"Someone needs to show me one first." Devlin wanted Robert to pick up the challenge. Right now he was itching for an excuse to plant his clenched fist in the center of this wealthy young man's face. "You think you can do that?"

Again Robert moistened his lips, his tongue darting like a lizard's between his dry lips. "I don't expect you to understand, but gentlemen do not brawl like savages."

"I've never claimed to be a gentleman, Melville. You should keep that in mind."

Devlin dropped his hand, the blood throbbing in his fingers from the pressure he had been exerting against the tree trunk. He turned and found Frederick and Edwin staring at him as though he were a keg of dynamite that might explode at any sudden move. They expected him to get them out of this mess. And he was wasting time wallowing in anger and self-pity. Two emotions he detested. God, the woman had him tied into knots, and he wasn't sure he knew how to break free of the tangle.

"Mr. McCain, I was just telling Frederick I think we should make a raft and float downriver." Edwin dragged the back of his hand over his brow, wiping away sweat as he spoke. "I'm sure you will agree, continuing would be foolhardy."

Devlin hadn't expected Melville to give up so easily. Still, there was logic in the argument; they knew what was behind them, but they didn't know what lay ahead. He looked at Frederick. "What's your thinking?"

"We're so close, Devlin," Frederick said, his deep voice rough with emotion.

"Close to disaster," Edwin said. "What do we do if we run into Van Horne? We don't have so much as a slingshot."

"There are weapons we could make," Devlin said.

Edwin stared at Devlin. "You can't mean you want to go on. You haven't believed in this expedition from the beginning."

Devlin sensed Kate approach, felt the heat of her body warm the breeze touching his neck. Each day of this trip would be worse than the last, each day of being near her without being able to touch her would be a blade sliding between his ribs. Still, he knew what this trip meant to Frederick; he knew what it meant to Kate. "I was hired by Mr. Whitmore to take this group to a place called Avallon. If he decides he wants to turn back, then we'll turn back. Otherwise, I'll do what I can to get us there."

"Do you believe in Avallon, Mr. McCain?" Kate asked, her soft voice stroking his back.

Devlin glanced over his shoulder. Sunlight poured into the clearing, tumbling over her, glinting on the gold of the tiny curls framing her beautiful face. Austin stood beside her, looking every inch the man who belonged there.

She belonged with the aristocracy, Devlin thought. He had been a fool ever to imagine he could pluck his beautiful rosebud from her English garden. He was ten times a bastard for ever allowing the fire to consume him. He should never have touched her. He should never have felt the soft yielding of her body close around his. Because he was doomed now, doomed always to remember the passion that had flamed between them, the passion that was no more than lust in Kate's heart.

"I believe in doing the job I was paid to do, Miss Whitmore."

Devlin turned back to face Frederick, hiding his pain behind a calm mask. "What is it going to be?"

Frederick looked at Kate and Austin. "You both know how I feel. This has been a dream of mine for too long to even think about giving it up. But I can't make that decision for either of you. Do you want to go forward or turn back?"

"If Mr. McCain thinks he can get us to Avallon, then I think we should continue," Kate said.

"I agree," Austin said.

Barnaby moved to Frederick's side. "That goes for me."

"This is madness." Red flags of color rose high on Edwin's thin cheeks. "We can't possibly continue."

"Edwin, you can take several of the Indian paddlers if you like," Frederick said. "They can put together a raft and go with you and Robert back to Santarém."

Edwin glanced to where his son was sitting beneath the palm tree. He stared for a long time, his shaggy brows pulling together over his sharp nose. "I think we'll take our chances with the rest of the group."

Frederick squeezed his friend's arm. "You're making the right decision."

Edwin cast his friend a dark glance before turning his gaze on Devlin. "So tell us, Mr. McCain, how do you plan to get us to Avallon?"

"There's an Indian village near the base of the falls. I think I might be able to convince them to part with a couple of canoes. In case I can't, I'll have the Indians start work on a dugout. I should be back in a week." Devlin glanced at the river, sunlight glinting on the swiftly flowing current. "If I'm not back in two, there's a good chance I'm not coming back."

"You intend to leave us here." Kate moved to his side, the warmth of her skin whispering against his arm.

Devlin kept his gaze fixed on the rippling water. "You'll be safer here."

She stepped in front of him, forcing him to look at her. "I think we'll be safer if we all stay together."

"You'll slow me down."

She lifted her chin, her eyes glittering with determination. "Better you return a few days late than not at all, Mr. McCain."

"She's right, Devlin," Frederick said. "I don't like the idea of you going alone. Too many things could happen. I'd feel better going with you."

Austin echoed Frederick's sentiment. Although Barnaby wanted to go along, Devlin asked him to stay with Robert and Edwin. Someone needed to keep the Indian paddlers and the three Portuguese servants they had hired in Santarém under control.

Devlin resigned himself to a difficult journey through the jungle, made all the more torturous by one beautiful English rosebud. "We'll make camp here tonight and get started early tomorrow."

Kate paused on the edge of the forest. She stared into the small clearing, listening to the rush of water tumbling over rocks, wishing for a way to escape the emotions swirling inside her. She had known they would come upon this place. It had taken only a day, and with every step she knew they were drawing closer and closer. Yes, she knew they would come upon this place, but if she had anything to do with it, they wouldn't make camp here.

She glanced to where Devlin stood near the charred remains of their camp fire. He was staring at the narrow falls, the water splashing over dark gray rocks, catching the golden rays of the late afternoon sun. Was he remembering?

"This must be where you made camp," Austin said, glancing back at Kate.

This is where we made love. The memories were so vivid here, they shimmered like ghosts in the sunlight, ghosts she couldn't escape. Austin was watching her, a curious look in his gray eyes, waiting for an answer.

"Yes, we camped here the first night out of the Kuraya village," she said, keeping her voice flat, expressionless, hoping to hide the tension drawing taut inside her.

"It's a perfect campsite." Frederick walked toward the hut Devlin had fashioned a lifetime ago.

"There's still a few hours of daylight left," Kate said, following her father, drawn like a mourner to a lover's grave.

Frederick paused outside the entrance to the little hut. "Katie, we'll need time to find dinner and lay a fire. I don't want us to be in the middle of a thick tangle of jungle when the sun sets."

"There are other clearings along the way." Although still green, the banana leaves covering the top of the hut were curling at the edges, dying.

"I don't understand why you want to continue tonight. We're all tired."

How could she begin to explain? Unable to help herself, Kate looked inside the hut. Orchids still littered the banana leaves on the ground, petals shriveled now, drained of life. Although she fought the memories, she couldn't force them into a shadowy corner of her mind. Too vivid: delicate petals caressing her skin. More vivid still: Devlin, his strong hands stroking her, his warm lips brushing her skin, kissing her, adoring her.

"Orchids?" Frederick asked, his voice far too gentle.

She met his look, seeing the questions in his eyes, the answers he already knew. "Yes," she whispered, feeling the heat rise in her cheeks.

Frederick smiled, a wistful curving of his lips. "Perhaps later, we can talk."

She didn't want to talk about what had happened in this place. She didn't want to think about it. Too painful. Too tempting. "Do we have to stay here?"

"It's late, Katie. It would be too dangerous to continue."

Truths, only a few of the many she needed to face. She glanced over her shoulder, wondering if staying here would be as painful for Devlin as it was for her. He was standing beside the stream, talking to Austin. Cast in profile like two Roman coins, it struck her how similar these men were, both tall and lean, with black hair and blue-gray eyes, noses straight and thin, cheekbones carved high. They could be related, perhaps brothers. Yet they were from different worlds.

If only Devlin could trade places with Austin Sinclair. If only he wanted to live in London, and travel, and . . . if only she didn't want the wrong man.

Devlin glanced at her, as though he felt the strong pull of her gaze. For a moment their eyes met, his stormy, as though he could see the ghosts haunting this place as clearly as she could. Yet before he glanced away, the expression shifted in his eyes, grew hard with conviction. He could forget what they had shared. He would forget her. And somehow that realization made her want to strangle him.

Devlin stood in the stream, bamboo spear raised, watching, waiting for the shadow of a fish to draw near. From the corner of his eye he could see Lord Austin Sinclair, standing as Devlin was with spear raised, hunting for dinner. To the monkeys chattering in the trees, they would seem equal, Devlin thought, casino owner and English marquess. And as much as he hated to admit it, Austin Sinclair fit well into both worlds. He also had to admit that if Lord Gallant walked back to camp empty-handed, Devlin wouldn't mind at all.

Something soft brushed Devlin's calf just below his rolled-up trouser leg, an orchid. He plucked the flower from the water, the withered blossom drooping in his grasp, the white petals edged in brown. As he watched, a bouquet drifted past him, a cluster of orchids, colors faded, fragrance spent, as dead as his dreams.

He glanced upstream to the campsite. Kate stood beside the water, head bent as she tossed decaying flowers into the water, somber, as though she were attending the burial of a loved one.

Devlin glanced down at the flower he held in his hand, a knot of pain tight in his chest. He slid his thumb over the damp petals, wishing he could bring life to the delicate blossom, knowing it was beyond his power. He tossed the flower into the water, where it swirled with the current that carried it away from him, carried it toward Austin Sinclair.

Austin didn't seem to notice the orchid, too intent on his task. With the reflexes of a jungle cat, he lunged forward with the spear, driving the point Devlin had whittled into the water. A moment later he pulled the spear from the stream, hefting a plump, three-pound fish into the air, its silver scales glistening in the sunlight.

"Dinner," Austin shouted, smiling as he waved the wiggling fish in the air.

"Great," Devlin said, returning Austin's smile. He glanced down at the water and murmured under his breath. "Just great."

Kate glanced up from the rippling water of the stream as she felt her father draw near. He was watching her as though she were a particularly interesting artifact he had recently drawn from the earth, a puzzle he would soon unravel. She stiffened, sensing he intended to unearth matters she wanted to bury. "I'll gather more wood for the fire."

"The fire can wait awhile," he said, slipping his arm around her shoulders.

She felt exposed, as though all of her secrets were being dragged from the shadows. "It will be late soon. We should—"

"Talk about what happened between you and Devlin."

"Father, I . . . I don't want to talk about Devlin. I don't want . . ." *to think of him, to remember things I should forget.* "Please, just let it pass."

He took hold of her shoulders when she tried to walk away from him. "I didn't think he was the type of man who would hurt you. I thought he was honorable, but if he took advantage of you, if he has no intention of doing the right thing, I'll have a discussion with the man."

"Devlin McCain did not take advantage of me, Father. He never tried to touch me."

Frederick frowned. "Katie, something happened between you. I can see it."

Kate stared at the top button of her father's sweat-stained white shirt, still fastened at his throat even though it was hot enough to blister during the day. "I seduced him," she said, her voice barely rising above a whisper, the shame of her actions constricting her throat. "And afterward, he asked me to marry him."

Her father opened his hands on her shoulders before he gripped her chin and forced her to look up at him. He was smiling.

"The first moment I met the man, I had a feeling about him. I knew he was right for you."

Kate shook her head. "You don't understand. I don't want to marry him. I don't want to marry anyone."

"You don't love him?"

"Love him? I barely know him." And yet, in a way, she knew him more intimately than anyone else in the world.

"I knew your mother less than a week before I asked her to marry me."

"You and Mother wanted the same things from life. You were meant to be together. What I feel for Devlin McCain is different. It's true, I desire him." *It's true I crave the sight of him, the touch of his hand, the sound of his voice. I want to bury my face against his neck, draw his scent into my lungs. I want to kiss him, taste him, hold him in my arms.* "But it isn't love." *It couldn't be.*

"I wonder." Frederick turned toward the stream. He stared for a long time at the glittering cascade of water tumbling from the river above before he spoke. "Love is rare, Katie. If you find it, you should take hold with both hands and never let go, hold it, nurture it, and see how love can change your life."

"I don't want to change my life. I like the way things are."

Frederick released his breath in a long sigh. "Then perhaps you don't love him." He looked at her, his brown eyes filled with grief. "Because if you did, you couldn't imagine life without him."

Life without Devlin McCain—the thought drove a spear of pain through her heart. And yet she couldn't turn away from everything she had always wanted from life. Devlin McCain would absorb her, obliterate everything that was Katherine Whitmore. He would take her away from her father, from her work, from everything that had ever mattered in her life. And in turn, she would end up breathing for him, existing only for him. His power over her was that strong.

No, she couldn't allow it to happen. She would forget him. She would conquer this obsession she had with the man.

Chapter Twenty-one

Devlin rolled the bamboo spear in his hand, turning the two fish impaled on the bamboo over the fire—two of the five fish Austin had caught. Next to him Lord Sinclair sat cross-legged on the fresh banana leaves they had both gathered, supporting a bamboo spear on his knee, holding the other three fish over the flames. Three papaya, that was all Devlin had been able to catch all day.

"Something has been bothering me." Frederick peeled one of the papaya, the long blade of Devlin's knife reflecting the dying rays of the sun. He sat across the fire from Devlin, his back braced against a palm tree. "It's been nagging me ever since we ran into Van Horne. I keep thinking about—"

"I'm going to take a bath," Kate said as she emerged from the hut, a towel and fresh clothes draped over her arm, a cake of soap in her hand. "So, gentlemen, please keep your backs turned to the stream."

"You should wait until morning." Devlin glanced up at her. "It'll be safer then."

"It's still light." She continued walking toward the stream,

297

obviously intending to ignore his warning.

Devlin laid the fish on the leaves and stood, blocking her path when she tried to walk past him. "Do you remember the anaconda we met the last time we were here, Miss Whitmore? Wait until morning."

Kate stiffened. "I don't care to be ordered about like a child, Mr. McCain."

"An anaconda." Frederick stared at his daughter with wide eyes. "Katie, perhaps you should do without a bath tonight."

"Unless I'm mistaken, each of you took a bath in that very stream." Kate's chin took on a mutinous tilt as she glanced from her father to Austin. "Since it wasn't too dangerous for you, it isn't for me." Her eyes were glittering with barely restrained rage when she looked up at Devlin. "Now, I intend to have my bath."

The scent of roses drifted from the soap she held clenched in her hand, teasing Devlin's senses. "Miss Whitmore—"

"Mr. McCain," she said, her voice dripping frost.

Somehow they had taken a turn and ended up where they had begun—feuding strangers forced to share their days and nights. Devlin could almost believe it had all been a dream, an illusion. He could almost believe he had never held this woman in his arms.

"Unless you intend to physically restrain me, I am going to have my bath."

Devlin frowned, fighting the urge to toss the little professor over his shoulder and carry her back to the hut. What came to mind after that was the main reason he sank to the banana leaves and allowed the stubborn female to pass. "Be careful."

"I appreciate your concern," she said, her voice telling another story.

Devlin thrust the fish back over the fire, listening to Kate's movements as she walked into the bushes behind him. Frederick quickly adjusted his position, moving to sit between Devlin and Austin, putting his back to the water.

"She always did have a strong will." Frederick grinned as Devlin looked at him.

"Stubborn." A soft whisper of clothes being draped across a bush not more than 20 feet away, a woman stripping away her clothes. Devlin clenched his jaw, trying to exile the images igniting in his mind.

"You were saying something was bothering you, Frederick." Austin kept his eyes focused on the fish he was roasting over the fire as though his life depended on keeping his gaze fixed on those fish.

Splash of water. In Devlin's mind he could see her walking toward the waterfalls, water sparkling in the sunlight, caressing long, shapely legs, lapping at smooth, satiny thighs.

"Did you notice that necklace Lady Judith was wearing?" Frederick tossed papaya peels into the fire, sending sparks flying upward. He seemed completely immune to the intriguing sounds of his daughter's bath. "I swear it was the necklace Mayfield brought back from Egypt a few months ago."

"Necklace?" Austin asked, obviously as distracted as Devlin was by the soft sounds of water being splashed against smooth, ivory skin.

Devlin glanced at the man sitting beside Frederick, knowing Lord Gallant was picturing Kate's luscious body in his mind. He clenched his hand into a fist, fighting the urge to strangle the man.

"One of Cleopatra's necklaces," Frederick said. "You remember, we went to a reception to view the pieces Mayfield had found in that dig he made near Alexandria. What was it, a month before we left for Brazil? You do remember? That necklace is one of the finest pieces I've ever seen of that period."

Austin moistened his lips before he spoke. "I assumed the one Lady Judith was wearing was a replica. The real necklace is behind glass in the museum."

"I've heard of Van Horne's reputation. The man has a collection of artifacts that rivals any museum, and that's only the pieces he allows people to see. Rumor has it, he has a hidden

collection, the artifacts even more rare." Frederick sliced the
fruit, letting juicy chunks drop to one of the plates Devlin had
fashioned from a dried palm tree. "I think it's quite obvious,
he has no scruples as to how he obtains them."

"You believe he stole the necklace from the museum?"
Austin asked.

"Yes, I think he did. It would be the crowning gem of any
collection. I think he had Lady Judith wear the thing to taunt
us. It would suit him to do something like that."

"I take it Van Horne has a habit of collecting people,"
Devlin said, glancing at Austin. "I wonder if he collected
someone who works in the museum, someone who would
have access to valuable artifacts?"

"I wonder." Austin gazed into the fire, his expression
growing bleak.

Devlin frowned at the first sour notes drifting to him on the
cooling breeze. Although it was well disguised, the words, at
least, were those of "Greensleeves." He looked at Frederick,
raising his brows at Kate's voice.

Frederick laughed. "Katie loves to sing. It's just a pity she
couldn't carry a tune in a wheelbarrow."

"It's a mystery, isn't it?" Austin said, grinning at Devlin.
"How a woman so enchanting to look at, can sound so . . .
well, to tell you the truth, I've heard cats in alleys that
sounded better."

Devlin wondered just how many times the marquess had
heard Kate sing. Fear had led Kate to part her thighs for
the bastard owner of a casino, fear of dying without ever
tasting the forbidden fruit. Had Kate imagined it was Austin
loving her, Austin who had slipped past the virgin barrier?
Had Devlin done nothing more than rob Lord Gallant of the
honor of deflowering his future bride? The suspicion jabbed
him like the tip of a dagger, opening wounds he had no hope
of healing for a very long time.

Frederick pulled his handkerchief from his pocket and
began cleaning his fingers as he spoke. "The rector at our
church in London asked me to withdraw her from the choir

when she was nine. It broke her heart."

"Better than breaking the congregation's eardrums," Austin said, staring at the fish, the white flesh turning golden above the fire.

Kate hit a shrill note and it took Devlin a moment before he realized it was a scream.

"Katie!" Frederick said, scrambling to his feet.

Devlin was already on his feet, the spear tumbling from his hand. He had to dodge Frederick, which put him a few steps behind Austin as the marquess sprinted into the water. Kate was near the waterfalls, rising from the water, shoving wet hair back from her face.

She gasped when she saw the men splashing toward her. She glanced behind her, making sure nothing was about to attack from the rear. She saw nothing but the glitter of sunlight on the tumbling waterfalls.

"What's wrong?" she asked as Austin reached her.

Austin frowned. "You screamed."

"I slipped on the rocks."

"Are you all right, Katie?" Frederick asked, turning to face the shore.

"You startled me, that's all." In the commotion Kate had forgotten her nudity, until she noticed the direction of Austin's stare; his gaze was fixed on her breasts.

The dying rays of the sun glistened on her bare skin, her breasts rising and falling with each quick breath, her nipples drawn into tight little buds by the cool air. Water lapped at her waist, the rippling stream little more than a gossamer veil. Kate drew a shocked breath, but before she could turn around, Devlin's voice cut through the heavy air.

"Cover yourself," Devlin shouted, his voice strained with emotion.

She glanced at him, catching the angry glint in his silvery eyes before she spun on her heel, presenting the men her back. "Now that you have all assured yourself I am fine, I would appreciate it if you would give me a little privacy."

"Yes, of course," Austin said. Yet Kate couldn't tell if she heard embarrassment or amusement in his deep voice.

She heard the splashing movements of the men as they hurried from the stream. Still, she sensed she wasn't alone. When she glanced over her shoulder she found Devlin standing onshore, his wet shirt and trousers molding his muscular frame. He was staring at her, an odd mixture of desire and anger in his stormy eyes.

"Mr. McCain, do you mind?" she asked, glaring at him.

"I sure as hell do. You've got about three minutes to get your pretty little behind out of that stream."

"You have no right to—"

"Two and a half minutes."

"You have no right to order me about as though I were your servant," she shouted, turning to face him, crossing her arms over her breasts.

"One minute."

A breeze licked at the water on her skin, chilling her. Yet her cheeks felt as though they were on fire. "I hardly think two minutes have passed, even if I were concerned about your ultimatum."

He smiled, a slight curve of his lips that left his eyes simmering with anything but humor. "Thirty seconds."

If he hadn't issued his ultimatum, she would have left the stream in less than three minutes. As the sun sank toward the horizon, it was stealing the heat from the air, leaving her shivering. But she refused to let this man dictate to her. "Your high-handed tactics will not work with me, Mr. McCain."

He entered the stream, marching toward her, each movement a smooth flow of power.

"May I remind you, Mr. McCain, you are working for me," she said, fighting the urge to run. The flare of anger in his eyes sent her stumbling back a step.

"Just doing my job, Miss Whitmore." He paused less than a foot away from her.

The heat of his body reached out to her. Through the wet cotton of his shirt the dark shadow of black curls teased her.

Tempting. How easy it would be to throw her arms around his neck, to press her chilled breasts against the warmth of his chest, to feel the heat of his powerful thighs branding her legs.

She was aware of the water brushing against her, sliding intimately between her thighs, water that had flowed against his legs before touching her skin. Heat shimmered inside her, a slow burn centered deep in her belly. The power he could wield over her body was humiliating. She chafed under that power. "Your job does not include giving me orders."

"My job includes keeping one stubborn woman from getting herself killed. Get out of the stream. Now."

A sudden surge of anger brought her up on her toes. "Go to blazes! I will leave this stream when *I* decide, not you. If you think—"

Her words ended in a squeal as he tossed her over his shoulder. "Put me down!"

He ignored her.

"You have no right to treat me this way!" She pounded her fists against his back. He curled his fingers around her leg, the mere touch of his warm hand on the back of her bare thigh a hot wind sweeping across the embers of desire smoldering deep within her. "Devlin McCain, put me down this instant!"

He kept walking, carrying her from the water. Through the damp curtain of her hair she saw her father and Austin as Devlin marched across the campsite. They were sitting beside each other in front of the fire, watching McCain carry her as though she were some trophy brought back from a hunting trip, a Sabine woman. And they were both smiling.

Kate wailed with frustration. She pounded McCain's back, kicked, wiggled, and he just kept walking, straight into the hut. When he dumped her to her feet, she flew at him with clenched fists.

"How dare you!" she shouted, thumping her fists against his shoulders. She landed another blow before he grabbed both her wrists. In one smooth motion, he pinned her hands to the small of her back and yanked her against him.

The air left her lungs in a whoosh as her soft breasts collided with the hard wall of his chest. Instantly, she was aware of every place their bodies touched, the heat of his body impressing the hard image of his muscles into her soft skin. Instantly, the memories emerged from shallow graves, memories made in this little hut, memories of passion and pleasure seared forever on her soul.

She felt the hard thrust of his arousal against her belly, heating the damp cotton of his trousers until she was sure steam would rise between them. Heaven help her, she wanted him. Right here. Right now. Even knowing her father and Austin sat no more than 20 feet away, even knowing Devlin McCain was a domineering male who would sever every hope she had ever had of living her life as an independent woman, she wanted him. She had to fight this horrible need.

"You have no right—"

"Have we come full circle, Kate?" Devlin whispered, his lips nearly brushing the tip of her nose, the sweet scent of his breath filling her senses.

Kate stared up at him, his eyes glittering in the shadows that veiled his face. Full circle. This was how they had begun. This was how they would end. In anger. There could be no other way. "I was right about you the first day I met you. You should be wearing animal skins and carrying a club."

He slammed his lips against hers. Brutal in his possession, and yet strangely gentle, tasting of need and desire and pain, his kiss was an ember set to kindling. She fought to escape him, turning her head. And yet she couldn't escape. The enemy lived within: her own aching need for this man.

He kissed her, long and deep, and when she felt the tip of his tongue against her lips, she parted to receive him. Slick and hot, he entered, dipping into her like a hummingbird sipping from a rose, taking sustenance, as though he drew his life from her. Her breasts grew heavy against his chest, throbbing with need. Deep inside, desire coiled, growing tighter and tighter, drawing on her until the sweet nectar flowed from her woman's flower.

No, don't do this to me, she wanted to shout. *Don't make me want you. Don't make me a traitor to myself.*

She struggled to release her hands from his grasp to push him away, only to find herself drawing him near. His muscles tensed against her breasts, and then he was lifting his head, ending the kiss. He looked as shaken as she felt, young and vulnerable and ashamed suddenly for what had happened.

He released her and took a step back. Kate whimpered at the loss; she couldn't help herself—her body was crying for his touch.

"I can't seem to . . ." He ran a hand through his hair, working furrows through the thick, ebony waves. "Damn!"

Yes, indeed. She felt damned.

"See if you can behave yourself, Miss Whitmore," Devlin said, keeping his voice a harsh whisper. "And I'll do my best to keep my dirty hands off you."

She pressed her fingertips to her lips as he left the hut. Her every nerve fluttered with life, every fiber of her body throbbed with need. She took a step toward the entrance, wanting to call to him, needing him . . . needing . . . Oh, would this horrible need ever die?

Devlin stepped from the hut into the small clearing. He drew deep drafts of air into his lungs, hoping the smoke drifting from the fire could sear the alluring scent of roses from his nostrils. He felt stretched, his body aching, as though he were strapped to a rack, every muscle tense and throbbing with need.

Across from him on the opposite side of the fire sat Frederick and Austin. When they saw him, they both glanced down to the fish they were roasting over the flames, unwilling to hold his look. Did they think he was a barbarian who should be roaming around in animal skins?

It shouldn't matter what they thought. But it did. As much as he hated to admit it, he wanted the respect of these men.

He wanted to respect himself. And at the moment, he could find little to respect. He had allowed jealousy to force him into acting like a . . . like a damn barbarian.

He didn't like what he was becoming—bitter and jealous and half insane with wanting her. He didn't want to be here. He didn't want to face the temptation of touching her. He sank to the ground, knowing there was nowhere to hide. They had weeks ahead of them. And somehow in the days ahead, he had to learn to cope with the desire threatening to destroy him.

He would learn to harden his heart, as well as his body. He had to kill his desire for her; he had to bury his love. It was the only way he was going to survive.

Chapter Twenty-two

It had been less than a week since Kate and Devlin had traveled this route on their departure from the Kuraya village. Yet vines had already started to reclaim the path Devlin had hacked out of the jungle. In places, Kate could believe they had never really passed this way before. In ways, she wondered if they ever had.

She stared at Devlin's broad back, the stained white cotton of his shirt clinging to muscles that flowed with each powerful swing of his arm as he hacked at the lush green vegetation. They were no longer the same two people who had fought their way along this path.

Another lifetime. What had happened between them seemed no more than a dream, an erotic fantasy conjured by her all too active imagination. The man who had barely spoken to her in the past few days was certainly not the man who had held her in his arms, the man who had made her body sing with a touch of his hands. She didn't know this remote stranger.

The late afternoon sun slanted across the mist rising from

the base of the falls, carving a rainbow above the tumultuous water. Devlin had set a slower pace on the trip down this trail than he had when they were alone, camping twice along the winding stream that ran parallel to the river; she suspected in deference to her father. The man could be surprisingly thoughtful of others. Just one more thing she needed to forget.

Devlin came to a halt where the stream and the river flowed together, forming a narrow channel leading to the village. He stood for a long moment, staring into the swiftly flowing water as though he could see his future in the dark water and wasn't pleased with what he saw.

Frederick sank to a driftwood log beside the river and lifted his pith helmet from his damp hair. "Are we close to the village?" he asked, dragging the back of his wrist across his brow.

"About a half mile." Devlin stared another few moments into the water before turning to face the older man. "I want you and the others to wait here while I go in. If I'm not back in an hour, I don't want you to waste any time hiking back up that path."

"You expect trouble?" Austin rested his foot on the log beside Frederick.

"I'm not sure what to expect."

Apprehension prickled the base of Kate's spine. "But they think you're a god. Surely they wouldn't try to harm you."

"The new chief might not like having his authority undermined by anyone," Devlin said, glancing at her.

It seemed an eternity since he had acknowledged she was alive, and his glance did little more than graze her, as though he couldn't stand to look at her. Perhaps he couldn't.

It's better this way, she thought. And yet she couldn't quell the hurt that came from knowing he could exile her from his life so easily.

"If you're expecting trouble, I should go with you," Austin said.

"If something happens, you'll be needed here, with

Frederick and Miss Whitmore." Devlin pulled off his boots and socks.

"Are you intending to go into the river?" Frederick asked. "Isn't that dangerous? There could be alligators, piranha."

"The current is too swift for piranha to be any problem. And the alligators . . ." Devlin shrugged, as though they wouldn't be a problem either. "Austin, would you mind cutting a few leaves from that bush over there?" he asked, pointing with the tip of his knife to a nearby barbasco bush.

"Of course," Austin said, taking the knife Devlin offered. He immediately started hacking at the bush, releasing a pungent scent into the air.

Kate stared as Devlin unfastened his shirt, revealing a growing wedge of golden skin and dark curls. Once she had wondered what it might be like to touch him. Now she knew, far too well. Silky curls. Warm skin. Intriguing memories.

"If you don't want your delicate sensibilities injured, Miss Whitmore, I advise you to turn away," Devlin said, peeling the damp cotton from his skin.

Kate stiffened at the patronizing tone in his voice. "As I recall, I didn't swoon at the first sight of your nudity, Mr. McCain. I doubt there has been anything added to your anatomy that will cause me to swoon from terror, or from rapture."

Devlin smiled, a chilling imitation of the smile she knew could be warmer than sunshine. "No, Miss Whitmore, nothing's been added." He flipped open the buttons in the front placket of his trousers as he continued. "And nothing's been cut off either. Despite the efforts of one castrating little female."

Kate's mouth dropped open. "Mr. McCain, I have never in my life heard a more insulting . . ." She hesitated as he stripped the sand-colored trousers and white drawers from his hips. The pure, savage beauty of this man stole her breath.

Oblivious to her open stare, he tossed his clothes on the log and took the barbasco leaves from Austin. Unable to help herself, Kate watched as he milked a leaf. She followed the swift movement of his hand as he smeared the sap across his wide shoulders.

Chiseled perfection come to life, Kate thought, staring at Devlin. More magnificent than the statue of Michelangelo's *David*. For this creation was carved from warm, golden flesh, and moved with a grace and power that captivated the eye. Too beautiful. Too compelling. Too infuriating.

She dropped her haversack on the ground and sat beside her father, turning her attention to a vine covered in small, blue flowers, following its twisted path upward along a banana tree. On a lofty branch a toucan sat, his bright little eyes watching her, his head tilted to one side as though he were trying to understand this unusual creature in his forest. Only when she heard a soft splash of water did she glance in Devlin McCain's direction. He was standing a few feet into the river, his back to her, water lapping against his thighs.

"Good luck, Devlin," Frederick said.

"Are you sure you don't want me to go along?" Austin asked, standing on the edge of the river.

Devlin shook his head. "Remember, don't wait any more than an hour. Take this," he said, offering Austin the knife, their only weapon.

Austin shook his head. "You might need that."

Devlin looked past Austin to Kate, his expression an unreadable mask of calm. She wanted to say something, but what? *Be careful, Devlin. Please, be careful. I would die if anything happened to you.* She could say nothing.

He glanced away and plunged the knife into the sand at Austin's feet. Without another word, Devlin sank into the water and began swimming toward the Kuraya village. Kate stared, watching his every movement, his arms arcing powerfully, slicing the water, his legs pumping, churning the river in his wake. She might never see him again; that thought made her shiver in the oppressive heat.

Mist from the waterfalls carried on the breeze, brushing Kate's cheeks, the deep-throated roar of the crashing water filling her ears. She shifted on the hard log, staring at the jungle, feeling the seconds tick away with the pounding of her heart. It was growing late, the sun no more than a glimmer of gold overhead in the swiftly departing tropical twilight.

"How long has he been gone?" she asked, glancing to where her father sat beside her.

"I'm not sure this watch is keeping good time." Frederick snapped the cover shut on his pocket watch as though he didn't want to see the time it displayed.

Kate swallowed past the knot forming in her throat. "It's been an hour, hasn't it?"

The look of pain in her father's brown eyes was all she needed to confirm the horrible suspicion growing inside her. Frederick jammed the gold watch into his trouser pocket and rested his forearms on his knees. "We'll wait a little longer."

"I shouldn't have let him go alone." Austin paced back and forth along the edge of the river like a caged tiger. "I should have followed him."

"We should do something," Kate said, coming to her feet.

"I think we . . ." Austin hesitated, pivoting toward the jungle, raising Devlin's knife at his side, his entire body growing tense.

Kate had no time to ask what was wrong before the Indians attacked. In moments they were surrounded by burly, brown bodies, spears held high, tongues jabbering in that language Kate couldn't understand. And then the Indians were shoving with dirty hands, prodding, forcing them into the jungle.

Kate tasted terror with the bile rising in her throat. With every step she fought the urge to turn and run. Was a spear in her back better than what lay ahead? And yet she couldn't surrender to death. Not yet. Not until she knew there was no possible means of escape.

Light spilled into the forest as the Indians pulled aside the barrier of brush and vines shielding the entrance to their compound. They were pushed into the middle of a celebration.

Flames leapt upward from the brush piled high in the center of the clearing, like orange demons dancing for the devil. Men swarmed around the fire, raising their knees high, then crouching low before leaping upward with a wail, the joyous shouts of victory.

Kate didn't realize she was trembling until Austin slipped his arm around her shoulders, until he held her close and she felt the solid strength of his body. She leaned against him, trying to fight the terror threatening to overwhelm her. Her father was beside her and dozens of undulating bodies surrounded them. She thought of all the horrible tales she had heard of primitive tribes in the Amazon. She remembered those shriveled heads she had seen here.

She glanced around the compound as they were forced to march past the fire. What had they done with Devlin? Was his head simmering in a pot? Had they . . .

The Indians parted before her, revealing a man sitting on a crate of canned peaches. "Devlin." She thought she had spoken the word, but the only voice she heard was Austin's as he shouted Devlin's name.

Devlin lifted his hand in a salute, a small smile playing at one corner of his mouth. "I don't suppose anyone brought my trousers."

Devlin stared at the flames as they reached in vain for the stars overhead. The men danced in rhythm to their chants around the fire, paying homage to the river-god. He scarcely acknowledged the women who placed bowls of baked *makashera, kashiri,* and platters of roasted meat in front of him. Any encouragement and he wouldn't be able to get rid of the ladies.

"I must say, we thought you were done for." Frederick turned a piece of meat over in his hand. "Good heavens, Devlin! Look at this."

Devlin frowned as he stared down at the narrow arm Frederick was holding, a small hand cupped at the end, tiny fingers curved toward the palm.

"Who have they roasted here?"

"It's a monkey." Devlin glanced down as he felt a woman slide her hand upward along his inner thigh. Sitting at his feet, she was smiling up at him, her dark eyes glowing with sensual promise, her dark nipples drawn into excited little nubs.

"You have yourself a harem." Frederick gingerly placed the monkey arm back on one of the platters, glancing at the six other women gathered at Devlin's feet.

"Whether I like it or not," Devlin said, gently lifting her hand from his leg, wishing he had his trousers. The woman giggled and wiggled closer to him, ignoring the polite rejection.

Sexual release. Devlin could ease the ache in his loins with this woman and any of the others who were looking at him with warm invitations in their eyes. Rutting, like two animals, satisfying a basic need, that was what he thought of when he looked at these women. Had Kate seen the same thing when she looked at him?

He glanced to where Kate was sitting cross-legged on the ground a few feet away, next to Austin Sinclair. Firelight reflected on the gold of her hair, tendrils escaping the thick braid that fell over her shoulder to frame her face in soft curls. She looked pale and fragile, like fine porcelain, staring into the fire as though she were completely sheltered from everything around her. Yet he knew the strength behind that lovely face, the courage and conviction he admired and loved.

"I wonder if they would part with any of their salvage." Frederick popped a slippery slice of peach into his mouth.

"Two canoes, four paddlers to help us reach the upper part of the river, and one box of canned peaches. Without anything to trade, that's more than I had hoped to get," Devlin said, glancing at the few crates of supplies the Indians had fished from the river. "I just wish they had dragged a rifle and ammunition from the wreckage."

"We'll do without." Frederick gave Devlin a confident

smile. "You're a resourceful man, Devlin McCain, an excellent leader. I wonder if you might consider accompanying us on other expeditions?"

"You plan another trip into the Amazon jungle?"

"Perhaps. It depends on what we find in Avallon. But there will always be something to explore. I thought we might journey back up the Nile after we return from South America. And I would like you to be with us."

Devlin glanced at Kate. She was smiling, leaning close to Austin Sinclair, listening to him as though he had just returned from the mountaintop with the holy tablets. Jealousy coiled inside him like an angry cobra. "I don't know anything about archaeology."

"You know how to keep an expedition moving in the right direction. That would take a great deal of worry from my shoulders. You might even discover you enjoy digging into the past."

"I don't think so." Devlin didn't want to be around when Kate became Lady Katherine Sinclair.

"Well, there's no need to decide now. We'll talk about it again later. After we reach Avallon."

Nothing was going to change his mind. He wouldn't live through the nightmare of being near Kate and her Lord Gallant for any amount of money. "It's late," Devlin said, rising to his feet. "When you're ready to retire, the hut next to mine has been readied for you."

As he moved toward his hut, his harem followed, two of the women managing to slip beneath his arms and lock their arms around his waist. The others tagged close behind. To insult the ladies would mean insulting the tribe. Two women slipped their hands into the hair on his chest. He glanced down at their smiling faces. Just how the hell was he going to get rid of them without starting a war?

He was going to sleep with all of them, Kate thought, watching as Devlin walked into his hut. They were young, pretty, and anxious to mate with Devlin McCain. "Do you know what that man is going to do in there?"

Austin's black brows lifted a fraction as he looked at her. "I have some idea."

"You would never do anything like that."

"Well, I . . . were there six women with him?"

She nodded. "I can't believe he could take advantage of those women."

"To them it's a great privilege. They look at Devlin as a god."

She watched the Indian men as they swayed before her, dancing now to a slower rhythm, sensual, pagan, firelight pulsing against naked skin. "And those women are all to be sacrificed to Devlin McCain."

"I doubt they look at it as much of a sacrifice."

No. Those women were anxious to feel his strong arms around them, anxious to taste his lips, anxious to . . . Kate wrapped her arms around her raised knees, her cheeks growing warm as her imagination took full rein of her mind. Good heavens, she couldn't stand the thought of another woman touching Devlin. "He has no right to use them."

"Is he to blame if he takes what a woman offers? When she knows he doesn't love her? When she knows he will never marry her? Does that make him the villain?"

"It makes him . . ." *Human . . . as human as I am,* she thought. But being human didn't make it right. "The man is a barbarian."

Had she become what she most detested in a man, lusting for a member of the opposite sex, using him to ease her own aching needs? She dropped her chin on her knees and tried not to think of what was happening in the hut behind her. Still, she couldn't stop the horrible pain throbbing like a ragged wound inside her.

"He knows we're out here. I don't understand how he could do this." *How can he do this to me?* At the sound of high-pitched giggles tumbling from the hut, Kate curled her hands into fists on her raised knees.

Think of something else, anything else. Yet she couldn't

banish the images from her mind. Jealousy surged in her veins, like a wildfire spread across dry grass by a hot gust of wind. Before she thought about what she was doing, she was on her feet, marching toward Mr. Devlin McCain's hut.

Kate hesitated inside the entrance, staring at Devlin, her blood simmering with rage. A fire flickered in the center of the hut. Smoke curled upward from the fire, a column of gray rising behind Devlin's naked body. The women surrounded him, stroking him with their hands, rubbing their breasts against him, giggling. And he was talking to them, low and steady, no doubt giving them instructions, touching a shoulder here, an arm there, backing up into one writhing body.

One woman was sinking to her knees in front of him, sliding her hands up his thighs, reaching for . . . Kate's fragile control snapped. "Get out!"

Chapter Twenty-three

Devlin glanced up at the sound of Kate's voice. She was storming toward him, her cheeks high with color, her eyes flashing with the rage he could feel radiating from her, as hot and condemning as the tropical sun. Breathtaking. Magnificent in her fury. The Indian women shrieked as Kate drew near, cowering as though they were facing an avenging goddess.

Kate reached down and grabbed the arm of one of the women. "I said, get out!" she shouted, dragging the whimpering woman to her feet.

The woman didn't wait for another command from this golden goddess; she didn't need to understand the words to understand the meaning—she fled. The other women scattered, running from the hut as though they feared a thunderbolt would follow, Kate's rage succeeding where Devlin's quiet persuasion had failed.

She stood before him, hands on shapely hips, chin lifted, breathing hard. Devlin's heart pounded like a fist against the wall of his chest as he held her blazing blue gaze. Why had she followed him? Jealousy? Did she care enough to fight for him? "You chased those women away as though you had a brand on me."

She released her breath in a rush. "You really enjoy having women prostrate themselves before you, don't you!"

"Did they look as though I was forcing them?"

"How could you do this to these poor women? They don't know any better. How could you take advantage of them?"

"I'm still the barbarian, is that it, Professor? Not fit to breathe the same air as one of your fine, English gentlemen."

"A gentleman would never dream of taking advantage of a woman."

"Your English gentleman is sitting outside by the fire. You'd better join him before he gets the idea you prefer the company of bastard barbarians over English aristocracy."

"A woman would be insane to prefer you over Austin Sinclair."

"Yeah." He wondered if she had any idea how much damage she could inflict with words, how easily she could break open the wounds she had carved deep inside his soul. "Unless she thinks she's going to die and never have that itch scratched between her thighs."

Kate gasped. "That's a horrible thing to say to me."

"Well, that's the funny thing about the truth, Professor. Sometimes it's not very pretty."

"And I suppose you got nothing from me?"

"Nothing more than what those women were offering." *Nothing more than a glimpse of heaven and a sentence to hell.*

"You . . . you . . ." she sputtered, thumping her fists against his chest. "I was insane ever to let you touch me."

Devlin grabbed her arm when she turned to leave. "I suppose you're the injured party here."

"Let go of me!"

He pulled her against him, wrapping one arm around her waist, the other upward across her back. She struggled in his hold, brushing her breasts against his chest, firm and warm, shaming him with the sudden surge of desire he had no power to control.

"Tell me why I'm the villain in this little drama, Professor. I don't seem to understand."

"You bastard!"

"Right. I am a bastard. But that doesn't give you the right to treat me like a piece of dirt under your aristocratic heels."

"I never . . . how dare . . ." She glared up at him. "It took more than a circumstance of birth to make you a bastard, Devlin McCain. Now take your filthy hands off me."

"These are the same hands, Kate, the same hands you once wanted on your sweet little body." Devlin slid his hand over the curve of her hip. "I'm the same man you welcomed deep inside you."

"A mistake," she said, her voice strangled by rage as she tried to break free of his embrace.

"Was it?"

"Yes." Kate clenched her eyes shut. "A mistake I'll never make again."

Pain throbbed deep and slow in his chest, a constriction of love he still felt for this woman. "Am I nothing more than a regret, Kate?" He brushed his lips against her neck, breathing the scent of roses into his blood. "Am I just a bad memory to be pushed aside, forgotten?"

"I will forget you." She pushed against his chest.

He would never forget her, no matter how hard he tried. She had pierced him too deeply. And somehow, he had to make her remember him. Somehow he had to find a way to touch that part of her she kept hidden from him. Somehow he would leave his mark on her. When she was lying beneath Lord Gallant, he wanted her to remember the bastard who had once touched her, the bastard who had once loved her with every fiber of his godforsaken soul.

Kate gasped as he opened his mouth against the sensitive skin at the curve of her neck and shoulder. His lips were like a brand, so filled with damp heat. If he thought he could seduce her out of her anger, he was mistaken. If he thought she would be a substitute for his Indian harem, he would soon find she was made of stronger stuff.

"Let go of me!" She pushed against his chest, but it was like pushing against granite, except that the skin beneath her palms was warm, like satin in sunshine.

He slid the tip of his tongue upward, circling her ear, coaxing a wayward whimper from her throat. Sandalwood blended with the musk of male skin warmed by the tropical night teased her senses. The heat of his naked body seeped through her clothes, drenching her skin.

Heaven help her, was this the reason she had come storming after him? He nipped her earlobe, his breath a sultry breeze against her neck. She arched her hands against his chest, the pads of her fingers sliding over the pebble-hard male nipples. Muscles tensed under her touch. She felt his deep breath, the slow rise of his chest, the soft exhale that warmed her shoulder.

Had she wanted this? Had she wanted to feel his arms around her again? She couldn't surrender to this madness. She had to . . .

He slid his hands over the curve of her buttocks and lifted her into the cradle of his loins, sliding the lush heat and promise of potent masculinity against her belly. Inside, she felt the dangerous shift of emotions, the melting of cold rage into warm desire.

This was madness!

Yet her body was already yielding to his. Like ice yielding to the heat of the sun, her body melted, soft and pliant, sliding against him, seeking all he could give her. She wanted him. She needed him. And she could have him, if only for this moment.

She turned her head, brushing her lips against his cheek, craving his kiss. She arched her hips, lifting into the hard thrust of his flesh, needing to possess him. She slid her arms around his smooth shoulders, wanting to hold him forever.

Devlin felt the sweetness of surrender in the softening of her body against his. Inside, he trembled with need. "Kate," he whispered, sliding his lips across her cheek.

At the first touch of his mouth against hers, she parted her lips, soft breath warming his cheek. He drew the tip of his tongue along the curve of her lower lip and felt her sink her fingers into his hair. He dipped inside her mouth, hot and sleek, touching the tip of her tongue, retreating, teasing, until she groaned deep in her throat, until her hands clenched and tugged on his hair.

Memory could do her no justice. Dreams could only deepen his hunger for her. He burned for this woman, a fire banked deep inside, a fire destined to consume him. But his own destruction didn't matter now; nothing mattered but the feel of her body brushing against his, a hungry flame burning in his arms, this summer goddess of heat and light.

He slipped his hand between their bodies and flipped open the buttons of her shirt, of her trousers. She didn't protest as he slid the shirt from her shoulders. She whimpered only when he broke their kiss.

"Where are you going?" she whispered, grabbing his shoulders.

"Nowhere without you." He slipped the straps of her camisole from her shoulders.

He kissed her breasts through the sheer silk of her camisole, stabbing at the pink crests with his tongue. She closed her eyes, a sigh slipping from her parted lips. Slowly, he undressed her, kissing every inch of the rose-scented skin he revealed, reveling in the soft, pleasured sounds his touch drew from her throat. He pulled the boots and socks from her feet, drew the trousers and lacy drawers from her hips, rediscovering the shape of her long legs with his hands, with his lips, with his tongue.

Soon she stood naked before him, the firelight worshiping her smooth, ivory skin. Devlin feasted on her beauty, storing away memories like a beggar who knows he will soon feel the horrible gnawing ache of hunger once again.

She opened her eyes. She looked at him where he stood naked before her. He held no guard against her, laying bare his emotions. Hope and love. Emotions that could betray him, emotions he could not deny when he looked into her eyes.

"Hold me." She slipped her arms around his neck. "Devlin, please hold me."

He closed his arms around her, cradling the silken warmth of her body against his skin. She glided upward, lifting on her toes, searing his chest with her breasts, teasing his thighs with the smooth satin of her legs, capturing his lips beneath hers. He surrendered completely to this woman, shoving his doubts into the shadows.

For now, she was in his arms. For now, he could love her as he dreamed of loving her. He wouldn't think of what the cost might be.

He slid his hands down the sleek lines of her back, warm silk beneath his palms. Her muscles tensed beneath his touch as he cupped the pouting curves of her rounded behind. When he lifted her, she slid her long legs around his waist, soft, damp curls teasing the smooth, hard flesh of his arousal. She tightened her arms around his neck, clinging to him, pressing against him as though she couldn't get close enough to him.

He carried her to the nearest hammock, settling her bottom in the intricate net of woven vines. With his lips against hers, with the sweet taste of her mouth on his tongue, he entered her, sliding into the welcoming heat and moisture of her sleek sheath.

She was made to receive him, fashioned in size and form to fit as no woman ever had in the past, as no woman ever would in the future. Yet even as he possessed her fully, even as he felt the voluptuous pulse of her flesh tugging his, he wondered if this would be the last time he would ever know such complete joy.

Kate felt suspended in midair, Devlin her only anchor, his feet planted firmly on the ground. With his hands on her hips he thrust her forward; the hammock swayed, her breasts brushed his chest, black curls teased her sensitive nipples. She glided with the motion, swinging away from him until she lost all but the velvety crown of his arousal. An instant of anticipation before he drew her near, before he was sliding into her once more, filling her with his heat and power until she thought she would shatter with the pleasure.

Flying. Over and over he sent her flying, pushing her away, drawing her near, warm skin gliding against her, hard flesh filling her over and over again.

She gasped as Devlin lowered his lips to her neck, the damp heat of his tongue swirling against the pulse throbbing with the pleasure he was conjuring inside her. Through the singing of blood in her ears, she heard the distant chant of the Indians in the clearing, the rhythm a counterpoint to the mating dance of this pagan god.

The fire cast their shadows against the wall, ancient drawings etched in charcoal, man and woman joined for the ages. And then there was no room for thought, as Devlin commanded her body.

Devlin whispered her name over and over again as he drove into her, as he felt her grow tense and urgent beneath him. She clutched at his shoulders, her body arching, her legs tensing against him, her body closing around him in a long, sweet shudder of release.

She trembled against him, surrounding him, her soft moans carried on broken breaths, shattering, as she dragged him with her to her kingdom of heat and light, as she consumed him with her fire. He surrendered to her heat, delivering his soul into her hands.

Their soft, ragged breaths and sharp, staccato heartbeats blended together as their sweetly sated bodies clung one to the other. The shadows on the wall flickered. In time the fire cooled, hearts slowed, breathing eased as they tumbled from a realm of magic.

When Devlin could collect his strength, he gathered Kate in his arms. He turned her gently, cradling her against his chest as he lay back against the hammock. There were words he wanted to say, words that collected in his heart, words he wondered if she would want to hear.

He felt her hand furl into a fist on his chest, her body tighten as though she were fighting something inside her. With his hand on her chin, he tilted her head. Tears, they were there in her eyes, catching the firelight like shimmering stars. He saw a horrible pain in her face. And inside he felt a reflection of her pain in his own broken hopes and dreams.

"I didn't want to make you cry," he said, stroking damp curls back from her cheek. "I never want to make you cry."

She shook her head. "I'm not crying. I've never been one of those weepy females," she whispered, a single tear escaping her tight control.

He cupped her face in his palm and swept his thumb over her skin, smoothing the shimmering droplet from her cheek. "I'm sorry. I never should have—"

"It's not your fault. It's me . . . it's how I feel." She traced a serpentine pattern against his shoulder with her fingertip as she spoke. "Those women, were you really going to make love to them?"

"No." Devlin smoothed his fingers over her temple, feeling the violent pulse of her heart. "I was trying to persuade them to leave. They didn't want to take no for an answer."

"You're not an easy man to resist," she whispered, her voice reflecting the misery he could see in the trembling curve of her smile.

"There's only one woman I want, Kate."

She shook her head. "I shouldn't have come barging in here. I don't know what's wrong with me. I don't know . . ." She drew a deep, ragged breath. "Will this ever go away?"

"What, sweetheart?"

"This jealousy. This feeling I have, this horrible need. I don't understand it. I don't want it!"

With her words, he felt hope rise from the ashes of his dreams. "Kate, it's all right to feel—"

"This isn't like me." She slashed at the tears she could no longer hold at bay. "I don't know the woman I'm becoming.

I can't seem to control my emotions. I . . . oh, I hate this! My father is out there. Austin Sinclair is out there. They probably know what happened in here."

Devlin felt a jolt of jealousy rip through him at the mere mention of Austin Sinclair.

"This isn't the person I always thought I was. The woman who ran in here like a screaming shrew, the woman who can't stop wanting to touch you."

She reached out with her hand. For a long moment she held her open palm above his shoulder, touching him only with her warmth, as if she were afraid to touch the skin she had so recently caressed.

Devlin watched her, seeing her confusion, wishing he could ease her pain. But he couldn't. He was the source of her misery.

She curled her hand into a fist and pressed her knuckles beneath her chin. "I don't know the woman who came storming in here. I'm not sure I like her."

"I know her," he said, slipping his fingers around her clenched fist. "I love her."

"No." She scrambled off the hammock, breaking free of his hold.

"Kate." He rolled to his feet. "Give me a chance. Let me show you I can be more than a worthless casino owner. Let me—"

"Please, don't." She pushed against his chest as he drew near.

"Doesn't this show you there's something between us? Can't you see we should be together?"

"No. We don't belong together."

"And what about what just happened? Did love have anything to do with it?"

"Devlin, I . . . I can't love you. I can't."

Her words froze the breath in his lungs. She wanted him for one thing, one thing alone—the fire he could ignite in her blue blood. He stood watching as she pulled on her clothes, feeling as dirty and worthless as he had ever felt in his life.

"Are you going to marry Sinclair?"

She looked up at him, her hands falling still on the top button of her shirt she had been trying to fasten. "You don't understand. It's not because of Austin. It's me. It's you."

"I don't fit into your life, is that it?"

"I've always been sure of what I wanted to do, how I wanted to live my life. I've never wanted to marry. Anyone. Do you understand? I've always wanted to live my life as I saw fit. My work has always been my love." She gestured with her hands, a fluttery movement of confusion. "And you turn everything upside down. This thing between us, it won't last. It's too fast. It's too intense. It isn't right, not for either of us."

"So you're just going to turn your back and pretend this never happened."

"What else can I do?" She looked so heartbroken, it was all he could do to keep from taking her in his arms. "You want forever; I can give you today. Will you take moments, knowing one day we'll go our separate ways?"

Devlin turned away from her, closing his eyes, the pain ripping at him with steel claws. He was sick of feeling dirty and used. He was sick of wanting something he could never have. "I can't be your stud, Kate. I care too much to be nothing but a warm body with the proper equipment."

He heard her gasp, felt her gaze burn into him before she ran from the hut. For a long time he stood staring at the flickering shadow on the wall, the shadow of a man alone.

Chapter Twenty-four

Morning sunlight poured into the clearing, streaming gold across the narrow beach. Five days of traveling the splinter channel and they were back where they had started, in the camp above the waterfalls. Of course, there were a few changes, Devlin thought—the paddlers and the bearers had deserted, leaving him with men who had never handled a canoe in their lives, unless he could convince the Kurayas to stay with them.

Devlin glanced up from the Kuraya Indian's expressive face as Frederick moved toward him. The Indian rattled away in his guttural tongue, flapping his arms as though he expected to lift off at any minute, trying to convince Devlin of his cause.

"How is it going?" Frederick asked, easing his way past one of the Indians to stand at Devlin's side. "Do you think they will stay with us?"

"That depends. This one offered to be my slave for a year, if I give him your daughter. That one just raised the ante to two years."

"If you give him . . . He wants Katie?"

"They both do." Devlin smiled, knowing how Kate would feel about being the object of such devotion. "Poor men don't know the trouble they'd be getting into."

One of the Indians pounded his chest and pointed to where Kate was leaving her tent, clutching her sketchbook to her breast. She glanced in Devlin's direction before hurrying toward the beach on the far side of camp, like a doe with the scent of a hunter in her nostrils.

She looked pale, the only color in her cheeks the dark, purplish smudges under her huge eyes. She had barely eaten anything in days, and from the looks of her, she wasn't getting any sleep. He felt the steel coils she had wrapped around his heart tighten until his chest throbbed with pain.

The Indian spoke rapidly, passionately for a moment, then fell silent. After Devlin replied, the man nodded. The others bowed their heads and touched their hands to their hearts.

"What did you tell them?" Frederick asked.

Devlin watched Kate pick her way across the tangle of vines snaking from the jungle into the river. "I told them Miss Whitmore was my goddess, and nothing on earth could take her from my side."

Frederick's hand closed on his arm, a brief squeeze of his fingers that told him Frederick was well aware of the way Devlin felt about Kate. Heat prickled the skin at the nape of his neck, a searing of shame for the self-pity he had been wallowing in the past few days. A man never won a poker game by folding his hand, and he realized he wasn't ready to walk away from this game.

"But they're leaving." Barnaby stared after the four Indians as they jogged toward the forest. "Won't they stay for you? With them thinking you're a god and all."

"It's better if they leave." Devlin turned to face the little man, Barnaby's hair shining like a copper kettle in the sunlight. "If they stay, they might be disappointed in me. No telling what they'd do when they discovered I'm only human." Human and stubborn. He was the reason Kate looked as though she had been dragged through hell.

"Well, then, there is really no question of going on," Edwin said. "Under the circumstances, I don't see how we can possibly go forward."

Frederick turned to face his friend. "We are closer to Avallon than we are to Santarém."

Edwin stared at Frederick from beneath shaggy, brown brows. "Since you have not seen fit to share with me the map to the city, I wouldn't know."

"I would say one or two days before we reach the channel leading to Avallon," Frederick said. "Another four, perhaps five days before we reach the base of the mountain."

"We will have easier going if we turn back. And we won't have Van Horne waiting to slaughter us."

Frederick held his friend's gaze a long moment before he spoke. "The decision has been made, Edwin. If you wish to return, you can take one of the canoes."

"What chance would we have without McCain?"

Robert laughed. "Father, do you really think we have a chance with McCain?"

Devlin chose to ignore the young man, the way he might ignore an annoying fly.

Edwin looked at his son. Regret. Disappointment. Anger. Devlin saw all of this in Edwin's face.

"Mr. McCain, I trust you will ignore my son's attempt at humor," Edwin said. "I'm sure you are capable of escorting us all safely to Santarém."

Robert Melville was the least of Devlin's concerns at the moment. "Unless Mr. Whitmore changes his mind, I'm planning to lead this group upriver to a place called Avallon."

"Frederick, please," Edwin said. "If you have no thought for your own safety, then think of Katherine."

"My daughter has never been one to look behind. We are going forward, to Avallon."

Edwin shook his head. "And when we reach Avallon, what do you suppose we should do to protect ourselves against

Leighton Van Horne? That's if we don't meet him on his
trip back to civilization."

"I have an idea," Devlin said, his lips curving into a smile
as he glanced at Frederick. And he also had an idea of how he
might put the rose blossoms back in Kate's pretty cheeks.

It would be foolish to venture any farther from the others,
Kate thought, glancing back toward the camp a few hundred
yards downstream. A haze hung above the ground, capturing
the sunlight until the air shimmered, lending a strange, dream-
like cast to the camp and the men gathered around Devlin
McCain near the edge of the jungle. She needed time alone,
time away from Devlin McCain's disturbing presence.

She sat on a boulder beside the river, opened her sketchbook, and leafed through the pages, stopping at the first
blank sheet. A vast tangle of green rose like a mountain
on the opposite side of the river. High in the trees behind
her, monkeys chattered and rattled the leaves, their familiar
screeches no longer frightening. It was the unknown that
frightened her. The future and the choices she must make,
these frightened her.

She pulled a pencil from the pocket of her trousers
and confronted that blank page. Since she had been a
child, she had loved to draw and paint. It was an escape,
capturing images on paper. And the images that surrounded
her—the primeval forest rising from the water's edge, the
river rushing headlong toward the waterfalls, the distant
rainbow streaking above the mist rising from the cascade—
all these images should inspire her. And yet the sketches
she drew were mechanical, lifeless scratches of pencil on
paper, until she began to sketch the haunting image of
Devlin McCain.

At the sound of a twig snapping, Kate lifted her head,
shielding her eyes from the sun with her raised hand. Her
father was making his way toward her, weaving his way
carefully over the vines and boulders and pieces of driftwood
littering the edge of the river.

"Catching up on your sketches?" Frederick asked, sitting beside her on the rocks.

She glanced down at her sketch, wishing she had thought to close the book, knowing it was too late to hide the drawing she had made of Devlin McCain's head and shoulders. "I seem to be a little distracted from work these days."

Frederick lifted the sketchbook from her lap. "I think you've idealized his jaw a bit."

"I don't think so. He has a rather strong jaw."

"And his nose." Frederick studied the sketch a moment. "His nose is hardly that straight."

"I think you're mistaken." She took the book from his hands. "Devlin's nose could be chiseled from marble."

"It seems to me only a woman in love would have sketched a nose that perfect." He tilted his head and smiled at her. "Of course, that couldn't be. Could it?"

She glanced away from his perceptive brown eyes. Dark green water flowed swiftly past the shore, lapping at the exposed roots of a nearby palm tree. "When I think about the future without him, I grow cold inside."

"So it seems you do love him."

"I keep hoping these feelings will go away. I keep hoping everything will go back to the way it was before I met him."

"Follow your heart, Katie."

She shook her head. "He wants to buy a ranch in California. I don't know if I can survive so far away from everything I've ever loved."

Frederick slipped his hand around hers. "And you can see no compromise?" he asked, resting their clasped hands on his knee.

"He wants to settle down, raise a family."

"I raised a daughter and never gave up my work."

Kate glanced down to the open book in her lap, tracing the compelling lines of Devlin's face with her gaze. "I doubt he would want to raise a family out of a trunk."

"I wonder if Devlin would really be happy on that ranch in California."

"He said he has been roaming all his life, searching for a home."

"Perhaps all he has been searching for is someone he could love, someone who would love him." Frederick frowned as he stared down at their clasped hands. "Perhaps all he needs is to feel a part of a family, to belong."

"I want to be a part of his life, Father. I know I do. It's just . . ." She squeezed his hand, wishing he could help her, knowing no one could. "I love my work. I love the excitement of each new discovery. Devlin would never settle for a wife who knows more about digging up pots than cooking in one. In time he would grow to hate me because I'm not really want he needs, and I would grow to hate him for turning me into a poor image of something I never wanted to be."

"So you're just going to give him up, turn your back on him?"

She stared at the river, reflected sunlight on the water hurting her eyes. *Turn your back on him.* She would never hear Devlin's voice, see his smile, feel the warmth of his skin. Her chest tightened, her heart squeezing with the horrible truth of what she must do. "I don't see how it could ever work between us."

Frederick was quiet a long while. She could feel him looking at her, but she couldn't meet his gaze. She knew she would only see disappointment in his eyes.

"Come on," he said, releasing her hand. "Devlin is going to show us how to use a native weapon and he wants you to learn as well as the others."

"He does?" Kate closed the sketchbook. She was utterly stunned to hear that Devlin wanted to teach her alongside the men. "I'm surprised he doesn't think it unseemly for a woman to learn to use a weapon."

"Perhaps there are still a few things you and that young man need to learn about each other."

Kate hesitated when her father turned to walk back to camp. As much as she wanted to live up to this sudden faith Devlin had in her ability, she was torn by the agony she knew would come from being near him. He was a temptation, a temptation she wasn't sure she could resist. If she should surrender to the feelings he conjured inside her, he could destroy her.

She didn't want to be near Devlin McCain, to be close enough to touch the warmth of his skin, close enough to inhale the intoxicating fragrance she would always think of as his. When she was close to Devlin, she couldn't think. "I'm not sure I want to learn how to use this weapon."

Frederick turned to face her, the sun full upon his face, revealing every line of his frown.

"You know the only thing I can bring myself to shoot is a clay pigeon."

"Katherine Louise Whitmore, when did you become a coward?"

"I'm not a coward!"

"You're afraid to face Devlin McCain."

"I am not afraid of Devlin McCain."

"Good, then come along. We shall need every hand when we run up against Van Horne again." Frederick turned back toward the camp. "And there is at least one hand I'm not at all sure of."

"You must be joking." Robert stared at Devlin with cold contempt in his dark eyes. "What do you imagine we are going to do with these?"

Devlin drew a deep breath and Kate could see him silently calling on every ounce of patience he possessed. "The Indians have been using blowguns for centuries."

Robert turned the hollow bamboo pipe over in his hand. "And what good do you suppose they will be against rifles?"

"We have surprise on our side. Van Horne isn't expecting us to show up in Avallon." Devlin turned away from Robert and glanced at the small group standing in a line in front of him.

Kate wondered if he were mentally clicking off their assets as Devlin looked from one person to the next: two old gentlemen, a dwarf, an aristocrat, a useless young man, and a woman he considered a rosebud. With a pang of guilt, she wondered what hope they had against Van Horne and his army.

When Devlin looked at her, there was a tenderness in his eyes, a warmth she hadn't seen in days. And there was more in his eyes, a confidence that made her believe they could face the devil himself and win, as long as they faced him together. That look in his eyes sent her heart careening into the wall of her chest with a mixture of fear and excitement. As he moved toward her she fought not to retreat.

"Let me demonstrate how it's done," Devlin said, stepping behind Kate.

The warmth of his body stroked her back. She flinched, jerking away from him, nearly tripping on the long blowgun she was holding. She glanced at Robert as his laughter rumbled in the steamy air.

"Looks like Katie is afraid of you, McCain," Robert said, grinning at Kate.

Heat flooded her cheeks. She hadn't meant to give anyone an opportunity to laugh at Devlin. "I'm sorry." She glanced over her shoulder at Devlin, expecting to confront his anger. The smile she saw on his lips and in his eyes caught her by surprise, like the sun emerging from behind dark gray clouds on a day when one expected nothing but rain.

"Shall we try again?" Devlin asked.

There was something in the deep, gravelly timbre of his voice that made her wonder if he might be speaking of things other than weapons. She nodded, unsure of her voice. The heat of his body drenched her back as he moved behind her, his warmth shaming the sun overhead, a warmth that whispered to the memories cradled deep in her soul.

"Hold the pipe so the end is elevated." Devlin slid his hand down her arm, his palm gliding over the damp cloth of her shirt, his fingertips finding the bare skin of her inner arm below the rolled-up shirt at her elbow.

Kate bit her lower lip, fighting the sudden shivering in her limbs. He covered her hand with his and squeezed gently.

"The darts are inserted into the base of the pipe." Devlin slipped one of the seven-inch-long darts he had made into the palm of her left hand. He guided her hand to the base of her blowgun and slowly slipped the dart into the narrow shaft. He leaned closer, brushing her cheek with his as he lifted the blowgun, controlling her movements with his big hands, bringing his arms around her.

Sandalwood and the spice that was his alone flooded her senses. He surrounded her, overwhelming her with the memories she couldn't deny. This was only a demonstration, she reminded herself, trying to halt the shivering deep inside her.

"Take a deep breath and press your lips against the mouth," he said, his sweet breath brushing her cheek.

She parted her lips, but it wasn't the cool bamboo she wanted to feel against her mouth. Moisture trickled between her breasts; her skin tingled with anticipation.

This was madness! She had to concentrate on what she was doing. She had to forget.

"Now blow, hard and sharp."

She tried, but her breath was lost in her lungs. Could he feel her hands trembling beneath his? Did he know what he was doing to her?

"Miss Whitmore?" he said, his lips dangerously close to her ear, so close he sent tingles rippling down her neck.

"What?" She turned her head to look into his face. He was smiling in a way that said he knew exactly what was happening inside her.

"You forgot to breathe."

You'll turn blue if you don't breathe. And I've never seen a blue rosebud, have you? She heard the echo of his words as clearly as she felt the memory of his bare skin sliding against hers. He was taunting her, tormenting her with memories.

"Put your lips against the mouth and blow."

She watched the movement of his lips as he spoke, sensual, playful, intriguing, the way they curved with his smile. And oh so tempting. Too tempting. She pressed her lips to the mouth of the blowgun and blew, flinging the dart a few feet toward the laurel tree that was her target.

"A little more breath next time and I think you might hit your target." Devlin released the gentle hold he had on her hands.

The warm breeze felt cool against her skin as Devlin left her. She felt restless. Her clothes scraped her damp skin with her every breath; her nerves sizzled with raw, throbbing need.

She stared at Devlin, his words lost in the clamor of emotions inside her as he addressed his troop. Sunlight slipped fire into his black hair, stroked gold across the finely chiseled planes of his face. She wanted to sink her hands into the silk of his hair. She wanted to feel the smooth slide of his skin against hers. Inside she felt a slow tightening of her stomach when she realized she might never hold him in her arms again.

It has to be this way. They could never have a future together, she thought, trying to shake the feeling of despair settling around her like a shroud. And he would never make love to her again, not without a commitment, a commitment she couldn't make.

"Are these things accurate?" Edwin asked.

Devlin turned toward the jungle and lifted his blowgun to his lips. With a single puff of breath, he sent a dart flying into the trunk of the laurel tree, piercing the wood with a sharp thud.

"I'm not sure how this is going to give Van Horne more than a headache." Edwin frowned as he looked at Devlin. "Unless, of course, we hit a vital organ. Then I can see where one of those darts would be deadly."

Devlin stared at the dart he had plunged into the heart of the laurel, but he seemed to be looking beyond the tree, beyond anything Kate could see. Was he looking into the past? she wondered.

"The darts become even more deadly when you apply curare to the tips," Devlin said, his voice devoid of emotion.

"Oh." Edwin glanced down to the darts he held in his hand as though he were holding a lighted stick of dynamite. "I see."

"All right, take one of the darts I've given you and slip it into the bottom of the pipe." Devlin moved out of the line of fire. "When I give you the signal, take a deep breath, put your mouth to the opening, and blow—short and hard. And make sure you take that deep breath before you put your mouth to the opening."

Everyone complied—everyone except Robert, who stood watching the others as though they were putting on a comedy for his benefit alone. Austin Sinclair hit the target on his first try. Everyone else . . . well, everyone else needed practice, Kate thought. She felt Robert lean close to her side and stiffened.

"I'd be careful how I looked at McCain, Katie," Robert whispered. "You don't want Lord Sinclair to think you've been a naughty girl."

Was it so obvious, this horrible attraction McCain held for her? "I suppose it's too much to ask you to mind your own business," Kate said, keeping her voice to a harsh whisper.

"But I'm like one of the family. Can't you see I'm only thinking of you?" Robert smiled, a sarcastic curve of his lips. "Don't suppose you're the only woman to be blinded by that chiseled face of McCain's. I've seen the type in more than one gaming hall. Handsome bucks who do nothing but live off of their rich wives."

"I suppose they have much in common with young men who live off of their fathers."

"Always a kind word for the downtrodden." All trace of friendliness left his eyes, although his smile remained, a chilling curve of his lips. "Never a smile for your old friend. I wonder if you can possibly understand what it's like to grow

up with a man who has never approved of anything you've
ever done."

"So you've simply given up trying?"

"I'm finally living up to all of my father's expectations
of me."

"I hope you feel satisfied proving him right." Kate lifted
her blowgun and aimed for the laurel tree; her dart fell several
feet short of the mark.

"You're getting closer." Devlin crossed the firing line,
retrieving the darts from the ground and the various wounded
bushes and trees. He moved like a jungle cat, each movement
fluid and powerful.

She turned and smiled up at Robert. "Pity you shall never
know how good it feels to try."

"Honestly, you don't believe for a minute this little scheme
of McCain's will work."

"At least he is doing something; he is trying to succeed."
She glanced to where Devlin was pulling darts from the laurel
they were using as a target, admiring the shift of muscles
beneath the damp white cotton of his sweat-stained shirt.
"You've decided to bury yourself alive."

"I suppose I should try to be more like that bastard casino
owner."

"If you were one-tenth the man he is, you would be sixteen
times the man you are now."

Robert shoved a dart into the end. Before Kate realized
what he was doing, he lifted the blowgun to his lips and sent
a dart flying, a dart aimed directly toward Devlin McCain's
broad back.

"Devlin!" Kate shouted, knowing it was too late to save
him.

Chapter Twenty-five

Devlin turned at the sound of Kate's voice. White-hot pain flared in his arm, a searing of skin and muscle radiating in all directions, stealing the air from his lungs. He lurched forward, bracing his shoulder against the scarred laurel tree, snatching for his breath. The darts tumbled from his suddenly numb hand to scatter at his feet.

"Devlin!"

He heard Kate's voice in the tumble of voices swirling around him, startled voices, shouting his name. He glanced back to find her running toward him, a look of terror on her beautiful face.

"Good heavens, Devlin!" Kate grabbed his injured arm in her slender hands.

Devlin looked to where the burn of pain centered and flared. A scarlet line had been etched across his upper arm. A slow slide of warmth trickled down his arm, the dark red flow of his blood staining his shirt. "What the hell happened?"

"I didn't mean to do it," Robert said.

Devlin glanced at the man standing behind Kate. Young

339

Melville was pale, looking as drained of blood as Devlin felt.

"It was an accident, I swear. I never realized I would hit you."

Devlin had little doubt the man was telling the truth. That knowledge only lessened by a cat's whisker his urge to strangle the man.

"Damnation, Robert!" Edwin shouted, red flags of color rising high on his cheeks. "Of all the stupid, brainless . . ." He turned away from his son and the bloody scene, marching toward the river as though he couldn't stand to be near a living soul.

Color returned to Robert's cheeks, a scarlet stain rising from his sweat-stained shirt collar. He stared at Devlin a moment, emotions Devlin could only guess at flickering in his eyes. Without a word, Robert turned and marched away, headed toward his tent.

Devlin wondered at the strained relationship between father and son. And he wondered what his own relationship might have been if he had known his father.

"My, but I'm thinking it's lucky those darts weren't tipped with poison," Barnaby said, smiling up at him.

"You'll have infection to worry about," Austin said. "In this climate any wound can be dangerous."

"Infection," Kate whispered, her fingers growing tense on Devlin's arm.

"I'll get your medicine box," Frederick said, patting his daughter's shoulder.

"Van Horne took it." Kate pulled her handkerchief from a front pocket of her trousers.

"We should find a way to stop the . . ." Frederick pressed his fingers to his lips, looking very much like a man who is about to be ill. "You're bleeding rather badly, Devlin."

Devlin clenched his teeth against the sudden surge of pain as Kate clamped her handkerchief against his wound, the wisp of white linen and lace rapidly absorbing his blood. He could feel her fear for him in the trembling of her hand as she held the stained cloth to his torn flesh.

"It's getting late," Devlin said, glancing at Frederick. "Why don't you and Lord Sinclair see if you can catch anything for dinner. Barnaby, you start gathering wood for the fire."

"So it's to be fish again." Barnaby walked between Frederick and Austin toward the river. "By the time we're done with this trip, I'll be able to swim my way back to Ireland."

"How deep is the wound?" Kate lifted the handkerchief, frowning at the blood flowing in a steady, red stream from the gash visible through the tear in his shirt. "Good heavens, I wish I had my medicine box."

She might not love him, but she cared for him. And maybe that was enough for now. "Come with me." Devlin took her hand. "I want to show you something."

"But your arm," she said, allowing him to lead her toward the jungle. "We should do something."

He smiled at her. "The Indians use the jungle as their medicine box."

Devlin paused a few feet into the jungle, allowing his eyes to grow accustomed to the shadows. Sunlight peeked through the emerald canopy overhead, setting the mist that hovered above the ground aglow with gold. Ferns and palm shoots lifted lacy green arms toward the light, hopeful for a sip of nourishment overlooked by the trees and vines towering above them.

Here the passage of time was little felt. Devlin stood as a man might have stood 200 years before him, as a man might stand 200 years in the future, breathing the moist air, tasting the humus on his tongue, witnessing the jungle as it was today.

Holding Kate's hand, he ventured farther into the ancient forest until he came upon a narrow stream fed by the river. Great pendants of orchids dripped from the trees, pale ivory, deepest scarlet, and all shades in between, hanging in cascades 20 feet long, reminding him of the morning he had surrounded Kate with fragrant blossoms.

He glanced down at the woman walking beside him. She was staring at the orchids, a frown marring her smooth brow. Was she also remembering?

It took him only a few moments to find what he was looking for: a broad-leafed vine with small, yellow flowers that had coiled upward along the trunk of a palm tree growing beside the stream.

"Would you cut a few inches from the stem of that vine?" Devlin slid his knife from its sheath. He turned it in his hand and offered the smooth, wooden grip to Kate.

"Is this an Indian remedy?" she asked, taking the proffered knife.

"I hope so."

He expected her to turn away; she didn't. She stood clutching the knife in her hand, watching him as he flicked open the buttons lining his damp shirt. As he stripped the shirt from his shoulders, her gaze flowed over him, skimming his shoulders, his chest, warm as summer, filled with the admiration of a woman appreciating the man before her, a woman who wanted that man.

Despite the pain in his arm, Devlin felt an answering flame to the fires he saw burning in her blue eyes, the need inside him growing, unsheathing talons that sank fully into his groin. He had the uneasy feeling the woman would be able to stir his blood if he were on his deathbed. Yet there was sadness in her eyes, a sadness he could feel as keenly as her desire, a sadness that allowed him to fight the beast awakening inside him.

He understood her, perhaps better than she understood herself. He was only beginning to understand this tricky emotion of love.

"The vine." He accepted the husky tone of his own voice for the desire he couldn't hide.

Kate flinched, like a sleepwalker startled into wakefulness. "Of course," she whispered, turning away from him.

Kate silently berated herself as she crossed the few feet of decaying leaves to the vine he had indicated. The man was bleeding and all she could think about was the way the muscles moved beneath the smooth skin of his chest as he had stripped away his shirt. There was something wrong with her. Something very wrong.

She heard the soft sound of splashing water and glanced over her shoulder. Devlin was kneeling beside the stream, rinsing his bloody shirt. As she watched, he bathed the blood from his arm, drawing handfuls of water over his skin, thick muscles dancing beneath golden skin with every movement.

She turned away from the intriguing sight of this man and hacked the vine with the razor-sharp edge of Devlin's knife, as though slicing it to pieces could excise the part of her she didn't understand, the demon deep inside her that could do nothing but want and want and want. A faintly sweet scent filled the air as she tore the tender, green flesh; a pale green liquid oozed from the wounds she inflicted.

When she turned toward Devlin, he was sitting on one of the roots that grew like buttresses from a tree beside the clear stream, his wet shirt draped over a nearby root. She was struck with the sudden feeling she had stepped into an enchanted forest and awakened a woodland god.

Mist hung in the air around him. The glow of sunlight painted the gold of his skin in sharp contrast to the dark green background, carved the contours of his smooth shoulders and arms. Black curls highlighted rather than hid the thick planes of his chest. Black hair, damp with the humid air, waved around his face. He was smiling in a way that made her want to press her hands to his cheeks and capture that beguiling smile beneath her lips.

"Is this enough?" She held out her hand, hoping he would think her trembling had everything to do with his wound and nothing to do with the way he made her feel. Several inches of emerald vine lay weeping in her palm, pale green tears slipping between her fingers.

"It should be." He dabbed his fingers into the sap overflowing her palm.

She drew a sharp breath as his firm fingers slid over her sensitive palm. He glanced up at her, an inquisitive look in his silvery blue eyes. She decided to ignore the questions she saw in those beautiful eyes. It was safer not to think of those questions, or the answers that might be hidden deep inside her.

"What is this vine called?"

"*Juju*." He sucked in his breath as he spread the sap over the gash in his upper arm. "Magic. I'm afraid I don't know the proper name for it. But I've seen the medicine men of two different tribes use it on open wounds. Something in the vine seems to prevent infection."

"Let me," she said, sitting beside him. With her fingertips she spread the cool, green salve over the ugly red gash, sensing the pain she was inflicting, feeling it in the way his muscles grew tense beneath her touch. "I'm so sorry this happened."

"It wasn't your fault."

"I was arguing with Robert. He became so angry he didn't think."

"I don't believe he did it on purpose." Devlin released his breath in a long sigh. "I'm not sure I've ever met anyone as self-destructive as he is."

"You're right about him. He is self-destructive. And I don't think I ever realized it until today." Kate glanced up, meeting the stormy blue depths of Devlin's eyes. "Edwin demanded a great deal from Robert, even as a child. I think this is Robert's way of rebelling."

"I guess there's something to be said about never having known your father."

She saw a sadness in his eyes, a shadow of hurt and humiliation there, a haunted look that made her glance back to the tangible wound in his arm. There were depths to this man Kate had never realized existed, layers of feelings she was tempted to explore. Yet she knew temptation would lead to destruction.

"When we were children, Robert was my best friend. But

now I wonder if I ever really was his friend. I wasn't there when he was troubled and needed someone to talk to. I wasn't there when . . . I was never there for him."

Slowly she drew her fingers over Devlin's open wound. "I've spent my life roaming from one end of the world to another. I've never thought of it before, but aside from Father, I've never really been close to anyone." *Perhaps that's why what I feel for you is so frightening.*

"Whenever you let someone get close to you, Kate, it's frightening."

She glanced up, afraid for a moment she had spoken her feelings, knowing in that instant when her eyes met his that he had somehow perceived her thoughts.

"There's always the unknown about a relationship." He cupped her cheek in his warm hand. "Will the other person accept you when he sees you at your ugliest? Will he return your affection? Will he leave and take your heart with him?"

Kate closed her eyes, feeling the weight of his love settle against her chest, a tangible thing, warm and vibrant, inviting, threatening. She resisted the urge to cover the warm hand pressed against her cheek with her own, to turn and press her lips to his palm.

"Like you, I've spent my whole life roaming from one place to another." He brushed his thumb over one corner of her lips. "But I've always wanted a place to settle down, a place to call home."

He took his hand away, leaving the warm print of his palm against her cheek, and the cold ache of regret deep inside her. The sounds of the forest filled the silence between them, the constant chatter of monkeys high overhead, the cackle of a bird that sounded too much like laughter.

"Will you be happy if you settle in one place?"

"I don't know." He smiled, a slight curve of his lips that whispered of wistful imaginings. "Will you be happy once you find your fabled city?"

She had once thought finding proof of Atlantis would be

the most wonderful experience of her life. Now she wondered if that were true.

"Of course I'll be happy." The scent of warm sandalwood drifted from his damp skin to tease her senses. She glanced at his chest, wishing she could brush her cheek against the silky, male curls, remembering the taste of his skin. "Father and I have been searching for years for proof of Atlantis, my entire life, really."

"And once you have it, once you realize your dream, then what?"

"There will always be a mystery to solve," she said, her gaze sliding upward along the strong column of his neck. She could see the shadow of his beard just below the surface of his smooth cheeks, the bristles gone now. Yet she remembered the intriguing feel of his beard against the smooth skin of her thighs; her skin warmed with the memory.

"Father believes there is a connection between Atlantis and the old legends of England and Wales and Ireland. He believes there is a chance King Arthur and Merlin were from Atlantis."

Devlin's lips curved into a smile. "One of the priests at the orphanage let me use his library. I remember devouring Malory. I guess there was a time when I believed in King Arthur and his Camelot."

"We might explore that possibility. We might return to Egypt." Why did it all sound so hollow? Why did it all sound so lonely? "Egypt is fascinating. Perhaps the first colony of Atlantis. It really is quite satisfying to discover a part of the past, to touch another lifetime." Why did she sound as though she were trying to convince herself?

"It sounds as if you plan to live your entire life roaming from place to place."

She held his gaze a long moment, searching for an answer to the questions churning inside her, knowing it was as elusive now as it had been since the first moment Devlin McCain had held her in his strong arms. She stood, appalled to realize her legs were far from steady.

"The bleeding has stopped," she said, avoiding the subject of her future, a future she had always felt so certain of, a future that suddenly felt foreign.

"The medicine men knew what they were doing." Devlin glanced down at the gash in his arm, his thick, black lashes tangling at the corners of his eyes. "Too bad every wound couldn't be treated so easily."

The sadness she sensed inside him spoke to the longing deep within her. It had been too long since she had felt his arms around her, too long since she had tasted his lips. He sat quietly, watching her with those stormy eyes, making her want him as she had never wanted anything in her life. "We should go back. You need rest."

She turned away from him, well aware of how close she was to the edge, knowing it wasn't fair to him if she should tumble over the brink. If she stayed here another instant she would be in his arms.

And then what? What could she give him? Nothing but a few moments when he wanted so much more, when he deserved a lifetime of love. She needed to get away from him. Yet she knew there was no shelter anywhere from the feelings locked deep inside her. She knelt by the stream and rinsed her hands, washing away the traces of his blood that had stained her fingers.

"Let's not go back to camp yet," he said, his gravelly voice a husky caress.

She stood, fighting the conflicting urges inside her. She wanted to run. Yet she knew the only place she wanted to run to was straight into Devlin's arms. She felt him rise behind her, felt the heat of his body embrace her as he moved toward her. "It will be getting late soon."

"We have hours yet." He rested his hands on her shoulders. "You're trembling."

"I was terrified when I saw Robert had shot that dart at you." Kate drew a deep breath. "I guess I'm still a little shaky."

"Is that why you're trembling?" He drew his hands down

her arms, skimming the linen of her blouse, sliding his palms over the bare skin below her elbows. "Or is it something else?"

"You know what it is." Kate closed her eyes and fought to keep from leaning back against him. "Why are you doing this? Why are you tormenting me?"

"I've been thinking about what it means to love someone." He laced his fingers through hers. Slowly he wrapped his arms around her, bringing their clasped hands to rest between her breasts. "We might not have forever, Kate, but we have this moment. I can't let pride stand between us. I can't go on watching you, knowing I'm the reason you've lost your smile."

"Devlin," she whispered, awed by what his offer had cost him, afraid of taking his gift. Pride had been the price for Devlin. What would it cost her?

He nuzzled aside the collar of her shirt and pressed his lips to the base of her neck. The soft warmth stole her breath.

"It's been a long time since I saw you smile, Professor," Devlin whispered, his lips brushing her skin. He drew a line with the tip of his tongue from her neck to the lobe of her ear, dragging a moan from her lips. "Tell me, how can I make you smile?"

This was dangerous. Far too dangerous. She should tell him to stop, tell him she had changed her mind, tell him . . . He tugged at her earlobe with his teeth, sending sensation shimmering down her neck and across her shoulder.

"I want to share the few moments we have left." He slipped his hands free of hers. "I want to hold you in my arms, love you, if only for today."

She swayed on her feet as he backed away from her, leaving her craving the heat of his body. She turned, looking at him with all the bewilderment she was feeling inside. He smiled, but in his eyes she saw a haunting sadness, a sadness she wished she could banish forever.

"Will you let me love you, Kate? Will you let me share this brief moment of your life?"

Three feet of warm, fragrant air hung heavily between them, a mist glowing in the muted sunlight like a barrier between two worlds. He held her with nothing but his gaze. He embraced her with nothing but the love she could feel radiating from him.

She thought of all the reasons she should turn away from this man, all of their differences, the danger of becoming more entangled in his life. Yet when he reached for her, offering his outstretched hand, all of those reasons crumbled into dust. There was no tomorrow. There was only today, this moment, and the man reaching for her with love and tenderness.

She slipped her hand in his. She felt the warm pressure of his fingers closing around her hand. She looked up into his face, tracing the artfully carved curves and angles, and crossed the barrier between them.

"Kate," Devlin whispered, holding her close to his heart. "My beautiful Kate."

Slowly they peeled away layers of cotton and linen and silk, touching, kissing, until the fragrance of orchids caressed their bare skin. Yet it was the caress of Devlin's skin Kate savored.

Intriguing friction—silky, male curls against her smooth breasts, the sweet abrasion sending delicious sensation spiraling from her aroused nipples. All of those sensations gathered like glittering sparks low in her belly, where she felt the compelling heat of his arousal, full, lush, throbbing with life.

"I didn't believe this would ever happen again." She slid her free hand upward along the smooth slope of his shoulder. "Except in my dreams."

He slid his arms around her waist. "Do I haunt your dreams?"

"Every night." She pressed her lips against the pulse point of his neck, feeling the swift throb of his heart beneath her touch. She didn't stop to think of what her own words revealed. She didn't want to know.

"Did I hold you like this in your dreams?" He slid his warm palms upward along her back, his fingers curving along the shape of her sides, his fingertips grazing her breasts.

"Yes." She arched under his caress, her breasts sliding against the naked heat of his chest.

"Did I kiss you like this?" His breath warmed her cheek with each word before he touched his lips to hers.

Dreams were a pale reflection of reality, she decided, parting her lips beneath his. Sunlight. This was what it would feel like if she could sip from the sun: hot and vibrant, filling her with light and warmth.

"I wonder." He brushed his lips against her temple. "What happens when two people share a dream? Do they meet on another plane? Do their souls mingle?"

She trembled at his words, at the way he was touching her, with his hands sliding over the curve of her rounded bottom, pulling her close, impressing his passion into her belly.

"Each night you've haunted me, Kate," he said, his voice husky as he lowered his lips to her neck. A soft kiss, before he parted his lips and she felt the searing swirl of his tongue against her skin. "Each night I've held you like this. Each night I've made love to you, sinking into your fire."

"Devlin." She held him close, her arms wrapped around his neck. "Make love to me." *Make me forget about that tomorrow when we shall say good-bye.*

He lifted her in his arms and lowered her to a soft carpet of lacy ferns. A whisper of sunlight found its way through the trees, glowing softly on his black hair. He kissed her, his emotions naked in every movement of his lips against hers. Love and regret, pleasure and pain, all there in the touch of his lips. He brushed his hands over her breasts, his fingers circling the crests, teasing, before squeezing the rosy tips gently. She moaned against his lips.

He kissed her neck, branding her with the sudden flick of his tongue. He drew a line of fire with the tip of his tongue across the slope of her breast, slowly banking the fires inside her, until anticipation simmered in every nerve. She sank her hands into his thick hair as he took one velvety nipple into his mouth. Silky strands stroked her fingers as he coaxed her nipple to rise and tighten and tingle with his hot mouth, as he skimmed her belly with his callused palm, as he claimed the soft folds hidden beneath moist curls with his long fingers.

He flowed down her body. She came alive beneath his hands and his lips and his tongue, her nerves gathering into a network of sensation, the sensation shimmering, consuming her.

"I love you, Kate," he whispered, lowering himself between her thighs.

She touched her fingers to his cheek as he slid into the welcoming heat of her body, her feelings for him overflowing her carefully constructed dam of self-protection. *I love you.* The words were locked in her heart.

"Remember me." He lowered his head, pausing with his lips a breath away from hers. "Just remember me, that's all I ask of you."

"Always." Never would she feel this way again. Never would she welcome another man into her arms. Never, not after tasting Devlin McCain's love.

He closed his eyes, a sigh slipping from his lips to warm her before he kissed her, before he carried her away to that distant realm where reality burned away into ashes, and love gave birth to hope.

Chapter Twenty-six

The thick tangle of forest began to thin with the gradual rise of the land as their canoes slid through the dark water of a wide, uncharted river, a rippling stream that would take them to Avallon. Men who had never had a callus before now sported blisters from the paddles Devlin had taught them to use. Yet no one complained, not even Robert, who had spoken little to anyone in days.

Anticipation hung in the early morning air, as thick as the mist that gathered every day. Anticipation that turned to dread with the charred remains of every campfire they found, evidence of Leighton Van Horne's progress before them.

"Katie!" Frederick said, grabbing her arm. "Look, there, up ahead."

As they turned a bend in the river, a mountain soared above the ragged forest a few miles in the distance, the lofty summit slicing through the morning mist to pierce the sky with jagged points, like black diamonds. The dark rocks came alive in the sunlight, flames of color leaping from crystals embedded in the mountainside.

"Just like Randolph described," Frederick said, squeezing Kate's arm. "This is it, Katie. This is it!"

"Yes," Kate whispered. They were close now, close to discovering the fact of their dreams. Yet she was having doubts about her dreams.

Frederick turned and shouted to the men in the canoe behind them, waving his arms so enthusiastically he set the narrow boat swaying.

"Easy now." Barnaby gripped the sides of the canoe where he sat behind Frederick. "I'll be telling you, I'm not much for swimming."

"There!" Frederick shouted. "Randolph's mountain!"

Austin waved in reply. Edwin and Robert, who shared the canoe with Austin, sat staring straight ahead. Edwin looked stunned, Robert sullen, his expression as closed as it had been for days.

"I think Mr. Melville is beginning to believe," Devlin said.

Kate turned back around to face the man sitting in front of her in the narrow canoe. Devlin was turned on the seat, his hip pressed against her knees, his smile making those knees turn to water. She lifted her shoulders, trying to ease the tension in her muscles. It seemed she was forever tense these days.

She spent every day sitting behind Devlin, watching him, wanting him. She spent every night lying awake in her tent, waiting for him, wondering if this would be the night he refused to come to her.

Yet every night he did come. Every night she discovered more of the mystery in his arms, more of the sensual world where Devlin ruled supreme. And every dawn he left her, with poignant memories of the night before, with pointed regrets for what the future would bring.

"And how about you, Devlin?" Frederick asked. "Are you beginning to believe?"

Devlin tipped back his hat, allowing the sunlight to stream across his face. He looked toward the mountain, staring a long moment before he spoke. "Yeah, I guess I am."

Something in his voice brought the hot sting of tears to Kate's eyes, a poignancy colored by hope and, at the same time, sadness. They were drawing near the end of their journey. Soon it would all be over, the search for Avallon, the nights spent in Devlin's arms. She watched as Devlin plunged his paddle into the water, each powerful stroke taking them closer to Avallon, closer to their inevitable parting.

She glanced away from Devlin, trying to fix her mind on something other than the conflicting emotions he always conjured inside her. Gray, gnarled trunks of trees rose little more than 20 feet above the capim grass covering the flat sweep of the plains. Among the trunks, stunted rubber trees and dwarf palmetto grew, their tops torn from the wind.

What was wrong with her? She was close to discovering the biggest archaeological find in history, and all she could think about was Devlin McCain. She wanted to touch him, she wanted to press her cheek against his broad back and breathe in the scent of his skin, she wanted to slip her arms around him and hold him so she could feel the warmth and life of him. At this moment, compared to Devlin, all the discoveries in the world seemed insignificant.

This power he held over her was frightening. Frightening, because she was beginning to wonder if she would always feel this way about him.

"We'll beach the canoes just up ahead." Devlin glanced over his shoulder at Frederick.

"But we're more than a mile away," Frederick said, bumping his paddle against the side of the canoe. "We could take the canoes right up to the base of the mountain."

"We haven't passed Van Horne," Devlin said. "That means he's up ahead, somewhere. I'd rather not cruise right into his camp."

"Oh, Van Horne, yes." Frederick scratched his chin with the butt of his paddle. "I had rather forgotten all about the man. I suppose we'll have to proceed with caution."

Devlin's smile was indulgent as he looked at Frederick. "I suppose."

At Devlin's orders, they landed the canoes a mile from the base of the mountain. There was no beach here, just a tangle of roots from the trees growing alongside the river, and tufts of grass at the water's edge. The soil was more clay than sand, the mud on the bottom of the river sucking at Kate's feet as she waded the few feet to the shore. She waited on the shore, watching as Devlin and Austin secured the canoes with ropes to a cedar tree growing beside the river.

"I'll scout ahead," Devlin said, slinging the vine strap attached to his blowgun over his shoulder. "The rest of you wait here."

A whisper of frost breathed against the base of Kate's spine, a cold premonition of danger seeping into her blood. She grabbed Devlin's arm, needing to feel his warmth and vitality, wanting to keep him safe. He looked down at her, and she knew he could see all the fear and confusion in her face with his silvery blue eyes.

"Don't worry, Professor," he said, a smile curving his lips. "We'll find your lost city."

"I'll go with you." Austin took his blowgun from the bottom of the canoe.

"I'd rather you stayed here," Devlin said, holding Austin's gaze. "Just in case."

Kate didn't want to think of what that might mean. "Let me go with you."

"I'll have a better chance of getting in there and out in one piece if I go alone." Devlin gently pried her hand from his arm. "This might take a while, so don't get nervous and go plunging after me. You just might get us both killed."

"You won't take any chances, will you?"

"I told you once before, I'm no one's hero. But I need to find out if Van Horne has found the city, and just what we're up against." Devlin held her hand, sliding his thumb back and forth over her knuckles. She knew he must feel the moisture on her palm, the sign of fear she couldn't hide.

"I don't need to be worried you're going to pop up behind me. Promise me you'll wait here."

"Yes," she whispered, forcing the word past the constriction of fear in her throat. Her promise won a smile from Devlin, a smile she wished she could tuck away and save for all the days of her life.

He turned and left her. In a matter of moments he disappeared into the stunted forest.

Kate felt a searing in her chest, a pain that went deeper than flesh, and from that pain came clarity, a certainty that crystallized in her heart: she would lose her soul when Devlin McCain walked out of her life.

It was there, just as Randolph had described it in his journal, an opening at the base of the mountain, the passage to Avallon. Devlin bent and poked his head inside the narrow cleft in the black stone of the mountain. Inside, the crevice widened slightly, the small cave filled with a curious sighing of the wind. He could see a glimmer of light shining from around a bend in the stone, a beacon beckoning him to a mystery.

He had found traces of Van Horne near the river, the charred remains of his campfire, his flotilla of canoes sitting on the shore. Yet there had been no guards. Why wouldn't he leave any guards over the canoes?

Devlin glanced over his shoulder. The backs of his ears tingled; he couldn't shake the feeling he was being watched.

Except for a few palmetto and stunted rubber trees, the land was clear for a half mile back toward the river. An island of wind-battered little trees stretched southward, separating him from Kate. The forest would be a good place to hide, if someone had a reason to hide. But for the life of him, he couldn't come up with a reason why Van Horne's well-armed men would be hiding.

Devlin glanced at the cleft in the black stone and drew a deep breath, wondering what was waiting for him on the other side. He stepped inside the narrow cave.

The passage was low and narrow, pure hell for a man of Devlin's size. He walked with knees bent, head bent, his shoulders brushing both sides of the ragged stone walls. In here there would be no chance to use the blowgun, leaving him vulnerable to attack from the front or rear.

The strange sighing of the wind grew louder as he crept toward the light, as if calling to him. Devlin only hoped it wasn't a siren luring him to destruction. With care for the poisoned tip, he slipped a dart into the base of his blowgun before he stepped from the small, curving cave into bright sunlight.

He had passed through the wall of the mountain and stood now on the rim of a gorge. He stared at the cause of the odd sighing sound he had heard in the cave. On the far side of the gorge, water emerged from the face of the mountain, falling in a white curtain, tumbling over black rocks 200 feet to the base of the gorge, where lush, emerald-green palms and ferns grew in abundance, and orchids dripped from the trees. Eden, it seemed.

Devlin turned in a circle, checking the walls of the mountain for Van Horne's men. The trail was there, winding up past the opening of the cave, exactly as Randolph had described it. He saw no living thing among the harsh, black rock. Still, he couldn't shake the uneasy feeling his every move was being watched.

He stood at the base of the trail a moment, staring at the point where the path bent inward on itself, judging the chances Van Horne had placed guards along the way. He would be as exposed as a duck on a pond. Still, if he wanted to get to the summit, he would have to take this trail.

Kate sat in the shade of an acacia by the river, staring into the rippling water, the swift current washing the exposed roots of the tree before slapping against the rocks below her feet. She concentrated on the splashing water, wishing it would drown out the voice of the man standing behind her.

"I knew this was a mistake," Edwin said. "What are we supposed to do if McCain gets himself killed?"

Kate pressed her back into the rough bark of the acacia and glanced to where her father was sitting on the ground beside her. There was no reason to be nervous, she assured herself. None at all. Devlin knew what he was doing. He was fine. Still, she couldn't keep the muscles in her shoulders from drawing into tight knots.

"Devlin McCain can handle himself," Frederick said. "Nothing is going to happen to him."

"I realize you have a great deal of faith in this man." Edwin spoke as though Frederick were a child who still believed in fairy tales and it was his job to deliver the ugly truth. "But I feel we must face the possibility that he is not coming back."

"It's too early to start building a funeral pyre, Edwin," Frederick said.

Kate tugged on a stalk of grass beside her, dragging the roots from the ground. Devlin had been gone a long time, more than four hours the last time she had checked with her father a few minutes ago. Too long.

"We should have turned back the moment we got free of Van Horne." Edwin's voice faded slightly as he turned away from her. "And now look what's happened. That young man is no doubt dead."

Kate glanced over her shoulder. She watched Edwin's agitated pacing, feeling the tension tighten inside her, twisting in her chest until she could barely draw a breath.

Frederick came to his feet and followed Edwin toward the forest. "Edwin, you are doing nothing but making our situation worse. There is no sense in worrying about something that will not happen."

Edwin turned to face his friend. "What chance do you suppose we will have, trying to make our way back out of this tangle?"

"Just once try to see the possibilities instead of the obstacles."

"I do see the possibilities." Edwin planted his hands on his hips. "I see the very real possibility Devlin McCain isn't coming back. I see the possibility we shall never see England again."

Kate stared at the mountain. Afternoon sunlight painted a rainbow in the mist hanging above the highest jagged peak, as though nature were drawing attention to the treasure waiting for them there. Yet what else waited for them? she wondered. A devil with an angel's face?

It was then that she realized she would turn her back on the mystery waiting atop that jagged peak if it meant keeping Devlin safe. But was it too late?

"You look a thousand miles away."

Kate glanced up to find Austin standing beside her. "Not that far."

"Just as far as the mountain."

Kate nodded. "Do you think Devlin is in trouble? Do you think we should go after him?"

"I think he'll be back soon." Austin sat beside her, curling one long leg on the ground. He rested his forearm on his raised knee, his gaze directed to the mountain. "If not, I'll go after him."

"I don't think I can take this waiting much longer."

Austin tilted his head and looked at her, his lips curving into a smile. The breeze tossed a lock of ebony hair across his brow. Something about Austin at that moment made her feel she was looking into Devlin's face, Devlin's eyes. Good heavens, would she see Devlin in the face of every dark-haired man she met?

"You care a great deal for him."

"I think I'm beginning to understand what it means to love someone," she whispered, echoing the words Devlin had spoken a lifetime ago.

"From what I've seen, you aren't alone."

"He asked me to marry him." Kate glanced down to the grass she still held clenched in her fist. "And I turned him down. At the time, all I could see were our differences."

"And now?"

She opened her hand. The broken blades of grass lay across her palm along crescent-shaped marks dug deeply into her skin from her nails. "Now I realize I don't want to live my life without him. I only pray it isn't too late."

Austin took her hand in his warm grasp, his palm sliding over hers, enclosing the slender blades of grass between their hands. "I have a feeling everything is going to be all right."

"I don't know what I would do if—"

"Devlin!"

Kate glanced over her shoulder at her father's shout. He was rushing toward the forest, toward the man walking from the shadows. "Devlin," she whispered, his name an answered prayer.

Relief came swiftly and with an intensity that left her shaking. Austin rose to his feet and helped her to stand, his hand warm around hers, his strong arm steadying her. Although her father, Edwin, and Barnaby swarmed around him, battering him with their questions, Devlin didn't seem to notice them. He was looking at her as though she were the only sight in the world he wanted to see.

She rushed to his side on shaky legs. Once beside him, she touched his arm, needing to feel the solid warmth of him. "You were gone so long, I was afraid something might have happened to you."

"I took a trip up the mountain." Devlin smiled in a way that tilted her heart upside down.

"Was it there?" Frederick asked. "Did you see Avallon?"

"It's there."

"I knew it!" Frederick shouted, slapping Edwin so hard across the back, the other man stumbled forward.

Kate's world shifted. She held tighter to Devlin's arm. "You saw Avallon?"

"I was in the city."

"What about Van Horne?" Edwin asked.

Devlin turned to look at Edwin. "No sign of him."

"That's wonderful," Kate whispered.

"That's damn curious," Devlin said. "He left his canoes on the beach, with no guard."

Austin shrugged. "He wasn't expecting to be followed."

"Here, you have to expect anything." Devlin glanced over his shoulder as though he were looking for someone in the shadows of the sparse forest.

"Devlin, my lad, sometimes you have to smile at your own good fortune," Barnaby said.

Devlin glanced down at the little man. "Why wasn't there any trace of Van Horne in the ruins of the city?"

Barnaby shrugged. "I suppose 'tis possible he might've decided to explore more of the mountain."

"Let's not question our good fortune. Let's go." Frederick marched toward the canoes.

"Van Horne is gone, Devlin." Austin turned and followed Frederick.

"To Avallon!" Barnaby shouted, running to keep up with Austin's long strides.

"Frederick, perhaps we should camp here tonight," Edwin shouted, following Frederick toward the river. "McCain is right. There is something strange about this."

Frederick dismissed his friend with a wave of his hand.

Devlin didn't follow the other men. He stood for a long moment, watching them, before he looked down at Kate, his brow carved into lines. "Stay close to me."

"You're worried."

"Something isn't right about this."

"But if Van Horne is gone . . ."

"That's just it. What happened to him?"

Her arms prickled as though brushed by ice. "Do you think we should wait?"

"I think your father has been waiting too long already. Nothing is going to keep him from seeing that city today." Devlin looked to where the other men were scrambling into the canoes. "I just wish I didn't have this feeling we were walking into some kind of trap."

Chapter Twenty-seven

Smooth rock paved the floor of the trail leading to Avallon like cobblestones, intriguing reminders that it could only have been cut by the hand of man. Crystals studded the wall of the mountain, spinning sunlight into rainbows; hexagons of malachite, layers of history revealed in the green stone, mushroom formations of glittering quartz, and shimmering green and blue nuggets of aquamarine.

It took less than two hours of traveling along the winding trail to reach the summit. Yet it seemed to Kate it had taken a lifetime.

With a cool breeze in her face, she stared at the vista before her. Mountain peaks stretched from northwest to southeast farther than she could see, dissolving into a pale blue haze on the horizon. A forest spread like a thick, emerald blanket from north to northeast, silver ribbons of water winding through the trees glittering in the sunlight. Yet it was the nearby valley that captured her gaze, and her imagination. It was there, exactly as Randolph had described, the great stone walls rising less than a mile from where she stood.

Avallon.

In minutes that took an eternity, they reached the city. Three arches marked the entrance, stones that had been carefully cut from the mountain and set in perfect symmetry. Kate stared up at the crown of the center arch, holding her breath as she traced with her gaze the symbols carved deeply into the black stone.

Looking up at that arch, she felt a shiver pass through her. It was as Randolph had described. The symbols were the same as those she and her father had traced back to what they believed to be a common source—Atlantis. She pressed her palm against the wall, feeling the warmth of the sun captured in the black stone, needing reassurance it was real.

"Afraid you're dreaming all of this?" Devlin asked.

Kate glanced up to the man standing beside her, the man who had brought her through hell to give her a glimpse of paradise. "If I am, promise me you won't awaken me from this dream."

"I promise," he whispered, his dark, gravelly voice brushing over her in a rough caress. "How does it feel when a dream comes true?"

"Incredible." Kate looked up into his eyes and wondered if she could make a dream come true for him.

Devlin looked away from her, his smile growing still. She knew he was hoping this dream didn't turn into a nightmare.

A wide avenue stretched beyond the arches. Fallen pillars and stones littered the paved street, ancient crystals in the stone sparking flame from captured sunlight. On either side of the street rose two-story buildings of precisely cut stone. In many the roofs had caved in. Stones were missing in a few, causing the structures to settle at odd angles.

Kate walked between Austin and Devlin, staring in amazement. Yet beyond her feeling of elation lingered a nagging anxiety. Devlin looked at every doorway as though he expected a devil to come charging at them. He kept glancing over his shoulder as though he thought they were being followed by someone other than her father, Edwin, Robert, and Barnaby. She sensed Austin's unease, saw it in the taut lines of his face. Apparently both he and Devlin couldn't accept their good fortune and enjoy the wonders spread out before them.

"It looks as though an earthquake destroyed most of the city." Devlin glanced at one of the buildings as they passed it. "The city once extended to the edge of the cliff. I found a few buildings standing outside of this street and the plaza up ahead. But just about everything is in ruins or half buried."

The street opened into a huge square. Planted in the center was a large black column with a statue on top, a figure of a man. The sculpture resembled the art of the Italian Renaissance, the bearded face finely chiseled, a laurel wreath resting on his thick crop of short hair. Bare from the waist up, a short tunic draped his hips. The statue stood with one hand on his hip and the other pointing north toward a building that spread stone wings along the entire right side of the square, an ancient temple or palace.

The eight square stone columns lining the front of the structure were still intact, lifting the pediment roof toward the sun. In the shadows cast by the roof sat a man and woman on the top step. They smiled when they realized Kate had noticed them.

Kate's breath caught in her throat. She reached for Devlin. At the same time he stepped in front of her and raised his blowgun.

"Who are you?" Devlin demanded.

"Don't shoot!" Austin grabbed Devlin's raised arm.

"Devlin, don't!" Kate shouted, clutching his free arm.

Devlin glanced down at her, frowning. "I'm not going to shoot unless they give me good reason."

"You have nothing to fear from us," the man said, his deep voice molded into the distinctive accent of the British upper class. He rose, tall, slender, his shirt and trousers as black as his thick mane of midnight hair, his clean-shaven features as finely chiseled as a statue.

In spite of the stranger's words, Kate could feel Devlin stiffen beside her. She tightened her hold on his arm, more to keep her own sense of balance than to prevent him from doing harm. Who were these people?

"Katie, do you think they could be . . ." Frederick didn't finish; he stared, as they all stared at this compelling couple.

The stranger offered his hand to the woman and helped her to her feet. She rose, her fair head reaching the man's broad shoulder. A tunic of emerald-green silk flowed around her hips as she descended the stairs, a braided belt of gold and silver cinching the smooth material at her narrow waist. Beneath the tunic, she wore close-fitting trousers of cream-colored silk.

When she stepped into the sun, the light revealed reddish highlights in golden hair that cascaded in rippling waves to her hips. She was stunning. And the man—there was something familiar about his handsome face, something familiar in his lithe stride, each movement conjuring images in Kate's mind of a jungle cat.

"We've been waiting a long time to meet you, Devlin McCain." The man extended his hand as he drew near.

Devlin's arm stiffened beneath Kate's hand, an echo of her own surprise rippling through him.

"Who are you?" Devlin demanded, ignoring the man's outstretched hand. "How do you know who I am?"

The man smiled, a slight curving of sensual lips that sent curious chills curling along Kate's spine. He seemed so familiar, so very familiar.

"The first question is simple to answer. The second will take some time." The lines crinkled around the stranger's blue-green eyes as his smile deepened. "I'm Rhys, and this is my wife, Brianna."

"We have a home near here." Brianna smiled as she looked at Kate. Her accent differed from her husband's, a soft lilt that whispered of the emerald green of Ireland. "I'm sure you must be exhausted from your journey. Please come with us. After you've changed and had a nice, hot meal, we'll be happy to answer all of your questions."

Frederick stared up at the man called Rhys. "This city, the ruins, they're the remains of a colony of Atlantis, aren't they?"

"The city was the first my ancestors built when they reached this mountain more than six thousand years ago." When Rhys spoke, there was a touch of pride in his voice, pride without conceit.

"The symbols. I've tracked them for years." Frederick looked past Rhys to the ancient temple. "Your ancestors must have been descendants of Atlantis."

"The legends of my people tell of a great expanse of land in what is now the Atlantic Ocean, where our ancestors once lived before the island was destroyed by a tremendous cataclysm." Rhys smiled as he held Frederick's gaze. "This island was known as Atlantis."

Kate could scarcely breathe. "Father, all of your work . . ." Had they finally captured the dream?

Rhys looked at her, his remarkable eyes filled with a wealth of understanding, as though he could sense the turmoil within her. "Your father's work is really quite remarkable. You should both be proud of your accomplishments." Again came his smile, and with it a warmth that embraced her. And yet there was something guarded about this man, ancient mysteries hidden behind a generous smile.

"You know about my work?" Frederick asked.

"We've been following your progress for years," Rhys said. "I particularly liked your book on the legends of Britain and their possible connection to Atlantis. I must say, you're quite insightful. We have several scholars who have arrived at similar conclusions."

"Oh," Frederick whispered. "Would it be possible to see their work?"

"I'm sure you have many questions," Rhys said. "And I'm certain you will be more comfortable at our house."

"And what if we decide we don't want to go with you?" Devlin asked.

"I suppose under the circumstances I would be as cautious as you," Rhys said, his voice deep and calm. "Still, there is no reason to fear us. If we had wanted to, we would have taken you prisoner the moment you approached the entrance to the mountain, as we took Leighton Van Horne and his fellow companions prisoner."

"You have Van Horne?" Devlin asked.

"Yes." Rhys held Devlin's gaze a moment as though he were studying the younger man, appraising him. "Please, come with us. I assure you, we mean you no harm."

Kate believed him. There was something about him, this man who could trace his ancestors to the dawn of civilization, a sense of integrity, a quiet, commanding quality that said he had no need to use tricks against them. She glanced up at Devlin, seeing the wariness in his eyes, knowing his trust would not be given as easily as her own. "I think we should go."

"Yes, Devlin," Frederick said. "We should go with them."

Devlin shifted his primitive weapon, slinging the blowgun over his shoulder. "I have a feeling we don't have a choice."

Rhys led them through a narrow passage leading from the square to a path that wove through the hills surrounding the ruins. The path was paved with black cobblestones that could have been there 6,000 years, each rock worn and smooth. Here the air was cool, the breeze scented by the wildflowers that grew in rolling waves of blue and white and yellow upward along the emerald hills. It looked natural, yet planned, like a garden or park.

Kate glanced up at Rhys, who walked beside her along the stone-paved path. Had he manipulated what seemed so natural? Her father walked on the other side of Rhys, bombarding the man with questions. Behind them, Austin and Devlin walked on either side of Brianna, and the others followed.

"You say Avallon was established more than six thousand years ago," Frederick said. "Why did your ancestors come here, to this remote place?"

"My people were scientists in an era when such knowledge was dangerous. After the cataclysm, when my ancestors were forced to live among primitive tribes, they used religious cults to shield their way of life in Egypt, Spain, Africa, and what is today Ireland, Wales, Scotland, and England."

"That's why there is such a similarity between the different ancient pagan religions," Frederick said.

Rhys nodded. "Some of our people involved with these cults were absorbed by them, overwhelmed by the power they possessed. They lost sight of our original purpose. They eventually saw the others as a threat."

"Corrupted by power," Kate said.

"The power to dominate kings and queens. In time, my people could no longer hide behind the shield of their religious cults. They were seen as witches and wizards, to be used or destroyed depending on the climate at the time. They sought shelter, a place where they could be free from persecution, free to establish a culture based on the exploration of the mysteries of nature."

"And what mysteries have you unveiled?" Kate asked.

Rhys glanced down at her, the corners of his eyes crinkling with a smile that held a touch of melancholy. "Perhaps too many."

The mystery intrigued her. She sensed this man knew much more than he would ever reveal to them.

Rhys looked out across a wide valley stretching to the east. "This is our city today."

In the distance she could barely distinguish the pattern of a small town nestled amid trees in the valley below. It would have remained hidden if Rhys had not pointed it out to her. All of the structures were built from stone and wood from the surrounding forests and hills. "It all blends into the background."

"We believe a person should not intrude on nature, but live in harmony with it."

Through the trees she could see a river glittering in the sunlight, a winding ribbon of gold as it flowed from the hills to Avallon. Kate stared at the distant city, her imagination taking flight, powered by legends of the magical people who had lived in a distant age. "You've created a city filled with Merlins."

"Not quite. We're all merely mortal."

"Where are you holding Van Horne?" Devlin asked.

Rhys glanced over his shoulder at Devlin. "He's staying at our home."

Kate stared at Rhys, not quite believing what he had said.

Devlin's voice was low, filled with emotion as he spoke. "That man belongs in prison."

"I'm afraid we have no prisons in Avallon."

"Have you really eliminated all crime?" Frederick asked.

"There are still those who deviate from acceptable behavior." Rhys resumed his pace, strolling upward along the tree-lined path, sunlight piercing the branches overhead, painting feathery patterns on the black cobblestones. "In place of jails, we have rehabilitation centers."

"And why hasn't Van Horne been placed there?" Kate asked.

"We are not accustomed to handling violent criminals. It's believed the Outworld, that is, the world outside the bounds of Avallon, will deal better with this man."

"Have you found your rehabilitation centers to be successful?" Frederick asked.

"Very. You see, one is not the same person after leaving the center."

Kate glanced to Rhys. "What do you mean?"

"It's possible to alter a person, to change the patterns of their thoughts, to erase memories, implant others."

Inside, Kate felt a shaking that came with the growing realization of how completely these people could control her if they wished. "You mean the rehabilitation centers can literally change a person's mind, alter them so they assume another identity?"

"Exactly." Rhys smiled down at her, a warm, generous smile meant to allay her fears. "We have also found the ability to alter thoughts helpful for people who have emotional problems, as well as criminals."

Kate tried to draw a deep breath and found it catching in her throat. "A person could just walk into this center and say 'I want to forget what happened yesterday'? Wipe the slate clean?"

Rhys nodded. "Something like that."

"And who determines when a person will be stripped of their identity?" Devlin asked.

"The Central Council makes the final decision." Rhys glanced back at Devlin. "Seven people who are elected by popular vote every seven years."

"And do these criminals get a trial?" Devlin asked.

Kate glanced over her shoulder. Sunlight filtering through the branches flickered over Devlin's face. He was frowning, staring at Rhys as though he wasn't sure he wanted to trust this man.

"Anyone accused of a crime is provided with an advocate when he faces the council." Brianna glanced up at Devlin as she spoke, a frown marring her smooth brow.

Kate glanced away, shivering deep inside. What would it be like facing that council, knowing they could steal all of your memories?

Rhys paused on the path. "This is our home."

Three stories, fashioned from stone and wood, the dwelling sat perched on the brow of the hill, like an eagle spreading wide wings. With its smooth curves and lines, at once simple and majestic, it was like nothing Kate had ever seen. There was no manicured lawn leading up to the house, nothing but stones, colorful wildflowers, and long meadow grass bending in the breeze—the beauty of nature allowed to rule supreme.

"Do you often walk from one place to another?" Kate asked as she walked beside Rhys along the path leading to his front door.

The breeze ruffled Rhys's thick hair, tossing the silky, black strands into waves around his handsome face. "I'm sorry, did you find the walk strenuous after your long journey?"

"No." Although they had traveled more than two miles along the winding trail, the pace had been leisurely, the paved path easy to traverse. "It's just that I expected . . ." Kate hesitated, looking up into his smiling face, the heat of her blush creeping into her cheeks. "Something a little more . . . advanced."

"I think you must be a fan of Mr. Jules Verne's novels," Rhys said, smiling down at her. "Were you hoping to find a city of glass and steel? People hovering from place to place, their feet never touching the ground?"

Kate laughed. "Yes, I suppose I was."

"We discovered a long time ago how dangerous our thirst for technology could be." Rhys climbed the stone stairs leading to his house, ten stairs in all, stretching upward to a wide, covered landing. "It nearly destroyed us. Through the centuries, we've learned to live with the land, to take what it offers, and give back what it needs."

"So your civilization has developed to a point where you find simplicity in life is valued above all else?" Frederick asked.

Rhys smiled. "We try to maintain a balance with nature. For example, our only energy source now comes from power captured from the sun."

"Power from the sun." Frederick paused on the top stair, turning to glance up at the clear blue of the sky. "Fascinating."

As they approached the front door, it opened. A young woman dressed in a tunic and trousers of sapphire-blue silk stepped onto the stone landing, her gaze darting past Kate to where Devlin and Austin stood. "You're here." She smoothed back a lock of her long, dark brown hair that had drifted with the breeze across her cheek. "I can scarcely believe—"

"This is our daughter, Alexandria." Rhys slipped his arm around his daughter's slender shoulders, cutting off her words. There was a silent exchange between father and daughter, swift and subtle, that brought a blush to Alexandria's cheeks, and made Kate wonder what the girl had been about to say.

After Rhys introduced Alexandria to everyone, he led the way into the house. A shimmering pool of light and warmth embraced them. Sunlight streamed through the skylight in the entrance hall, tumbled in a golden cascade through diamond-paned windows at the landing of a wide mahogany staircase. The brilliant light stroked the mahogany wainscoting, radiating a reddish-gold warmth.

Frederick walked beside Rhys toward the staircase, his booted heels tapping on the white marble floor, echoing on the paneled walls, a noisy counterpoint to the silent tread of the man from Avallon. "How many people live in Avallon?"

"About ten thousand, in an area half the size of Wales," Rhys replied, his tolerance for Frederick's questions never wavering.

Rhys and Brianna led Kate and the others up the wide staircase to the second floor. A bouquet of flowers three feet in diameter stood in a crystal vase on a round mahogany table below the windows on the landing, the warmth of the sun coaxing perfume to rise from pink roses and white lilies.

"We're far less formal when we're in Avallon," Brianna said as they reached the second floor. "We have a smaller staff here than we do in England. It's more difficult to find people interested in domestic service here."

"You have a home in England?" Kate asked.

"Yes." Brianna glanced at her husband. "We once spent a great deal of time in England."

"Your room is this way," Rhys said, taking Devlin's arm. At the friendly touch, Devlin stiffened, causing Rhys to drop his hand. For a moment the two men stood facing each other, Devlin stiff and wary, Rhys composed and friendly.

"Under the circumstances, I too would be wary." Rhys turned to lead the way down the long hallway. Devlin and the other men followed.

Brianna led Kate to a room at the end of the hall, in the opposite direction of the men. Wooden panels painted white covered the walls of a room that might have been in a manor house in England. The furniture was French in style, white with gold trim. The sofa and chairs were covered in the same rose damask as the drapes and the counterpane. "I didn't expect the interior of this house to seem so familiar."

"We Outworlders have managed to leave our mark on Avallon."

"You're not originally from Avallon?"

"I'm from Ireland. It's quite common for the people of Avallon to find their mates in the Outworld." Brianna drew back the drapes from one of the four large windows in the room, brass rings singing against brass rods. "You'll have a fine view of the ruins from this room."

Below, a garden spread from the house to a wide green lawn, yew forming a star pattern, roses, lilies, and gardenias blooming within, along with beds of other blooming flowers and plants. It could have been an English garden, but the sight beyond the garden came from a distant world.

Kate stared out at the ancient city rising a mile to the south, black stone glittering in the late afternoon sunlight. "You speak of the ruins as though they were as common as Hyde Park."

"I suppose I think of the ancient city the way someone who lives in sight of the pyramids might think of them. Fascinating, still able to conjure a mystery." Brianna threw open the drapes at the next window. "And yet commonplace."

"Do you spend much time here?" Kate opened the drapes at one of the other windows, allowing sunlight to flood the room.

Brianna turned in the light flowing through the mullioned windowpanes. "More and more, now that our son has taken over some of his father's duties in England."

"His duties? Do they have anything to do with Avallon?"

"Yes. You see Avallon has what you might call 'diplomats' all over the world."

She looked at this woman, wondering how on earth Brianna could have a son old enough to take on any duties. Even standing in the sunlight, the woman looked no older than 30. And yet, she had a daughter Kate suspected was close to 20, and a son old enough to take over his father's duties. "People age well in Avallon."

"Thank you." Brianna smiled, a peach-pink blush rising in her smooth cheeks. "The people here have delved deeply into medicine, and they keep us shamefully healthy. Although I'm afraid our youthful appearances are becoming difficult to explain to acquaintances in the Outworld. In the last few years Rhys and I have become frightfully reclusive. I wonder sometimes if we shall have to assume other identities to once again move freely in the Outworld."

"Do they have reasons for keeping their medical discoveries from the rest of the world?"

"It's against their law to interfere in the Outworld. I suppose because they know how dangerous their discoveries could be if misused."

"But think of all the people they could heal."

"Yes. They could do immeasurable good. Or immeasurable harm."

"If they don't wish to interfere, why do they have 'diplomats' all over the Outworld? Why do they maintain any contact with us?"

"Imagine Avallon as an island. Even with advances in medicine and technology, there has always remained the need to explore, to enjoy other parts of the world, to meet new people. There is far too much beyond the boundaries of Avallon to keep everyone satisfied hidden on this mountaintop. And there are those who believe the only way to remain secure is to monitor the progress of the Outworld, to maintain some influence there."

"The power to influence kings." Kate stared out at the

ruins that glittered in the sunlight. "I wonder how many people from Avallon I have met in the world beyond this mountaintop?"

"More than you would ever realize." Brianna opened a nearby door. "This is your dressing area. The far door leads to your bath. You'll find fresh clothes in the closet. I hope you don't mind, we obtained your measurements from your dressmaker in London."

"It seems you truly were expecting us."

"Yes." Brianna glanced at the closet door as though she didn't want to hold Kate's gaze. "Although you'll find several gowns, dinner is informal, as are most other occasions in Avallon. A tunic and trousers are all you'll be needing most of the time you're here."

"A society that accepts ladies in trousers. How amazing."

"One of the nice things about Avallon is that women have an equal place here. I'll leave you now. I'm sure you're anxious to have a real bath."

Kate followed Brianna across the bedroom, a thousand questions spinning in her head.

"Please make yourself at home." Brianna paused in the doorway. "When you're ready, come down to the drawing room, which is the first room to the right at the base of the stairs. We'll be gathering there to go in to dinner."

Chapter Twenty-eight

Electric lights in the shape of flames flickered in the crystal chandelier above the long mahogany table in the dining room. Carved panels of mahogany lined the walls: they captured the golden glow of the lights, surrounding the diners in a pulsing warmth. Kate twisted her fork in her fingers and stared across the table at the empty space above the mantel behind Austin. She could see a hook, a place to hang a painting. Yet the panel was bare. It seemed . . . odd. She took a bite of lobster, the creamy wine sauce tangy with lemon.

"I get the impression you've known of our expedition from the beginning." Frederick focused his attention on the dark-haired man sitting directly to Kate's left, at the head of the table.

"Yes." Rhys swirled his wine in his glass, the beveled edges of cut crystal sparkling in the light. "The man who sold you Connor Randolph's journal is from Avallon—the journal itself is a fabrication."

"You arranged for Mr. Whitmore to obtain that journal," Devlin said. "You wanted him to come here."

Kate glanced at Devlin. Brianna sat at the opposite end of the table from her husband. She had arranged for Devlin to sit on her right, beside Alexandria.

"You're very perceptive, Mr. McCain," Rhys said. "I'm afraid putting the journal in Mr. Whitmore's hands was all part of a plan."

"I'm not sure I understand," Frederick said. "Why go through the trouble of planting a journal? Why not simply bring us here?"

"You were only part of the scheme." Rhys contemplated his wine as though the pale liquid might reveal a secret.

Although Devlin was dressed like the other men, in a soft white silk shirt and black trousers, although he looked every inch a gentleman, Kate could sense the savage power pulsing inside him, the power she felt each time he took her into his arms.

Devlin glanced in her direction, catching Kate staring like a lovesick schoolgirl. He smiled, a slow slide of sensual lips that whispered of intimate moments shared in the hours between midnight and dawn, a smile that coaxed heat into her cheeks.

"A quest was established by the Central Council of Avallon to verify the character of one of our own people, a man who was looked upon with suspicion," Rhys said.

Kate dragged her gaze from Devlin. "A quest, like one of King Arthur's knights?"

Rhys tilted his head and smiled at her. "Yes, I suppose it is like an ancient quest. But you have to realize, some of the old ways don't always die. Without the quest, without testing his honesty, his character, he would not have been allowed to assume his place in our society."

"What was he to do?" Kate asked. "What exactly was his quest?"

"He was assigned the task of . . ." Rhys hesitated. "You might say he was your guardian through the jungle."

"Our guardian!" Kate sat back in her chair, staring at her host as though he had suddenly sprouted an extra head.

"The man no doubt failed his quest. We were nearly killed more than once. And that man," she said, glancing to where Leighton Van Horne sat on the opposite side of the table, between Edwin and Austin, "was very nearly our executioner."

Leighton Van Horne smiled at her, the angelic innocence of his face spoiled only by the glitter in his eyes.

"Mr. Van Horne's interference was not foreseen," Rhys said.

Edwin shifted in his chair, looking at Van Horne from the corner of his eye, as though the fair-haired man was a viper about to strike. Kate could only wonder why their hosts had invited the man to dine with them. It was as if Rhys and Brianna had assembled the actors, to reveal each part they had played in this drama.

"Lady Judith is the reason we're sitting here today." Kate looked to where Lady Judith sat on Brianna's left. Judith stared down at her plate, color rising to stain her smooth cheeks.

"We're aware of Lady Judith's intervention on your behalf." Brianna smiled as she looked at Kate.

"So am I." The venom in Van Horne's voice spread thickly along the length of the table.

Judith curled her hand into a tight ball on the white linen beside her plate, her gaze fixed on Van Horne's smiling face. Fear. Kate could see it in Lady Judith's eyes, she could sense it coiling inside the other woman, as tangible as the shudder that shook Judith's narrow shoulders.

Brianna leaned forward and covered Judith's hand with her own. "You have nothing to worry about, dear. Mr. Van Horne is no longer in a position to harm anyone."

Van Horne smiled at his hostess. "I'm as meek as a kitten."

A chill crawled along the nape of Kate's neck. Never in her life had she met anyone as cold as Leighton Van Horne. She truly believed the man was capable of anything. "As for guardians, the only guardian we have had through this ordeal is Mr. Devlin McCain. It is thanks to him we survived at all."

Rhys glanced into his glass. "Yes, I understand Mr. McCain did an excellent job."

"You would be looking far and wide to find a better man," Barnaby said, nodding his head to Devlin. "Brave, he is, and honest, resourceful. Yes sir, a fine man."

Devlin shifted in his chair. He frowned at Barnaby, who was seated across the table, next to Lady Judith. Kate was sure she could see color rise in Devlin's cheeks. He looked uncomfortable, and utterly disarming.

"I for one shall never forget Mr. McCain's heroism." Van Horne raised his glass to Devlin in a silent salute. "Perhaps one day I shall be able to repay him for all he has done for me."

Devlin glared at Van Horne, his silvery blue eyes catching the light, illuminating the anger there, the look that said there was nothing he would like better than to strangle Van Horne with his bare hands. Kate held her breath, wondering if Devlin could control his anger enough to stay in his chair.

"Your council had no qualms in risking our lives," Edwin said, glaring at Rhys.

"You came on the journey of your own will, Edwin. As did the rest of us," Austin said. "We were all well aware of the dangers we might encounter in the jungle."

Edwin's lips flattened beneath his thick, drooping mustache. He looked past Austin to Rhys. "You have manipulated all of us into acting as pawns for some infernal game of yours."

Rhys regarded him a long moment before he spoke. "The game was not mine. You see, the man who was tested is our son. If we had not agreed to the test, he would have lost the privileges of his birthright."

Van Horne laughed. "He must have been a very naughty boy to warrant such treatment."

Although Rhys displayed no outward signs of anger, Kate

could sense it simmering just below his calm surface. "His only crime was being raised in the Outworld, without any of the usual training a person of his backgroun receives."

"Didn't you realize what would happen to him if you didn't give him the training your council expected?" Kate asked.

Rhys looked at her, his beautiful eyes betraying a horrible sorrow. "We had no hand in our son's upbringing."

Kate glanced at Brianna, seeing her husband's pain mirrored in her eyes. What had happened? she wondered.

"And what happens now?" Devlin looked at Rhys. "Now that this little game is over."

Rhys studied Devlin, as though he were weighing his words carefully. "You will remain our guests for as long as you like. And then we will provide transportation back to England."

"And Van Horne?" Devlin asked.

"His memory of Avallon will be erased before he is sent to Pará. We have magistrates there who will see he gets the punishment he deserves."

"Just like that?" Robert asked. "You're going to let us walk out of here? Aren't you afraid we'll tell everyone about your little city? Aren't you afraid we'll lead an army back here?"

Kate held her breath, waiting for the answer to a question that had been buzzing in her brain.

"You would not be able to find this place again," Rhys said. "You see, the route you took no longer exists."

Robert shook his head. "Just like that, you've moved rivers."

"You might say we have closed a few corridors."

Robert stared at his host a moment. "We could still tell everyone about you."

Kate looked past her father at the foolish young man seated next to him. Robert had no idea when to stop.

"Without proof, no one would believe a word you had to say, we would make sure of that. And, if matters got out of hand, we would make sure you did not cause trouble. You would soon forget all about Avallon."

Kate clenched her napkin in her lap. What was the procedure for erasing a human mind? she wondered.

"Well, I have all the proof I need, even if I shall never be able to present it to the world." Frederick tilted his wineglass toward Rhys. "I know now Atlantis truly existed, even if I cannot tell a soul."

"Although I find this story interesting"—Edwin blotted his lips with his white linen napkin—"I must say, we have seen no proof of these ancient myths this man has been spinning."

"Really, Edwin," Frederick said.

Edwin stared across the table at Frederick. "As far as those ruins having any connection to Atlantis, I say poppycock."

Frederick leaned forward, dragging his white shirtfront into the cream sauce on his plate. "I can show you how they all relate. The symbols carved into the buildings, the architecture, the—"

"All conjecture," Edwin said.

"Careful, Father." Kate dabbed at his shirt with her napkin.

"Thank you, darling." Frederick swiped at the blotch on the front of his shirt. He looked at Rhys. "I don't suppose you have any artifacts that might serve to enlighten a skeptic?"

Rhys smiled as he held Frederick's gaze. "I would take great pleasure in showing you some of the relics of my people."

"And your son," Kate said. "When shall we meet him?"

"Soon," Rhys said.

When she met the man, Kate intended to tell him just what she thought of the care he had provided as their guardian angel.

"These pieces belong in a museum." Edwin paused in front of one of the glass cases in the gallery, this one holding bronze statues and bowls.

The room looked like a museum, Devlin thought, glancing at the collection of medieval shields displayed on one wall. Except this room was brighter than any museum he had ever seen. Lights recessed into the swirls of plaster on the ceiling flooded the room with a soft glow that reflected like sunlight on the glass cases, the white marble walls and floor.

"Then you believe they are authentic?" Frederick asked, turning to face Edwin.

"I believe they are very old, fourth century B.C., probably from Egypt." Edwin looked across the case at Frederick. "But they have nothing to do with Atlantis."

"I don't understand why you can't—"

"Frederick, you're grasping at straws."

"It's obvious . . ."

Devlin turned away from the two men, dismissing their argument. There were other, more important matters that concerned him. He took his host's arm and drew Rhys a few feet away from Edwin, Frederick, and Kate.

"There is something disturbing you, Mr. McCain," Rhys said, smiling as he met Devlin's concerned look.

"Van Horne disturbs me."

"You can't understand why I don't have him locked up somewhere." Rhys glanced to where Van Horne stood across the room, gazing into a glass case containing several polished swords. "I wanted to give you and the others a chance to see him this way, powerless."

Devlin shook his head. "From what I can see, you have only one man guarding him."

"Lawrence is well trained. If Van Horne should try anything, he would soon find himself overpowered. And if by some chance he was able to escape this house, there is nowhere for him to go."

"I hope you're right. I hope you aren't underestimating the man."

"Mr. McCain," Brianna said, touching his arm, "we have a wonderful library. I wonder if I might show it to you."

Devlin glanced down at the woman. Each time he looked in her eyes he sensed Brianna was keeping a secret from him and the others, and she didn't like it. Not one bit. If he could get her alone, away from her husband, he might be able to persuade her to part with her secrets. "Yes, I'd love to see the library."

Kate glanced over her shoulder, barely listening to Edwin and her father. She was more concerned with finding Devlin than she was with listening to their argument. They were all there, wandering about this incredible room, everyone except Devlin and Brianna.

"If you're looking for your muscular friend," Van Horne said behind her, so close she jumped, "I saw McCain leave with our beautiful hostess a few moments ago."

Van Horne smiled as she pivoted to face him. She looked up into his eyes, eyes as cold as the North Sea, demon eyes glinting in the face of an angel.

Kate glanced at the man guarding Van Horne. He was standing at the far end of the gallery: tall, broad shouldered, dressed in close-fitting black trousers and a black shirt that seemed to be joined to form one piece. Except for a small, odd-looking silver pistol attached to a narrow, black belt at his waist, the man looked unarmed. She hoped her hosts were not underestimating Van Horne. She hoped there were other guards in the house.

Van Horne tilted his head, gilt strands of silken hair brushing his shoulders. He glanced at the guard, then back down at Kate as though he could read her mind. "We shall see."

He strolled away from her, joining Edwin at a small glass case in the center of the room. A chill crept over her skin as she watched Van Horne. The man was evil, pure, undiluted evil.

Devlin couldn't shake the feeling he was a lamb being led to slaughter.

"Do you play chess?" Brianna led the way across the hall toward the library.

"Yes, I do."

"My son and Alexandria love to play as much as Rhys and I do."

"Perhaps we can play later."

"Oh, I'd enjoy that very much." Brianna smiled up at him, her gray eyes filled with a warm affection that made Devlin all the more wary.

Electric lights in gold fixtures were glowing in the library when they entered. Devlin stood for a moment in the center of the room, his feet planted on an Aubusson carpet of gold and blue. This was a library such as he had always dreamed of owning. Two stories of books on mahogany shelves, a carved wooden balustrade curving along the length of the second-floor gallery. Double glass doors sheltered each set of bookshelves, and an arch trimmed in gold curved above each pair, providing alcoves for small pieces of sculpture and other pieces of art.

"I have been told you have a great love for books. I can see by your expression it's true."

"Did you do research on all of us?" Devlin looked at her. "Or is there something about me that made you curious?"

"I wish to know everything about you." She smiled, a slow curving of her lips that whispered of sorrow. "You see, I've been waiting a very long time to meet you."

"Your husband said the same thing." He held her gaze, seeing expectancy in her eyes, feeling his skin growing warm, the nape of his neck prickling. "What's the real reason you brought us here?"

"We've told you the truth, but not all of it. Please, sit with me." Brianna gestured toward the sofa and upholstered armchairs near the lifeless jade marble hearth. "It will take a while to explain, and I would like to wait until Rhys joins us."

Devlin stayed where he was, watching as Brianna took a place on the sofa. He knew he had to hear what these people had to say. And he had a feeling he wasn't going to like it.

* * *

"Katie, come take a look at this." Frederick waved for her to join him. "This looks Celtic."

Frederick stood aside for Kate to look into the small glass case. Inside, a gold medallion about three inches in diameter sat on a pedestal of pink alabaster.

"Second century, I would say," Kate said.

"I would say closer to the third," Edwin said. "The inscription appears to be in Goidelic, or something close to the ancient Gaelic."

Frederick glanced at Rhys. "May I take a closer look?"

"Of course." Rhys pressed his fingers to the base of the case and the front panel of glass slid open.

"How old is it?" Kate asked, brushing her fingertip across the carved face of the medallion.

"No one is quite sure. This one has been in my family since before recorded history." Rhys offered the medallion to Kate. "You may hold it."

The thick piece of gold was heavy, much heavier than she had anticipated, and warm, as if it were capturing the heat of her palm. A square-cut emerald shimmered in the light as she turned the medallion, the gem forming the eye of a bird that was carved into the center of the disk, a bird such as she had never before seen, with a crown of smooth feathers sweeping down his long neck.

Kate resisted the urge to bolt as Van Horne drew near. She didn't intend to show the man how much he frightened her.

"What does it say?" Van Horne asked, staring over Kate's shoulder at the ancient symbols carved around the edge of the medallion.

"Nothing of any importance," Rhys said. "I'm afraid it's simply a good luck charm."

"An ancient good luck charm." Van Horne followed the gold medallion with his gaze as Kate placed it in her host's hand. "I wonder if it would bring me luck."

Rhys cast Van Horne a glance before replacing the medallion on the pedestal and closing the panel. "Are you still a skeptic, Mr. Melville?"

"You have some interesting artifacts, but nothing we couldn't find in Egypt, or dredge from peat bogs in Ireland." Edwin glanced down into a glass case. "Nothing here convinces me your ancestors formed the ancient cults of civilization. Certainly there is nothing to convince me your ancestors had anything to do with the mythical Atlantis."

"You see, even if you were to take this room back with you to England, I'm afraid most people would have Mr. Melville's attitude." Rhys smiled as he turned to Frederick. "Skepticism is a formidable shield."

Frederick shook his head. "Edwin, look at these scrolls," he said, taking his friend's arm. "Katie, help me make this man see reason."

Kate didn't want to examine another artifact. She wanted to talk to Devlin. She wanted to discuss the future, not the past. She glanced over her shoulder at the door as her father ushered her toward one of the many glass cases in the room. Rhys was leaving the gallery.

Chapter Twenty-nine

Devlin resisted the urge to shift in his chair, his discipline keeping him still. For too many years his profession had demanded he mask any sign of nerves. He lowered his gaze from the bookcase behind the sofa in the library to where Rhys and Brianna sat across from him, their clasped hands resting between their bodies on the gold brocade upholstery.

"What I said at dinner was true," Rhys said. "You and the others were brought here on a quest designed by our Central Council to test our son, a quest both Brianna and I opposed."

Devlin followed the slow movement of the other man's thumb as Rhys slid it back and forth across Brianna's taut knuckles. The room grew warmer with each passing moment, with each word Rhys spoke, like the gathering of heat just before a summer storm.

"When our son was very young, we journeyed with him to Ireland. Brianna wanted to be with her sister when Maura gave birth. She delivered a son, a little boy who didn't live to see the first light of dawn. We stayed with her a fortnight, hoping to give some comfort. The day before we were to return to England, Maura disappeared, taking our son with her."

Devlin drew a deep breath, trying to ease the tension in his muscles. He flexed his hands on the rosewood arms of his chair, staring at the clasped hands of the couple across from him, feeling the warm air press against him, growing heavier and thicker.

"We had twin boys, you see." Brianna's soft voice barely reached Devlin across the six feet of carpet separating them. "In the note Maura left us, she said it wasn't fair that we should have two beautiful boys, while her son had died before ever having had a chance to live. We discovered she had taken a ship to New York City, but couldn't find a trace of her after she arrived."

Devlin kept his gaze fixed on their locked hands. Moisture beaded on his brow, trickled across his temple. Suspicion grew inside him, it urged him to stand, it begged him to get away from these people and the story they were weaving around him. Yet he couldn't move. He needed to hear this. He needed to know.

"We searched for years, without finding a trace of our lost son," Rhys said. "Then, eight months ago, one of our people at the British Council in Pará saw a man who was the image of our son's twin brother. This man was under investigation, suspected of murdering his partner."

The air turned to stone in Devlin's lungs; he could feel the weight pressing against his heart. "You're talking about me."

"Yes, we are."

Devlin looked straight into the other man's eyes, seeing the truth there, the truth he didn't understand. "Are you trying to tell me I'm your son?"

Rhys held his gaze an eternity before he spoke. "Yes."

"My God!" Devlin sprang from the chair, clenching his hands into tight fists at his sides. "If this is true, you've known who I am. For nearly a year, you've known who I am."

"We wanted to bring you home immediately," Rhys said. "But the council refused to let you take your rightful place until you had been tested."

"Please try to understand." Brianna stood and moved toward him. "We tried everything we could."

Devlin backed away as she drew near. "Why?" There was so much anguish in that single word, a lifetime of humiliation.

"We had no choice." Rhys released his breath in an unsteady sigh. He rose and faced Devlin. "If we had gone against the wishes of the council, you would never have been able to take your proper place in Avallon."

Devlin swallowed hard, forcing back the emotions forming a knot in his throat. "I see. You were afraid I wasn't good enough."

"No." Tears reflected the light like stars in Brianna's silvery blue eyes. "It was never like that."

"Please try to understand. If you hadn't been tested, you would have lived as an outsider the rest of your life."

"Tested?"

"The quest. I admit, it was a primitive rite of passage, brewed by the Central Council. I believe they were truly at a loss as to how to handle the situation." Rhys held Devlin's gaze as he continued. "You see, there were those on the council who believed you might have murdered Gerald Fielding for his share of the gold."

"And you?" Devlin stared at these two strangers, his father and the woman who had given him birth. "Did you think I was a murderer?"

"Never," Brianna whispered.

"We had faith in you. Always."

"Faith enough to manipulate my life." The muscles in Devlin's throat ached with the need to scream his frustration, to vent his rage.

"Please, don't turn away from us. We've waited so long, searched a lifetime." Brianna reached for Devlin, but the look he gave her stopped her cold. "Pierce, please, give us a chance to—"

"Pierce?"

"That was the name we gave you, Pierce Montgomery Sinclair," Rhys said, his deep voice calm and soothing, like a cool stream of water pouring over the hot coals smoldering inside Devlin.

"Sinclair," Devlin whispered, thoughts spinning like a whirlpool inside his head. "Austin Sinclair is my brother."

"Your twin brother." Rhys went to a round table placed in front of one of the arched windows nearby. Photographs in various frames of carved wood and gold reflected in the mirror finish of the mahogany surface. He lifted one of the frames and handed it to Devlin. "Under that beard of his is a face you would recognize from looking in the mirror."

The photograph was like none Devlin had ever seen. Instead of the stilted images impressed in shades of gray, this photograph captured the young family in vivid color. A red-and-white plaid blanket spread across emerald grass, sunlight glowing golden on the figures of a man and a woman, Rhys and Brianna, looking very much as they looked today. Devlin stared at the two little boys sitting between their parents, two little boys who shared the same features.

"Once we knew you had been placed in an orphanage in New Orleans, we were able to trace what had happened," Rhys said quietly. "When Maura arrived in New Orleans, she was ill, complications from her difficult birth, we believe. A proprietor of a brothel took her in, with the hopes Maura would join the establishment. Shortly after, Maura died, and you were taken to the orphanage."

Devlin's face grew warm as he stared at the young boys in the photograph, as he wondered which smiling face was his. Tears stung his eyes, tears he refused to shed. He could remember nothing of this day, nothing of the happiness he could see on the faces of these strangers. He had once belonged here. He had once been surrounded with love and warmth. And this life had been stolen from him.

"So my brother came along to make sure I lived up to expectations."

"No. He wanted to be with you, to lend any support he could," Rhys said. "The council granted permission for him to accompany the expedition, under certain restraints. He couldn't tell you or anyone else who he was. He couldn't interfere. Someone else was assigned the task as watcher."

Devlin lifted his gaze to his father's face. "Who?"

"Barnaby Shalleen."

Devlin's chest constricted as though Rhys had landed a physical blow. He had trusted Barnaby. And now he realized the friendship he had cherished had been no more than a lie. Into his mind came the image of a woman with hair of sunshine and eyes the color of a summer sky. "The Whitmores, are they part of this?"

Rhys shook his head. "They were chosen because of Frederick Whitmore's interest in Atlantis. We believed he would risk everything to glimpse the ancient city. The challenge was to get them here safely. The council wanted to know you could be trusted. They wanted to test your loyalty, your honesty, your strength. They were more than satisfied with your performance."

Devlin glanced down at the photograph he held. Yet it was Kate's face he saw in his mind. Kate, the one reality in this tapestry of illusions. "And if I'd failed their little test, what would have happened?"

Rhys rested his strong hand on Devlin's arm. "We never once believed you would fail."

"So now I've got your council's blessing." Devlin pulled away from Rhys. "Now you can welcome the suspicious stranger into your home without fear he'll steal the silver."

"It isn't like that. We were thinking only of you." Brianna swiped at the trail of tears coursing down her cheeks. "Please, try to understand. Give us a chance to be a whole family again."

Devlin handed her the photograph. "I'm not sure I want to be part of this family."

"Devlin," Brianna whispered as he walked toward the door. "Please, give us a chance."

The pain in her voice pierced him. Yet he couldn't turn around; he couldn't face her or the man who was his father. Not now. Perhaps never.

Devlin marched from the room. He wasn't sure where he was going. He wasn't sure what he was going to do. He wasn't sure of anything anymore.

"Devlin!" Kate shouted.

He hesitated in the hall, turning to find Kate rushing toward him, her footsteps echoing against the white marble floor. Her beautiful face revealed every emotion to him, her concern for him so strong it enveloped him like a warm embrace.

"What's happened?" she asked, grasping his arm. "You're upset."

She looked up at him, the blue of summer in her eyes, fear for him naked in those eyes. She was real. She was free of deceptions and lies, and his love for her was the only truth that remained in his life. "I'm going for a walk. Will you come with me?"

"Anywhere."

Devlin tossed a pebble over the edge of the cliff. Kate watched the dark stone tumble in the moonlight, arc, and fall into the river far below. Black rock flowed in a smooth path from where they sat on the edge of the cliff to the river. Moonlight glinted on the crystals embedded within the stones; it fell upon the water, spinning the river into a rippling ribbon of silver. Behind them the ruins of Avallon stood like a dark specter whispering of ancient mysteries. Yet the deep voice of the man beside her commanded Kate's attention, the story he unveiled making her clench her hands into fists on her lap.

She wasn't sure how many hours they had walked, or how far, before they had found their way back to this place. She had remained quiet, sensing the storm of emotions raging inside Devlin. She had not probed. She had known in time he would share his turmoil with her. Yet the truth he revealed caught her unprepared.

Kate pressed her back against a pile of stones, all that was left of an ancient home. She felt lost, caught up in the pain she sensed rather than heard in Devlin's voice, as though she had been swept up into a whirlwind.

A boy lost. A man found. A family that had not accepted him without a hideous test. She squeezed her hands, pinpoints of pain flaring in her palms where her nails bit into her skin. How could they? How could they have put him through this?

And yet, she had met these people. She had seen the sorrow in their eyes.

Devlin's voice faded into the cool breeze. He was staring out into the darkness. Moonlight stroked his face, painting the portrait of a pagan god. *Yet he is only human,* she thought. And he was hurting, as if they had taken a knife and cut him.

"When I was a boy, I made up a story about my real parents and why they'd left me at the orphanage."

Unable to keep from touching him another moment, Kate rested her hand over the fist he held against his raised knee. He didn't look at her. Yet he didn't pull away from her touch. Jasmine grew wild here, the flowers belonging to no one and everyone, sharing their perfume with the evening breeze.

"My father was a sailor, you see, and when his ship vanished, my mother went looking for him. Since she couldn't take me with her, she left me at the orphanage. She wanted to make sure I'd be safe. And one day they would both come back for me." He closed his eyes and rested his brow against her hand. "I never told anyone, but I held on to that fiction for a long time. When I was twelve, I knew no one would ever come for me. That's when I started looking for . . . something I never found."

"Devlin," she whispered, stroking his shoulder with her open palm. "You have to give them a chance."

He looked at her, moonlight and pain reflected in his eyes.
"A chance for them to make me jump through a few more
hoops?"

"They lost their little boy. They will never have back those
years, never know what it was like to watch him grow, to
tuck him in at night, to read him stories, to see his eyes
fill with wonder on Christmas morning." Kate felt a strange
stirring come to life inside her. As she spoke she imagined
what it would be like to watch her own child on Christmas
morning, a child she and Devlin had made. "Don't deny them
the chance to know you now. Don't deny yourself the chance
to know them."

"Do you have any idea what it's like to belong nowhere,
to belong to no one?" He looked away from her, staring out
across the plains that stretched beyond the river. "All my
life I've been on the outside, a stableboy, a hired hand, a
gambler, always looking through windowpanes, always just
out of reach of the warmth I could see inside."

"Your parents agreed to this quest so that you would never
have to be on the outside again. They want you to be part of
their family, a very important part. They want you to take
your place in Avallon. They want you to have everything.
You simply have to give them a chance."

Devlin drew a deep breath. "There's so much time behind
us."

"And so much time before you. Don't waste it, Devlin.
You have to give them a chance. It's your only hope to be
whole again."

Devlin slid his fingertip back and forth across her knuckles, a loving touch by a man who had so much love inside
him, love he had never been able to share with anyone.

"You just might be right, Professor. What good is a gambler if he isn't willing to take chances?"

Kate felt the tension release inside her, a moment of ease
before she realized she must also take a chance. "This has
been a voyage of discovery for both of us."

He looked at her, a silent question in his eyes.

She slipped her hand into the silky, black strands waving at his nape. "You've found a family, and I've found something I never thought I wanted, something I don't want to live without."

"What?"

"You." She hesitated, doubts shimmering inside her, fears of a future path she had never planned to take. "I love you. I want to marry you, Devlin. I want to spend my life with you."

He stared at her a long moment, as though he were turning each word over and over in his mind. "You want to marry me?"

"Yes. I want to be with you, now and always."

He slipped his hand from beneath hers. "I thought you weren't interested in marrying anyone."

"I wasn't. Until I met you."

Pebbles scuttled beneath his feet as he stood. The small stones tumbled over the cliff, bouncing against the side of the mountain on their downward plunge. Devlin stood staring at her as though he had never seen her before.

Looking up at him, Kate felt a tightening around her heart, fear spinning a web of steely threads. The silvery blue eyes that had looked at her with such warmth and love, stared at her now chilled by another emotion. Her skin grew cold, as if she stood naked in a frigid December wind. She rose, her legs shaking with the growing fear inside her. "Devlin, what's wrong?"

"Seems funny, you suddenly deciding to marry me. Now that my name is Sinclair." He took a step back when she reached for him. "Your little change of heart wouldn't have anything to do with the fact there's a duke in the family, would it?"

Kate gasped. "How could you think I would . . . Devlin, you don't really believe I—"

"God, what a damn fool I was." He swept his hands through his hair. "I believed you. I believed you never intended to marry anyone."

"I never did intend to marry anyone."

"The fact is, you never intended to marry a bastard casino owner."

"Devlin, it isn't like that."

"You're one hell of a liar, Professor."

"I never lied to you!"

"Oh, I see. You just decided you couldn't live without me, is that it?"

Tears burned her eyes and she fought to keep them from falling. She wouldn't cry in front of this man. She wouldn't show him any of the pain he could inflict with his horrible accusations. "How could you believe I'm the type of woman who would marry for money or title?"

"It's real easy from where I stand, Professor."

"It looks as though we never did know each other, Mr. McCain." Kate spun on her heel and marched along the path that meandered along the edge of the cliff and cut through the center of the ruins. If she stayed another instant with this man he would see the tears she couldn't stop, the tears spilling in hot streams down her cheeks.

She had gone no more than a few yards when a shadow separated from the ragged remains of a wall beside the path. A man stepped from the darkness, his blond hair glowing like silver in the light.

"Are the lovers quarreling?" Leighton Van Horne's lips drew back from even, white teeth in a chilling smile.

Kate froze, her heart colliding with the wall of her chest. She glanced around, looking for the guard, seeing only the shadows of ancient Avallon. "What are you doing here?"

"I told you we would see." Van Horne lifted a small, silver gun to his side, the same type of gun she had noticed on the guard's belt. "It looks like I won."

Kate turned and ran toward the man who stood on the edge of the cliff. "Devlin!"

Devlin turned at her shout. Before she could take another step, Van Horne's hand closed around her arm. He jerked her back so hard she lost her balance and plowed into his chest. He staggered back a step, yanking her arm upward, wrenching her shoulder, forcing her to her feet. Through the tears of pain flooding her eyes, she saw Devlin rushing toward them.

"Stay back, McCain," Van Horne shouted. Kate moaned as he shoved the barrel of the gun into her ribs. "I'll kill her."

Devlin halted a few feet in front of them, hands tight fists at his sides, broad shoulders rising and falling with his breath. "Let go of her, Van Horne."

"I don't think that would be a good idea at all."

Devlin glanced down at the gun, then back to Van Horne's face. "If you hurt her, I'll take you apart with my bare hands."

Power and rage radiated from Devlin. Although Van Horne held the gun, Kate felt the shudder of fear that passed through him. Splinters of pain darted along her arm as he tightened his grip on her.

"I was wondering how I might provide myself with safe passage out of here. Miss Whitmore will be my ticket."

Devlin relaxed his hands at his sides, then curled them into fists once more. "You won't get away."

"We shall see. I took our host's good luck charm on my way out. It's only fair, since I had to leave behind something of great importance to me. But one day I shall retrieve my necklace. You see, I always get what I want." Van Horne lifted the gun, pointing it directly at Devlin's broad chest. "And right now, I want to repay you for all you've done for me."

As if in a slow-moving dream, she saw Devlin lunge forward, felt Van Horne shift the gun. "No!" She rammed her elbow into Van Horne's body, hitting his diaphragm, driving the air from his lungs in a loud *whoosh*.

Devlin grabbed her arms, dragging her from Van Horne's stunned grasp. She tripped over a low stone wall when Devlin released her, falling flat on her behind.

The men struggled a few feet away from her, two tall silhouettes against the black sky, grunts and curses splintering the cool evening breeze. They were close to the edge. Their scuffling sent rocks tumbling over the cliff, bouncing in bright sounds until they plunged into the river below.

Kate grabbed a rock from the ground beside her. Van Horne still had the gun in his hand. Devlin fought to pry it from his fingers. The silver metal absorbed the moonlight, glowing before the gun disappeared between them.

She stood, gripping the rock, intending to smash Van Horne over the head, but they were twisting with their struggle, shifting places. One quick turn by the men, and she might hit Devlin. Behind her, footsteps pounded on the stones, and voices echoed against the stone walls of the ruins.

"Over here!" She stepped over the low wall, clutching the rock in her hand.

A low, muffled pop; the gunshot barely disturbed the quiet of the night. Yet to Kate it was an explosion.

Devlin and Van Horne stood locked together, no longer struggling, the gun buried between them. They stood staring at each other, utterly still, as if waiting to see which one of them would fall.

Kate was barely aware of the noises behind her. The blood pounded in her temples as she held her breath and waited. Devlin looked at her as his knees buckled and he sank toward the ground.

Blood! There was blood on his shirt, growing in an ever-increasing stain from a wound in his chest.

"No!" Kate refused to believe the truth starkly etched by moonlight. The rock tumbled from her hand.

Van Horne stood above Devlin, staring down at him, the gun limp in his hand.

"Drop it, Van Horne!" Austin shouted.

Kate glanced up as Austin moved to her side. There were other men with him, dressed in the same type of black uniform Van Horne's guard had worn.

Van Horne looked up, his blond hair ruffling in a sudden breeze. He took a step back, pausing on the very edge of the cliff, the gun bobbing in his hand at his side.

"Drop the gun," Austin shouted.

Kate sank to her knees beside Devlin, fear closing like a steel claw around her throat. *God, please, let him live.* Gently she turned him, cradling his head on her lap. Thick, black lashes rested against his pale cheeks.

"You can't get away." Austin gestured with his pistol. "Drop the gun."

"Justice, is it?" A smile slowly slid along Van Horne's lips. He looked like an archangel, tossed from heaven, intent on making hell his domain. "I think I would rather take my chances with the devil."

Before anyone could move, Van Horne turned and jumped. One moment he was standing on the edge of the cliff, the next he was gone, the guards swarming around the empty space he had left on the edge of the cliff. Wild laughter drifted upward as he plummeted toward the river far below.

Devlin lay still in Kate's embrace, his blood soaking the white silk of his shirt, pooling on the black stones beneath him. Austin dropped to his knees beside his brother. "Is he . . . is he alive?"

"Devlin," Kate whispered, touching his cheek. When he opened his eyes, she nearly collapsed with relief. "I thought you—"

"Go back to England where you belong, Professor," Devlin said, his voice strained with pain. "Get the hell out of my life."

He pierced her heart with his words, more sure and deadly than a blade. Kate sat back on her heels, staring into the depths of Devlin's silvery blue eyes, seeing only emptiness where there had once been so many dreams.

Chapter Thirty

Austin glanced away, willing his stomach to stay steady. He stared at the blue brocade drapes shielding the French doors leading to the balcony of Devlin's bedroom. A prick told him Dr. Carrick had inserted the needle into his arm. He had never cared for needles. Still, Devlin had lost a great deal of blood. The transfusion would help save his brother's life, he reminded himself.

Austin looked to where his father stood at the foot of the bed, seeing the anguish there in his face, the guilt for what had happened to Devlin. How had everything gotten so out of hand?

Miscalculations. Devlin and the others had nearly been killed on the journey. And now this.

"Father, I think Van Horne had help," Austin said, pulling a necklace from a pocket in his trousers.

"I want you to stay still, young man." Dr. Carrick glanced over her shoulder, her light brown brows drawn into a frown over the straight line of her thin nose. "We don't want that needle breaking, do we?"

"No." Austin felt his stomach curl in at the edges. "No, we certainly don't."

Rhys came around the edge of the bed, careful to stay out of the way of Dr. Carrick and her two assistants as they worked to save Devlin's life.

"I spoke with Lady Judith this afternoon. She said Van Horne had told her he had a friend on the expedition. She assumed it was one of the men we hired in Santarém, but I'm not so certain. Take a look at this." Austin handed the necklace to his father. "I took it from Van Horne's room before dinner. I believe it's genuine."

"Egyptian." Rhys turned the necklace over in his hands, studying the ornately carved piece of gold. "It's a beautiful piece, exceptional, really, but what does it have to do with this?"

"Van Horne is a collector of artifacts. From what Lady Judith tells me, he is obsessed with them."

"That helps explain why he took the medallion."

"The medallion!" In Van Horne's hands. It was worse than Austin had realized. "Even if he lived through that fall, Van Horne won't make it out of the jungle," he said, trying to reassure his father.

Rhys drew a deep breath. "He could."

"Still, he has no idea what he possesses."

"If he manages to use it by accident, it could be a disaster." Rhys stared down at the necklace, sliding the gold between his fingers. "Since the man is a collector of artifacts, I don't see what the significance of this necklace could be. Obviously this is a piece any collector would want to possess. It's priceless."

"It's supposed to be in the British Museum. It was on display at a reception a month before we left London for Brazil."

Rhys frowned as he looked down at his son. "Tell me what you suspect."

Kate sat beside her father on one of the two sofas that flanked the fireplace in Devlin's sitting room. She glanced at the gold-and-crystal clock on the gray marble mantel, noting the hands had barely moved since the last time she had checked the time. Two hours and 15 minutes since they had carried Devlin home. She shared this vigil with Devlin's family and the members of their expedition.

The door leading to Devlin's bedroom opened, drawing Kate's attention like a magnet. She stared at the man standing on the threshold, as did the others who had been waiting for word. Her father took her hand, his palm damp, as damp and cold as her own.

Rhys glanced around the room, his gaze touching Kate before resting on his wife, who sat beside Alexandria on the matching sofa directly across from Kate, both women pale, their expressions tight with worry. Kate could see nothing in Rhys's eyes or his expression, nothing but a handsome mask, nothing to reassure her.

"The doctor was able to repair the damage," Rhys said. "Devlin will be fine."

Kate released the breath she hadn't realized she had been holding. A low murmur of voices filled the room, collective relief and joy draining away the tension. Devlin would be all right. Yet with the knowledge came a sudden pain, a realization that he was lost to her as surely as if he had died.

"I have recently acquired an interesting piece." Rhys pulled a gold necklace from a side pocket of his black trousers.

Kate stared at Rhys as he drew near. Was he really discussing artifacts at a time like this? She glanced down at the necklace he held out for her father to examine, her curiosity growing. "That looks like the necklace Mayfield brought back from Egypt." She glanced at the door leading to the hall as it opened. Two men dressed in black uniforms entered, closing the door behind them, blocking the entrance.

Frederick didn't touch the necklace, but sat staring at it, as though he were staring into the grave of a loved one. "Is it genuine?"

Rhys drew his thumb over the carved gold. "Yes."

Frederick closed his eyes. "I was afraid of that."

"Father, I don't understand." Kate glanced up at Rhys. "The necklace was in the museum. Where did you get it?"

"From Lady Judith." Without looking up from the necklace, Rhys continued. "Perhaps you will tell us how Leighton Van Horne obtained this from the museum, Mr. Melville."

Robert leaned forward in his chair. "I don't know what you're talking about."

"No." Rhys turned, facing Edwin where he sat beside Robert. "But I suspect your father does."

"Now, see here." Edwin came out of his chair. "I had nothing to do with replacing that necklace with a replica."

Rhys smiled. "I think you did."

"So it seems we have a viper among us," Barnaby said, rising from his chair by the windows.

Edwin glanced at the two guards who stood at the door. "Frederick, tell them this is ridiculous."

"I kept hoping there had been some mistake," Frederick said. "You helped that man track us. You helped him escape. He killed the guard, Edwin. He tried to kill Devlin."

"You were the one," Judith said. "Leighton said he had a friend on the expedition."

"You have no proof of any of this." Edwin ran his hand over his mustache. "Why, that necklace is more than likely a fake."

"I've contacted one of our people in London." Rhys slipped the necklace into his pocket. "It should be fairly simple to find enough proof to convict you, Mr. Melville. So you see, it's useless to maintain this pretense."

"Father, is it true?" Robert asked.

Edwin looked down at his son. "You and your gambling." He lashed out with his hand, slapping Robert hard across the cheek. "How did you think I was going to pay all of the debts?"

"I didn't give a damn how you paid them." Robert lifted his hand to his torn lip, color rising to stain his cheeks. "I wanted to ruin you. How does it feel, Father? Knowing your only son hates you enough to try to destroy you."

Edwin closed his eyes, his shoulders curling forward as though bowed by a great weight.

"Edwin, why didn't you tell me you were in trouble?" Frederick asked. "I could have helped."

"I thought I could get out of the mess on my own. It seemed so simple." Edwin sank to his chair. "Van Horne came to me; he had purchased all of Robert's gambling notes. He told me he would dispose of them if I would help him expand his private collection. He wanted that necklace, and he was willing to do almost anything to have it. I thought at the time, who would ever know if I replaced the real necklace with a fake? Van Horne had the replica made, and late one night, I replaced the original. After I stole for him, he owned me."

"You told him about the journal and map," Frederick said.

Edwin shook his head. "He was in the anteroom of my office when you came to see me the day before we left for Brazil. He overheard us discussing the trip. It fascinated him. It was then he decided to go treasure hunting."

"We could have all been killed," Frederick whispered.

Edwin looked at Frederick, his face pulled into tight lines that made him look years beyond his age. "I'm sorry, old friend, so very sorry."

"What will happen to him?" Kate glanced down at her tightly clasped hands, unable to look at Edwin another moment. "He was only a pawn in Van Horne's game."

"I understand your feelings. But a man died because of his actions." Rhys studied Edwin for a moment. "I will give you a choice, Mr. Melville. Face the council, or return to London for trial. I warn you, if you choose the council, you will not be the same man you are now after they pass judgment."

"Edwin Melville has no reason to go on existing." Edwin smiled, a twisting of lips that spoke of sorrow. "I choose your council, with the hope they can make a better man of me."

Kate rested her hand on her father's arm. When he looked

up at her, the tears she saw in his eyes made it all the more
difficult to keep her own tears at bay. They had come here
looking for a dream. They had both found a nightmare.

Kate stared out the window of her sitting room, listening to
her father explain all the reasons they should stay in Avallon.
In the distance the ruins stood as they had for 6,000 years,
glittering in the sunlight of a new day, mysteries yet to be
solved. Still, she had lost her appetite for mysteries.

Three days had passed since Devlin had been shot. Although
Devlin refused to see her, Austin and his family kept her
informed of his progress. She knew he would soon be up
and about, as strong as ever. And she knew she had to leave
before that happened.

"We can leave for London this afternoon," she said. Lady
Judith had decided to stay, as had Robert. He had entered one
of the rehabilitation centers this morning, beside his father.
They were each looking for a new life in Avallon. Kate
hoped they would find happiness here. "An underground
train of some sort will take us to Pará. Rhys has provided
for his private yacht to carry us home. He said it would take
three days. Can you imagine, the entire trip in three days."

"Katie, Devlin isn't even out of his sickbed. And the ruins,
we haven't had a chance to explore them. Not to mention
these people. They have the future here. Why, the powder
Austin gave you after you were bitten by that snake saved
your life. Imagine a powder that can neutralize the venom of
a viper."

Kate kept her gaze on the ruins. It had been somehow
comforting to learn there truly had been a snake. At least
some things on the trip had not been illusions.

"Why, just yesterday I saw a device Rhys used to commu-
nicate with London, some type of telephone. He was talking
to the man as if he were as close as the next room. Why,
I could spend my life here, exploring, learning. Think of
it, Katie, we could stay. Rhys said we could stay, here in
a colony of Atlantis."

"I can't stay, Father." Kate drew her hand down the curtains, smoothing the rose silk damask beneath her palm. "But I will understand if you wish to remain behind."

"What's happened? Why do you want to leave? Devlin is facing a great emotional challenge. Don't you want to be here? Don't you want to help him?"

Kate felt a thickening in her throat, an expansion, as if her emotions were centering there, gathering to conspire against her. "More than anything in the world."

"I don't understand."

Neither do I. Dear God, neither do I. How had it all gone so wrong? "He doesn't want me here. He doesn't want me in his life."

"He loves you."

"If he loved me, would he refuse to see me?" She kept her eyes focused on the ruins, her father a figure in the periphery. He was staring at her, but she couldn't hold his look. She couldn't let him see the pain she knew was in her eyes. "He thinks I'm some kind of little snob who only wants to marry him because he is suddenly a member of the aristocracy."

Frederick stared at her, his mouth open, his eyes wide with disbelief. "That's preposterous! Why, young Asheboro made a fool of himself following you about like a puppy. And he's a duke, for heaven's sake. And there was that Frenchman, what's his name, the Count of something or other. And the—"

"Father, you and I know I don't care one whit for money or titles or pedigree. But it doesn't alter the fact that Mr. McCain believes I have such a low character, I would marry him because of his change in circumstance."

Frederick shook his head. He turned and paced to the door, then turned and marched back to where Kate stood by the window. "I'm sure it's only the shock of everything he has been through. In time you can be sure he will come to see—"

"No. I once believed we were wrong for one another. Now I know that's true. If you wish to stay I shall understand."

Frederick took her hand in his. "I couldn't stay without my little girl."

Kate looked down at their hands. All her life he had been there for her. She wanted to tell him how very much she loved him, how very much she needed him right now. Yet she couldn't. Her throat was too tight to allow a single word to escape without releasing the tears that seemed to hover constantly at the back of her eyes.

How many tears had she cried in three days? Enough to make her eyes puffy and sore. Enough to make her feel humiliated and all too foolish. Yet no amount of tears could wash away the pain.

Never again. She would never trust another man. Never would she lay her soul bare, or offer her heart with such reckless abandon.

For years Kate had known exactly what she wanted from life, and it had nothing to do with getting entangled with a man. It had nothing to do with Devlin McCain. It was time to forget him. It was time to get on with her life. It was time to heal.

Chapter Thirty-one

Afternoon sunlight streamed through the lace curtains shielding the drawing-room windows of the Sinclair town house in London, casting a tangled pattern across the chessboard. Devlin stared at the chess pieces, trying to concentrate on his next move. After two months in Avallon, his parents had persuaded him to visit England.

His parents. It still sounded strange to his own ears when he referred to Rhys and Brianna as his father and mother. Yet it felt good to be a part of their family.

He had everything he had ever wanted: a home, people who cared about him, a future with more opportunity than he had ever dreamed. Yet it wasn't enough. All he had gained could not ease the longing at night, could not fill the emptiness gnawing inside him. All he had gained could not equal a tenth of what he had lost.

Devlin had been in London only three months. Amazing how quickly the elite had accepted him. Hell, they more than accepted him; they devoured him. The Sinclair name meant money and power and social position. A lost heir, an earl, he was a sensation, sought after by every hostess in the city, fresh prey for every matchmaking mother in England.

Three months. He had been in London in time to see the last traces of snow dissolve into the first buds of spring. He had attended parties and balls and formal dinners. He had gone to theaters and museums and galleries. He had taken daily rides through Hyde Park. And yet, he had not glimpsed Kate's face.

Kate. She was in town. Devlin knew where she lived. He had ridden past her door so many times his horse knew the way by heart. A three-story town house of white stone in the heart of Mayfair, a castle. And each time he passed that big, stone house, he caught himself staring up at the windows like a peasant pining for the princess inside, anxious for a glimpse of her.

He needed to forget her.

Why did he still dream of her at night? Why did the thought of her haunt his every waking moment? Why the hell couldn't he get her out of his blood?

He would forget her.

A trace of roses could betray him. More than once he had caught the fragrance adrift in a room filled with people. More than once he had moved through that room, searching for Kate, finding only strangers. More than once he wondered if he had been wrong to force her out of his life. More than ever before he wanted her in his life. Was he fooling himself to believe he could stay away from her?

He would always love her.

"Are you going to move anytime before dinner?"

Devlin frowned as he looked across the chessboard at his brother. Austin had shaved, leaving no doubt the two shared identical features. And Devlin was discovering they had more in common than he had originally suspected. He moved his knight and leaned back against the blue silk brocade of the wing chair, seeing disaster even before Austin moved his bishop.

"Checkmate." Austin smiled, a curving of lips that gave Devlin the uncomfortable feeling he was looking into a mirror. "You seem a little distracted lately. Has finding yourself one of the most sought-after bachelors in town taken its toll?"

"Do you ever attend any parties where there aren't mothers trying to sell their daughters on the marriage market?"

"Not many."

"I don't know how you stomach it."

"That's one reason I usually spend very little time in the social circles of London." Austin fingered one of the pawns he had captured.

Bitterness, Devlin could hear it in his brother's voice, bitterness born of experience. Bitterness, Devlin could feel it flow like poison through his own veins, seeping into his every pore, destroying soft tissue, eating away until nothing but that bitterness was left inside him. "How can you ever be sure a woman isn't just after your money, or your title?"

"I suppose you can't be sure, although legend says when you meet your *Edaina*, your soul mate, you will know. I thought I met her once. I was wrong." Austin stared down at the pawn he held between his fingers. "Sometimes, I wonder what it might be like to live without a title appended to my name." He looked across the board, meeting Devlin's gaze. "You've had that opportunity."

"Yeah, I've had that opportunity. It's a real eye-opener."

Austin rolled the pawn between his fingers, looking at Devlin as though he could see straight into his brother's soul. "When you find a woman you love, a woman who loves you, who isn't interested in money or title or position, you should grab her and hold her and keep her for all of your days."

Devlin drew his hand into a fist on the arm of the chair. In the five months since he had discovered his family, only once had Austin questioned Devlin about Kate. Perhaps because Devlin had made it clear he didn't intend to discuss her. Perhaps because there had been so many other things to concern them both. Chief among those things was the fact that Van Horne and the medallion had not been found.

"Yeah, well, the next time you see a woman who isn't interested in money or titles, point her out to me. I'd like to meet her."

"There are some women who find themselves sought after for similar reasons, especially if they possess both wealth and beauty." Austin glanced down at the porcelain chess piece he held between his fingers. "I remember hearing of the fool Asheboro made of himself over an heiress to a shipping empire."

Devlin had met the Duke of Asheboro. The man walked around with his Roman nose so elevated it was a wonder he didn't run into the furniture.

"Seems the woman couldn't turn without tripping over him. One night, he hired a string quartet to play under her bedroom window. The story has it the young woman tossed a pitcher of water from her balcony, drenching all of them, including Asheboro. Seems she didn't care that he had just become a duke. You see, money and titles never had meant anything to her. Rumors are she turned down half the aristocracy in London as well as a few scattered around the world."

A woman who didn't care for titles or money. Devlin stared at the pattern cast by sunlight on the chessboard, the weight he had been carrying around his heart growing heavier as he thought of Kate, as he wished she had been able to look beyond title and social position. "The woman must be a rare gem."

"She is. Beautiful, intelligent, brave. The type of woman a man could walk through hell with, and think he was traveling through paradise."

A spark shot along Devlin's nerves, a sudden wrenching of suspicion inside him. "Is this woman married?"

"No." Austin leaned back, smiling as he held Devlin's gaze. "Although I did hear she had planned to marry."

"What happened?"

"The man she fell in love with deserted her. Seems he preferred to become the rage of London."

Heat crawled upward along the back of his neck until Devlin's ears tingled. "Do I know him?"

"I'm not sure." Austin glanced down at the pawn he was holding. "I think you did know him. Maybe you need to become reacquainted."

"What makes you think the woman ever intended to marry this man?"

Austin looked up and stared into Devlin's eyes. "She told me she was going to marry him, the day he left her behind to search for an ancient city on the top of a mountain."

"Before we . . ." Devlin stared into his brother's eyes, seeing the truth there, feeling like a man who had just been sentenced to death. "Kate told you she was going to marry me?"

"She told me she was beginning to understand what it meant to love someone."

Devlin closed his eyes, his brother's words settling around him like a shroud.

"She said she didn't want to live her life without you."

"Before she knew," Devlin whispered, forcing the words past the constriction in his throat.

"Before she knew you were anything other than a casino owner. You see, she saw the man behind the rough facade. She fell in love with him."

"That man is a damn fool."

Kate dabbed paint in one corner of the canvas, bringing a pale bloom to life. Fading sunlight peeked through the leaves of the oak in the garden behind her father's house to tumble across the canvas, wet oils sparkling beneath its touch. Although the roses nearby were just coming to life, filling the warm breeze with perfume, it was not their beauty she captured with her brush. It was a memory. A memory she had long ago realized she would never excise from her heart.

When she heard footsteps on the flagstone path leading from the house, she knew it was her father. Time to dress for dinner. And although she had no appetite, she would eat, just as she got up every morning and bathed and dressed and went through the day. Small habits, little rituals, the basic routine of a life, all that was left to her now.

Silently she cursed the man who had shown her there could be so much more in life. Silently she cursed the man who had taught her to love and hate and ache with a deep, unhealing pain. Silently she cursed the first day she had set eyes on Devlin McCain.

For three months Devlin had been in London. At first she had risen each morning, feeding like a starving beggar on the certainty he would come to her. Yet Austin had been the one who had come to see her, torturing her with features so like Devlin's.

Each day the newspapers were filled with stories of Devlin, the long-lost Earl of Hatherleigh, the younger son of the Duke of Daventry, the man who had inherited his father's third title. Each day there was a new account of him in the social columns, a hint of this lady or another who might one day be his bride. And each day Kate had grown colder inside, as though life slowly drained from her, until all that remained was a shell who went on existing.

This had to stop! She wouldn't let the man destroy her. She wouldn't think of Devlin McCain. In two weeks she and her father would leave for Egypt. She would drown herself in work. Work was all she needed. In time Devlin McCain would be nothing but a faded memory.

The footsteps paused. She sensed her father was watching her, worrying about her, as he had been for months. She took time putting away her brushes; she needed time to shake off her air of despair, to mold her lips into a smile before she turned to face him. The words she intended to say were swamped in a sudden rush of emotions when she saw Devlin standing on the path behind her.

"Hello, Professor."

He looked impossibly handsome, standing in a shaft of sunlight slanting through the leaves overhead, black waves tumbled around his face by the breeze. Taller than she remembered, thinner too, perhaps, his black coat of superfine wool hugging broad shoulders, his white silk shirt and necktie emphasizing the golden brown of his skin.

She fought the almost uncontrollable urge to run into his arms, to fling herself back into the emotional whirlwind that had all but destroyed her. "What are you doing here?"

"I wanted to see you."

He looked at her then, as though he were comparing her to a memory, his gaze roaming from the crown of her tightly bound hair to the tips of her black kid shoes peeking out from beneath her plain, blue gown. So intense was that gaze, so intimate, her skin tingled, as though he were stroking her bare breasts, her hips, her thighs with his strong fingers.

Why hadn't she worn something else today? She fidgeted with her skirt. Why did she have to look like a dried-up old maid on the day he chose to call? The devil take it all! She refused to care what he thought of her looks. "I'm not carrying your child, if that is what you have come to discover."

He looked startled, as if the thought had never occurred to him, while she had spent days in suspense, waiting with alternate fear and hope that she might one day give birth to his child.

In the end she had realized he had left her nothing. Except the memories that taunted her. The memories that made her reach out in the middle of the night for the warmth of his body, only to find the chill of her reality. "Now that you have seen me, you can leave."

He held her gaze, his silvery blue eyes filled with a warmth she thought never to see again. "I've missed you, Kate."

She turned away from him, feeling the sting of tears in her eyes. *Don't do this to me!* she wanted to scream. *Don't make me hurt any more than I do.* "From what I've heard, you haven't lacked companionship."

"Jealous?" he asked, and she could hear the smile in his voice.

"Not any longer." Kate stared at the stone birdbath nestled in the center of the rosebushes. Sunlight reflected on the blue mosaic tiles on the bottom of the basin. It was empty. Someone had forgotten the birds. "I've buried all of those terribly primitive emotions you were always so good at dredging from my soul."

"All of them?"

She looked straight at him. "Every one."

He brushed his knuckles back and forth across a full, white rose that nodded in the breeze beside him. He studied the blossom as though it were some rare species rather than an ordinary English rose. "You didn't stay long in Avallon."

"There was nothing for me there."

He stroked the flower with his fingertips, slow, gentle caresses drawing the petals together at the summit, reminding her suddenly of the feel of those fingertips against her bare skin. Why had he come here? Revenge? Guilt? "You seem to have adapted well to your new life, Lord Sinclair."

"You were right." He glanced up from the flower. "I needed to give my family a chance. It was the only way I was going to feel whole again."

Would she ever feel whole again? She stared at the ivy-covered wall at the end of the rose garden, one segment of the whole that surrounded the garden, red bricks joined one to another, blocking out the world. "Pity, finding yourself the younger son, settling for the title of earl while Austin remains the marquess and heir to your father's most coveted title."

"Titles don't mean a damn to me."

"Really," she said, allowing that single word to drip with skepticism.

He was quiet a moment. She could feel him watching her, willing her to look at him. She refused.

"Do you ever think of me, Kate?"

"No. Never." She spoke the lie with all the conviction she could muster. "Now, please go away. Leave me alone."

"I think of you." From the corner of her eye she saw him move toward her. "Truth is, I can't stop thinking of you."

"Yes, I understand you've been living like a monk since you told me to get out of your life."

"I regret those words, Kate."

She clasped her hands at her waist as he drew near, the heat of his body stroking her side, like spring sunlight streaming across a dormant rose. "I regret more than words."

"Do you?"

"More than you could ever realize." He was too close, his heat conjuring flames from the ashes of emotions scattered within her, love and hope stirring in the blaze, fighting to rise like a phoenix from the flames. She wouldn't allow it.

"Your painting doesn't look a thing like this garden." He brushed his fingers over a loose curl that rested against her shoulder, touching her through the linen of her gown. Warmth flowed through her veins, awakening every nerve, curling around her breasts. "But it does look like a place I remember. A savage paradise where I first held you in my arms and tasted the sweetness of your body."

"You never held me, *Lord Sinclair*. You never touched me." She curled her shoulder to escape his touch, knowing it was too late. Deep inside, a sweet ache throbbed, an ache only he could ease. And oh, how she hated him for the power he wielded so ruthlessly over her. "Devlin McCain, the man I made love with, the man I loved, died in the jungle."

"No, he didn't. He wandered around lost for a long time, but he finally found his way home." He leaned forward and pressed his lips to the sensitive hollow behind her ear, sending shivers whispering across her shoulder. "You're my home, Kate."

"What's wrong, Lord Sinclair?" She turned to face him, hitting the easel with her hip, sending it crashing to the ground, canvas and paints spilling across the grass. "Can't find a woman to warm your bed? Is that why you've suddenly decided to come calling?"

"I can't find a woman to warm my heart." He rested his warm hands on her shoulders. "Come back to me, Kate. I'm lost without you."

Pain closed around her heart at his soft words. Lord help her, she wanted to believe him, she wanted to lay her heart at his feet.

He moved closer, strong fingers holding her gently. She could break away from him. She would! He lowered his head, lips parting, warm breath streaming across her cheek, sweet as the breeze after a warm summer rain. It had been a lifetime since she had tasted his lips. A lifetime since she had stood in the warm haven of his embrace. A lifetime since she had felt the fire stream through her veins. She wanted . . .

She couldn't! She wouldn't! She refused to be turned upside down and pulled inside out again, not by this man, not by any. She turned her head, avoiding the kiss she craved with every fiber of her body.

"You think you can just waltz up to me and sweep me off my feet, is that it?" She jerked away from him. "Get out of here! I never want to see you again."

He looked at her a long moment, the pain she had seen reflected each morning in her mirror, there in his eyes.

"I understand why you're angry." He smiled, and she felt her resolve waver. "I guess I'll just have to find a way to prove how much I love you. I do love you, Kate. More than my life."

She had heard him speak those words before, and she had learned just how little they meant to him. "I don't want your lies. All I want is to be left alone."

"I have no lies to give you. I have only my heart."

She turned her head as he began to walk away from her. She wouldn't watch him leave. She wouldn't shout the words that would bring him back to her side. She would conquer this weakness.

She stared down at the painting that laid on the grass. The damp oils of the landscape shimmered in the dying sunlight; a thin cascade of water tumbled over black rocks into a narrow stream; orchids dripped from the trees surrounding a small clearing in the jungle, all spattered with paint. Ruined.

She had been willing to sacrifice her every dream for that man. She had been willing to turn her life into anything he wanted. And he had cast her aside. He had believed she was no better than a whore, a woman who would sell herself for money and title. He had shown so little faith in her. And that was what she couldn't forgive: his lack of trust.

At the sound of footsteps on the flagstone, she drew a deep breath. She didn't want to face anyone.

"Katie, are you all right?" Frederick asked.

She tried to force her lips into a smile. Impossible. Impossible to lie. "Why did he have to come strolling back into my life? Just when I was learning to live without him."

She felt her father draw near. He slipped his arm around her shoulders and turned her, holding her head against his shoulder, flooding her senses with the fragrance of bayberry, conjuring memories of all the times he had held her on his knee and dried her tears.

Only this hurt went deeper than a scraped knee. And in his comforting embrace it was all she could do not to surrender to the tears clawing at her eyes. She knew tears wouldn't wash away the pain.

"When did my little girl start lying to herself?" he asked, stroking her arm. "You know you're never going to be over that man. He's a part of you."

"No, he isn't." Kate tried to draw air into lungs that had grown shallow.

"He loves you, Katie." He kissed her brow. "And you love him."

She shook her head.

"Try to understand what happened to him on that mountaintop. Try to understand the turmoil he was in when he turned away from you. Try to accept him now. It's the only way either of you will be happy."

"I don't need him. I have my work," she whispered, her voice dissolving into the emotions crowding her throat. She swallowed hard, fighting the need for Devlin that crippled her defenses. "I can live without him."

"I know you can," Frederick said, stroking her back. "But the question is, do you want to live without him?"

"Well, now, isn't this a touching scene."

The voice came to Kate from a nightmare. That voice sent her heart careening into the wall of her chest with a sudden fear that sucked the breath from her lungs and sent her blood pounding through her veins. She turned as one with her father, staring at the specter who stood near the vine-covered wall that surrounded the garden and sheltered it from the neighboring residences.

"You!" Kate whispered.

Van Horne smiled as he began to move toward them, the last golden rays of the sun stroking his silvery blond hair. "You look as though you've seen a ghost."

Kate backed away as he drew near, grabbing her father's arm, halting when Van Horne pointed a revolver at her heart.

"I assure you, I'm quite real, Miss Whitmore." Van Horne smiled, a slow slide of finely molded lips that left his eyes glittering like ice in the sun. "As real as this gun and the bullets I will put into you and your father if you do not do exactly what I wish."

Chapter Thirty-two

"There has to be some way to change her mind." Devlin turned as he reached the glass-fronted bookcases at one end of the library. Without pausing, he stalked the windows on the opposite side of the room, prowling like a jaguar in a cage, frustration fueling his every move. "I'll be damned before I let her shut me out of her life."

Austin stood with his shoulder braced against the jade marble hearth. He glanced down at his brandy snifter as Devlin approached, gaslight glinting on the cut crystal as he swirled the amber liquid in his glass. "I suppose you could always court her."

Devlin paused in front of his brother, frowning at the smile Austin couldn't quite hide. "Court her?"

"You know, flowers and trinkets and hanging about her house." Austin looked at Devlin, his eyes sparkling with mischief. "Of course, I wouldn't recommend hiring a string quartet to play beneath her window."

"You mean, make a fool of myself."

"I would say you've already done that, little brother."

Twenty minutes separated them in birth, 20 minutes that had forever doomed Devlin to be the younger brother. "I'm glad you're getting so much pleasure out of this."

"I have complete faith in you." Austin sipped his brandy. "Of course, I also have complete faith Kate will lead you on a good chase before she agrees to be your wife."

Devlin shoved his hands into his pockets and stared out the windows that faced the garden. Moonlight poured like liquid silver over the bushes and plants, the trees dark silhouettes.

In his mind he saw another garden, this one untouched by man. He saw a young woman asleep on a bed of orchids, her smooth skin kissed by delicate petals. With the memory came inspiration. "Do you know where I might get my hands on some orchids? Enough to fill a room?"

"I think we might be able . . ." Austin paused as the door to the library swung open and Frederick Whitmore stormed across the threshold.

"He has her!" Frederick shouted, waving a note in his hand as he rushed toward Devlin and Austin. "Van Horne has my daughter."

A bolt of fear shot through Devlin, sparking through his every nerve. "What happened?"

"He just appeared, out of nowhere." Frederick shoved the note at Devlin. "He wants to meet with you."

Devlin snatched the note from Frederick's hand and read the few lines scrawled in black upon the white parchment.

"What's he asking for?" Austin asked, touching Devlin's arm.

"He'll meet with me tonight, to exchange Kate for the necklace." Devlin handed the note to Austin.

"He chose a theater." Austin looked up from the note. "Very public."

"So how the hell do I get my hands on that necklace?" Devlin asked.

"I'll contact one of our men who specializes in getting into tight places. We should have the necklace in time to meet him." Austin stared at the note as though he were trying to read more than the few lines scrawled in black upon the white parchment. "We can't let Van Horne get away. We have to get the medallion."

Devlin's blood pounded in his temples as he stared at his brother. "We have to get Kate out of that maniac's hands."

Austin held Devlin's gaze. "I doubt he intends to let either of you walk away, whether or not he gets that necklace."

Beneath the soft light of crystal chandeliers, people poured into the velvet-lined seats of the theater. Men in elegant black evening clothes escorted women in every shade of the rainbow. Precious gems glittered in the gaslight: diamonds, emeralds, rubies, sparkling, sending shards of light in every direction. Yet shadows cast by swags of dark blue velvet surrounded Kate where she sat in the box beside Leighton Van Horne. It was as if she existed outside of this world of laughter and color, trapped in Van Horne's hell.

"I do appreciate a good comedy," Van Horne said. "I understand this one has gone over very well in New York."

Kate glanced at the man sitting beside her. Van Horne was sitting back in his chair, smiling at her, looking as though he were out for no more than a night at the theater.

"I'm afraid your father's coat is a little too short in the sleeves. But I must say, you look beautiful." He slid his fingers from the white silk rose on the shoulder of her evening gown down to the emerald silk shaping the modest, round neckline. "Another time, another place, I think you and I might have—"

"You aren't going to get away with this." She leaned away from him, pressing against the velvet cushion of her chair.

Van Horne laughed deep in his throat. "We shall see."

Chimes sounded in that world outside this shadowy box. Kate stared at the audience, searching for Devlin, wondering if she might somehow find a way to escape.

The lights grew dim. *Stay away, Devlin, please stay away.* She knew Van Horne would kill him. She sensed it was part of his plan.

"Turn around, my dear Miss Whitmore," Van Horne said. "We have company."

Kate turned and found Devlin standing before the curtained doorway, the starched white linen of his shirt glowing in the faint light.

"Are you all right, Kate?"

"I'm . . ." Kate hesitated as Van Horne touched her arm with the cold steel of his revolver.

"The lady is unharmed." Van Horne slid the gun barrel back and forth across her bare skin above the white glove that rose just above her elbow.

Devlin shifted on the balls of his feet, his expression betraying none of his emotions. Yet Kate could sense the barely restrained rage inside him. Memories swept around her like a tornado, yanking her back in time, back to a moonlit mountaintop.

She clenched her hands into fists in her lap, reliving the struggle once again, hearing the explosion of the pistol, seeing Devlin fall to the stones, bloody and broken. "Devlin," she whispered. "Please don't." *Don't do anything that might cause this man to harm you.*

Devlin frowned as he looked at her.

"You should listen to her, Mr. McCain." Van Horne pointed the pistol at Devlin's chest. "We can all walk away from here if you cooperate."

"Let her go, Van Horne."

"Did you bring the necklace?"

Devlin reached into his coat pocket and withdrew the ancient piece of gold. It shimmered in the faint light, glowing as it had around the neck of Cleopatra 2,000 years ago.

Van Horne stared at that ornate piece of gold as though it were a lover returned to him. "Set it on the chair and back out of the box."

Devlin shook his head. "I'm not going anywhere without Kate."

Van Horne ran his tongue over his lips. "I'll let her go once I'm safely away from here."

Devlin moved toward the railing of the box. "You want a hostage, you take me."

Van Horne wagged the revolver at Devlin. "I fear you might be more than I wish to handle."

Laughter rippled from the lower floor, a counterpoint to the tension rising inside Kate.

Devlin thrust his hand over the railing, holding the necklace suspended above the lower floor of the theater. "I wonder what would happen if I dropped it?"

He tossed the necklace into the air; it opened like a golden bird stretching its wings, capturing the glow from the stage like sunlight.

"No!" Van Horne came out of his seat.

The necklace tumbled back into Devlin's hand. "Do we trade?"

Van Horne glanced over the railing. Kate could almost see the man calculating how he might retrieve the necklace should Devlin toss it from the box. "I'll shoot, McCain."

"And you'll lose the necklace, Van Horne." Devlin held the necklace over the railing, dangling the gold from one finger. "I doubt you'll be able to find it in the mess that would follow a shooting. Want to take the chance?"

Van Horne grabbed Kate and dragged her from her chair, his fingers biting into her upper arm. She clenched her teeth to keep from moaning at the sharp pain.

"I'll kill her," Van Horne said, his voice a harsh whisper as he shoved the muzzle of the gun into Kate's side. The sudden blow dragged a moan from her lips.

Devlin's eyes narrowed. "Harm her, and I throw this thing as far as I can."

Van Horne licked his lips. He flexed his hand on Kate's arm, his gaze riveted on that shimmering piece of gold dangling from Devlin's finger.

"Let her go, Van Horne."

Save yourself! She wanted to scream the words as she looked at Devlin, seeing him now as she had that night on the edge of the cliff, knowing he would risk his life to save her. She couldn't let him.

"Damn you, McCain," Van Horne whispered, swinging the gun from Kate, aiming directly at Devlin's chest.

He would shoot him, out of sheer, perverted rage. Kate rammed her shoulder into Van Horne's side, catching him by surprise. As the sound of his grunt filled the air, she brought her fist down on his wrist, knocking the gun from his hand. She twisted in his grasp, breaking free.

"Now!" Devlin shouted, grabbing Kate in his arms. He turned and brought her down to the floor, covering her with his body.

Over Devlin's shoulder she saw Austin rush into the box, followed by two men. All of them were holding pistols. All of them were aiming directly at the tall, blond-haired man who stood beside the railing.

"It's over, Van Horne," Austin said, moving toward Van Horne. "Come with us."

Van Horne smiled. "You wouldn't shoot an unarmed man. Would you?"

Before Austin could reply, Van Horne turned and began shouting, his voice soaring above the voices of the actors on the stage, rising in a clear tone, shouting one word over and over again.

"Fire!"

Screams ripped through the theater. In a single movement, Van Horne vaulted over the railing, standing for a moment on the ledge, staring at Devlin. "Another time, McCain!"

Austin lunged forward, knocking over a chair, reaching for Van Horne, but it was too late. He had already crouched and dropped to the floor.

"The exits!" Austin shouted to the two men behind him.
"Go!"

Austin swung his long legs over the edge of the railing.
Kate gasped as she realized he intended to jump. Austin
crouched and grabbed the narrow ledge, lowering himself
before dropping to the lower floor. The two men dashed
from the box, the drapes billowing in their wake. Devlin
scrambled to his feet, dragging Kate with him.

Below, people were dashing toward the exits, pushing,
screaming, trampling one another in their panic. In the swirling current of people, Kate saw Austin fighting his way
toward the stage. She caught a glimpse of Van Horne before
he disappeared behind the dark blue curtains framing the
stage.

Kate clenched the railing. "He's going to get away."

"There's a small army surrounding this theater," Devlin
said, his voice deep and sure. "They aren't going to let him
walk away from here."

Kate turned to face him, looking up into his clear, silvery
blue eyes. He smiled, and she felt the world tilt. The noise
and panic crashing all around them faded into a distant buzz,
as though she were stepping into the calm eye of a storm, a
safe haven where nothing could harm her.

Devlin touched her cheek, a soft brush of warmth across
her skin that whispered deep inside her. "I've been trying to
think of ways to coax you to come back to me, Professor."

Kate thought of all that had come before. He had risked his
life to save her time and time again. He had given his love
when she offered nothing in return. He had taught her there
was more to life than a solitary existence. And she loved him.
She would always love him.

He brushed his thumb across the corner of her lips. "Tell
me, what can I do?"

"Hold me, Devlin." She slid her hands upward along his
arms, the heat of his skin radiating through the smooth,
black wool to warm her palms. "Hold me, and never let
me go."

"Kate," he whispered, reaching for her, wrapping strong arms around her.

She threw her arms around his neck, surrendering completely to the power of the man lifting her from the floor, allowing him to surround her. Tears pricked her eyes and she buried her face in the warm curve of his neck, breathing in the scent of his skin: sandalwood and man.

Images of a pagan god standing naked in the sunlight flashed in her mind, a portrait of potent male beauty forever impressed in her memory. And she would treasure that portrait and the man for the rest of her life. When he let her feet touch the floor again, her legs were trembling.

"My beautiful Kate. Sorry doesn't begin to tell you how I feel for what I've done to you."

"It doesn't matter now," she whispered.

He smoothed his thumbs over her cheeks, catching the tears she couldn't stop. He kissed her, a gentle brush of firm lips across hers that left her hungry for everything only he could give her.

"Marry me," he whispered. "Tomorrow."

"No."

She smiled as his expression pulled into a frown, confusion swimming in the silvery blue pools of his eyes.

"Kate, I thought you—"

She pressed her fingertips to his lips. "If you don't mind, I would like to be married in ancient Avallon. I want your parents and my father, Austin and your sister, and Barnaby to be there, to watch as our dreams become reality."

He smiled, his lips curving beneath her fingertips. He slipped his fingers around her wrist and lifted her hand from his lips, placing her open palm over his heart, holding it there with his hand. "We can leave first thing tomorrow morning."

Kate absorbed the solid beat of his heart beneath her palm. "I suppose you expect me to tell you I love you?"

"It would be nice."

She tugged one corner of his necktie, loosening the black silk. He was too buttoned, too civilized for the Devlin she adored. "Going to believe me this time, Mr. McCain?"

He leaned forward and kissed the tip of her nose. "Try me."

"I love you, Devlin."

He closed his eyes, his breath escaping on a long sigh. The wealth of emotion in that simple sound left her shaken. He had lived his life alone, looking for a home, searching for a place to belong. He had known pain and humiliation. He had survived, strong and proud. Yet beneath it all, he was as vulnerable as she was.

"Do you believe me this time?" She pulled studs from the front of his shirt, letting them fall to the dark blue carpet.

"I don't know." He looked down at her, his silvery blue eyes reflecting his love for her. "I might need to hear you say it a few more times before I really start to believe you love me."

"Then I suppose I'll have to tell you every morning, every night." She nuzzled her nose into the inviting pelt of black curls and golden skin revealed by his partially open shirt. "I love you, Devlin."

He slipped his hands into the hair at her temples, combing the golden strands with his fingers.

"I love the taste of you, the heat of you. I love the sound of your voice, the touch of your hand. I love your strength, your courage. And I love that vulnerable little boy you keep hidden inside." She tasted him with the tip of her tongue, smiling against his skin when she felt his muscles tighten beneath her touch. "I want to be with you, Devlin. Now. Always. Forever."

He slipped his arms around her, holding her close to his heart. "Forever."

Chapter Thirty-three

Avallon was impervious to the world once again. A stone had been rolled into place at the base of the mountain, closing the entrance to the mountaintop, shutting out intruders. Morning sunlight tumbled over the edge of the narrow gorge near the ancient entrance, flooding the lush garden below, peeking through the low entrance of a banana-leaf hut.

Kate stirred as a finger of sunlight brushed her face. A sweet fragrance filled her senses, coaxing her from her dreams.

Orchids. Red and white and pink, the flowers spilled across the blue silk sheet beneath her; they covered the blue cotton blanket tangled around her naked hips.

"So he did understand," she whispered, lifting a soft, white blossom to her cheek.

Yesterday, after their wedding ceremony, Devlin had raised one black brow at her suggestion for their honeymoon site, but he had agreed. And now she knew he understood her need to be here, so near the entrance to what had been a mystery, so like the place where she had first glimpsed heaven in his arms.

No one from Avallon came to this place. They were alone in this little paradise, the banana-leaf hut Devlin had fashioned their only shelter, the air-filled mattress and bedding Brianna had insisted they take, their only comforts. Except for the comfort they found in each other's arms.

She slid her hand over the pillow where he had rested his head, the silk cool beneath her palm. Where was her husband?

They were safe here, she assured herself, folding back the blanket, safe from the evil of Van Horne. The devil had escaped their men in London.

Austin had left Avallon a few hours after the wedding, headed for New York, hoping Van Horne's sister might lead him to the man. Kate prayed Austin would remain safe. She knew she was the only reason Devlin hadn't accompanied his brother.

She stepped from the shadows of the hut into the full light of morning. Sunlight stroked her bare skin, tingling the tips of her breasts.

Air fragrant with orchids and the crisp scent of moss and ferns filled her senses, leaving a tang on her tongue. Above the soft, swishing sound of the water that tumbled in a white cascade from the side of the mountain into a nearby pool, birds sang high in the trees, as if proclaiming their joy for the beauty of this morning. And amid this lush paradise, Devlin stood in the pool beneath the waterfalls.

Golden light tumbled in the water, sliding over his shoulders, his back, sunlight and water merging to bathe this prince from an ancient race. Watching him, knowing they were joined for all time, she felt warmer of both body and spirit than she had ever felt in her life. And yet beneath the joy, beneath the contentment, a kernel of fear remained, like a fossil trapped in ice, the uncertainty of a future she had never imagined for herself.

She pushed aside her fear. She wouldn't think of it now, she thought, slipping a white orchid behind her ear. She wouldn't think of anything beyond this moment.

* * *

Devlin watched Kate approach. She came to him, this summer goddess, thick hair tumbling around her bare shoulders, cascading to her hips, capturing the sunlight, shimmering like spun gold. Through the swaying veil of her golden hair he caught glimpses of her, pink nipples peeking at him, the smooth curve of her belly enticing him. In spite of the cool water licking over his skin, heat flickered in his blood.

He walked toward the edge of the pool as she drew near, the water sleeking between his thighs, rippling like silk. "Good morning, Professor."

"Good morning, Mr. McCain." She tossed her hair over her shoulders, lifting the golden veil.

With his gaze he followed the play of sunlight as it danced across the pale curves of her breasts, as it glided golden fingers over the lush swell of her hips. Deep within his belly, desire pulled into a tight fist that beat against his flesh in the same rhythm as his heart.

"Do you suppose I might join you?"

"Oh, I think that's possible." He reached for her, placing his hands on her small waist. He lifted her into the pool, where he held her against his body, her long legs brushing against his, water bubbling around him, lapping at her waist.

She slipped her arms around his shoulders, sliding the lush heat of her breasts against his chest. "They told me in Pará you were the best man to lead me through the jungle."

Water from the cascade splashed against his shoulders before tumbling across her breasts. Her nipples responded to the cool caress, drawing up into tempting, pink buds against his skin. His body responded to her, his blood surging in his loins, his heat rising against her.

"I wonder if you might consider taking the job."

"Well, now, Miss Whitmore, I suppose for the right price I might be persuaded to be your guide."

Kate wiggled her hips, brushing the smooth skin of her belly over the rising pulse of his arousal. Devlin drew in a sharp breath, flooding his senses with the delicate fragrance of the damp orchid in her hair and the roses lingering on her skin.

"Perhaps a kiss?" She covered his lips with hers. She teased him, darting her tongue between his lips, stroking the tip of his tongue, then retreating, time and time again. When she pulled back in his arms, his breath was ragged.

She smiled, a provocative curve of lips made red from their kiss. "What do you say?"

"That was nice. But you're asking me to risk my life, Miss Whitmore." He drew her with him as he backed toward a wide shelf of rock hidden beneath the water. When he felt the smooth rock against his knees, he sank back, sitting, the water lapping at his chest. The main flow of the waterfalls splashed on the rocks nearby; a narrow stream of the falls cascaded on the rocks overhead, raining soft mist and glistening droplets over them. He pulled her onto his lap, astride, the sleek skin of her thighs enbracing his.

"It's very important to me, Mr. McCain. I'll pay anything you want."

"Anything?" He pressed his lips to the delicate hollow of her collarbone. He slid his tongue across her wet skin, tasting springwater and woman.

She tilted back her head, her hair swirling in the bubbling water, long strands brushing his chest. "Anything."

Devlin growled deep in his chest, a primal sound of deep, elemental need. He wanted to devour her, to cherish her, to plunder her sweet flesh, to surrender every inch of his own flesh to this woman. His blood grew thick, pulsing hot with the lust that had only grown as his love for her had grown.

"My *Edaina*." With his hands on her waist, he lifted her. She arched in response, like a supple cat, offering her breasts to him. And he took her offering, taking one pink bud between his teeth, gently abrading it, laving it with his tongue, drawing it deep into his mouth with a sweet sucking that turned her breath into ragged sobs.

She clutched at his shoulders, water splashing softly across her arms, spraying his warm cheeks. A moan rose from deep in her throat as he abandoned her fully aroused nipple to the cool spray of the water, only to torture and tease the other one. And inside, he endured his own torture, the beast of his desire sinking steel claws into his groin.

"Devlin." Her voice was a sultry whisper of need as she pressed against him. She slipped her hand into the water, finding him, slender fingers wrapping around his pulsing need, guiding him home.

He cupped the pouting cheeks of her rounded behind and pulled her closer, a provocative brush of damp curls and warm skin against flesh that threatened to burst with his need for her. "Luscious enchantress," he whispered, easing into the heart of her soft warmth.

"Irresistible barbarian." With the tip of her tongue, she stroked his lower lip, teasing, retreating, coaxing him to follow.

He took her mouth in a penetrating kiss, plunging his tongue past her lips, pulling her flush against him, thrusting with his hips, taking hot possession of her. Each joining with this woman amazed him, each time a renewal of faith, a pledge of dreams fulfilled.

She tightened her hold, gripping him with her hands, her legs, with muscles that contracted deep within her. Water, soft and sweet as a spring rain, poured over them as they moved in an ancient dance, man flowing into woman, woman welcoming man. Her skin slid sleekly against his, his every nerve coming alive and tingling.

Soft cries tumbled from her lips, a song of joy to her lover's ears. She slid her hands across his shoulders and tangled her fingers in his hair, holding him with a fierce tenderness, as though she were afraid someone or something would rip him from her. He loved her with every sinew of his body, showing her nothing could ever rip them apart.

Deep within her, he felt the pulsing of her flesh, the spiraling of feminine release that squeezed him tightly and pulled him over the brink. Together they broke the tethers of this world, soaring as one, rising to that place of mystery they had discovered and claimed as their own.

He held her clasped against his chest, his arms crossed behind her back, feeling each delicious ripple as her body relaxed against his. Her thighs grew soft and supple once more along his thighs, her breasts slowed their rapid rise and fall against his chest, her breath eased into a steady flood of heat warming his shoulder. Through the heavy mist of pleasure clinging to his senses, he felt her lips brush the skin beneath his ear, her tongue tickling his skin.

"Well, what do you say, Mr. McCain? Will you be my guide?"

He laughed against her cheek. "Anywhere."

She rested her head against his shoulder, one wet tendril of her hair streaming over her shoulder, curling around the curve of her breast. "Sitting here with you, I could almost believe we are the only people on the face of the earth."

"You're all I need." He lifted the orchid from her hair and brushed the petals across her cheek. "My luscious wife."

If he hadn't been holding her so close, if he hadn't been locked deep within her body, he might have missed the subtle stiffening of her muscles. "What's wrong, love?"

She shook her head. "Nothing."

"I have this funny notion about marriage." He slipped his fingers under her chin and tilted her head until she looked at him. "I believe a husband and wife should be honest with each other."

She hesitated a moment before she spoke, her words tumbling one after the other. "I love you so much it scares me."

"I know I hurt you once, Kate, but I swear—"

"It isn't that." She cupped his cheek in her hand, her fingers curling beneath his ear. "It's . . . I . . . I'm not sure how to be a wife."

He smiled. "Seems to me you've been doing a pretty good job."

She shook her head. "This is just one small part of being a wife. It's easy with you. But the rest . . . We've never discussed the future."

"No, we haven't. So let's see, what should we discuss?"

She drew her teeth over her lower lip. "What do husbands and wives discuss?"

Husbands and wives. What did he know about husbands and wives? "I guess we'll have to learn this together."

"How do we begin?"

"Well . . ." He brushed the orchid over her cheek, capturing glistening droplets upon the velvety petals. "Do you want to have children?"

She lowered her eyes to his shoulder, smiling. "Yes, I think I would like very much to have your children."

"We're all right on that subject."

"I'm an archaeologist, Devlin. I always thought I would travel all my life. And now . . . I want to be a good wife, I really do. I want to make you happy. I'm just afraid. Afraid I won't be any good at it. I don't know anything about making a home."

"All my life I've been looking for something. Call it home, if you like." He brushed the orchid along her bare shoulder, the petals gliding smoothly along her wet skin. "But it isn't a place. It's a sense of belonging. It's caring for someone and having someone care for you. I've found that, Kate, with you."

"Oh, when you say things like that, you completely knock me off balance." She smiled, a shy curving of her lips that brought light into her summer-blue eyes. "And my work? I had planned to visit Egypt. Of course, that was before Father and I had Avallon to explore. Still, sometime, I thought we might go there. Of course, if you don't want to . . ."

"I'd enjoy making love to you under an Egyptian moon." He kissed the tip of her nose. "Think of the possibilities, Professor."

"I shall try to be everything you ever wanted." She traced the curve of his lower lip with her fingertip. "I only fear I might fail, and be nothing at all."

"I'm in love with the woman I married." He cradled her face in his hands, pressing the orchid petals against her skin, releasing the fragrance to drift around them. "I never intend to change her. You see, she *is* everything I've ever wanted."

Author's Note

In 1754 a Portuguese explorer dispatched a report from the Brazilian jungle to his viceroy in Bahia, describing an ancient city he had discovered high on a mountaintop in the interior. He also reported catching glimpses of fair-skinned people dressed in odd clothing near the city. He and his group vanished.

In 1925 Colonel P.H. Fawcett, a respected explorer and former member of the British military, plunged into the jungle to find this lost city, which he believed was far older than Egypt. He disappeared. Others have tried to locate the lost city, but no one has ever returned.

Does the city exist? Was it a colony of a civilization older than Egypt? The mystery captured my imagination.

I hope you enjoyed your journey to the lost city of Avallon as much as I enjoyed writing it. In my next novel, *Deceptions and Dreams*, I return to Avallon.

Although innocent, Sara Van Horne has lived with a horrible scandal all of her life, a scandal that set her father and New York society against her. She never imagines the thief she catches in her Fifth Avenue home is a man who can trace his ancestors back to Atlantis, a man who is a nineteenth-century knight on a mission to retrieve an ancient medallion. Will this knight who has stolen her heart destroy or cherish her for all time?

I love to hear from readers. Please enclose a self-addressed, stamped envelope with your letter.

Debra Dier
P.O. Box 584
Glen Carbon, Illinois 62034

DECEPTIONS & DREAMS

DEBRA DIER

Sarah Van Horne can outwit any scoundrel who tries to cheat her in business. But she is no match for the dangerously handsome burglar she catches in her New York City town house. Although she knows she ought to send the suave rogue to the rock pile for life, she can't help being disappointed that his is after a golden trinket—and not her virtue. Confident, crafty, and devilishly charming, Lord Austin Sinclair always gets what he wants. He won't let a locked door prevent him from obtaining the medallion he has long sought, nor the pistol Sarah aims at his head. But the master seducer never expects to be tempted by an untouched beauty. If he isn't careful, he'll lose a lot more than his heart before Sarah is done with him.

___4582-6 $5.99 US/$6.99 CAN

MacLaren's Bride
Debra Dier

BESTSELLING AUTHOR OF *LORD SAVAGE*

She is a challenge to the gentlemen of the ton, for they say she can freeze a man with a single glance of her green eyes. Meg Drummond wants nothing to do with love—not when she has seen her own parents' marriage fall apart. And though she promises to marry an Englishman to spite her father, she has to find someone to win her stubborn heart. Then Alec MacLaren charges back into her life, unexpectedly awakening her deep-seated passions with his wicked Highland ways. He kidnaps and marries her out of loyalty to her father, but once he feels her tantalizing body against his, he aches to savor all of her. He knows he needs to break through the wall of ice around her heart, gain her trust, and awaken her desire to truly make her...MacLaren's Bride.

___4302-5 $5.50 US/$6.50 CAN

Dorchester Publishing Co., Inc.
P.O. Box 6640
Wayne, PA 19087-8640

Please add $1.75 for shipping and handling for the first book and $.50 for each book thereafter. NY, NYC, and PA residents, please add appropriate sales tax. No cash, stamps, or C.O.D.s. All orders shipped within 6 weeks via postal service book rate. Canadian orders require $2.00 extra postage and must be paid in U.S. dollars through a U.S. banking facility.

Name_____
Address_____
City_____ State_____ Zip_____
I have enclosed $_____ in payment for the checked book(s).
Payment <u>must</u> accompany all orders. ❑ Please send a free catalog.

A Rogue's Promise

PEGGY WAIDE

Eighteen years ago, deep in the mountains of China, Lady Joanna Fenton's father found a sacred statuette. The two-headed dragon is reputed to beget prosperity, but for Joanna, it brought nothing but heartache. Her father was obsessed with the piece until his death. Now, the artifact itself has disappeared.

Her search takes her to the darkest establishments of London, and from those rat holes steps a friend. He is a smuggler, a man who has forsaken his noble heritage for the shadows. A man who sees that she does not belong. And when MacDonald Archer swears to aid her, Joanna realizes the secret to true happiness is not in Oriental charms or spells, but in love.

SIERRA
Connie Mason

Bestselling Author Of *Wind Rider*

Fresh from finishing school, Sierra Alden is the toast of the Barbary Coast. And everybody knows a proper lady doesn't go traipsing through untamed lands with a perfect stranger, especially one as devilishly handsome as Ramsey Hunter. But Sierra believes the rumors that say that her long-lost brother and sister are living in Denver, and she will imperil her reputation and her heart to find them.

Ram isn't the type of man to let a woman boss him around. Yet from the instant he spies Sierra on the muddy streets of San Francisco, she turns his life upside down. Before long, he is her unwilling guide across the wilderness and her more-than-willing tutor in the ways of love. But sweet words and gentle kisses aren't enough to claim the love of the delicious temptation called Sierra.

_3815-3 $5.99 US/$6.99 CAN

Dorchester Publishing Co., Inc.
P.O. Box 6640
Wayne, PA 19087-8640

PATRICIA GAFFNEY **Fortune's Lady**

"Like moonspun magic...one of the best historical
romances I have read in a decade!"
—Cassie Edwards

They are natural enemies—traitor's daughter and zealous
patriot—yet the moment he sees Cassandra Merlin at her
father's graveside, Riordan knows he will never be free of
her. She is the key to stopping a heinous plot against the
king's life, yet he senses she has her own secret reasons for
aiding his cause. Her reputation is in shreds, yet he finds
himself believing she is a woman wronged. Her mission is
to seduce another man, yet he burns to take her luscious body
for himself. She is a ravishing temptress, a woman of
mystery, yet he has no choice but to gamble his heart on
fortune's lady.

_4153-7 $5.99 US/$6.99 CAN

Sweet Treason

Patricia Gaffney

Exquisitely beautiful, fiery Katherine McGregor has no qualms about posing as a doxy, if the charade will strike a blow against the hated English, until she is captured by the infuriating Major James Burke. Now her very life depends on her ability to convince the arrogant English officer that she is a common strumpet, not a Scottish spy. Skillfully, Burke uncovers her secrets, even as he arouses her senses, claiming there is just one way she can prove herself a tart . . . But how can she give him her yearning body, when she fears he will take her tender heart as well?

___4419-6 $5.99 US/$6.99 CAN

Dorchester Publishing Co., Inc.
P.O. Box 6640
Wayne, PA 19087-8640

Please add $1.75 for shipping and handling for the first book and $.50 for each book thereafter. NY, NYC, and PA residents, please add appropriate sales tax. No cash, stamps, or C.O.D.s. All orders shipped within 6 weeks via postal service book rate. Canadian orders require $2.00 extra postage and must be paid in U.S. dollars through a U.S. banking facility.

Name_____

Address_____

City_____State_____Zip_____

I have enclosed $_____ in payment for the checked book(s).

Payment <u>must</u> accompany all orders. ❏ Please send a free catalog.

        CHECK OUT OUR WEBSITE! www.dorchesterpub.com

Belle

Melanie Jackson

With the letter breaking his engagement, Stephan Kirton's hopes for respectability go up in smoke. Inevitably, his "interaction with the lower classes" and the fact that he is a bastard have put him beyond the scope of polite society. He finds consolation at Ormstead Park; a place for dancing, drinking and gambling . . . a place where he can find a woman for the night.

He doesn't recognize her at first; ladies don't come to Lord Duncan's masked balls. This beauty's descent into the netherworld has brought her within reach, yet she is no girl of the day. Annabelle Winston is sublime. And if he has to trick her, bribe her, protect her, whatever—one way or another he will make her an honest woman. And she will make him a happy man.

___4975-9 $5.99 US/$7.99 CAN